THE DRAGON'S HIDE

The Shadow's Dragon Book 1

DUSTIN PORTA

D.K. HOLMBERG

ASH
PUBLISHING

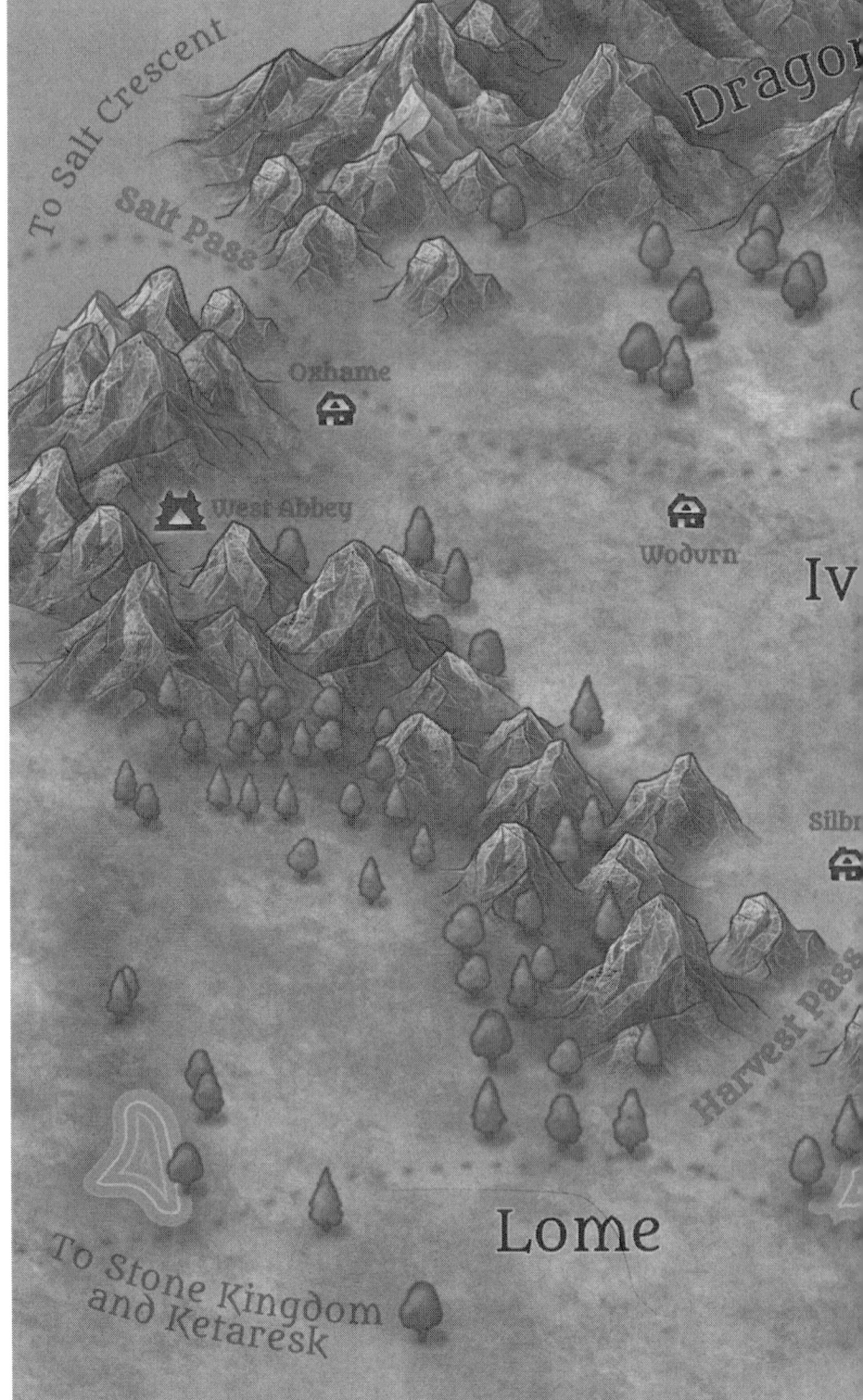

Chapter One

THE HUNTER

THE FOREST OVER SIGNET LAKE SHOULD HAVE BEEN FULL OF noise in the evening. Bats leaving their mountain caves to hunt in the cooling air, squirrels and songbirds bedding down as the nighttime scavengers took their place. Those were the sounds Treylen heard each summer since arriving at the abbey so long ago.

Peering from behind a high boulder, on the mountain trail between the abbey and the fishing village below, Treylen squinted into the darkness and heard—nothing. A voice spoke into his thoughts.

Even the deer have fled.

His eyes flicked around, searching, but the rest of him remained still. Treylen answered with a thought of his own.

I didn't spook them.

There was another long silence, then a hissing reply.

Not slow as you're moving.

Treylen allowed himself a slight shake of the head, turning his focus back to the trail. Wildcraft was not one of the tenets taught at the abbey, but for all the time young assassins devoted to it, it might as well have been. In the waning light, it wasn't much use to him. The trail ahead was washed out. Nothing unusual about that. Any traveler passing by would be hard pressed to do so without leaving prints of some kind. Thick briars lined either side.

I need to see. He sent another thought.

You are asking?

I'm just giving you fair warning.

So kind of you, bondmate.

Treylen had learned to ignore the edge of sarcasm. Rime could be petulant, and uncooperative, but the best way to handle it was to pretend he wasn't bothered. Besides, if his bondmate were any less of a pain, he might feel guilty for stealing as much power as he did.

Bah.

A swirl of prismatic colors hovered outside his thoughts. Treylen extended his mind toward it, seized it, and pulled it inward, like a desperate man downing a drink. He closed his eyes so the flash of the dragonmind entering his consciousness wouldn't give him away and focused on the dragon sight.

When he opened them again, the forest was bright before him. Those colors that swirled in his head now swam through the evening woods, glazing the washed-out trail, the forest canopy, and the brambles that lined the hillside. Nobody had been through here.

Treylen let go of all but the slightest trace of the dragon-mind; a faint shimmer still highlighted the outlines of the leaves.

Greedy.

He ignored the dragon.

Treylen had been hugging the boulder since before the sun touched the eastern mountain. He eased away from it and into the shadow of a nearby pine. The needles carpeting the hillside masked his footfalls, and so long as he stepped carefully and favored boulders when the ground got steep, they showed no sign of his passing as he crept along the mountainside overlooking the path.

Someone else could have done the same. Treylen scanned the canopy again.

You didn't see anything?

If I did not see it, it is not there.

Rime was cocky, but he'd be a better lookout if Treylen gave his sight back. He blinked away the last of the dragon-mind and the world went dark. It was reassuring how the shadows swallowed him up again. Treylen moved at a spider's pace. The trees grew thicker as the path turned downhill toward a small clearing. He didn't like the idea of stalking prey that couldn't be seen or heard. Especially when he knew they were out there, stalking him.

Honestly, Rime, what do you think?

The dragon paused a moment before responding.

The ambush will be here, bondmate.

I think you might be right this time.

Always right.

Though he'd released it, Treylen could feel the dragon-mind burn a little brighter at the insult, flickering just outside of his own thoughts.

This is where I would do it. If I were laying the trap. They're here. We just can't see them.

Another long pause, then the flickering subsided.

Smells of pine tar. Raw earth. Lavender, Rime said.

You think traps?

Pitfall maybe. Watch your feet, assassin.

This is pointless. I think we should get…

A faint screech called his attention to the canopy, where a blur of motion streaked from one branch to the next.

Watch for snares up there.

If I don't see it, it is not there, bondmate.

So much for stealth. Treylen chased after his dragon, leaping from rock to rock like a shadow, racing up a fallen log and vaulting over a briar patch to land on another boulder. It was dark enough now that the trail was no longer visible. The opening in the canopy where the trail cut through the trees showed the lamps of the village reflecting off the lake far below.

As Treylen's foot touched the boulder, it slipped. He fell. He tapped into the dragonmind again, drawing on his bond-mate's speed and sight. The world slowed. Everything once again was drenched in shimmering color. A sapling grew just beside the boulder, and Treylen shot a hand out, steadying himself—finding his footing on the slippery stone, short of tumbling into the briars and rolling down the hill.

Treylen heard a clatter somewhere in the trees as Rime lost his night sight and missed the branch he'd been leaping for.

Glancing down, he scanned the underbrush for threats. Nothing leaped out from behind him. But what had he slipped in? It smelled like pine sap, drizzled over the top of the boulder.

The colors danced around in a swirling pattern. It was a thing alive with magical potential. Someone had drizzled a glyph onto the boulder in pine sap.

A figure burst from the underbrush and slapped a hand onto the far side of the boulder with a shout.

"Crotus!"

A sharp crack sounded as the mess of pine sap expanded outward, spilling over the top of Treylen's boots before hardening into a crystalline resin. It all happened in a flash, even with his dragon speed. Treylen tried to move but both feet were entrapped. Treylen's eyes snapped toward the figure. A young woman in the dark cloth of an assassin, a black dragon mask covering her face, the same as his.

"Who taught you that glyph?"

The flash of a blade answered him as the woman lunged.

Treylen dodged as well as he could with his feet fixed in place. She slashed again and he leaned backward, the resin holding him from falling over. Her other hand produced a second dagger, this one aimed for Treylen's gut. He had two daggers of his own stashed on his back and no time to reach for them.

But he had something that she didn't. Dragon speed.

Her dagger came down, and Treylen wrapped it with his own, turned it aside, and guided it so the strike flew wide. The other dagger slashed at his legs, still fixed in place. Treylen punched the knife hand and the dagger clattered to the ground.

The woman inhaled sharply, cradling her hand, then lunged again, blade pointed at his heart.

"That's a mistake." Treylen pulled at the dragonmind, speed surging again. He wrapped his hand around the attacker's as he snagged her elbow, letting the momentum of her lunge carry her up and over him. The other assassin let out a small shriek as she tumbled into the brambles. Rime's voice cut into his thoughts and chided him.

You draw too much power.

At least I'm not dead.

The ribbons of magic were still trapped in the amber that held his feet. She was clever, for a novice. The power word she'd used had activated a crotus glyph—a blistering spell that imbued the sap with heat and caused it to bubble up— but she'd chained it to a second glyph, entropos, which imbued it with decay, aging the amber so it crystalized around his boot.

Treylen followed the fire energy latent in the sap, touching his finger to the amber and tracing the fire glyph as he spoke a power word to match it.

This was going to hurt.

"Flavus!" He scratched the rough edge of his glove against the amber and it burst into flame.

The whole boulder lit up, Treylen's feet included, brightening the clearing around him. He turned just in time to find the woman scrambling up to strike at him again. A swift mule kick sent her into the brambles with a flaming footprint on her chest.

He could stop then and douse the flames, or leap into brambles himself and beat them out on his opponent's face. He took the obvious route. Diving after her, he almost missed the trip wire. It caught his shin and snapped. Of course, there were more traps. Treylen rolled into the brush, thorns shredding his dark clothing, opening small gashes across his face. The mask saved him from the worst of it. From above came a snap and a twang. Then something large whipped through the air just where he had been standing.

It was clever, he thought. But he knew this sort of trap. He also knew assassins. If he spared even a moment to look for what had nearly taken his head off, he would wind up with a dagger in his back. Instead, he rolled, drawing his own dagger and popping up on one elbow.

The clearing was empty.

Flames roared on the boulder and up one of his feet, but Treylen bit his cheek and pushed the pain aside.

Where was she? He squinted down the mountain. Leaves rustled near the trail. How could he have let them get the drop on him like this? He was too predictable.

She's getting away.

Slow her down, then.

I cannot see.

Oh.

Treylen released the dragonmind as he darted down the mountain, handing most of the power back to Rime. The light was all but gone from the gray moonless sky. His boot still burned like a funeral pyre, but he pushed through the pain. The chase would stomp it out.

The trees that clung to the mountain laid down a thin carpet of pine needles, and tree roots held clods of earth and stone. Racing down, it was more a poorly controlled tumble than a foot chase. But trail running was another of those unofficial tenets passed down between students at the abbey.

Treylen rode it the rest of the way down before snagging a vine to arrest his tumble as he reached the trail. Just ahead, he saw another flash in the trees. The small, glimmering shape of a dragon detached from a branch and landed on something in the brush down below. His prey let out a shriek, followed shortly after by the high keening noise of an injured dragon.

I'm bloodied.

Treylen sprinted up the path. Traps be damned.

Coming!

He didn't dare draw on the dragonmind now. Rime would need every bit of it to protect himself. When he rounded the bend, he saw a dark shape wriggling on the ground, tangled in a net of fishing line—four-legged, but small and long, like a mink, with scaly ridges up its back and two leathery wings not much good for flying. Usually Rime was a dark blue like a storm at sunset. But panicked like this, he flashed white, green, purple—his color-changing scales gone mad.

"I've got you, lizard, calm down already."

He wasn't too entangled. Drawing a dagger with one hand, Treylen gripped the net with the other and gave it a shake. The diminutive dragon thumped to the ground, then snapped back to his senses, chuffing at the air, head darting around before his color changed, and he seemed to disappear into the shadows of the footpath.

She went downward.

"Good," Treylen said, snapping his fingers. "Come on." Now that they were together, he could speak out loud. It wasn't any quicker than telepathy, but it reminded the dragon who was leading this hunt.

Rime let out an indignant hiss and scurried up Treylen's still-smoking pant leg, ducked inside his jacket, and popped out under the cowl to look him in the eye. The assassin's cowl was a hooded collar that buckled onto the jacket. It was bunched around the neck and draped over the shoulders like a short cloak.

You slowed me.

"I didn't touch it." He hadn't stolen any of Rime's speed going down. Well, maybe just the tiniest bit for balance. What was Rime thinking going after an assassin, one-on-one? That was as profitable as a badger wrestling a bear. "Don't underestimate her next time."

He leaped off the path, down the mountain again. The trees here were thicker, the slope easing off as they neared the lake. There was movement on one of the lower trails.

"She thinks she's getting away."

It's working, then.

Treylen snagged a branch and pulled on the dragonmind to catch the top of a sapling, using it to vault a clearing full of brambles and land in a roll on the lower path. A sound like a cracking whip echoed from up ahead—another yelp and a flurry of shivering leaves.

"Got her."

Treylen couldn't keep the grin from his face as he rounded the bend and found the young assassin dangling upside down, a snare around one ankle.

"You know what the monks say." Treylen laughed. "The best trap is the one that brings home dinner." He crossed his arms casually as he approached, resisting the urge to draw his daggers.

There will be a fledgling, Rime said.

The assassin still held on to one of her daggers and sawed at the wire that had snared her foot.

"There's a way out. But that isn't it."

Treylen struggled to look boastful and keep the nervousness out of his voice. He strutted up, just short of her reach. When she lashed out at him, he snatched the dagger from her hand.

"I figured you'd set your ambush up there, then run here when it didn't go your way."

"You didn't figure anything." Her eyes darted toward the upper side of the path.

Do you see him? He sent the thought toward the dragon.

I see the small one.

"If you say so." He twirled the dagger, then held it to her neck.

Treylen felt his dragon tense and braced himself. A screech came from the trees to his right, and Rime launched himself from Treylen's shoulder, colliding midair with another dragon— green, and even smaller than he was. They landed in a hissing tangle on the path and rolled into the brush. Treylen didn't turn his attention from the assassin hanging in front of him. She'd tried to disarm him while her dragon struck, but he'd twisted her hand and pinned it in a wrist lock. She cursed, but didn't scream.

"I think you're out of this game."

"Maybe." She grimaced. "But I played my part."

The soft twang of a bowstring behind him sent a chill up his spine. Treylen rolled to the side, throwing his dagger on instinct. It buried itself in a tree. A short bow clattered to the ground, like someone had tossed it there...as a distraction.

There hadn't been a sound, but a rough hand slipped around Treylen's neck from the nearby bushes and a dagger pressed into his back. He tried to spin, but felt the point pierce his shirt and bite into skin.

"Is it over?" the voice said in his ear. A pale dragon twice the size of Rime landed on Treylen's shoulder and crawled down his shirt, tearing at his pocket and nosing inside.

"Fine." Treylen grunted.

"Felicity seems to think you're holding out."

"I don't have anything."

"The nose doesn't lie."

The dragon sneezed, then came out with a chunk of dried

meat, swallowing it whole. It ran down Treylen's leg and into the brush, where the sounds of the struggle between Rime and the smaller dragon filled the woods.

"Alright, then…" The attacker eased the dagger away. Iveran assassins all carried the same blades—Queen's Fingers —half an arm's length, and curved at the end, the hilt wrapped in black leather with a sword-breaker guard. They were forged in the Stone Kingdom before the war. It was identical to the ones Treylen carried. He released his hold on Treylen's neck. Treylen spun, rubbing the spot on his back and giving the other man a hard look. Aaron was light-skinned, stocky, and a hand taller than he was despite being younger. But then everyone who came to the abbey was younger than Treylen these days.

Aaron chuckled, somewhat grimly, then cocked an eyebrow at the dagger jutting out of the tree. "That was unsporting."

Treylen felt his cheeks redden. "You'd have dodged it."

"Maybe, but the fledgling couldn't have." He turned his attention toward the third assassin. The young woman's eyes were closed, face puffy, tangles of brown curls spilling out from under her hood. She slowly spun as she hung from one ankle over the path. "Another time, Volanti, we'll show you how to get out of that."

"Show her now," Treylen said.

"She'll burst a vein. Come on now. Grab on to me."

Shifting her weight onto one muscled shoulder—Aaron always cut the sleeves off his darks, even though it defeated their purpose—he wrapped an arm around the half-conscious assassin, then lifted her up and used the other arm to loosen the snare from her leg. He seemed to contemplate tossing her over his shoulder, before gently dumping her onto the path instead.

"Is she alright?" Treylen asked.

He did care after all. Sometimes it just took Aaron to

remind him when the game had ended. There had been a time that he didn't care. When he was young and hot-tempered. Bos, the last mentor at the abbey, had died and the students were left to fend for themselves. The monks, for whatever reason, never saw fit to request a new dragon rider be sent up to mentor, or the generals never saw fit to send one. One by one, every assassin who'd trained under Bos was called into service. Until only Treylen remained to teach the new recruits. The fact that he was never called up to serve had only made him angrier. If Aaron hadn't come along, learned so quickly, and taken so easily to the mentor role, Treylen might have stayed angry.

That was years ago now. Treylen wasn't angry anymore, and between the two of them, they managed to keep up at least some of the standards that Bos had set.

Volanti wouldn't have lasted long before Aaron came along. Not because she was small. Size was no asset to assassins. But she was slow, and clumsy, a deadly combination. Treylen had nearly turned her away on arrival. But Aaron had seen a cleverness in her. And based on the glyphwork she'd demonstrated tonight, he'd been right.

"Any more hazards we should be aware of?"

"Not mine." Treylen rubbed his back again. His hand came away bloody. "What the hellcaves was that tripwire up there?"

"Nothing too deadly, I think. The fledgling set it."

"You know not to underestimate her."

"I'm not a fledgling," Volanti groaned from the side of the trail.

"But your bondmate is." Aaron frowned at the sounds of fighting coming from down the hill. "Rime! Ketcher! Felicity! Knock it off."

He's right, knock it off, Treylen thought. Only his own bondmate would be able to hear him, but if one of the dragons were instigating, Treylen suspected it was Rime.

Nasty weasel, this one, Rime answered. He always fought with the others, but something about Volanti's bondmate, Ketcher, brought out the fledgling in him.

You're the eldest. Don't encourage it.

Aaron must have seen the look on his face because he put a hand on Treylen's shoulder. "Felicity will break it up."

Treylen wasn't so sure about that. But the fighting stopped, and after a moment, Felicity appeared, dragging Ketcher by the scruff. She dropped him in front of Volanti, who was sitting up now and looking much less red in the face, and the young dragon whined and scurried up into Volanti's arms.

Rime appeared just behind them, and climbed onto Treylen just long enough to sniff at the pocket where Felicity had stolen the treat, then leaped off and glided into the darkened trees.

Treylen looked from Volanti, still looking a bit queasy, to the grinning Aaron, who'd picked up his dragon and was scratching her nose and whispering to her.

"Alright. I think we've trained enough for the night." Treylen pulled himself up so that Aaron didn't tower over him quite so much. "You did well, both of you. Good spellwork. The knifework will come. Now let's get back. They can start dinner early."

It was fully dark now, the last hint of gray gone from the sky. The lights of Signet Lake Village flickered over the water down below.

Treylen untied his snare and coiled the wire before tucking it into the assassin's toolkit on his belt. He spared one last glance at Aaron's short bow that was still lying on the ground, and at the dagger he'd driven into the tree, before trudging up the mountain toward the abbey.

The others would follow once they'd caught their breath and Aaron would retrieve the dagger for him. He needed to cool off and clear his head. The chill air higher up near the abbey would do the trick. As he climbed near the upper limits of the forest, a soft ringing caught his ear, and Treylen borrowed Rime's sight to scan the trees. Perched in the upper branches of a twisted pine sat a lone pigeon, late getting back to the roost. Then Treylen saw why. Around one leg was tied a bell and the distinctive shape of a message tube. The kind that was only used for official business.

"Hellcaves." Treylen gritted his teeth and gripped the lower branches, climbing up slowly so as not to spook it.

What is the matter, bondmate? Rime said. *It's nothing,* Treylen thought. The last thing he wanted to do was let Rime know that a bird was nearby. But his mind was already turning. Why this day? There were no recruits coming. No shipments of dragons' eggs to the abbey. Messages meant change, but this wasn't the time of year for changes. It was winter, and they were just settling in to another season of hard training.

He'd almost reached the top when Rime burst from the branches, snapping and scrambling up the trunk as he tried to seize the pigeon in his teeth. It squawked and took to the sky as Rime got a mouthful of tail feathers.

"Damn it, Rime." Treylen slumped in the branches as he watched the pigeon flutter up toward the abbey.

What do you think it's doing here? Rime asked, unapologetically.

"I don't know," Treylen said, "but we had better hurry back and see if we can find it. They don't put bells on them if they aren't important."

Chapter Two

THE HEARTH

THE SOUND OF PIGEONS TOLD TREYLEN HE WAS NEARLY HOME. The great hall of Coops Abbey was perched in a shallow alcove halfway up the sheer rock face of the mountain. It funneled echoes from the dovecote building where the birds were kept, so that visitors approaching from the Signet Lake trail were greeted with a swell of reverberating cooing.

The effect was both soothing and disorienting.

The first time Treylen had climbed it in the dark, he'd frozen in fear and clung to the narrow ledge until dawn. Sunrise and the sight of all Iverna Valley spread out below had only made it worse, and he'd been stuck there until one of the monks came out to get him. But that was six winters ago.

Now, sprinting up a pathway half the width of his boots, the thought of it made him laugh. The sound from the birds, the faint pinpricks of light from the village, and the stars mirrored in the lake below lent the feeling of flying. The wall to his left fell away, and Treylen knew he'd reached the alcove. No need for dragon sight here. He leaped blind and caught the edge of a roof tile.

Hauling himself up, he padded up the spine of the great hall, stepping heavy enough to alert the monks to his return.

They'd start dinner if they hadn't already. It was said that in other lands the monks had gods to worship. But in Iverna, they gave devotion to the queen…and to the assassins, who served as her hand and who, by Iveran law, were to be treated as an extension of the royal personage.

That didn't stop Sister Ono from yanking his ear when he wasn't listening. Monks were funny like that.

Treylen hopped over the cupola and ran down the ridge of the roof. When he reached the far gable, he leaped down into the dark again, grunting when he hit the courtyard wall that separated the training yard from the cliff's edge.

He scrambled up, then raced along the top of the wall, feeling the way with his feet. Cold air gusted up from the lake far below. Another leap brought him to the dovecote tower—a glorified pigeon loft made of stone, with a honeycomb of holes covering the outside, nooks and nest boxes stacked within. When he hit the side of the tower, it exploded with angry flapping, followed by smaller, indignant coos as he used the pigeonholes to scale it. Rime burst out of the upper pigeonholes, amidst another cacophony of fleeing birds and flying feathers. At the top of the dovecote was a shrine to the Dragon King—built before the ascension of the Iveran queens. An old stone roof supported by four stone serpents covered a flat altar. A mess of sticks, bones, and scarves stolen from the monks' closets formed a mound in the middle, with coins and bits of silver throughout. Rime scurried up and flopped into his nest with a sigh, rolling on his back and scratching his belly.

Treylen reached the top of the tower, holding on to one of the serpent columns and letting one foot dangle. He borrowed just enough dragon sight to see feathers sticking out of his bondmate's mouth and the look of self-satisfaction about him.

"If you keep hunting them, they'll stop roosting, then where will you get your eggs?"

I was only helping.

The dragon arched his neck, opened his mouth, and hacked something up from his craw. A small metal cylinder clattered to the stone—the canister from the messenger pigeon.

Treylen had always had a rebellious streak, but Rime was a terror, especially toward the monks and their poor pigeons. The two of them had a lot in common. Even if they never got on quite as well as bondmates were supposed to.

"Bad Rime." He scratched the dragon under the chin and tugged the feathers from his mouth. "Keep an eye on the trainee for me. I think she hurt her ankle."

I think you hurt it, Rime replied, *and you nearly murdered the large one.*

"Hush. You aren't my mother."

If I was, we'd be fed better.

Rime's fondness for Treylen's mother was based entirely upon the one time she'd visited and had brought a bagful of treats. That, apparently, had been enough to buy the dragon's boundless devotion. The queen forbid Treylen ever speak ill of his mother when Rime was around.

"Go check on the others."

Treylen didn't wait to see if his order was followed. He snatched up the cylinder and stared at it with foreboding. Every instinct told him that he should either open it now or chuck it from the cliff and forget it ever existed. But he was duty bound to give it to the head monk. Treylen had not proven his loyalty for so long to get branded a traitor.

He tucked it into his belt. He borrowed just enough dragon sight to see the cliff face that rose above the abbey, and to make out the small cave opening just beside the dovecote tower. Leaping across, he landed inside. The assassins' chamber wasn't quite high enough to stand. Finding a lamp by the entrance, he touched his finger against the wick, then used the oil to trace a glyph on the wall of the cave.

"Flavus."

The glyph burst briefly into flames. Quickly, he touched the wick to the flames to light the lamp. The first time he'd tried it, he had drawn the glyph onto the lamp itself and nearly burned down the abbey.

Four small alcoves lined the back of the cave, each just big enough for a bedroll and a few possessions. One was empty now, but new trainees would come in a month, and they'd be crammed in shoulder-to-shoulder. Then he and Aaron would do their best to thin the ranks out again. Some would be called into service, others would fail to bond with their dragons, or simply not make the cut. A few, like Aaron and Treylen, might be passed over for one reason or another, forced into a second training, or third, or sixth…

Treylen shook his head as he stripped off his black leathers and sweaty linens and dressed in the red cloth of the monastery, leaving the shirt off so he didn't bleed on it. He grimaced when he touched the wound on his back.

"I'll sew it up for you," Aaron said, hauling himself inside the cave.

"I can do it over dinner."

"Suture yourself, then." Aaron laughed, eyeing the alcoves. "I can't wait to be out of here."

"Yeah, me too."

"If you wanted out, you'd have been gone years ago. I'm ready for service."

Treylen shook his head, untying the leather dragon mask and tossing it onto his bunk. He mussed his hair and stretched, walking over to the opening. "You're ready," Treylen said, clapping his friend on the shoulder. "I'm ready. Everyone is ready except for Rime."

"He would go wherever you tell him to go. He's still your bondmate."

Treylen looked out at the stars that hung over Iverna. It was true; once an assassin's dragon was large enough to defend themselves, the pair was expected to go into service.

Typically, that service began at a safehouse, learning espionage behind enemy lines. That meant cities, spycraft, disguise, and deception, a very different sort of life than Treylen had become accustomed to.

It was a difficult life, but it lasted only until the dragon was large enough for riding. Then they would come home, and a different sort of training would begin. But Rime wasn't growing. That changed things quite a bit.

"You'll be out before I am," Treylen said. "Someone has to teach when you go."

"That's a frightening thought."

Treylen laughed. "Bring Volanti's things when you come down. She can sleep in the great hall until her ankle heals."

"And you can't get them?"

"I don't want to get blood on them."

Aaron nodded and made a sound of concern but went back to undressing. Treylen leaped out the opening and caught the pillar of the dovecote, then climbed down and crossed the courtyard, toward the great hall.

To most, the great hall was an old, simple lodge perched on a ledge halfway up a mountain cliff. Treylen, who'd grown up with an architect and a stonemason for parents, saw it in greater details than he really cared to.

The warm shadows of the timber roof with its wood shingles, rough-hewn king posts, and dowel-pinned tenons lent a homey feel to the structure. A freestanding firebox with a circular hearth, clad in mountain rock, dominated the center of the room. There was a kitchen on the back side of the fire and a row of lofted beds, between the old-style crucked beams that gave the outer walls of the hall its rounded shape, as if to give the impression of being inside the belly of some great mother dragon.

The construction fit with the purpose of the abbey. A place where young assassins and dragons were sheltered from the wars of the world and raised up to their full potential.

Though Treylen's parents would have said it was a place where promising young apprentices ran off to squander their family's good name and hide from responsibility. That was, they would have said it if speaking such a thought weren't treasonous to the queen.

Without meaning to, Treylen summoned more of the dragonmind. It was easy because Rime was near. He let the details of the building blur with shifting flows of light and energy, magic coursing through the hall, heat from the fire, strength from the ancient timbers and the old, sluggish magic in the hearthstones. With that heightened awareness came new sounds. Mice scratching behind the walls. Pigeons going back to their nests. One of the dragons climbing in through the cupola.

You're doing it again. Rime's voice cut through his thoughts.

Was I?

For no reason...

Treylen looked around to find Rime lounging on one of the rafters. *It's not like you needed it.*

I am dragon. I always need it.

He blinked the dragonmind away and stepped through the door.

One long table dominated the front of the hall. It was big enough to seat twenty, but only four sat around it now. Volanti slouched in her chair, dragon mask still covering the top half of her face, one boot off, and her swollen foot propped on the table.

The other three were monks. Courd and Cenna were siblings from a noble family. The third, Ourbeth, was an orphan from the dragon mountains far to the north and raised by the monks there. He had arrived just last year. He'd carried the last shipment of dragon eggs to Coops Abbey and decided to stay. According to him, life was easier here, and the duties of the monks in this chapter less backbreaking than what was required of them in the north.

They were a nice bunch, if lazy.

The harder-working monks were in the kitchen on the other side of the hearth. Brother Dobb was up to his elbows in a wash basin while Sister Ono ladled stew and brought bread out from the fire.

Treylen walked to the back and into the kitchen space. There weren't walls to separate the great hall, but a row of flour-covered tables, well-worn chopping blocks, and hooks bearing smoked meat and dried vegetables delineated the kitchen from the living space.

"Can I carry something?" he asked, leaning over the table.

"What?" Sister Ono thumped her cleaver on the butcher block. "You look about to fall over. Tell Courd to see to your injury and get a shirt on. Food's coming out now."

A head popped up from a pallet in the back of the hall, then four wrinkled monks emerged from the gallery. There were three men and a woman, all with canes and each holding on to the other, like a pack of baby deer out for their first walk —Trema, Micender, Boneau, and Fild. There wasn't much for an elder monk to do in a mountain abbey but sweep the court-yard, sleep the day away, and race to the feast table in the evenings for their soup.

"Oh, now they arise to partake. Where were they when the pot bubbled over, or the bread needed turning? I should send them back to their families and be free of the drain on the abbey's pantry."

It was an empty threat. Half the monks who lived at the abbey had no family to begin with, and none who served could expect to return to them. It was a calling to the end. And those who were still young enough to make the climb were too round from Ono's cooking to hug the narrow ledge. Treylen chuckled and snagged a hunk of bread while her back was turned before sneaking around the hearth to join Volanti.

She was leaning back with her foot still on the table, eyes closed, breathing slow, heavy sighs.

"You still have your mask on."

Volanti cracked one eye open and glared at him through a wreath of stray curls. "It's the only thing holding my head together."

She has been groaning and wincing, Rime cut in.

"Did you hit it? Do you want me to look at it?"

"It's just pounding."

"Let's see it, then."

Volanti groaned again and tugged at the lacing. The dragon masks were made from stiffened black leather that covered the upper half of the face. Tooled ridges along the eyebrows and ears gave the look of a dragon's features, and a curved beak came down over the nose. She pulled off the black hood underneath. A shallow gash ran up her cheek, but the bleeding had stopped. There was no wetness in her hair that would indicate a head wound.

Treylen reached into the tangle and felt her skull, trying not to wrinkle his nose. She was comely for a fighter, but she reeked of soggy boot leather and lavender oil.

"I don't feel anything." He checked the other side. Long ears stuck up through her curls. They weren't true elven ears, of course. Treylen had never seen an elf. They must've had some tall ears indeed if all Iverans possessed them, simply because a couple elves had ruled this valley in ancient times. He checked the scalp behind them. "You won't have these much longer."

"You think?" she squinted, grimacing.

"You've bonded with your fledgling. It's time."

"But I like them."

"We all liked our points. You can keep them if you like. On a necklace. Or in a jar…" He flicked one of her ears. It was meant to be gentle, but she grimaced again, jerking her head away and sitting up with a scowl.

"You're fine. You could wash your hair, though." He wiped his hands on his pants and moved around.

"My hair doesn't allow over-washing."

"Unscented oil, then. Rime sniffed you out on the mountainside."

Sister Ono emerged from behind the hearth, each hand carrying another trencher with stew and glazed roots, roast venison, and the obligatory pigeon eggs.

"I'll be doing your ears, Volanti," Sister Ono said. "You needn't worry. I cropped Treylen's and he only cried a little. But he cried over everything back then."

"It's not the pain, Sister Ono. I just worry they'll heal badly."

Ono set the trenchers in front of the two of them, then reached over to seize Treylen's head under her arm, turning it, and presenting his ear to Volanti like a silversmith proud of her wares.

"See the curve here." She ran a finger along the top of his ear as Treylen tried to squirm away. A thin scar on the edge was the only evidence it had once been as high as the top of his head. "Pretty as a rose."

"Look like a rat's ear to me."

"The Jaul have rat's ears, then. Most people do, you know, aside from us. Well…" She touched her own ear, self-consciously, glancing at the other monks. All except one of the elders had their ears cropped short.

"Why is that?" Volanti asked. "I know why I need it. But you'll never have to spy in Jaul or hunt a Seeran horselord."

"We do it for you, my dear," Ono said, running back to the kitchen and emerging with three more trenchers for the elder monks. "It wouldn't do to mangle the queen's ears. I must practice on someone."

"Tell that to Aaron," Treylen said.

"I can only stitch the ears; I cannot make one sit still for it."

"She'll be glad when I'm gone." The door slammed shut as Aaron entered, smiling. "I only remind her of her mistakes.

Treylen chuckled and Volanti hid her laugh. Aaron played with his mangled ear. It wasn't that bad really. A tad smaller than the other. Were his head not so big and his hair so short, it would hardly be noticeable. Ono huffed and stomped into the kitchen to get stew for Aaron while Dobb finished up with the washing.

"No, it's good to have you around as a cautionary tale. Now join hands." Ono took a seat beside Aaron and placed her hand into his, reaching across the table to join hands with Treylen. Volanti and the monks completed the circle. Back in the kitchen, the scrubbing stopped for a moment.

Heads were lowered.

"Queen Olysya Rewenis Ivera, daughter of Olumus Rewenis, son of Olysya Nevelyn, daughter of the line of Ivera. You whose eyes see every secret, whose ears hear every name, whose hand touch every land. See our devotion and know its fervency. Carry our prayers to the king of dragons, raising the fiery peak ever higher until Iverna touches the sky. I know she listens."

The last line was repeated around the table.

The irony was not lost on Treylen, that he was to serve as the queen's ears one day, and so was essentially saying a prayer to himself. But he knew better than to make light of it with the monks around.

He muttered the last bit and tore a chunk of bread to dunk in the stew. It was heavenly.

Chatter picked up again and Brother Dobb went back to scrubbing while the rest sunk into their meals. The monks were excellent cooks. Unoriginal, maybe. But what they lacked in variety, they made up for by serving one massive feast—and only once a day. After hours of fighting and running the trails half-starved at sundown, they could boil a boot in Ono's kettle, and still it would taste divine.

He ate ravenously, then got up to help himself to seconds. Walking around the fire, he caught the dragons, all three of them, tearing into a rack of venison that had been hung beside the fire to smoke.

"I didn't hunt that for you three. Aren't you full on pigeons?"

Ketcher cocked his head at him. Felicity scurried off and climbed onto Aaron's lap. Rime choked down a hunk of meat, then went back in for another as if he hadn't heard.

"Oh, I'm too hungry to care." Treylen let it be and helped himself to another ladle of stew and enough bread to choke an ox. If there was one thing they were never wanting for, it was food stores here in the abbey. The queen made sure of that. A shipment came every other week to the village below. Part of training was hauling the goods up the mountainside.

If Treylen ever saw the queen, he would have to thank her.

He waddled back to the feast table and dove into his second helping.

"Treylen," Ono asked, "will you sit still now and let Courd mend your wound? You don't look well."

"He is a bit ashen, isn't he?" Aaron said. It wasn't his injury that bothered him. It was the message in his pocket.

"He can stitch it, if he needs the practice," Treylen said, looking back. A small puddle was forming on the floor behind him. Aaron must've stabbed him a bit deeper than he realized.

"Then you can fix my ankle," Volanti said.

"Nothing to do for it," Treylen said, then turned to Aaron. "Did you bring her things down?"

"You'll sleep here," Aaron said, "for tonight at least."

"I'll brew some willow," Ono said, standing and rushing off to the kitchen to put the kettle on.

"What are you doing? Get off of there!" Ono yelled, and Treylen heard a towel snapping and claws scurrying over floorboards.

"That reminds me," Treylen said, "Rime got another messenger pigeon."

"What? When?" Ono came back to the table and loomed over him.

"Just earlier."

He pulled the small canister from his belt and held it up to her. Ono snatched it away and cracked the seal, gently teasing the small piece of rolled paper out of its casing. The room went silent, and everyone held their breath as she unrolled the paper. She held it before her nose and squinted, before frowning at Treylen.

"It's for you."

"Is it my father again? Is he telling me how poorly his search for a new apprentice is going and reminding me that I'm shaming the family?"

"He would never say such a thing."

"He doesn't have to."

"It's from the commander of the queen's southern army."

He sat in stunned silence for a moment before he managed a response. "What?"

"You are to go south to the Harvest Pass to speak with him."

"When?"

"Urgently."

"But why?"

"You don't see?" A sad little smile crossed Sister Ono's face.

"See what? What does he want with me?"

One of the elders looked up from their stew to shout at him.

"It's your time, boy. Tithes to the queen! You're finally being called into service."

Was it really that time? After all his training, Treylen didn't know if he was ready. "You don't really think that?"

"It's past due, we all know," Sister Ono said.

I don't think it, Rime muttered into his thoughts.

"This is a summons from the general, Treylen. It's not an invitation to tea…"

Ourbeth and Cenna chuckled. Ono stared at him, stony-faced.

"In any case, you're going to answer it. I have half a mind to send you now. But tomorrow should be good enough, or he would have sent a messenger instead."

That is it, then? Rime whispered in his thoughts. *We leave our home?*

We don't know anything yet, Rime. But I'm not waiting. If General Bourin wants us, we're leaving now.

Chapter Three

THE BATTLE

No place in Iverna was far from any other. You could cross the entire valley in four days—less with a fast horse. And no traveler in Iverna need worry about the dangers that plagued the lands over the mountains. The queen's assassins watched all within her realm. At least that was what people said. Treylen had never seen another assassin on the roads. Perhaps they were there, but didn't show themselves.

The road from Signet Lake meandered west before it joined with the queen's road and turned south to Harvest Pass. It was only a day's walk, but even quicker if you knew the game trails along the foothills of the southern mountains. They ran through the night on familiar trails and arrived just before morning.

Cries of battle greeted sunrise over Harvest Pass as Treylen climbed the white stone staircase to the wall where General Bourin would be camped. The sounds of combat set his nerves on edge, even though he knew that he was well above the killing fields.

So much blood in the air.

You'll have to get used to that someday, Treylen answered, though the pit in his stomach grew with every step.

The stairs were made of blue-flecked limestone from the lakeside quarries north of Queenseat. It would have been much easier to quarry from the mountain itself, but all the great holdings of Iverna were clad in the stone. It was the marker of the Iveran queens.

It wasn't just the material that felt familiar to him. These were new stairs, barely weathered. They'd been quarried and carved some years ago—as was normal for these grand constructions—and only recently carted south and set in place. The chamfered edges and sloppy corners bore the deep chisel marks of an apprentice stonemason, bored with his work and hurrying to finish.

The uneasy feeling deepened.

*Killing each other down there…*Rime's words drew his attention back to the pass.

As he rounded the mountainside, the battle came into view. The staircase ran along the cliffs before reaching a white stone wall that stretched partway across Harvest Pass. Another wall was being built on the other side. Between the unfinished walls, a quarter mile of wooden palisade blocked the pass.

That was where the battle raged.

Rows of Iveran soldiers stood behind the palisade, polearms at the ready, steel helms glistening, white capes flapping in the wind.

Across the wall, the enemy formed a motley caravan that moved up the pass from the south. When the Jaul empire conquered a new land, their first action was to begin recruiting soldiers. And they paid well. There were Seeran horselords with their thundering splint mail, wild-eyed northerners under the three-antler flag of the elkbone mercenaries, and poorly armed farmers from Lome, the land just south of the pass. Between each group were the square shield-walls of the Jaul legionaries.

All eyes were on a single breach in the palisade where the timbers had been torn aside. Elkbones charged through, wearing antlers on their heads and dark furs over their shoulders, screaming war cries. More of them scaled ladders and spilled over the top, throwing themselves into the Iverans. A rider in full plate and a cloak of red drove his barded warhorse through the gap in the wall and sank his lance into the nearest Iveran soldier, urging the elkbones onward. The Iveran line contracted around the opening. The formation shook, but it held. Arrows rained down from the wall, only to be answered by a barrage from the Jaul archers below.

Rime made a hissing noise in Treylen's ear. *He is waving at you.*

It took a conscious effort to tear his eyes from the carnage.

On the opposite side of the pass, a stone landing was carved into the cliff face, where the wall met the mountain. A lone tent pitched on this landing had served as the headquarters for the commander of the queen's southern army since Treylen's grandfather's time, when Lome had fallen to the Jaul. The queen stubbornly refused to allow any shelter to be built at the outpost. To do so was to admit that Iverna had lost the war outside of their valley and was truly cut off from the rest of the world.

Someone stood in front of the tent, waving across the battlefield at Treylen. He squinted over the pass. A sandy-haired man in light silver chain, white leather boots, and a cape of flowing silk stood beside the tent and gestured for Treylen to join them. Treylen jumped from the walkway to land on the stone wall, jogging out behind a row of archers and ballistae positioned on the wall. The soldiers who operated the machines looked warily at him, then quickly away when they realized what he was.

Treylen stopped at the end of the wall, looking down at the gap where the battle raged.

Are we going to fight? Rime said, poking his head out of Treylen's jacket.

"We're not getting involved. I will meet you at the wall."

Treylen pulled the dragon from his jacket and dropped him on the stone. Then he backed up, got a running start, and leaped down to the battlefield. He landed just behind the Iveran lines, behind the palisade. The sudden appearance of an assassin startled the soldiers, but they backed away to give him room. Treylen stopped to see Rime leap and spread his wings to glide over them. A stray arrow shot out from the enemy side but fell short. Treylen jogged behind the ranks, waving a quick salute to the commanding officer as he darted past. He gave a wide birth to the breach in the wall.

He'd almost reached the opposite wall when a boom sounded, something struck the nearest stretch of palisade, and it shattered. Treylen dodged a falling log as soldiers around him staggered back. Cavalry poured through the breach, and the Iveran nearest screamed as he was trampled under hoof. The rider buried his lance into the chest of another, then drew a saber, slashing as his horse waded into the Iveran ranks, weapons glancing off his heavy plate. More charged through behind him.

The line was faltering. The charge had cleared the opening, and now the Jaul foot soldiers were pushing in behind them. He could change that quick enough and be on his way. This wasn't his fight, and as a trainee, he was not approved to kill just yet. But that didn't mean he couldn't help just a little.

Treylen leaped between the horses, dodging the slash of a saber. He ducked beneath the saddle and drew a dagger, slashing the underside to cut the leather straps. As the Seeran leaned to chop at another Iveran, his saddle slipped, and he went over. As heavy as his armor was, he would be stabbed before he could stand again.

Treylen jumped to the next horse. The heavily armored horses stood shoulder-to-shoulder as they pushed forward. Their hooves were just as deadly as the weapons the riders wielded. Treylen swung under the next in line. Hanging underneath the horse, he cut, then moved to the next and cut again, clinging tightly so as not to fall into the frightful churning of mud and blood under-hoof.

An elkbone shouted at Treylen as he crawled out from under the last in the line, and the warrior brought an axe down. Treylen pulled on dragon strength to knock the heavy axe aside, then slashed the arm, and the man dropped his weapon. Treylen didn't stay to cut him down. He leaped, landing atop one of the horses whose straps he had cut. He grabbed the rider and pulled him off, falling back into the ranks of Iverans who swarmed them now.

Treylen wormed free of the pile, and found himself at the foot of the opposite wall. The unfinished construction made for easy climbing as he gripped the block and hauled himself up, stopping near the top to look back and see the Iverans reclaiming control of the breach in the palisade.

You said not to get involved. Rime was waiting and hissed at him when he reached the top of the wall.

"Don't be jealous, you'll get your chance," Treylen said, scooping the dragon up and running along the top of the wall, past another roll of startled archers and ballistae.

He reached the cliff on the opposite side, then hopped up the last of the stairs to the command post and knelt on the landing. Four soldiers leveled their poleaxes at him. Treylen lowered his head toward the general. Rime stayed clinging to Treylen's shoulder, but bowed his head as well.

"Stand down," the general said in an even tone. "You are Treylen Corbel, son of Aldus and Laurelei."

Treylen glanced at the soldiers looming to either side of him. "I am not at liberty to say, Lord General."

"You're late." The general raised an eyebrow, glancing at the battle below with the Iveran lines reformed, thanks to Treylen's intervention.

"Your message only just arrived, Lord General."

"Were the swallows late to their nests this summer?" It was assassin's code, meant to be sprinkled into conversation unnoticed, but the general was getting straight to the point. He was asking him to verify his ranking and abbey of origin.

"Not as early as the cranes, Lord General. It was a mild summer on the lake this year."

"Very good."

A scream from below pierced the air. Out of the corner of his eye, Treylen saw the line of soldiers buckle. The Seeran riders had made it through the breach again, their lances outreaching the Iverans' poleaxes. Jaul legionaries hurried through and secured their shield walls along the Seeran flanks while elkbone berserkers slipped between them like a dark tide of furs and antlers. The Iveran ranks buckled. The general didn't give it a second glance.

I smell a dragon, Rime said, head twitching.

"Now stand up and let me take a look at you."

Treylen stood to attention as the general eyed him up and down, nodding appreciatively at his darks, but frowning at the small dragon on his shoulder.

"I saw your mother and father at the palace, you know. They have become something of a favorite among the houses of Lakehold and Wetherdin. Queenseat, of course. I haven't seen you since you were a little thing." The general grinned and crossed his arms across his chest. "You were playing ball around the quarry while your father and I sourced the stone for the barracks at Tillage. Let's off with that mask and get a look at you."

Treylen cringed, not at the general's surprising familiarity with his family, but at how freely he spoke of such things. Assassins were supposed to be like shadows. Unseen. Unheard. Unnamed...at least until they became dragon-riding battle assassins and their names became legend. Now there were four Iveran soldiers who'd heard enough of Treylen's history that he would have been justified in slinking into their tents at night to slit their throats—if he chose to.

The general seemed to notice the guards who flanked Treylen for the first time and waved a hand at them.

"Out with your eyes, then."

The soldiers turned their backs in unison.

Treylen untied the lacing of his mask and slipped it off.

"Yes, I see the resemblance." General Bourin smiled, then reached out and touched one of Treylen's ears. "He would weep at this. They have healed well, though. You could be a man of Jaul. Pity."

"We do as she asks, Lord General."

"Call me General Bourin."

"I'm only a trainee. I don't speak for the queen yet."

"Right. That brings me to why I summoned you here."

"It wasn't for this?" Treylen nodded toward the battle raging in the pass. The Iverans had brought their heavy cavalry forward. With poleaxes at their backs, they had pushed the Jaul and their allies back to the breach.

"This? No, you've trained near enough to here to know this is nothing. Every season they come to make their mercenaries earn their coin. A big enough push to keep us garrisoned here and to pull a few cohorts from the Eastern Pass. That is where the real war is waged. And with an attack like this one"—he looked down at the battlefield as a chill passed over him—"you can be sure they'll be making a move in the east soon. But we have little to fear here. We have held Harvest Pass for a hundred years. We will hold it for a hundred more."

"I would ask why you have summoned me, then."

"It has come to my attention that you've been at the abbey for some time."

"I trained under Bostra Avex. He wasn't replaced."

"I am aware. And your dragon…Do they feed them at Coops Abbey?"

A great bang filled the air, causing Treylen to jump and Rime's claws to dig into the flesh of his shoulder. Light flashed from the Jaul line, and the soldiers of Iverna staggered back from the palisade.

"What was that?"

"That is the other reason why you're here," the general said. Treylen slipped the mask back over his face and stepped toward the edge to watch. No sooner had the Iverans regained their footing than another legionary shouted and smacked a hand against the side of her shield. Light flashed across the front of the metal and an invisible wave of force struck the Iverans. Polished helms went flying. White capes tangled with poleaxes as their wielders lost their footing.

I need your sight, Treylen said to Rime before reaching out to the dragonmind.

The elkbone mercenaries let out a cry, then rushed forward to strike at the fallen Iverans. One of the mercenaries ran a hand over his battle-axe, speaking what could only be a power word. Treylen could see the flows of magic coalesce around the power word, pulling together in the air and following the berserker's hand as it smacked against a glyph on the handle. Fire magic surged through the patterns, as if ash or sulfur had been worked into the grooves cut in the axe handle. It flared along the length of the pommel, and burst forth from the blade in a slashing arc. White-hot fire separated the nearest Iveran's head from her shoulders. The axe glowed hotter in the berserker's hands, and he cried out, slashing again with the glowing weapon even as it burned through his gloves.

Treylen's dragon sight revealed more magical patterns in the mass of soldiers behind him. It was hard to see in the chaotic energy that naturally arose from the violence of the battle, but they were there. Glyphs carved onto shields, axes, and swords.

"They aren't battle assassins?"

"You think the queen would allow the Jaul to have dragons?"

"Never. But…they aren't wizards, are they?"

"I wish that Jaul would use its wizards so recklessly. They would be easier to hunt."

"So what are they?"

"They are nothing. But the weapons they carry have been plaguing us for some months now."

"Someone is making these? It shouldn't work like that."

Another burst of fire cut through the Iveran ranks, then the Seerans on their horses poured through the breach. Rime made a chittering noise and ducked inside Treylen's jacket.

"I see Bostra taught you well," the general said. "Tell me, if it isn't possible to forge such a weapon, then how could it be?"

Treylen shook his head. "It shouldn't be. I could scratch a glyph on metal, maybe. But…"

"It wouldn't last," the general finished the thought for him. "Tell me why."

"The magic would change with the temperature, or the moon, or whoever holds it. You can't trap magic in a glyph. A glyph's just a tracing of what's already there."

"He's in Tabron. Just a day from here," Bourin said.

"Who?" Treylen asked.

"What does the name *Norris Duremo* mean to you?"

Treylen blinked, scratching under his mask. It was familiar. But why? His old life felt so far away ever since he had committed himself to the art.

"A Norris Duremo studied under my father. We learned draftsmanship together in Lakehold."

Another blast went off and a section of the palisade splintered.

"What do you remember about him?" the general pressed.

"He was better than me. He apprenticed under my father. Then he just quit and went off to the university. I had to take his place."

"It must have been difficult for your father to lose someone he had made a part of his legacy." There was a note of disappointment in his voice.

"I don't know why Norris couldn't have stuck with it. He actually liked it." Treylen stared at his feet, thinking back to the day when he'd told his father that he would also be quitting. Sounds of battle pierced his thoughts, and Treylen clawed his focus back to the matter at hand. "What does Norris have to do with this?"

"Did your friend ever tell you what he would be studying there?" the general asked.

"I'm sorry, Lord General, we were not close."

"Norris Duremo is from a prominent family in Queenseat, I'm sure you know that. Somebody within his family had friends in the university, in the department of magical science."

"Norris is a wizard now?" Treylen said. The general laughed at that.

"We haven't had a wizard for years. No, but in the time since you knew him, he's risen to a prominent position among the university's glyph scribes."

"So my father was right about him wasting his talent," Treylen said, shaking his head and laughing to himself. Glyph scribes were even less respected than regular scribes. They spent years studying individual glyphs...how the shapes changed with the seasons and the materials used to draw them. It meant reading about the stars and the moon and the shapes of magic. All those years of study to cast the simplest spell that assassins could do out of instinct, without any book learning at all. The general did not seem to share Treylen's amusement.

"You may not see any value in the study of magic, but our enemy does. Early this year, Norris Duremo went missing from his rooms in the university. All of his work went missing along with him. At first, we suspected an academic rivalry, but we now believe he was recruited by the Wizard's Tower in Jaul."

"He betrayed Iverna?" Treylen asked, rubbing his temple. The very idea of that sort of treason made his head hurt. He turned and put his hands on his knees, watching the pass below. There was another blast. More of the palisade wall fell away and the Jaul spilled through yet another gap. He looked away.

"The Wizard's Tower must have offered what the university could not. Respect. Power. The opportunity to grow in his abilities, to study under real wizards."

Treylen scoffed but held his tongue.

"What are you thinking, assassin? Out with it," the general said.

"I'm sorry, Lord General." Treylen suppressed a laugh. "It's just…a wizard can't do anything that I can't do."

"Have you ever fought a wizard, Assassin Treylen?"

"No," Treylen said. He was fairly certain that nobody had even seen a wizard in Iverna.

"Few do and live to tell of it, even among your kind." Treylen nodded his acceptance of the general's claim. Whether he believed it or not didn't matter.

"So Norris has become a wizard now," Treylen said.

"Doubtful," said the general. "By all accounts, he was a promising talent, but his research was not in performative magics, but in new applications and materials.

"I see," Treylen said, more confused than ever.

"It means he didn't care about casting spells. He studied inscription, and the magical properties of metals."

Another blast went off and the line broke. Jaul soldiers rushed in, pushing the Iveran line back. They had begun to take control of the palisade wall. Treylen looked to the general, worried, but he seemed unconcerned.

"A few months after his disappearance, these weapons began showing up."

"I still don't understand how it's possible," Treylen said.

"The university doesn't either, but there you are."

Something in the crowd caught the general's attention. He pointed, and Treylen turned to see a group of archers near the rear of the enemy forces draw their bows back. They aimed high and released. A cloud of arrows rose up, streaming toward their position on the parapets. Treylen tensed, ready to flee as soon as the others did, but the general hadn't moved.

"Can you deal with those, Assassin?" the general said, and Treylen understood.

"Yes, Lord General." Treylen drew his daggers as the arrows streamed in.

I need all the speed you've got, he said to Rime, eyes flashing with the dragonmind. Treylen took a deep breath and focused on the incoming barrage. The first landed, and he struck out with a blade, cutting the shaft in two—it clattered harmlessly to the stone. Then another, then two, three, four at a time. Rime let out a slow, anguished whine as he summoned all the speed he could muster. The battle below seemed to slow like molasses, yet the arrows still streamed in fast, and thick. Behind him, the general grinned, arms crossed over his chest, as he looked on. He glanced up as a high one sailed in and Treylen vaulted back, leaping in the air over the general's head to kick it away as a second snagged the leather of his boot.

Treylen landed as the cloud of arrows thinned, and he knocked the last of them aside, then went back to snap off the shaft of the arrow that stuck out of his boot. A sharp pain bit into his heel, but it wasn't deep—the boot had taken the worst of it. He kept his eyes on the archers as they readied another volley. "Well done, Assassin Treylen. I see now why the monks say you are long overdue for your first assignment. Keep an eye to the sky now. I'll put a stop to this."

The general turned his back on the battle and faced the cliff behind them.

"Dragon." His voice boomed.

Treylen nearly leaped from the parapets as a massive, camouflaged shape peeled away from the mountainside. It was half the size of the command tent, colors shifting before resolving into a deep cerulean. The dragon moved silently to crouch on the ledge before the general. It was long, like Rime, but easily twice the size of a heavy warhorse and saddled in black leather with polished steel. Two large sacks hung from either side of the saddle. The dragon craned its neck to bring its head level with the general's.

Rime hissed from within Treylen's jacket.

Keep it together. Treylen put a hand on the bulge where his bondmate hid.

"The Jaul casters have revealed themselves. Is she ready?" The dragon tossed its head. "It's time, then."

The general pointed, and the dragon spread its wings, a rumble escaping from its throat as it glanced briefly toward Treylen before taking to the air. A dark figure appeared from behind the crenellations. They leaped from the wall and landed on the back of the dragon, which carried the rider high above the mountain pass.

"Who is that?" Treylen asked, reaching out to snag another arrow that whistled toward them.

"Rak'tsoro. Battle assassin to the third regiment," said the general, "and the queen's primary wizard hunter."

Foxbane, the elder, Rime answered at the same time. The word elder was subjective. Thirty years was old by bondmate standards, but those who were unbonded—feral dragons that lived in the northern mountains—had no concept of lifespan so far as Treylen knew.

The pair spiraled high over the wall, then turned southward, toward the rear guard of the enemy's forces.

"I've heard of her," Treylen said, cutting another arrow down.

Everyone has heard of her, Rime hissed.

"Never thought I would get to see her fight."

"It's a thing of beauty." The general put his hand on Treylen's shoulder. The dragon and rider spiraled higher. A wave of terror passed over the enemy army as the soldiers caught sight of them.

No sooner had a hush fallen over the pass than another shape detached from the cliffs on the opposite side, like a wildcat pouncing on a rabbit. A lanky dragon plunged into the enemy forces, driving straight into the Jaul legionaries. The standard-bearer toppled over as the dragon collided with his horse. An assassin leaped from the dragon's saddle, daggers drawn, cutting down one soldier, then the next, before hopping back onto the dragon and taking flight again.

Rak'tsoro and Foxbane began their dive, turning in the air as they fell. The assassin drew her daggers, then plunged each of them into the sacks tied on either side of the dragon's saddle. Streams of yellow powder spilled from where Rak't-soro tore them open, pouring out in a spiral as they plummeted toward the battlefield.

"Ballistae fire!" the general shouted. A soldier burst from the command tent and ran to the wall, racing down the length of it, repeating the order. Each pair of archers dropped their bows and wheeled forward a massive crossbow with a lance-like bolt, doused in oil. They brought a torch up to light it, then loosed the projectile into the ranks of the Jaul.

Near the back of the enemy army—far enough that Treylen could only see with the aid of dragon sight—was a ring of standard-bearers and signal flags. Knights in full plate armor surrounded a commander on horseback. The man looked pale as he craned his neck to watch the assassin descend upon him.

The enemy must have been waiting for this moment, as a

large net shot out from each side. The archers who had been firing on the command tent turned to shoot up at the battle assassin. But it was a futile effort. Foxbane dodged the net, taking an arrow in the side, but nowhere vital.

Rak'tsoro leaped from the saddle as her dragon crashed into the enemy, tossing riders from their horses, scattering foot soldiers, and shrugging off swords with a hide like scale mail. Rak'tsoro landed in the center of the space her dragon had cleared. The last of the sulfur spilled out from the bags on the dragon's saddle and Rak'tsoro stepped into the pile it formed. She began to trace a shape, ducking under spears and blocking sword strikes. Treylen could see the patterns of magic coming together as the powdered sulfur rained from the sky around her.

She completed the glyph, barked the power word, and struck her blade to the sulfur. Walls of fire streaked into the sky, forming a ring around the assassin and her target. Soldiers rushed in to defend their leader, only to be pushed back by the intensity of the flames.

It's amazing, Treylen thought. *Just like Bos said. You know they trained together.*

His rider isn't bad either, said Rime.

You know who I'm talking about. But yes, they're both amazing.

They fight as one.

Flames obscured the combat, but a spray of blood erupted through the curtain of fire, steaming as it spattered the shields of the enemy. More nets were thrown toward them—the enemy had some kind of ballista of their own for flinging them. Most were pushed aside, but a few made it through the fire. Behind the curtain, a shape took flight, riding the drafts of air until the pair escaped the flames, charred netting falling away from them. They rolled to duck beneath a volley of arrows, then made a pass along the ramparts of the cliff, saluting General Bourin before wheeling over the battlefield again.

A trail of smoke began to stream from the dragon's nostrils. He opened his mouth, roared, and a stream of fire poured out onto the soldiers below. Smoke filled the air, and a cluster of cavalry scattered as the horses threw their riders, tripped over one another, and raced to avoid the flames.

The other battle assassins finished their kills and took to the sky. Just when it looked like Rak'tsoro and Foxbane might go into another dive, the standards waved. Horns sounded the retreat as commanders pulled back, lest they be the next to feel the battle assassin's wrath.

"You see," the general said. "They always rout in the Harvest Pass. In the east, it is harder. Though they rarely fight to a man, even there. The elkbones wouldn't have it. Mercenaries must live to spend their coin, after all."

Slowly, the mass of enemies routed. Those who had pushed through the palisade found themselves trapped as the Iverans crowded in from either side to cut them off. Two who still held weapons inscribed with magic prepared to blast their way out, only to be pounced upon from the air by the second dragon and their assassin as soon as they revealed their glyphs.

"Now we will get a better look at these objects."

"I thought we were losing," Treylen said.

"This time it was a ruse. But we *were* caught off our guard when they first appeared on the battlefield. Wizards used to stay out of the war. Battle magic and flight were once the sole domain of Iverna. Now it would seem we have lost one of our great advantages.

"And our control over the skies grows thin. Jaul may not have dragons, but we have lost too many in recent years." The general pointed at the other dragon and its rider as they took flight again, soared over the wall, and flew away northward. "Those two were on loan from the tower. We were fortunate for a lull in the conflict at the War Pass long enough to spare them."

"I didn't know it was getting that bad," Treylen said. Had any of the riders he'd trained been killed?

"I know that you have been without a mentor for some time at the abbey. And I commend you and the monks for the work you've done in their absence. Unfortunately, I don't foresee the situation changing. Far too many in the queen's service have been lost. I have pulled some into service prematurely, but those engaged in espionage are still very much needed. Although the day may come that we turn to unbonded spies."

"Is it really that bad?" Treylen asked, though he knew it must be true. Why else would they have left him on his own when Bos died?

"It is troubling. The last was Reyem. My own honor guard. I sent him south to Ketaresk. We hadn't heard from them since South Kysik fell. I had feared the Jaul finally overran them as they have every other land on the continent.

"Still, I hold out hope. I haven't seen any Ketaresk soldiers fighting for Jaul. I thought maybe their ports were blockaded. Reyem was to fly by night across the Stone Kingdom, then enter Ketaresk from the sea. He never returned."

"You want me to be your honor guard?" Treylen asked, astounded.

The general laughed, glancing at Rime.

"Not unless you can ride that lizard. No, you are to go into Lome. The city of Tabron is where they stage their assaults on the pass. You will find your safehouse north of the city. Once you have arrived, a spy master will assess your capabilities. You will begin the next phase of your training, and when you're ready, they will direct you toward your first objective."

"To kill Norris Duremo?"

"Kill him if you must, but alive is preferable, along with his research. The books are just as important as the man himself. As well as anything you can glean of troop movements, battle plans, or the fate of Ketaresk. It's important you do nothing else to alter the situation in Tabron. Stay in the shadows, don't leave a trace of your presence. Don't let yourself be seen."

"That sounds easy enough."

The smile fell from the general's face. "If it were easy, we would still have eyes in Tabron. I would not be putting into service an assassin whose bondmate is not yet grown. But nothing is easy anymore. We're shorthanded, and you are the only agent who knows what the scribe looks like. Now come inside and I'll give you the lay of the land before we toss you into it."

The general spun on his heel, not waiting for Treylen to follow.

Treylen paused a moment to watch the archers on the wall loose another round of ballista fire at the retreating army, while behind the palisade, the Iveran soldiers rounded up those who surrendered.

He took one last look at Rak'tsoro and Foxbane, still circling over the battlefield, before following the general into his command tent.

Chapter Four

THE MAP

AARON, VOLANTI, AND SISTER CENNA PEERED OVER Treylen's shoulder as he unrolled a sheet of parchment on the flagstones, setting his daggers on either side to weigh it down.

It was past noontime, and the monks were doing their exercises across from them in the courtyard. They'd started cooking early when they heard that Treylen would be leaving, and smells from the kitchen already filled the air. The three dragons chased each other through the dovecote, terrifying helpless pigeons. Treylen would have stopped it, but Rime's sour mood was improving, so he let it go.

The journey back to the abbey had felt much shorter than the way out—though Treylen had probably been distracted.

"I've never seen all Iverna," Volanti whispered, gazing at the map before them.

"You wouldn't have," Cenna said, "especially if you came from a lowborn house. The queen would not like it."

"Maybe you should get back to your exercises, then," Aaron said. "This is for the queen's eyes only."

"I have seen plenty of maps," Cenna said, turning her nose up.

"It's fine," Treylen said. "Monks' eyes belong to her too."

Cenna nodded but grew quiet, her hand going to her face.

Treylen took in the shape of Iverna. The land within the valley was dotted with farming villages. At the center was Lake Iverna and the twin cities, Queenseat and Lakehold. But Treylen's eye was drawn to the edge of the map. The Elkbone Badlands over the east mountains, the Great Desert over the west, and over the south, the farmlands of Lome. Beyond Lome, off the edge of the map, would be the Stone Kingdom, Libbat, Kysik, and queen knew how many other lands that had fallen to the Jaul Empire. Somewhere beyond even that was Ketaresk, where General Bourin's honor guard had disappeared.

Volanti knelt beside him. She touched a finger to the parchment and traced the mountain range around the outside, pausing at the gap in the eastern mountains. A drawing of the Assassins' Tower stood just before the War Fields.

"Will they send you there?"

"You know I'm not allowed to say."

"The tower is for dragon riders," Aaron said, kneeling.

Treylen studied the map in silence. Maybe he could tell them. A few secrets between assassins wouldn't hurt anyone. He turned to Sister Cenna.

"You should go back to your exercises."

Cenna glared like she might spit on the parchment, then spun and stomped into the great hall to find her brother, who had no doubt found some other way of avoiding their exercises.

Treylen nodded toward Aaron. "It's what we were afraid of. They haven't sent another instructor because there aren't any to spare."

"Are we losing the war?" Volanti's voice was reedy.

"What did he tell you?" Aaron asked.

"Nothing. It's the same as it has always been. Ketaresk is quiet. But they're so far away, that could mean anything."

"You would tell us if you knew something." Volanti clutched at her sleeve like she might run off into the air.

"I'll head out tonight." Treylen pulled away. He pointed toward the bottom of the map. Just over the mountains from Coops Abbey, a road ran south into Lome. Treylen followed it toward the edge of the map and tapped on a city. Then he raised his finger to his lips, looking around to make sure none of the monks were watching.

"Tabron. What are you doing there?"

"Whatever the queen asks me to."

Aaron cleared his throat with a rumble and stood. "We know where to look for him when he goes missing. I think that's plenty, don't you?"

"Right." Treylen pushed the daggers off the sides of the parchment, then rolled it up again.

Volanti leaned against the courtyard wall, absentmindedly playing with her mask, before putting it back on again. "How are we supposed to learn without a teacher?"

Treylen shrugged and collected his daggers. "The monks helped me. They all know the glyphs, even if they can't use them. Cenna's knifework isn't bad. And Sister Ono knows marksmanship. Better than Aaron at least."

"I can teach all that of just fine," Aaron said.

"Yes, Aaron can teach you how to toss your bow through the woods."

"I won fair, and you know it." Aaron chuckled.

"Aaron never trained under Bos, but he's good enough."

"That's generous," Aaron said.

"I'm always generous."

"So is Rime when his belly is full."

Treylen laughed, shoving the parchment back into its container and jabbing it against Aaron's ribs.

"See," Aaron said, "you're quite decent when it suits you." He offered a meaty palm, then hauled Treylen to his feet.

Treylen walked to Volanti and helped her up. She was still limping from her swollen ankle.

"Will you show me the spell before you go?" she asked.

"I think your spellwork is better than mine already."

"There's one you haven't taught yet," she said. "You did it when I first got here?"

"That one's easier than you think," Treylen answered.

"It might be, but I didn't have dragon sight when you did it."

"Okay, then." Treylen put his hands on his hips and looked from Volanti to the courtyard, where the monks were just finishing their exercises. "Let's have a last match before I go? If you think you can dodge it, I'll show you the spell."

Aaron stepped between them and put an arm over each of their shoulders.

"As much as I would love to see you fillet each other, you have to meet your handler in one piece. And I can't train Volanti if she's burned to a cinder."

"I suppose you're right. I don't want to make a bad impression by showing up injured. At least not any more injured than I already am."

"Speaking of which, Assassin Treylen, what is that coming from your boot?" Ono stood behind him, arms folded. He looked down to see a trickle of blood on the paving stones.

"That's nothing," Treylen said. He had forgotten about the arrow he'd taken to the boot. It had gone numb while he spoke with the general, and he'd been in such a hurry to get home, the details of his new mission turning in his mind. He had pushed the dull ache aside, heels barely touching the ground as he sprinted along the mountain trails to get home and tell the others.

"Let's see it, then," Ono said.

Treylen sat on the stone and began to take the boot off, but winced, a sudden pain shooting through his leg. "Oh, that isn't good."

Volanti limped over and knelt beside him, taking his foot gingerly in her hands. Felicity flopped down while Aaron watched with his hands on his hips. "There's an arrowhead wedged into the leather. You have to pull it out to get the boot off."

"I know now." Treylen groaned.

Volanti pulled one of her gloves on to grip the sharpened prongs. She yanked the arrowhead out. Blood spurted from the hole in his boot and Treylen fell backward. Sister Ono clicked her tongue.

"How'll I walk on that?" Treylen groaned.

"You should have thought of that before you ran home on it," Ono said.

"I'm just getting your boot off," Volanti said, working at the laces.

Treylen felt Aaron grab his shoulders as Volanti yanked on the boot. He groaned again, but it didn't hurt so bad with the arrowhead removed. Once the boot was off, Ono slipped the stocking off. It fell to the ground with a splat. Volanti turned the boot up and a trickle of blood poured out of it. Treylen winced as Ono bent and prodded his heel. Then she uncorked a bottle and poured something over it that made it burn.

"Oh, that's not bad at all." Aaron leaned over him. "Didn't even hit the bone."

"Alright," Treylen said, tiring of the spectacle. "Everyone get out. Go do something. Not you, Sister Ono." He met her eyes. "I'm sorry—ouch, will you leave it already?"

"I'm going to stitch it here and now. Ourbeth! Fetch the salve!" She waved off Aaron and Volanti and the two of them shuffled inside. They brought her kit, and she cleaned the wound, then began to stitch it. "They will miss you when you leave. You've been a good teacher here."

"Is that what it means? Or are they just on my last nerve?" Treylen beat his fist against the flagstones as her needle punctured his heel.

"Come now, Treylen, stop mewling. Bos taught you better than that. This is the queen's foot, you know. Her pain, not yours. You remember your oaths? Use them."

Treylen closed his eyes and followed her voice. He focused, not on the dragonmind, but on his own. On the waves of pain that throbbed from his heel. The arrow must have struck a nerve as it came out. He pictured it, like a flow of magic, and followed its patterns, isolating them, imagining what they would look like if they were drawn on the stones, not through his body, not a pain from his heel, but something distant and disconnected, something he could set aside, or offer up to his patron. His queen's pain, not his own.

He was calm then. Cold. And perfectly still. He opened his eyes and nodded, but Sister Ono was already finished.

"It's not a wide cut. It's deep, though. I'll wrap it tonight before you go." She wiped her hands on a cloth and glanced behind her. "Now go apologize to them. They're hurt that you are leaving."

"They'll be okay."

Her face fell and she turned back to the great hall. "We'll eat soon, then send you on your way."

Sister Ono walked off, leaving Treylen alone in the courtyard. Wind gusted up the mountain cliffs on the other side of the courtyard wall. It swirled around the alcove and brought more kitchen smells to his nose. It would be ready before long.

He hoped that Volanti would forgive his irritation. She was always pestering him for just one more lesson in glyphs. Something told him she'd master the spell before she was walking again. He marveled to think what she'd be capable of once her dragon speed developed.

There stood a gnawing sound, and Treylen saw Felicity sprawled out beside him chewing on one of her claws. She flicked her tongue at him, then rolled over to scratch her back against the stone.

He reached over and gave Aaron's dragon a scratch on the chin, then he pushed himself up to hobble around and pack his things before dinner.

Chapter Five

THE STARS

Aaron followed Treylen up Coops Mountain as he made his way to the peak where his contact would meet him. A hearty dinner and warm goodbye from the monks and Volanti helped to ease some of the sting of leaving.

"Do you think you'll be back?" Aaron asked, hauling himself up over a boulder. Treylen should have turned Aaron back before now. It wouldn't do to meet his contact with a novice in tow.

"No," Treylen said. Anger needled at him through the dragonmind, Rime still upset about leaving. But he didn't need any of his dragon's feelings right now. He had enough of his own.

"I can't believe it's finally time for me," he said.

"What do you think you'll be doing?" Aaron asked.

"I don't know."

"Well, I hope it's something grand for you. Do you think you'll get to infiltrate any palaces?"

"I've seen all kinds of palaces—well, sketches for building them."

"Will you do spycraft?"

"I'll be learning it."

"Can I choose your name?" Aaron gave him a boost up a small cliff.

"What name?" Treylen turned and pulled Aaron up behind him.

"Your alias. You'll need a Jaul name if you're hiding among them."

"Do you know any Jaul?"

"I have ideas. Cren'pin."

"That's it? Is there a family name?"

Aaron stopped on the path. He thought about it for a moment.

"Eelbucket."

"Cren'pin Eelbucket?"

"If I hear something about an Eelbucket who killed someone in Tabron, I'll know it was you."

"That's bleeding awful."

"That's why they'll talk about it."

"No one's supposed to talk about aliases. They're forgettable. That's the idea."

"Then you'll have to write to us."

"The queen would have my fingers cut off."

"Knot a cord, then, to mark your kills. Leave it somewhere I'll find it."

"I can do that."

Treylen jumped down on the path and winced at the pain in his foot.

"Take it easy." Aaron landed behind him. A screech sounded above, and Felicity glided overhead—she still hadn't mastered flight—crash-landing at the top of the next ridge and scrambling on top of a rock, scouting the terrain.

"Trail goes to the right," Aaron said. Treylen nodded.

Why don't you get out there? he thought to Rime, nudging the bulge in his jacket where Rime had burrowed into the lining. There was no answer.

"Felicity says goodbye. She will miss him, you know," Aaron said.

"I think Rime will miss everything."

"He'll perk up."

Aaron looked up at his dragon, then back to Treylen.

"We should leave you here. The trail fades near the summit, but you'll be alright."

"I didn't ask you to come in the first place." Treylen grinned. Aaron held a hand out.

"May that you see me next we meet."

"May that you see me," Treylen echoed, the old assassins' oath.

They clutched hands a long moment. A chill wind gusted down the mountain, tearing at their cloaks and whistling through the boulders. And then they parted, Aaron turning back to Coops Abbey, Treylen with Rime in tow, marching toward the flat-top summit.

How he would get across the mountains and south to Lome…was still a mystery.

The sun grew lower as Treylen approached the peak. Felicity stayed on the top of the ridge and watched them climb until Treylen shook his fist at her. She flapped into the air and fell out of sight.

Are you going to be like this all day? he asked Rime.

Waiting for you to change your mind. Rime squirmed around in the lining of his jacket.

It's not my mind. It's my posting.

You wanted this, Rime snapped.

I ought to make you climb.

He didn't, though; a quiet Rime was a blessing. And Rime didn't stir again for the rest of the climb. By the time he reached the summit, the last reds of sunset hung over the mountains to the south. High, jagged peaks and steep cliffs marred with rockslides stretched southward.

If he squinted, he could almost see a goat trail winding

down from the peak and up the nearest mountainside. Beyond that, it was even rougher and more impassible. To his knowledge, no one had ever walked across these mountains. But knowledge only extended as far as the queen permitted. Maybe in the daylight, it would look different.

A small cairn marked the center of the summit.

"Do you see anyone?"

Rime didn't answer. But a little nudging sent him out. His color shifted, he disappeared against the shadows of the summit, and the scuttle of claws told Treylen he was checking the perimeter.

After a minute, he hadn't returned. Treylen loosened the buttons on his jacket and lowered his hood, fanning the sweat off from the climb.

"Where's our guide? He told us sunset. We can't be that late."

Maybe they changed their mind, and we should go back, Rime said. Treylen ignored it.

"Do you remember the first time we came here?" Treylen said. "Bos took us here to sleep rough in the winter. I have good memories of this place."

I remember being cold, Rime said.

"You were the size of a salamander. You spent the whole trip in my pocket."

I miss my nest, Rime grumbled.

"You used to like it here too," Treylen said.

A small depression in the center of the summit formed a shallow pool just deep enough to drink from. Treylen walked the perimeter of the pool. A low wall of stacked boulders ringed the summit, just high enough to crouch and build a small fire behind, if you were cold and camping, and had brought your own fuel along as Treylen used to. At the far end was a small stone structure as high as his chest. Four pillars carved in the shape of serpents supported an old-style roof, also of stone. The bones of a dragon curled in the center, along with coins and bits of jewelry—shiny things that dragons liked. One white skull rested on the ledge.

"I can't believe he's still here." Treylen knelt in front of the shrine. It was old, even older than the one at the top of the abbey. The eye sockets seemed to look out at him, their expression soft and gentle.

It is a holy place.

"The monks wouldn't say so."

Creatures still know the domain of the dragon king.

"Is that something dragons talk about?" Treylen reached out a hand, running it along the bleached crest of the familiar dragon skull.

We don't talk as much as you think. In truth, dragons didn't talk to one another at all. There was an animal communication. They could pass feelings along, warnings and ideas. But supposedly, only the eldest dragons could speak to anyone who wasn't their bondmate.

"What do you think it was like for him, when Bos died?"

I wouldn't know.

No one survived the death of a bondmate. Humans might linger for a while before passing. But dragons never did. Windfell must have come here straightaway after Bos's death, curled up on the bones of the dragons before him, and succumbed to grief. Treylen might not have thought to look for him here if Bos hadn't told him of the importance of these places.

Treylen felt his throat tighten. He shifted the skull so it rested more comfortably and stood, brushing the dirt from his knees. The sun had just about set again. Night wind whistled between the rocks. Rime hopped from his shoulder and scurried up into the shrine, scratching and nudging the older bone shards out of the way before rolling on his back and curling up in the center.

"Now you like it here?"

He made a soft noise and nuzzled against an old saddle blanket at the center of the nest.

"Alright, then. We might as well have a fire to wait."

Treylen gathered a few sticks and found a chunk of old charcoal half buried in the hardpack. When he'd built a small pile, he cleared a spot to draw a glyph on a burned patch of ground using the charcoal.

Casting the Flavus spell would be harder here, but the dragon sight showed the patterns of old fire magic left behind from the long-ago campfire. And the scattered coals would channel the spell better than earth ever could.

He drew the glyph more meticulously than normal, keeping it small and making slight changes to accommodate the wind.

"Flavus!"

Energy flowed into the glyph as Treylen spoke the power word. Low embers pulsed in front of him. He swept the pile of tinder onto the glyph, and the flame caught as he piled the rest of the old dry scrap on top.

"There. No tent needed." He glanced back at the dragon. Rime yawned and tucked his head under his wing, the shrine and the ritual of the fire having finally chased his foul mood away.

Treylen leaned back against the shrine, warming his feet and trying to ignore the eerie feeling of the dragon skulls staring up at him. He pulled up the hood on his cowl and fed another stick into the fire. Then a voice he had never heard before spoke into his thoughts.

You are late.

Treylen shot to his feet and spun. He was backing away from the wall, looking for the source of the soundless voice, when his back struck something solid. It was large and looming, and it hadn't been there a moment earlier.

For the first time since his first day at the abbey, Treylen was paralyzed with fear. Stale, sooty breath washed over him from above, then the massive shape behind him swelled against his back again.

The sun is down and then some.

The voice in his head was deep, sonorous, and most surprisingly, it was not Rime's. Was that even possible?

"I, umm…"

You make us wait again.

A dragon's head craned over him, tongue flicking in irritation. It was the same dragon that had been on the ledge with the general. Rime appeared out of the shrine, then ran up Treylen's side, stretching out toward Foxbane with a screech that made Treylen jump. Another puff of stinking air washed over them as the dragon sniffed at him.

The pressure of the dragon's chest against his back eased. Foxbane stretched to his full height, his tail knocking over the cairn as it swished in irritation. A trail of smoke snaked up from between his teeth.

Rak'tsoro!

Treylen flinched. A squat, black-armored figure stood on the cliff's edge, hands folded behind her back. No one had been there a moment ago. Had they?

The spiked epaulets on her shoulders marked her as a war-tested battle assassin. Her short blue cape snapped in the breeze. Her boots crunched on the rock with the short, rapid steps of someone who had very little patience. Despite it all, Treylen couldn't help but think how she wasn't any taller than Volanti was.

The dark horns that topped her helm came up just to Treylen's forehead. He let out a nervous laugh.

"You know that Bos told me…"

A hand gripped his cowl and yanked him down. Her other hand produced a burlap sack, which she slipped over his head. Rime squealed and leaped off. Treylen raised his hands out of instinct, but a pinch at the nerve on his neck made his legs go to rubber. He fell to his knees and the sack was tugged down over him. His feet were shoved inside and tied up.

"Ah, hold on. I'm just—"

Be still, Foxbane boomed in his thoughts.

Rak'tsoro whistled, and the dragon responded with a low clicking, then the wind whipped around him and beating wings drowned his protests. Treylen heard the creak of saddle leather and cried out as claws tore into the sack, grabbing hold of him and hoisting him from the mountaintop.

Rime! he called out through the dragonmind. No answer, but he could see a little through the holes in the sack. As he climbed higher into the air and the dusk-lit mountains of Iverna shrank beneath him, his connection to the dragonmind remained. Rime was with them, somewhere.

Though he feared at first they would take him north to face the judgement of the queen, it was clear they flew south-ward toward Lome. Even if he could send his thoughts through the dragonmind to speak to Foxbane, he didn't dare. Nor did he dare to squirm in the dragon's grasp. Those claws digging into his flesh were the only thing keeping him from falling to his death.

Soon, darkness fell completely, and the stars came out. It really wasn't all that different from that feeling of running along the ledge outside the abbey. The moon rose, its hard white casting the tops of the jagged mountains in stark relief. Gradually foliage began to appear again, here and there between the ridges. Then a dark winding path that might have been a river, and finally a forest. Not the steep mountain forest of stubborn pines that grew around the abbey, but thick tufts of oaks or elms spread out over rolling hills, flat enough that Iverans would have cleared them all for farmland. Lome had plenty of farms, with room to spare. They didn't need every acre of it to feed the armies.

Foxbane descended, skimming along the canopy. Leaves whipped at Treylen in his sack. He squeezed his eyes shut and braced himself. There was a bank to the left, a downward lurch, then the claws released him. He'd practiced falling every day at the abbey. But never once in a sack.

A short drop, then he hit the ground. Thick grass cushioned him, but they'd come in fast, and he rolled, only stopping when he collided with some bushes.

Treylen squirmed around and found his dagger. He was about to cut himself out, but he thought better of it. He slipped the dagger back into its sheath and lay there—cold, panting, eyes closed—and tried to will the bruises away. Grass crunched beside him, and a hand gripped the sack, pulled it upright, and tugged the rope loose from the top of it. The sack fell away, and Treylen found himself sitting on the edge of a clearing in a quiet forest, clutching his knees. Rak'tsoro trudged back to Foxbane, whose colors had shifted so his massive form was barely visible in the tall grass.

Grabbing hold of the small trees that he'd crashed into, Treylen slowly got to his feet, checked himself for injuries, then checked his toolkit and daggers. Shakily, he picked one foot up and stepped out of the sack, brushing himself off and looking around again.

Mountains rose on either side of them. Thick trees crowded the clearing. They were well hidden, at least. The sound of water came from somewhere nearby. Rak'tsoro rubbed a hand over Foxbane's neck, moving around him and tightening various straps on his saddle. Treylen wasn't sure what to do. He bundled up the sack and tucked it under one arm, taking a few cautious steps forward.

Rak'tsoro opened a saddlebag and dug around inside. She pulled out a handful of something small and dark, then turned to Treylen. Her voice was low and strangled—an old injury maybe.

"If you'd been on time, we'd have beat the moonrise."

"I'm sorry."

"He has rangers in these woods."

"Who?"

Rak'tsoro held a piece of dried meat up to her shoulder and Rime appeared, snatching it and choking it down without

chewing. The spines on her gauntlet glistened in the moonlight as she scratched the small dragon under the chin, then
held her fist out toward him. Treylen put his hands together,
and she dropped the fistful of dried meat into his palms.

Rime scurried down her arm and hopped onto Treylen's,
snatching a bite before he could tuck it away, then burrowing
into his cowl, beneath the hood.

Rak'tsoro glanced around the clearing, then sent her
dragon off into the woods. Saplings shook every now and then
as he squeezed between them, circling their hiding place.

"You knew Bostra Avex?" Rak'tsoro's voice was flat.

"I trained with him."

"I'd thought most of those were dead already."

"I didn't know that." Another wind rustled the trees.
Treylen watched Rak'tsoro, mind brimming with questions he
wasn't sure he should ask. The spot on his neck tingled in
memory of where she'd struck his nerve. His head ached; he
must have hit it on the way down. He held out the sack toward
her. She made no move to take it.

"Take off your mask."

"Why?"

Rak'tsoro crossed her arms, leather armor creaking. Her
eyes narrowed.

"So that I would know you if I'm tasked to kill you
someday."

"Oh." Treylen lowered his hood, then unlaced the mask.
The air was cool on his cheeks. Rak'tsoro reached out and
pulled off the stocking that covered his hair. Then she untied
her helm and removed it, followed by her mask, leaving her
own stocking on.

Her eyes flashed, and she took his chin in her hand,
studying his ears. The metal spines of the gauntlet pressed
into his jaw, still cold from the mountain air.

Treylen watched Rak'tsoro's face. Her mask had been
older—older styled, older dye, and bearing the scars of count-

less battles. Most of those scars carried over to her face. There were long dagger marks, cheeks blistered from fire, a torn lower lip that had healed with a split on one side, eyes dark and heavy-lidded. The skin under the mask was smooth, with a few wrinkles, but her gaze was hard.

Finally, Treylen couldn't help himself.

"You knew Bos?"

The glove tightened on his chin, then she released him and pulled the mask back over her eyes. "What did Bostra tell you?"

"Nothing," he said, and she crossed her arms again. "Only, you rode through Seera and passed as horselords."

"And…?"

"Drove a cavalry down a river and killed a prince."

"That is all?" she asked. Treylen swallowed, nodded.

Rak'tsoro shoved the stocking back into his hand and gestured for him to put the mask on. "Keep the sack. Where's your bedroll?

"I thought stealth would be more important."

"Travelers carry packs. You'll stick out like a fool in a flourmill. Where's your bow?"

"I don't use one."

Her lip curled up like a wolf's. Foxbane appeared from the shadows.

"I'll have the general's map." She held a hand toward a strap on his belt that held the tube with the map of Iverna.

"Of course." It surprised him because he'd forgotten what he carried, but it made sense. The queen wouldn't want such a wealth of information to fall into the wrong hands.

"Whose eyes were on this?" Rak'tsoro asked, jerking it from his hands.

"No eyes that aren't the queen's." Treylen shook his head, a bit too vigorously. Rak'tsoro sneered, but tucked it under one arm.

"There's a path through those trees, by the river. Follow it south to the crossroads. Don't let them see you. If a ranger spots you, they die. Find the Dragon's Hide and wait there."

"What's that?"

Rak'tsoro growled, ignoring the question. She put her hand on the pommel of the saddle, then turned back.

"Foxbane tells me that you abuse the dragonmind. It does not belong to you. Do you understand?"

Treylen nodded, though he could hardly keep the trees around him from spinning, let alone focus on what she was telling him.

"I think so."

Rak'tsoro hauled herself onto the saddle and urged Foxbane into the sky. Treylen had to throw himself to the ground to avoid the great wings as they unfurled. Dragon and rider took flight, leaving him, Rime, and a field of flattened grasses behind.

At least they were alone.

The forest quieted a moment later. The leaves fell still on the trees. Rime rustled in the pouch where Treylen had tucked the meat. Treylen scooped him up and settled the dragon onto his shoulder as he sat up again, relief giving way to new worries.

Can't go back now, Rime said, strangely calm after his ride over the mountains.

No, Treylen thought. *We're in the Jaul empire now.*

Chapter Six

THE BOATSNATCHERS

RAK'TSORO WAS A LEGEND.

Not just because Bos had talked about her. Or because the assassins Treylen had trained up with aspired to be her.

Every child of Iverna knew the name. And every household had a hobby horse or two with dragon wings. More often than not, it was named Foxbane.

It was strange now as he crept through the forest south of the clearing, that Treylen felt more wary of the sky overhead than the rangers lurking in these woods.

There were other stories children told—of ghostly dragons stealing children from their beds when they misbehaved, of the queen's shadowy fingers creeping into nurseries at night to slash the throats of restless sleepers, of strange ghouls who lived in attics eating tattletales. It all seemed a little more believable this night.

It took a conscious effort to remember *he* was what was lurking in the darkness. *He* was what was whispered of around the fire. And if any throats were going to be slashed tonight, *he'd* be the one to do it.

Do you smell it?

"Bones of the king!"

Treylen's heart leaped half out of his chest as Rime dropped onto him from the branches.

"Do I smell what?"

Mud and water.

"They said the path was by a stream. Which way?"

See for yourself.

Treylen sighed, then glanced at the sky again. He'd been relying on the moonlight up till now.

You may use the dragonmind.

Treylen found the dragonmind for the first time since they'd dropped him in this forest. The trees seemed to dance with lights and colors. The magic here was different than on the mountainside. The dense leaves of the canopy, the deep, rich soil of the hills, and the soothing motion of water nearby all painted strange new patterns over everything. New shapes and colors intermixed with the familiar magics. Some he knew the names for, or recognized the shapes the magic took and knew the glyph to draw to harness it. Others were a mystery.

Smells of mud and water found his nose.

You see it?

"I can smell it now."

He let the dragonmind go and pushed through the trees to his right. The sounds of water grew, and they came out on what appeared to be a hunting trail. The sky to the south was filled with stars…flickering slightly. Was that a smoke trail in the sky? A quick glimpse using dragon sight confirmed it. There would be a village a few miles to the south.

Rime dashed into the water and Treylen let him splash around a minute before creeping down to drink and fill his water skin. The river was more of a stream, deep enough to wash up in, but ripples in the black water caught the moonlight, showing shallow rocks and branches just below the surface. Treylen kept his eyes fixed on the bushes across the water. In Iverna, feral dragons—those who were not bound to an assassin—sometimes snuck into farmers' fields to steal chickens. But they were small and mostly peaceful and kept to the northern Dragon Mountains. Packs of wolves sometimes crept down from the mountain forest to kill a goat or two, but they never disturbed his camping there.

In Lome, the animals were different. There were tales of wolves here whose haunches were the height of a man, with teeth like daggers, who grew fat on the livestock of this fertile land. There were tales of boars the size of small houses, and cats who hunted in the dark. And of course, there were these rangers he had been warned about. Treylen felt a prickling across his neck. It was unwise to be exposed like this, splashing around in enemy territory.

"Let's go." He stoppered his waterskin and backed away from the river's edge. Rime joined him.

We'll follow from the trees. I don't want to get caught out there, Treylen said.

Last time you did that we stumbled on a trap.

Last time there were assassins looking for us. He kept a little dragon sight, careful after Rak'tsoro's warning not to borrow so much that it hindered Rime. It didn't take much dragon sight to see well here. So much of the magic of growth bubbled out from the trees that he could draw a crotus glyph just about anywhere.

Treylen made his footfalls soft, a task made just a little harder by the wound on his heel. He scanned the forest floor for twigs, careful not to snap any as he weaved back and forth.

It will take all night this way.

There was a snap—and Treylen's eyes shot up toward the river.

Was that you?

I'm behind you, Rime said.

People thought of predators as moving, chasing down. But anyone who hunted knew a predator's greatest weapon was its stillness.

Assassins could be still as death.

Treylen waited, breathing slowed, hands frozen near his daggers. Rime crept up onto his shoulder and perched silently. For all his impatience, he was still a dragon, and a dragon was still a lizard, and all lizards were the masters of stillness. That didn't keep Rime's mind quiet, though.

Your mother will worry when letters are unread.

I don't answer them anyway, Treylen said.

Ono writes back to her. Rime seemed determined to distract him.

Then she won't have to worry, Treylen snapped.

Will worry more, now that we are gone. This kind of talk made him regret ever confiding in the dragon. Had they been resting on his bedroll, it might have been construed as well-intentioned. Long, honest talks with one's dragon were the way that bonds were strengthened. Rime just liked to needle him. More often than not, it was at the most inconvenient moments.

I wasn't of any use to them the day I left my apprenticeship. They stopped really caring then.

I hadn't hatched yet, Rime answered.

No, Treylen said, *you don't know anything about it. Now quiet. We are listening to the woods.*

Treylen tried to remember that Rime was still a young dragon, not a fledgling like Volanti's bondmate, Ketcher—though his underdeveloped wings said otherwise—but still a youth by any measure. Treylen was not. Had he stayed in the family business, he would be a landed citizen by now, with a drafting house in Lakehold or a stone yard in Queenseat, maybe a family of his own. So would Norris, the glyph scribe. The same decision had sent the two of them in very different directions, and yet…

Something moved, bringing his attention back to the forest.

A fur-covered shape climbed over a tree just ahead. Two more slunk up from the riverbed.

If they had been a forest cat, he might not have outwaited them. But otters were a curious bunch. The ones he'd seen in Signet Lake had always liked a chase. But the ones in Signet Lake were Rime's size. These otters were giants. The height of war-hounds, but twice as long. He'd heard of them before in the ghost stories his grandfather liked to tell. His grandfather had called them the *Boatsnatchers of Lome*.

Now he knew that they were real.

And now they had his scent.

The lead otter's nostrils flared, mouth half open as it tasted the air. The teeth were jagged and cracked from gnawing bones and river rocks. The eyes were black, searching.

Do you think they can climb? Treylen asked.

I know they can, Rime thought.

It can't hurt trying. Treylen waited until the otter looked down to crawl over the fallen tree. He borrowed dragon stealth through the dragonmind, and the shadows coalesced around him, muffling his footfalls, and further obscuring his movement. He sidestepped toward a larger sapling and wrapped his arms around it. The otter looked up and he froze again.

It scanned the forest.

He wrapped his legs, shimmying up, a little at a time.

The otters searched in short bursts like hunting dogs. Each time they moved, he climbed a little, until the leaves at the top started to shake and he couldn't go any farther. He was well in the air now, but the nearer they came, the more he wondered if those long, muscled bodies could stretch up to rip him from the tree without the back feet even having to leave the ground.

Can we kill them? Rime whispered into his thoughts. The first otter was nearing the base of the tree, close enough that he could see the steam from its breath.

Anything can be killed if you know where the stab it, Treylen said.

The boatsnatcher stopped and sniffed the air. The fur on

its back bristled and a low groan rolled out from its throat. The ones behind it did the same. Then its head turned up.

It sees you!

Don't move. Treylen fought the urge to draw his dagger.

Rearing onto its back legs, it stretched up, claws tearing into the tree, dragging long gashes into the trunk where the bark tore away. Then it dropped down again. Turned, and urinated on the tree.

It hasn't seen us. Yet.

The second otter had caught up now. It growled and snapped at the first, while the third passed them, sniffing the air. When it passed the place that Treylen had been standing when he first saw them, it snarled. The other two stopped bickering to watch it. The otter growled and put its nose to the ground again. It sniffed left, then right, and turned away from the tree, toward the river, excited grunting coming from it as it ran, faster than he would have thought was possible, stopping every now and then to check his scent. The others followed, turning at the river, headed back toward the clearing where he'd fallen.

Once the noises disappeared around the bend, he slid back down.

We don't have long, Rime said. The dragon had crept off him and disappeared into the trees when it seemed like they'd been spotted. That was probably for the best. One bite from those massive jaws would be all that it took.

I know. Come on. He hurried through the woods again, quickly finding the road and sprinting south.

I see you trust the road now. Rime chuckled.

I need speed, he said.

You do, Rime answered. Treylen found the dragonmind and borrowed as much speed as he dared, racing toward the smoke trails of the nearby village. A moment later, Rime landed on his shoulder, giving him another start.

A little faster, Rime said, looking back.

Treylen didn't look. He drew more speed and pushed them onward, sprinting until he felt his chest would burst and his legs give out. He slowed, still at a running pace, and Rime settled inside of his hood, peeking behind them every so often with an irritated snort.

Finally, he seemed to calm. Treylen turned his attention to their surroundings. The woods were quiet as he slowed to a jog. His foot ached. The wound on his heel felt like it had torn its stitches. No time to look now.

"Did we lose them?"

Hard to say. Better keep moving.

Rime looked at the river beside them, Treylen didn't need the dragonmind to know that he was nervous.

"Let's keep moving, then."

Are you sure you don't want to go back in the woods and sit awhile?

Treylen was too tired to answer. He pushed himself to jog a little faster and kept moving toward the curl of wood smoke that beckoned southward. He could only hope that at its end, they find a warm hearth, a comfortable bed, and someone who could tell him what came next.

Gradually the path widened and veered away from the river's edge, toward the trail of smoke in the sky until the trees thinned out. Grass grew longer on either side and a few faint lights appeared in a field ahead, along the edge of a wide road that intersected with the forest trail. Fog from the river hung low between the trees and around the buildings—a light rain was beginning to push it away. There were five or six structures that he could see among the scattered trees, maybe more behind them in the fog. Treylen hid behind a wide-branched elm. A low stone wall ringed the village; at waist height, it wasn't keeping any boatsnatchers out. It might have once braced palisades, though it had been so long since the armies of Iverna moved outside the Harvest Pass, it wasn't surprising that a village so small would be entirely undefended.

What do you think, Rime?

It looks to be a village, the dragon said.

Where is the Dragon's Hide?

Why don't you knock on a door and ask?

We're not supposed to be seen.

We will see someone eventually.

Treylen laughed. The dragon had a point. He wasn't going to stroll around, but if he encountered anyone outside of his meeting place, it would be best if he didn't have to kill them.

He unlaced the mask and tucked it away, removing the stocking and running a hand over his head. He stepped out onto the road, trying to remember how normal folk walked. He tugged on the back of his cowl, so it covered the daggers.

He stepped quickly, walking along the wall that bordered the road, until he reached a gap where a lone street ran up between the buildings. Treylen pulled his hood up; no need to reveal too much of himself to the people of this village. If anyone saw him, he was just a tired traveler hurrying to get out of the rain. The road was turning to mud. It only got muddier when he passed through the wall and between the buildings.

There were ten or so houses with low, thatched roofs. Rain dripped over darkened shutters. Treylen passed a stable with some horses that whinnied at him.

A lamp hung above an arched wooden door. A shingle hung in the shape of a crest, with the pattern of dragon's scales across it and a carving depicting a foaming tankard mounted at the center.

The inn was larger than the other buildings, resting on a foundation of stacked fieldstone. It was coal-black, as if every inch of it had been singed with fire, and it stood three stories tall. Each floor was a little smaller than the last, giving it the appearance of logs stacked in a funeral pyre. A crooked wind vane rested at the peak.

He'd studied these kinds of architect's tricks. The fire-blackened siding was an old style of weatherproofing. All the steep rooftops and harsh angles made the building feel taller and grander than it really was. If it weren't for the two elms that loomed over either side and put it into perspective, he might have mistaken it for an old fortress or the ruins of some pagan temple.

"Hide yourself."

He waited until Rime was settled into the lining of his jacket, then stepped toward the entrance. A loop of hardened leather nailed to the door served as a handle. He slipped his hand through it and pulled. The door swung open, and a warm light and smells of cooking greeted him, along with the faces of a half-dozen mercenaries and the flaming eyes of a skeletal dragon.

Chapter Seven

THE DOORWAY

TREYLEN FROZE IN THE DOORWAY AS A TABLE OF ELKBONE soldiers stopped chewing and looked up from their dinner. The dragon stared at him from the ceiling. Its great limbs draped over the rafters, tail curled around a knee-braced timber that stood between the tables, and its head hung from an anchor beam just above the oaken bar top by a piece of rope looped under the jaw so that it stared toward the door.

All throughout the skeleton were candles that dripped with wax, their flames flickering through the rib cage. More balanced along the tail and talons, as if it were some morbid chandelier.

What's the matter? Rime asked, but he could hardly answer. *Just stay put.*

An old man with a patchy beard and a hunched back leaned across the bar top and barked at him to shut the door.

"If you stand there any longer, you'll let the dead in. Rain and vapors, and he stands in the doorway like it's a summer day."

The strangely accented voice tore his focus from the ghastly display, and Treylen stepped inside. There was a staircase in the back that led up the second room, a wide stone hearth along the wall, and an old, heavy grandfather clock tucked into a dusty corner between the two. The tables were empty except beside the hearth, where the six elkbone mercenaries waited—half-chewed food hanging from their mouths, hands near their weapons. The innkeeper shouted at him.

"Throw the shutters if you like, milord. We'll let the weather in. Hellcaves, I'll fix a picnic for us. What say you, Amelia? A round of good ale for the boys and we'll all eat out on the green?"

The north men chuckled, all but one turning back to their meals. A skinny fellow in thick furs, soot on his cheek, and two black teeth in the front of his mouth, swallowed the last of his ale and leaned his chair back against the hearth. He put his feet up on the table, watching Treylen as he walked toward the bar.

Treylen hesitated. He'd spent so long on the mountain with only the monks and his fellow assassins—this was all a lot to take in. The old innkeeper straightened his leather skullcap, then spat onto the bar and bent over it, scrubbing with a rag. He glanced up again, winking as Treylen approached.

"Sorry about that," Treylen said.

"Whatddya want?" One eye bugged out as the man stared at him, frowning when his gaze passed over Treylen's cowl and the bulge under one arm where Rime had tucked himself. He gestured to a stool, just beneath the dragon's skull. Wax dripped down the back of it.

Treylen pulled the stool out and took a seat. His foot still ached, but he'd have to push the pain away a little longer. The old man slung a mug of something warm onto the bar in front of him. His face twisted up as he peered over Treylen's shoulder at the mercenaries, startling Treylen as he shouted into his face.

"Amelia? Did you hear me? I wasn't tuggin' your boot over the ale, lass. Top those mugs before the boys die of thirst. Now, what'll it be?"

"A room." Treylen coughed. "Food."

"A good room?" the man asked. Treylen shook his head. "Sleep in the stables, if you like?" Treylen shook his head again. "I've room in the back, then. Warm enough. Spot on the floor for ya."

"That's fine," Treylen said.

"I'll see what's left in the kitchen. You eat warhorse?" Treylen shook his head again. "Hmm. Don't go nowhere."

He glanced over Treylen's shoulder, then left his rag and shuffled back into the kitchen, keeping a hand on the bar to steady himself.

Treylen studied the room again, avoiding the eyes of the skinny mercenary. Eventually, his gaze settled on the dragon. Where had that come from? Was it from early in the war? Or something newer? Who had their rider been? Could any of the assassins who trained alongside him have a dragon that size by now? No, it must be as old as the inn itself. This would have to be the dragon whose hide had given the inn its name. The scales stretched across the shingle that hung outside might just be the real thing.

Slowly, anger began to boil up in him.

What is the matter? Rime asked again. *Is it the dead one?*

You smelled it? Treylen asked. Rime didn't elaborate. But at least he wouldn't startle and blow their cover.

The door to the kitchen slammed and a woman about Treylen's age came out carrying a pitcher in one hand, a bowl in the other. She wore a stained barmaid's dress, hiked up on one side so she didn't trip on it. Her eyes, tired and dull, passed over Treylen without meeting his gaze. She pushed the bowl down the bar so it slid to a stop in front of him, spilling a bit of soup into the beer that puddled around his drink, before crossing the room to top up the elkbones' tankards and leaving the pitcher on the table in front of them.

Treylen had never seen an elkbone up close before. He'd heard that they weren't human, but always had attributed it to

Iverans' fear of outsiders, or the fact they dressed in thick fur jackets, wore horns on their heads, and came from the badlands north of the dragon mountains. But now he saw that he'd been wrong.

They were all large, weathered-looking, and dressed in heavy furs, but what set them apart from human men were the antlers growing from their heads. Of the six, only one had a full-sized crown of branching antlers. The others were a mix of broken, blunted, or intentionally sawed short. The full rack belonged to the skinny man who'd been eyeing Treylen since he'd entered. The mercenary took a sip and leaned back again, watching Treylen with renewed interest.

Is that stew? Inside his jacket, Rime made a low rumbling noise.

They are watching, Treylen reminded him. *Stay quiet now.*

Treylen looked around for a spoon before finding one that had sunk into the stew. He fished it out and sipped a bit of the broth. It wasn't bad. In fact, it reminded him a little of the monks' cooking at the abbey. He ate around the chunks of stringy meat that sat heavily at the bottom, not sure he could stomach meat right now even if he knew it wasn't warhorse.

The laughter from the table behind him had resumed, and one of the elkbones drunkenly shoved the skinny one's feet off the table and pulled him in to drink with the rest. Treylen felt he could relax a bit.

The old man poked his head out, his one good eye bulging at Treylen, then disappeared into the kitchen again. When he was sure no one was looking, he snagged a chunk of meat out of his soup and dropped it down the collar of his jacket.

Quietly, he thought, dropping another in as Rime sniffed it out and choked it down.

"Come from Iverna?" A voice at his side made him jump. The barmaid held a tub of soapy water in one hand, a mop in the other. She leaned against the stool, far too close to his face.

"No, no. Not Iverna. Tabron…is where I'm going."

Treylen fought to keep the panic from his voice, but his eyes must have shown it. The barmaid flashed a half-drunk smile—a dimple on one cheek and a gap between her front two teeth.

"Oh yeah? Them elkbones over there just come from Iverna. That's why they got the coin, you know. They almost brought a dragon down in the pass yesterday."

A cheer rose behind him. One of the mercenaries shouted, his accent even deeper and stranger than the Lome tavern folks.

"Best battle of me life. Missed that wyrm by an arrow tip. Got out by the skin o'me arse. Can't say as much for that poor beggar playing legate."

Treylen raised a mug toward the soldiers, then turned back to the bar and took a long drink—mind working. A legate was a commander of the Jaul legionaries. If the poor bastard in question was not in fact a real legate, then the leader of the Jaul army had not been killed by Rak'tsoro. The entire rout had been a fake.

What was the reason, then? Push long enough to bring the dragons out to kill them? Flee before too many casualties were taken? Try again another day?

He realized the young woman had not left him. She tucked the mop beneath one elbow and leaned closer.

"Tabron isn't where you're from?" She batted her eyelashes furiously, lisping a little as she talked. The table behind him grew quiet.

"It, uh. Well, Tabron isn't…Where do you think I'm from?" Treylen's mind spun. How did people who weren't assassins talk to one another? He'd been in the abbey so long that he'd forgotten how to talk to outsiders. Some spy he made.

"You know what I think? I think you're…"

There was a crash as the door behind him slammed open.

The barmaid's eyes went wide. The soft, drunken smile fell away, and a grim sort of terror shot across her face.

Treylen spun, his hand almost going to his daggers again. Out of the corner of his eye, he saw the barmaid disappear into the kitchen.

A broad-shouldered figure filled the doorway.

Chapter Eight

THE RATS OF OXBRA'DAL

For a moment, Treylen imagined one of the boatsnatchers had followed him in. Then the man stepped in from the rain, removing his dark green cloak and his pointed woodsman's cap. He shook them off and smoothed a feather that stuck out from the band of the hat. He wore green leather gloves and high boots with a long leather jerkin that matched his weathered skin.

The woodsman put his cap back on and lumbered to the corner of the bar, groaning as he pulled an axe off his back and leaned it against a bar stool with his cloak, two seats down from Treylen.

Were those notches carved up the handle?

Then he pulled a stool around the end of the bar and sat so that the door was at his back, and Treylen and the rest of the bar were in front of him. He was even larger up close, back straight as a board even after he settled into his seat. A wild beard and tangled hair crowded his small features into the center of his face. A short, pointed nose with wide nostrils, below eyes so narrow and close-set, they seemed little more than bleary slits under heavy brows, the mouth lost entirely within the mass of whiskers.

"Oh, milord." The innkeeper burst from the kitchen with an armload of tankards. He held one under a tap, then slung it onto the table in front of the new arrival. "Always honored to host his emperor's ranger on a night such as this."

"Hmm." Still sitting straight as a rod, the man wrapped a gnarled fist around the drink and brought it to his face, tilting it into his beard until the tankard was empty. Two rivulets ran down the sides of his beard to drizzle on his lap. Treylen had to assume at least some of the ale made it into a mouth. His eyes never moved from Treylen.

He slammed the mug down with a grunt and ran a glove across his face.

"Quite the thirst, milord." The innkeeper set the last of the dishes beneath the bar and hobbled over quickly to take the tankard and fill it again.

"Hrrm…working," the man grumbled almost unintelligibly. Then rapped his knuckles on the bar. The barkeep nodded and hurried to get the tankard back to him.

"Hard work, no doubt, keeping the emperor's forests secure."

The man palmed the tankard again, raised it up, and sent another deluge down his beard as he drank with long, ravenous swallows—eyes still fixed on Treylen.

What's happening? Rime scratched inside the jacket and Treylen tensed.

Be still. Had the man's eyes narrowed? It was hard to tell.

A fist thumped against the counter to Treylen's left, making him jump. One of the elkbones set the pitcher on the counter. This was the brawler—three blunted points on one side, a broken stump of an antler on the other.

"Another round." They pushed it toward the innkeeper, who looked nervously at the woodsman who had almost drained his drink. Bits of coinage jangled at the ends of leather tassels that ran up the seams and through the lapel of the elkbone's fur-lined coat—it was much finer in its

construction than the barbaric pelts that he'd imagined
when he'd seen the north men from a distance. The elkbone
tore a copper free from his jacket and dropped it on the
counter.

"Yes, yes." The innkeeper took the pitcher with two hands
and held it under the tap. Treylen watched him, rather than
look at the men on either side.

What was he doing here? This all seemed like foolishness.
He'd surely be found out. If the barmaid hadn't made him
already. Where had she gone anyhow?

"Strange moon tonight," the elkbone said.

"Mhrrm." The man thumped his tankard on the bar and
let out a long breath. He rapped the table with his fingers and
the poor innkeeper looked from his tankard to the pitcher,
then let go of the pitcher with one hand and reached for the
cup, without turning off the tap. He sloshed the ale from the
pitcher into the tankard and set it back in front of the guest,
then focused on filling the pitcher again.

The elkbone grunted his displeasure but didn't say
anything. Treylen could feel the mercenary's eyes on his face.
It was unnerving, though not quite as unnerving as the man
on his right.

"Amelia! Stew for the lord ranger," the innkeeper
called out.

"Mnah." The woodsman shook his head and brought the
mug back to his lips. Drinking a little slower this time.

"No stew, Amelia! See to the table now, would you?"
Treylen shifted in his seat and the innkeeper glanced back at
him. "With you in a moment, son."

"Strange weather." The elkbone leaned on the bar beside
him and belched.

"Aye." The innkeeper looked at him and Treylen. "The
season is quickly turning for the worse, I think. Swallows will
have cleared out of the barns, if they weren't already." He
shut off the tap and returned the pitcher.

The elkbone took it back from him, then lowered his head toward the woodsman. "Milord." He returned to his table.

"Are ye well into your cups there, milord?" The innkeeper grabbed his rag and sopped some of the beer up from the bar. The woodsman gave a small nod, and set his tankard on the table, still half full.

The old man turned to Treylen. "And the gentleman from Tabron? Would a shank of lamb be to your liking or shall we get you settled in the back?"

"I think I'm tired," Treylen said, making the mistake of meeting the woodsman's eyes again. His gaze was implacable. The clock in the corner ticked away.

"As you wish. Pardon, milord. One to tide you over." The innkeeper placed a full tankard on the bar as the woodsman took another sip. "I'll just show the young traveler to his quarters. Come with me, if you will." He'd started away, gesturing for Treylen to follow, when the woodsman made a noise.

"What is that, milord?" The old man stopped and looked back.

"Stew."

"Ah. So the ale has roused the appetite after all." He faced Treylen. "Just a moment, then we'll get the rooster bedded down for the night."

Is that man strange to you? Rime asked.

You don't know the half of it, Treylen thought. It was hard to tell if the woodsman was looking at or behind him. His face didn't move. Logs crackled in the hearth and tumbled over, sending sparks up among the rafters. The skinny mercenary with the impressive rack hopped up and nudged the wood deeper into the fireplace.

"Warbard…" the woodsman mumbled.

"Milord?" The elkbone removed his hat—an odd-shaped cap with slots to accommodate the antlers—and held it to his chest, flashing a black-toothed smile.

"'Rats of Oxbra'dal'…" The woodsman set his empty tankard on the bar and took the second.

"Aye, milord. I know it." He waited for something more, but the man had gone back to his ale, eyes pinning Treylen in his place.

"Right, then, 'Rats of Oxbra'dal.' How does that one go?" The mercenary hummed a bit as he dug into his pack on the floor and produced a small lyre and a bow to drag across the strings, fumbling with the tuning before giving up and playing the first chord. It was a bright, driving tune that felt a bit off-kilter, but marched frantically up the strings, working steadily into deeper and darker chords. The woodsman sat impassive, except for one finger that tapped a steady rhythm on the bar top.

The bard broke into the first chorus. His voice was sickly sweet, like rotten apples.

"Rats of Oxbra'dal.
Your cat's upon the heath.
You run, you hide, you soon will find your tail between her teeth.
Oh, Rats of Oxbra'dal…"

I like this, Rime said.

The woodsman had drained the last of his tankard. He swayed in his seat, finger playing with the pool of beer that he'd spilled over the counter. The stare boring into Treylen was so unnerving that Treylen didn't bother to look down until after the man was finished scrawling the crotus glyph across the bar.

It didn't seem possible. But it was there.

"Crotus…" the ranger burped the power word and slapped his hand against the counter. The ale bubbled up in an instant, then burst with a yeasty fog that billowed out to fill the room. Treylen had tumbled backward, landing in a crouch just as the stool he'd been sitting on shattered, bits of wood flung everywhere. An axe head cut through the fog and cleaved the end off of a table, just short of splitting Treylen's head in two.

You'll crush me, Rime screamed in his thoughts.

Come out. He shook the dragon from his jacket, then summoned the dragonmind and scooted backward just before the axe came down to split one of the floorboards.

His shoulder collided with a pair of boots, and he looked up to see an elkbone mercenary.

Hands seized his collar, and Treylen reached up for the man's antlers and jerked them downward just as the next strike came. The axe buried itself in the back of the soldier.

The elkbone screamed. Chairs toppled over behind him as the others shot to their feet. The warbard was still playing somewhere over by the hearth. Strangest of all, the ranger was humming to himself as he yanked the axe free and brought it around again.

That was when Rime struck. Leaping from the rafters to land on his face, his claws raked across the ranger's eyes. The man swiped at him, but Rime was gone. It gave Treylen time enough to get out from under the bleeding elkbone.

His companions were coming after Treylen now. He slipped around the first soldier, plunging a dagger through his kidneys. The second swung a war hammer and Treylen dodged it, rolled under a table, and flattened himself against the far wall. The fog continued to grow, but with the dragonmind, he could just make out the shapes moving within it as they searched for him.

The warbard sang his song. Those Rats of Oxbra'dal were getting disemboweled and gobbled up in droves. Rime would be singing in his head for the next two weeks.

Was that a spell he used? Rime dropped beside him, color shifting as he disappeared against the floorboards.

Yes. I don't know how, though.

Treylen inched along the wall toward the door to the kitchen. The two-handed wood axe came sailing through the fog and buried itself in the wall by Treylen's chest. Then the ranger came at him, a hatchet in his hand. Dragon speed helped him parry easily enough, but the ranger was still shockingly fast, and any hope he had of escape was dashed by the mercenaries coming around from the side. Another with a war hammer, and two with axes of their own.

Treylen sprang backward, bolted over a table, and drew heavily upon the dragonmind to launch himself into the rafters. A sword bit into his thigh and he leaped again, falling on the next beam over. The ranger growled, then the hatchet sailed through the air. Treylen dodged it, leaping back to the next rafter. In the fog, the shape of the ranger turned to retrieve his two-handed axe from the wall. Two of the mercenaries were dead. The others searched blindly around the room.

Now was his chance.

Let's get outside, Treylen said.

He let the dragonmind slip a little. He couldn't have Rime hindered, wherever he was. A dragon skeleton blocked the rafters in front of the door, so he dropped down by the hearth, the bard's singing obscuring his footfalls. Treylen rolled under a table, then popped up and made for the door.

He was almost there when the lyre smashed into the side of his head.

Chapter Nine

THE HANDLER

THE ROOM WENT FUZZY. STARS SWARMED IN FRONT OF HIS EYES like rats. The bare floorboard pressed against his cheek. Treylen felt a hand grip his arm and wrest one of the daggers away. He rolled over, slicing aimlessly with the second dagger, but a boot caught his arm and pinned it. The woodsman's axe came down through the haze of steam. Firelight shone on the blade, and for a moment, Treylen imagined himself as another notch carved onto that handle. Then it struck with a thunk, wedging firmly into the soft wood floor. The handle pinned his throat.

"Hold him." The hands on Treylen's wrists tightened. He saw a burly elkbone on his left. To his right, the bard let out a sickly cackle. The ranger dropped his knee on Treylen's gut.

"Your name," the ranger growled. His fingers tightened on Treylen's face. He pressed the axe handle against his neck. Treylen struggled to buck him off, but the man only shifted more weight onto his knee. His guts felt like they'd burst from his belly.

Where are you? he called out to Rime. There was a screech and the dragon sailed over, tearing into the ranger's neck. A puff of flames erupted from Rime's mouth, swirling around the ranger's face and setting his beard alight.

The man released his hold on Treylen's head and snatched the dragon, wrenching him off and throwing him against the hearth with a smack. Treylen struggled but couldn't budge him. The bard cackled in his ear.

Stay back, he said to Rime. *It won't do any good.*

There was no answer. Though with Rime, that could mean anything. He'd lost his connection to the dragonmind when he fell. Now he reached for it again, but it wouldn't come. Either his mind was too clouded, or Rime wasn't there. He hoped his bondmate was okay.

The man grabbed his face again and leaned over him, beard still in flames.

"Your mission."

Treylen coughed at the smell of burning hair and shook his head. The hand squeezed tighter. The man leaned closer and mumbled, breath reeking of ale, "Take his boots off."

"Milord?" one of the mercenaries asked, confused.

The ranger's eyes bulged, and he growled, letting up on the axe for a moment to fumble at his belt. He came up clutching a buck knife and tossed it onto the floor behind him.

"Skin his feet," he muttered, then leaned into Treylen again, beard smoking. "Iveran?"

Treylen nodded—vigorously. Teeth flashed behind the beard. There was a tug as the mercenary began unlacing the first boot.

"Name," he demanded again. Another tug and the boot came off. The mercenary grabbed his foot, and pain from yesterday's injury shot up his leg.

"Mission?" the ranger grumbled.

He felt the pressure of a blade against his toes. Treylen pressed his lips together and shook his head. The bearded man smiled, leaning closer.

"You'll talk…" He burped, the air burning Treylen's

nostrils. Then the ranger's eyelids drooped, and he slumped forward.

"Milord?" The bard sank to the floor too.

Treylen saw that the third mercenary had already fallen, tongue hanging to the side, mouth foaming. The remaining elkbones ran for the door before they fell, twitching, then going still.

Treylen breathed. Slowly, his panic subsided. Again, he felt for the dragonmind. He found it, and with it, the strength to lift the man off his chest. He rolled the bodies off him, sitting up and taking in the scene. Tables overturned, chairs and barstools lay in pieces, bodies piled around him. The fog in the air was beginning to thin. Rime slunk over from the fireplace and crawled onto him.

"Were you really breathing fire?" Treylen put a hand on the dragon and scratched his head.

Don't know what came over me.

"You did well."

"Hah." A laugh came from the rafters. "I've never seen a more sorry performance in my life."

Treylen leaped to his feet, slipping in the blood from his heel. An assassin sat in the rafters, black mask over a strong chin, with a shock of short silver hair, black boots swinging. One hand rested on the brow of the skeletal dragon that glowed in the candlelight.

The assassin dropped with an easy grace, then strolled over to lean down and check the pulse of the ranger.

"He had better be dead. I gave him enough poison to kill a bear."

Treylen took another step back, scanning the rafters. "You're my handler?"

"Supposed to be. You know there was a time we'd both have our throats cut for a mess like this?"

Rime glided over to land on the assassin's shoulder. He

scratched Rime beneath his wings, producing something from his toolkit. Whatever it was, Rime gobbled it up.

He thrust his hand out. "Marziel, spymaster."

Treylen limped over and grabbed the man's hand. "Treylen Corbel."

The hand crushed down on his, punishingly. "Never give your family name. It makes you vulnerable."

"But Bostra Avex—"

"Riders aren't like us," he cut Treylen off, raising a hand toward the skeleton in the rafters. "When you're a battle assassin, you'll get your name back. And by the time you're a rider, all Iverna will know it. But if this is any indication…" He spread his hands toward the carnage that surrounded them.

The door opened and another assassin stepped out of the kitchen, dressed in black.

"It's not his fault," she said. "He's from Coops Abbey. They haven't had a trainer since Bos died." She was tall, with long arms and fair skin, a single scar on her cheek and a voice that might have been called rich if it had any emotion to it. Treylen recognized her immediately.

"Apogee!" He almost ran to her, but seeing the bodies on the floor, he hesitated.

"You know this fool?" the man asked.

"It's been a while. I was leaving when Treylen came in."

"How standards have fallen." Marziel crossed his arms. He had an easy confidence that reminded Treylen of Aaron. Though he was closer to General Bourin in age, which made him easily the oldest assassin Treylen had ever seen.

It was strange to be conversing with dead bodies lying around. Treylen decided he ought to explain himself.

"Rak'tsoro dropped me in the woods. She said to go to the Dragon's Hide. Then Tabron—"

"No." The man held up a hand. "Keep it to yourself. We can't get lax with our secrets. We've lost too many that way. I know enough about where you are going and what skills it will require."

Apogee stepped over a body and put her hands on Treylen's shoulders, then she checked his ears.

"Look at you. What would Bos say?"

"He would roll over in his grave," Marziel said. "Who's teaching at the abbey, then?"

"Well, I was. Where's Snarefoot?" He looked to see if the dragon was hiding in her jacket, before realizing that her bondmate would have grown considerably by now.

"How did it come to this?" Marziel scoffed. Then his expression changed to one of resignation. "You can fight at least, just got unlucky with the warbard. Usually they're more precious with their instruments. What were you thinking, walking in here with your darks on? You might as well have worn the queen's colors as a cape."

"He kept his cool, though," Apogee said. "I thought that I could break him, but he didn't falter."

She leaned in and smiled. The gap between her teeth sparked a realization.

"It was you?" The barmaid who'd been prodding him for information. "But you don't…"

"Look like that?" She pulled her head back so her cheeks plumped and smiled with a vapid grin that made her scar look more like a dimple. She drew her shoulders in and stooped. Even her voice shifted. "This any better, traveler?" Her eyebrows fluttered. Then it all fell away, and she was Apogee again. "A little rouge helps. The hard part is holding it all night."

"Where'd you learn that?" Treylen asked.

Her face went flat again. But it was Marziel that spoke first.

"She already had a grounding in it when she came to me. You should have learned these things at your abbey."

Treylen closed his eyes. *I feel like an idiot.* He sent the thought to Rime.

I have always thought so, Rime responded. He had expected that answer. Still, it cheered him to hear the dragon's voice. Just a minute ago, he'd feared him dead.

Think of all the time we wasted, Treylen thought.

You trained from dawn till dusk, bondmate. And then some. It was very boring. It must have counted for something. He was impressed with your fighting, just got unlucky. Treylen nodded as he listened. The last bit had helped. It wasn't much consolation, but it was the longest the dragon had spoken in months.

When he opened his eyes, the others were watching him. The man scratched Rime's chin. And realization dawned a second time.

"You were the innkeeper."

"It's my inn, after all." Treylen tried to imagine this man with a hunched back, bulging eyes, and a patchy beard. He couldn't see it.

"How did you do that?"

Marziel scoffed at the question. "Unlike my apprentice, I don't do parlor tricks."

"I'm not your apprentice anymore," Apogee countered.

"You've been here all this time?" Treylen asked. It had been five years at least since he had seen her. He hadn't known her well. But he had looked up to all the assassins he'd trained under that first year.

"No." She went quiet for a minute, maybe talking to her dragon. She might be large enough now that she stayed out in the stables.

"Apogee's come back to help me with things. I was her handler, but she came to me already well prepared. You, I'm sorry to say, don't have the training or the time to spare. I've orders to rush you off to your assignment. Seems someone in the upper ranks thinks that it is time sensitive. No"—he raised a hand as Treylen opened his mouth—"the left hand must never know what the right is doing. That's how the queen would have it."

"But if it's so important…"

"Whether or not it's important is another thing best kept to yourself. Discretion is an attribute that assassins seem to lack these days." He narrowed his eyes at Apogee a moment. "If I could cut your tongues out, you all might live a little longer."

Apogee frowned and looked at the floor. Rime scurried down the man's back and ran off into the kitchen.

Don't eat anything poisoned. Treylen warned him.

"What a mess." Marziel scanned the room, then turned back to Treylen, a look of resignation on his face. "You did a few things right. Showed nerves of steel at the bar. There were eyes on you from four sides, and you didn't flinch. He made you from the moment you entered the forest, but you had him second-guessing. You kept your mouth shut, that's half of deception right there. Queen's shadow," he cursed. "Why'd you have to bring him in here?"

Marziel walked to the woodsman and rolled him over, then searched the body. Not finding much of interest, he stood, shaking his head.

"When I saw things taking a turn, I did what I had to. The elkbones aren't from here. No one from the badlands was going to come looking for them—not that I am happy to kill a bard. But they'll be looking for the ranger."

"Why?" Treylen asked.

"What did you learn about rangers during your training?"

When Treylen didn't answer, Marziel closed his eyes and pinched the bridge of his nose. He seemed to be doing some kind of breathing exercise.

Apogee put a hand on Treylen's shoulder. "They're Emperor Jaul's eyes in his wild places. They watch the border. They work alone."

"But they talk," Marziel said. "That's the real danger of

the ranger networks. They keep an eye on their enemies and pass word along. They work together where their ranges overlap. We can't know when he'll be missed. This close to Iverna, it won't be long. Which means we have no time to waste. Your training starts tonight. Sit there." He pointed to a chair in the center of the bodies. Then looked at Apogee. "Fetch some clean water and salve. Get his foot wrapped."

She nodded, then ran up a staircase beside the door to the kitchen.

"The first thing you should learn is always sit with your back to a wall and facing the door. Your naivety served you this once, in that you looked too much a fool to be an assassin. But, the day will come that it doesn't."

Marziel mimed stabbing a knife into Treylen's kidneys.

"I will remember."

Marziel nodded, then gestured to the ranger again.

"He still caught you by surprise."

"He cast a spell," Treylen said. "How is that possible? They don't have dragons."

"I saw that." Marziel looked troubled, staring at the bones that hung in the rafters. "And it shouldn't be possible. But it was a crotus glyph. You don't need dragon sight to cast crotus in a forest like ours. Someone had to have trained him, though."

"A wizard?" Treylen asked.

"Someone who knew the moon cycles. He would have to have been very well studied in the arcane."

"I know my glyphs."

"But can you draw them without dragon sight? Could you predict the way a crotus glyph shifts with the seasons?"

"I don't think I'd ever need to." Treylen laughed. But Marziel didn't seem to think it funny.

"In the right location, with the right ingredients, you would be surprised what can be cast without dragon sight. Let's keep moving. Whiteroot poison. Do you know it?"

Marziel grabbed the elkbone nearest to Treylen and rolled him over, showing the foam around his mouth.

"I know how to harvest it," Treylen said. "That's all we learned."

"It'll serve you here, but you won't find it closer to Jaul. Too bitter for regular ale. But I brew mine sour so it's harder to detect. It kills quickly."

"I've never seen an elkbone up close before."

"You won't always see them. They come to fight, then they go home. You might find them at the inns between here and Ketaresk and in marketplaces. They like to shop. But they always return to their warlords."

"Do their women fight or is it just the men?" Treylen asked, and Marziel laughed.

"Oh, child. You're Iveran through and through. Not all nations of Pentearth have elven blood in them. Those are the women." He pointed to one of the hammer-wielders.

Aside from a little less hair on their faces, he couldn't tell the difference. "Don't you think it's strange the women have antlers?"

"No more than the men. They shed them each year, you know. Bloody mess when they're rutting." Marziel checked the pockets of the mercenary, then removed the coins that hung from the tassels of the jacket, holding one up for Treylen to inspect. "This is ancient Seeran. That is unusual. The Jaul would have taken this out of circulation. That means this coin was likely paid to one of the warlords during the Seeran conquest."

"What does it mean?" Treylen took the coin. It was the same shape as the others, round with a hole through the center, but rather than the face of the emperor, it showed horses.

"It could mean nothing. It could mean that one of the warlords who had fallen out of favor with the Jaul has had a change of fortune. Whether that means that his war bands have left his hold and pledged fealty elsewhere, or that Jaul has made peace with those who fought for Seera, is not for us to say. It might also mean nothing. Sometimes a coin is just a coin."

"How do we figure out what it means?"

"You're the eyes of the queen. Your job isn't figuring. You see something strange, you remember it. Parchment is the greatest traitor. You tell me. Then you forget. Do you understand?"

Treylen nodded. It was a lot to take in. And he still hadn't quite gotten over being shoved in a sack and flown over the mountains, let alone nearly having his foot almost flayed.

Rime, get back in here. We're starting.

He knew the dragon wouldn't pay attention, but it was hard to face on his own. Apogee returned, and Rime was on her shoulder. She had a bandage, a bowl of water, and a jar of salve. She knelt and started working on his heel.

"This one." Marziel rolled the first mercenary aside and dragged another over—the one he had stabbed in the fight. "Your first kill?"

It hadn't really struck him yet, so much death had happened so quickly. "It was."

He looked at the body for the first time. It was a young man, much younger than he was. He resembled the others—a son, or a nephew. The antlers, Treylen realized, weren't broken like the others. They were just the button horns of a young buck. His furs looked new, unlike the pelts worn by the rest of them, with few coins sewn onto the jacket.

Marziel tore a copper piece from one of the tassels and tossed it to him. Treylen caught the coin.

"Keep that until you get to Tabron. Then I want you to spend it. Once you've spent it, you'll let him go. While you are at it, you can let go of your feelings toward future killings. The queen doesn't want them. I don't care if you're proud or ashamed of this. We don't keep track. We don't keep trophies. We do as we are told, and we do it quietly."

Treylen turned the coin over in his hand, noting the strip of leather that hung through the hole in the coin's center. Aaron had asked that he knot a cord, after all, and this one already had a knot on one end. He put the coin, with its tassel, into his pocket.

"A good cut," Apogee said, gesturing to the wound on the body.

"A lucky one," Marziel added. "These furs aren't decorative. If you'd struck wrong, it wouldn't have pierced the jacket. You should've aimed here." He pointed to the sternum, where the furs hung open. Then he noticed something, unbuttoning the dead man's coat. "It has a lining."

He drew his dagger—a Queen's Finger, identical to Treylen's blade—then sliced the lining of the coat and pulled it open. There was nothing inside.

"Always check, if you have time. You never know what might be sewn into a coat. Money. Messages."

"I've never found anything," Apogee said, finishing up with Treylen's bandages.

"It never hurts to look. Unless the kill is meant to seem an accident, of course."

"I don't think he'll have trained in staging accidents," Apogee said, handing Rime back. Rime was twice as heavy as he'd been before he snuck off to the kitchen. He settled in his spot inside Treylen's jacket.

"No," Marziel said, "he had to have learned that. Tell me that you know accidents."

"I'm good with traps," Treylen said.

"Tell me you know the difference between a trap and an accident? Hellcaves, this is hopeless. How's his foot?" he asked Apogee.

"It will need more work tomorrow."

Marziel nodded, then drew himself up to his full height.

"Are you tired?"

"I've been traveling all night."

"Well, I won't begrudge you a bed simply because your training is lacking."

"Thanks for that."

"You just have to earn it. Let's get these bodies to the back. If another poor jackass wanders in from the storm, I would hate to have to add him to the pile. Your first test should be easy. I'd have you cart them to the forest, but that would wake up half the village. You'll have to carry them one at a time. Be sure to bury them deep enough that nothing digs them up. Apogee, you'll supervise. You'll be well tired out by tomorrow night. Then you can sleep."

"Isn't that a little harsh?" Apogee asked.

"I'd say the elkbones got the worst of it." He walked behind the bar and ducked down to fetch something.

"Shouldn't we put the room back together first?"

"Oh, I'll take care of that, m'dear." When Marziel stood up again, he was the innkeeper, old and gnarled looking, his jaw twisted at an odd angle, one eye squinting and the other bulging. The patchy beard had somehow been reattached. The leather skullcap covered his head, and his back was bent into a disfiguring hunch that made him look to be half his height, and covered by a dirty shawl. His voice had returned to that of the strange old man.

"Go on now, get milord ranger into the back along with the other fine gentlemen. I'll sweep up and keep appearances. I'm still the proprietor here. I'd hate to lose any more business."

If he didn't know any better, Treylen would have thought this was the man's true form and the other was the fake. For all the talk about not doing parlor tricks, the master assassin was putting on a performance worthy of the queen.

Chapter Ten

THE DREAM

TREYLEN HAD ALWAYS DREAMED OF DRAGONS. SOME OF HIS earliest memories were of waking up to check beneath his bed and out his windows, to see if dragons had really been visiting. A few times, he'd even spotted one gliding over the city.

Sometimes in the dreams, he'd been a rider like Rak'tsoro. Other times, he was their prey, hiding in the mountains from the great Dragon King, who'd risen from the dead to prowl for dinner. Fear and fascination, his dreams had run the gamut. That early connection had been a part of what had driven him toward the abbey. Later, once he had learned to touch the dragonmind, he wondered if those early dreams had greater significance. Perhaps the dragonmind had always been there, even before he met his bondmate.

Once he had learned to connect with it, the dragonmind came easily in his dreams.

This time, Treylen dreamed of summer and white stone warming in the sun. He and a flight of dragons were on the top of the Assassins' Tower near the War Pass, lounging and basking in the midday heat. In this dream, Rime was fully grown—fat in the middle and saddled in a black leather barding.

Treylen lay on him like a cushion, absently scratching at the dragon's flank. Rime blinked at him, then curled his head around to rest on Treylen's legs. The others lay around them. Felicity had grown stocky and taken on a slightly golden color. She was sleeping at Treylen's feet and wore a white saddle studded with rubies. Ketcher was stretched across the stones beside him, long and lean, but large enough for a saddle of his own. Foxbane and Windfell were also there, along with all the other dragons that Rime and Treylen had trained under at the abbey. They were all talking pleasantly, and Treylen could hear the dragons, as clearly as if they were his own bondmates.

This was odd, but he didn't think much of it. Foxbane had been able to speak to him, so maybe he had taught them all to do the same. With the bond, he felt the comfort of the drag-onmind and the companionship of the dragons, bright and warm as the summer sun.

Treylen tried to follow what they were saying, but each time that he thought he understood, a dry cracking sound would find his ears and wrench his focus away.

He tried again, listening carefully. They were talking about his friends, Aaron, Volanti, and the rest. They were missing. They had gone off toward Ketaresk unprepared and been captured by Jaul.

Another crack interrupted. It was a scraping, crunching noise. A set of talons reached up from the edge of the tower. A skeletal dragon's head rose up, candles glowing in its eyes.

But what were the dragons saying about his friends? It was his fault. He'd been the one to train them, after all. Now the dragons were deciding what to do about him.

Another skeleton appeared beside the first one, clambering over the edge of the stone. This one was smaller, and Treylen couldn't help but feel that he knew him. Looking at the others, he realized that Windfell, Bos's dragon, had withered away, until he was nothing more than a collection of bleached bones, baking in the sun. Treylen felt his connection to the dragonmind fray, and then snap.

A suppressed terror began to build within him. It was like the uneasiness that he felt when he used dragon sight too close to the old places and saw the magic of entropy and decay.

And the more that feeling grew, the more they crowded around him. Dozens of the skeletal dragons climbed up onto the tower. Rime and the others seemed not to mind, even as Felicity withered away from the absence of her bondmate, bones clattering to the ground.

Another part of his connection to the dragonmind snapped. As his fear grew, he felt his connection with Rime growing thin. Rime raised his head to look at him. There was a trust in those eyes that he didn't see often in waking life. A rumbling sound built toward the north.

"Wait here."

Treylen moved Rime's head and stood, stepping carefully around the skeletal dragons to reach the edge of the tower. He put his hands against the stones and looked out. From this height, he could see the War Pass to the east, Lake Iverna the west, against the faint silhouettes of Lakehold and Queenseat. To the south were the fields of Iverna Valley, and on the horizon beyond them, the faint purple of the mountains that housed Coops Abbey.

Another rumble called his attention north, to the mountains of the Dragon Lands. A pillar of smoke rose from the center of their tall, black peaks. It rumbled again, and something emerged from those mountains. The ancient bones of the last Dragon King shone white in the summer sun and cast a stark contrast against the black mountains behind it.

Its flesh had withered away, but somehow in this dream, it was flying in the air. The great dragon circled overhead, then landed, still looming over the massive tower. It leaned down, leveling its head with his. Fear clutched at his heart and Treylen took a step back, reaching for Rime but feeling only dry, dusty bones beneath his hand. He felt the connection to the dragonmind snap.

Then the sun disappeared, and Treylen was alone. Only himself and the darkness and the rumble of the Dragon King.

"Treylen!"

His eyes snapped open, and he was in a room at the Dragon's Hide. Apogee leaned over him wearing her barmaid's dress, a lamp in her hand, and a bundle of fine fabric under one arm. Rime wasn't there, but when Treylen felt for the dragonmind again, he found it still within his reach.

Where are you?

Downstairs. The dragon did not elaborate.

Apogee tossed the bundle of fabric onto the foot of his bed.

"What time is it?" Treylen pushed himself up, arms aching.

"It's evening," she answered. Marziel had been kind enough to let him sleep, once they had finished burying the bodies. It had been after noon by the time they'd filled the hole and spread leaves and branches across the forest floor to hide their work.

"Time for more training."

Treylen rubbed his eyes, still not sure if he'd slept for a day and a half or just a few hours. He decided on the latter.

She pointed to a chair beside the bed, where fresh gauze and a bowl of water rested, along with more salve. "Wrap your heel and come downstairs. Wear that." She pointed to the silks. "You are the son of a minor lord from the Stone Kingdom. You have been a disappointment to your family and so you've come to stay with an uncle here and find employment in Tabron. You took the west road through the Salt Crescent. And it was uneventful. You aren't from the stone cities, so if anyone asks, you don't know what they're like. Do you have any questions?" She was already moving toward the door.

"A lot."

"Well, keep them to yourself. Your first task is to keep your mouth shut. When your uncle gets here, you'll have some answers." She ducked out the door.

"Wait," Treylen called after her, but she'd already pulled it shut.

What's going on? He sent the question to Rime.

There's boar roasting in the kitchen, Rime answered.

Something about the tone of his thoughts told Treylen that Rime was already gorging himself on raw boar meat.

I guess this means we won't be sleeping tonight, Treylen thought.

I will be.

Treylen got out of bed and dressed in the silks he'd been given. He would've preferred to wear his darks underneath, but they'd been coated in mud after he finished digging, and Marziel had insisted he leave them outside his door before he slept so they could be laundered.

How could Marziel and Apogee find the time to wash them, roast boar, mind the tavern, run the inn, and whatever else they had to do to keep up appearances, all while maintaining their disguises? Something told him most of these duties would soon fall on him, and he was grateful for the few hours of sleep that he had gotten.

He left his daggers and most of his toolkit in the room, not having any way to hide them on his person, but kept a smaller knife, a snare wire, and some lock picks tucked into his belt.

After he was dressed, he wrapped his foot, then found a pair of stockings against the door, along with fine leather boots, and a hat so garish he doubted whether he was really supposed to wear it. But it had been placed deliberately atop the boots, so Treylen did as he believed that he'd been told and put it on, then headed out into the hall and down the stairs toward the smells of sour ale and roasting meat.

The soft notes of a lute greeted him on the staircase. Though it was past dark, new lamps had been lit around the bar. The fire blazed and the candles of the dragon chandelier cast a cheerier atmosphere than the one he had encountered the evening before. It was also more crowded.

Treylen descended the staircase from the third floor, but stopped halfway down the second flight of stairs. A table full of elkbone mercenaries stared at him from below, ale halfway to their lips. For a moment, the music stopped. Then the largest of the elkbones with the greatest collection of coins sewn to his vest raised a finger toward Treylen and broke into a fit of laughter. The others joined him, rocking in their chairs.

"Oh, west-man, do a turn for us," he roared.

The one beside him, already red-faced and well into his ale—judging by the number of empty tankards hung from his antlers—leaned forward, hiccupping.

"Hang your hat, milord." He tilted his antlers toward Treylen. The big one wiped tears from his eyes, gasping for air and clapping his companion on the back. Tankards clattered to the floor.

The table roared again.

Treylen pulled the hat off and stuffed it under one arm. He marched past the elkbones, ignoring their jeers. Scattered chuckles came from a few patrons seated at the bar, as well as a booth in the corner with three ladies. The bard, a middle-aged man with a potbelly and silver bells stitched to his jacket, smiled as he went on playing.

The old man—Treylen struggled to think of him as Marziel—went to the end of the bar and leaned on it for support, spitting at a spot and scrubbing with his rag.

"I thought that I might let you sleep, milord, after nearly getting yourself killed last night," the barkeeper shouted. There was a mischievous glint in his eye.

"What do you mean?" Treylen stopped at the edge of the bar and waited there uncomfortably, looking to see how many of the other patrons had been listening.

"Took quite a tumble, you did," he said, drying a mug with the same rag before filling it from a teapot and setting the steaming drink on the bar in front of Treylen. A short, round woman sat at the middle of the bar beside an even rounder man. She was red in the face and quite drunk, while he was asleep with his head on the counter. A steady drip of wax from the candles on the dragon skull formed a pile on his back. The woman smiled at Treylen.

"Horse threw him in the storm," Marziel said. "Showed up last night soaked to the bone and half froze."

"Oh dear," the woman said. "Any sign of your horse?"

Treylen took a long drink of his tea and shook his head.

"That's just awful. Well, I'll put together a search party, first light, and we'll get the animal located. Where did you say you lost it?"

"Won't be needing that," Marziel said before Treylen could answer. "I'm afraid it ran off toward the Harvest Pass."

"Oh dear, I'm sorry. Poor thing."

"Don't pity him too much, Hilde. He's to meet his uncle today. Lucky boy." The innkeeper winked at him.

"Oh yes?" The woman raised an eyebrow.

"None other than our Mauridin Tromweft."

"Oh, lucky indeed. We do love when our Mauridin comes to visit."

"We do, we do." He worked at the spot on the counter. The woman turned on her stool and put both hands on Treylen's shoulders.

"Well, if there is anything that I can do, you need only ask. I'm the mayor of the crossroads. And this is Bortleby." She patted the sleeping man on the back, then drained her cup. "We're all good folk here."

The innkeeper took the tankard, filled it, and handed it back.

"You're the mayor?" Treylen asked, and Marziel shot him a look that told him to watch what he said.

"Ten years running. It doesn't pay, but I volunteers me time."

"Small town, isn't it?"

"That's a bit rude," Marziel said under his breath.

"No, that's okay," the mayor said, her eyelids drooping as she raised her fingers. "We are ten households. All good folks, right, Marcus?"

The innkeeper nodded.

"You're Marcus?" Treylen asked Marziel.

"Aye. Didn't catch *your* name, milord, so out of sorts were ya' last night."

"Oh." An Iveran name would probably get his throat cut. "It's, uh…"

"Quite a tumble you had, wasn't it? Just a moment, I've tankards to fill." One eye narrowed in warning as he hobbled out from behind the bar to collect the tankards from the elkbones.

"Yes, sorry, the name is, uh…"

Don't use Aaron's, Rime said, too late.

"Cren'pin?" Treylen's voice wavered, but he cleared his throat and tried again. "Cren'pin Eelbucket."

A tankard cracked him on the head, and Treylen saw stars again for a moment, then pushed himself back up from the bar.

"I'm sorry, milord, are you all right?" The innkeeper came around the bar with his arms full of empty tankards. "Cren'pin, eh, now that's a funny name, milord. Almost sounds made up, don't it?"

"I thought Eelbucket was a Lomish name." The mayor leaned over, breathing ale into his face. "Are you related to the Westbridge Eelbuckets?"

"I'd reckon not," Marziel interrupted. "As last night, milord Cren…pin… told me he had no family, save his uncle, from outside of the Stone Kingdom, isn't that right, milord?"

"That's, uh, yes. Indeed."

"Right. Well, let's not let the mayor and I bother you all night. Find a table that suits you, perhaps there in the back where you'll have some bard-song to drown out our lowborn chatter, eh, milord?"

Treylen pulled himself up straight and nodded.

"Yes. I think so." He took his drink and started toward the back.

"Oh, milord…" Marziel called. "Don't forget your hat. I know how you Stone Kingdom folk are about them." There was a warning in his tone.

"That's right." Treylen went back for the hat. Marziel made a gesture to show he was serious, so he put it on.

"Very fine, milord. I'll have some supper sent out to you, then."

Treylen hurried to the back corner that the innkeeper had indicated, glad to be alone for a moment.

Cren'pin? Rime chided. *You're lucky everyone here is drunk.*

He probably brought the strong stuff out tonight to make it easier for me, Treylen thought, rubbing the lump on the back of his head.

I don't think he intends to make it easier for you, Rime answered.

Where are you? Treylen scanned the rafters, but he was nowhere in sight.

Near enough.

That was the answer he'd expected.

Have you found the dragons? Treylen asked.

Not yet, Rime said. *Strange, don't you think?*

It wasn't really that surprising, after having seen the way that Foxbane could hide from them. Treylen sipped at his tea and stared into the shadows overhead. The bones of the dragon candelabra cast strange patterns through the rafters. *When do you think we'll start training?*

This is your training, Rime said.

Do you think?

Oh yes, Rime said. *I think this is the training. And perhaps a test.*

Chapter Eleven

THE FAVORITE UNCLE

TREYLEN SAT A LITTLE STRAIGHTER IN HIS CHAIR AND SIPPED his tea, trying to look the part of a minor noble from the Stone Kingdom.

Why the Stone Kingdom, he wondered. And why the coast? It was south of Lome and its coast was to the west, near the Salt Crescent. He'd never learned anything about it aside from that it used to belong to a race called the lowsater, before the Jaul drove them out, and that its cities were carved into the mountains.

It was strange to imagine a minor noble from a kingdom like that walking freely through these lands. But that was the way of empires, tearing down borders and forcing nations together. Treylen imagined Jaul like some great mold, creeping out from its rotten core and spreading across the land, bringing more and more kingdoms under its corruption until only Iverna stood unblemished, in the center of it all.

The people here seemed happy enough under the boot of the Jaul. It seemed half the town was here. There were three tables with ten patrons between them, all in simple peasants' clothing, laughing and drinking. Clean plates stacked neatly at the center of the tables told him they were waiting for the boar to finish roasting.

The elkbones likely wouldn't make it to dinner, they'd drunk so heavily already. These were in a better mood than the group from the night before. From time to time, their attention would return to his hat and there would be another round of laughter at Treylen's expense. This was more the temperament he had imagined from elkbones. What had they to be upset about? They were paid whether they won or lost.

Although Iverna boasted of being the last northern land to stand against the Jaul, the badlands had never been conquered either. That was half because elkbones had no central rulership, and half because they were already in Jaul's employ. They'd fought against the Jaul in the old times, but after the tide of the war turned, Emperor Jaul had coin enough to hire them himself. It would only be a matter of time before Jaul had no more use for the mercenaries, and the legions conquered them as well.

The bard nodded again at Treylen. He leaned beside the hearth, strumming softly on his lute. The couple at the bar laughed and joked with the innkeeper.

What was his name again? Treylen thought.

Marziel, Rime answered.

No, the innkeeper.

Marziel calls himself Marcus when he's the innkeeper, Rime said. *The names are different, but they sound the same.*

Smart of him. If he makes a mistake, he can say they misheard him.

"Good evening, traveler," Apogee called out in her singsong barmaid's voice. "You look much better this evening. What can I get for you?"

"Ale?" Treylen asked, looking at his tea.

"Anything else?" She flapped her eyebrows at him wildly and leaned across the table. This drew one of the elkbones' attention and he put in a request of his own, though his accent was thicker than the others, and Treylen couldn't tell if he was speaking in the common tongue or some elkbone dialect.

"Stew," Treylen said, struggling to keep his attention on the room.

"Fed the stew to the pigs, milord," Marziel shouted.

"I'll bring you a plate of the boar. If that's alright, milord," she said, and Treylen nodded.

"Keep your mouth shut," she whispered. "And do let me know if you need anything at all." Her hip bumped against a chair as she floated away, stopping to put a hand on a pair of antlers and trade a laugh with the mercenaries.

I don't think you're ready for this, Rime said in his head.

Treylen focused on watching the bard, rather than risk being drawn into another interaction with the elkbones or the locals. He sat as straight as he could and tapped his hand on the table, trying to look regal and important. It occurred to him that because of his family's work, he had grown up around minor nobility from Lakehold and Queenseat, and few were quite as full of themselves as the high nobility were. He slouched a little.

"Any Stone Kingdom songs you like, milord?" the bard asked. Treylen flinched. The whole point of focusing on the bard was to divert attention from himself. How had the bard even heard about him? Had they made an announcement to the whole town that some traveler had shown up in the middle of the night? It hardly seemed like a good way to keep a secret.

"I think I like your music better. Play what you will."

Someone came up behind Treylen and a firm hand clasped his shoulder. Treylen startled again, looking up. It was only Marziel. But not Marziel in the form of Marcus the innkeeper. This Marziel wore a bright silk shirt and a wide, flouncy hat in the same style as Treylen's. He looked more or less like himself, but haler, with a broad smile and a twinkle in his eye. When he spoke, it was with a degree of cheer and joviality that felt incongruous with the serious man that Treylen had met last night.

"Bard, do you know 'Rats of Oxbra'dal'?"

"I think I do, milord." The bard scratched his head, then checked his tuning and dove into it. The tune was a little brighter on the lute, but it still set Treylen's teeth on edge. His nerves couldn't take much more of this tavern.

"My boy, stand up and let me take a look at you." Marziel hauled Treylen from his seat and wrapped his arms around him as if Treylen were his favorite nephew who he hadn't seen for a decade.

"My Cren'pin, it's good to see you." Marziel sighed. It was a warmer embrace than he'd ever received, and Treylen sank into it, the ache of yesterday melting away for a moment, until Marziel whispered in his ear.

"If this were Jaul, they'd gut you where you stand. Play it up a little. You're a lord. And speak a bit higher—you're my nephew, not my brother."

"I'm not afraid of a few elkbones," Treylen whispered.

"What about the good mayor?" Marziel squeezed a little too tight, rocking side to side as if overjoyed. "Could you bring yourself to cut her throat? If we're found out now, it will fall upon you to dispose of her. And the rest of the villagers."

"Oh." Treylen swallowed. So those were the stakes.

"I've come to like these people. I'd rather not murder them today." He hissed into Treylen's ear again. "Now don't say you forgot the name."

"Uncle Mauridin," Treylen squeaked.

"Louder so they can hear you," Marziel whispered.

"Uncle Mauridin!"

Marziel pushed him away and held him at arm's length. "My, I hardly recognize you. How is your mother?"

"Oh, you know." Treylen looked around and saw the whole tavern looking at them. "She's well."

"I'm so glad to hear it." He clapped Treylen on the shoulder, then pulled a chair out for himself, dropping a handful of coins onto the mantle beside the bard before sitting.

Treylen eased back into his seat.

"I heard you took a tumble last night."

"Yes. I'm walking a little better today," Treylen said, trying to sound a bit younger. Thankfully, the bard's playing had picked up and gave them some privacy, but he wasn't about to break character.

Apogee came out of the kitchen with their food and drink.

"Amelia," Marziel said, "it smells wonderful in here, where's Marcus?"

"He should be out in a bit," she said, "he's just carving the boar."

"Give him my compliments.

"I'll be sure to," she said.

Treylen took his stein and looked inside, making sure there weren't any remnants of white powder from the night before. It was full of water.

"My ale is a little weak," he said to Apogee.

"It shouldn't be," she said. "That's our best ale."

"Are you sure it isn't a little watered down?"

"I'm sorry, milord, that's the strongest we make," she said, frowning at him when no one was looking. Marziel laughed and slapped him on the back, nearly hard enough to knock the wind from him.

"I think my favorite nephew is becoming a lush. Now get some food in you before you drink your ale."

"Will that be all, milord Tromweft?"

"Please, it's Mauridin. We're all family here, isn't that right, Hilde?"

The mayor swayed in her seat.

"Oh, Mauridin, we do love these visits of yours. Will you be wantin' a horse or did the wagons leave you with one? I didn't see them come through this time. It must have been quite early."

Apogee gave a clumsy barmaid's curtsey, then hurried to collect and fill another round of tankards for the elkbones.

"No need, Hilde," Marziel said. "I've already rented a pair from Marcus. I think we'll look down the road a ways. My nephew lost some baggage when he was thrown. And if we don't see the horse while we're out, we'll go into the woods tomorrow to look for it. Have you met Cren'pin?"

"I have, milord. Please, you'll let me send some men with you. It's not safe in these woods, you know."

"You forget I trained with the rangers, Hilde. The boy'll be perfectly safe with me."

"I don't like the sound of it, but it's your decision, milord. Just stay clear of the riverbank. There's otters again, I'm afraid."

"Oh dear. Would you like me to deal with them?"

"That's kind of you, milord. We'll hire a war band to clear them out soon enough. Don't trouble yourself."

"Very well. If you change your mind, you need only ask."

"I thank you, milord." The mayor raised her drink toward him, then turned back. "So generous," she said, nudging her husband, who mumbled, then put his head back on the table.

Marziel checked to make sure nobody was watching, then focused his attention on Treylen, his voice low and serious. "Your acting is bad, but you carry yourself right. Did you come from money?"

"In a sense." Treylen sipped the water, then found his cutlery and began cutting into the slabs of boar on the plate in front of him. The meat sat in a rich mushroom sauce. He was grateful to be allowed to eat the food. He'd half expected Marziel to make him go hungry as punishment for the previous night.

"Good answer. You're a bit too common, though. You're supposed to be a lord, so you should puff yourself up a bit, talk down a little more when you're speaking to commoners."

"I thought I was a minor lord. That's not how the ones

that I know talk."

"You come from money. They wouldn't talk to you the way that they would talk to these people."

"We weren't that wealthy. I just don't think a minor lord would act like that. It's not realistic."

"Deception isn't about what's realistic. It's about what's expected. Most of these folks won't have met a minor lord. They are far less common in Lome than in Iverna. You give them one that meets their misconceptions, they won't stop to question it. You try and teach them better and they'll only want to know more. Mauridin is well liked, but he's a jackass. If someone asks me a question I don't like, then I can pretend I didn't hear it, smile like a fool, throw some coin their way, and ask for them to go fetch me supper. You'll find it is to your great benefit to have a lord within your repertoire. The greater a fool and the more minor their title, the more quickly they will be forgotten, and any inconsistencies in your story will be chalked up to false bravado."

"That makes sense," Treylen said.

"This will be your default alias. If you're seen without your mask, if you're spotted and caught off guard, then you're just some minor noble from another province, who's lost his horse and in need of assistance. It helps to have a default whose appearance is not too different from yourself."

"Is this your default alias?" Treylen asked, taking a drink of water and trying to will it to taste like ale.

"Sometimes. But it's hard work to be this much of a rube. Barmaid! Have a dance with me! We'll show my nephew how they do it in Tabron." He jingled a handful of coins at her.

"I would, milord," Apogee said, rushing to bring out food for another table, "but I'm needed in the kitchen."

"Another ale for me, then, and a round for the good soldiers."

A drunken cheer went up from the elkbones.

"See?" he whispered. "The attention is the disguise sometimes. Now, you'll call me Uncle Mauridin, never just Mauridin. Your mother is my sister and she asked me to help you find work in Tabron. I'm an intermediary for a trading company out of the Salt Crescent. We split our time between the coast and the badlands, and in between we stop over in Tabron, but I prefer the comforts of a quiet tavern in the woods over the bustle of the city. Can you remember all of that?"

Treylen nodded.

"What's more, the people here don't know much about the Stone Kingdom, even less of the coast. That's why we're using it for our alias. Mauridin prefers not to speak of his homeland. His wife and children—your aunt and cousins—were killed in a raid by the Ketaresk navy and the grief is just too much. Perhaps that's why he's always so chipper." There was a sadness in his eyes that seemed almost genuine. Then he laughed a warm Uncle-Mauridin laugh and slapped the table.

Treylen wasn't sure how to react to all that. He nodded again and sawed delicately at a piece of boar, politely moving it onto his fork like a gentleman.

"Good. Remember it," Marziel said. "And don't eat like that. You're from the Stone Kingdom." He speared his meat and held it like a drumstick, ripping a chunk with his teeth. "See?" he said, with a mouthful of meat.

Treylen did his best to copy, which got a laugh from the bard. The man had noticed something was off, or he suspected it. Treylen shot a worried look toward Marziel.

"Don't mind him," Marziel said, taking another bite. "He knows more than he should, but if he was going to rat me out to the rangers, he'd have done it years ago. Lazy bag of bones." Then he shouted, "Bard! Play 'Tip of the Scales.'"

The bard gave an exaggerated bow and swept the coin from the mantle into his hat, winking at Treylen. Then he started in on another tune. This one was more familiar to Treylen. He'd heard it often from the tavern on those nights he and the trainees had slipped down into Signet Lake Village to practice their stealth and swipe a few pints. Thinking of that, and all that time he had spent—had wasted—training others when he should have been preparing for his next advancement, Treylen felt a heaviness in his stomach. Pride and shame wrestling with one another.

"You know I'm not incompetent," Treylen said.

"Is this Cren'pin talking or my apprentice?" Marziel tore another chunk of boar from his fork.

"We worked hard to keep the abbey going. I'm a good fighter. I've trained good fighters."

"I can tell you have skill." Marziel sighed. "And the fact that you are far too old to be apprenticed is not owing to any fault of yours. "

"I don't know why Rime hasn't grown," Treylen said.

"It doesn't help that you steal his magic," Marziel answered.

"The monks didn't think so."

"I have seen him eat. I know the monks don't starve their dragons. So where does the food go? It feeds his power. And you steal it away."

Rime must've been in the kitchen, otherwise he would have chimed in already to agree.

"Rak'tsoro said something like that too." Treylen pushed the food around on his plate with his fork.

"It means you have a strong bond. Most trainees struggle with the dragonmind. Even some riders do. You just have to learn to be respectful of it. Only take what you need."

"I need it to fight," Treylen said.

"We will work on that." Marziel tapped on the table. "It's funny. Strong as your bond is, neither of you seem to acknowledge it."

"We don't always get along," Treylen admitted.

"I'm afraid I can't help you much with that."

Treylen nodded and drained his drink, eating the rest of

his meal in silence. Marziel's head bobbed along to the music as he sipped his ale, toasting the elkbones again. After a while, he got up to walk around the tables and chat. All the locals seemed to know him. At one point, he even ducked his head into the kitchen and pretended to have a conversation with the innkeeper who was, supposedly, carving what was left of a very large boar. Most everyone was too drunk to notice anything unusual about that.

He sat down again, clapping Treylen on the back and squeezing his shoulder with affection—not in the familiar way assassins leaned on each other and put their hands on each other's injuries, but a warm, fatherly sort of affection.

He relaxed a bit in his chair and listened to the music. His second tankard actually had a splash of ale at the bottom.

"How come Rime hasn't found your dragon yet?" Treylen said at last.

"What makes you think he hasn't?" Marziel asked with a strange grin.

"He'd have told me."

"You trust him to tell you everything he learns?"

"I know him. He'd have mentioned it."

"I see." Marziel chuckled darkly, then got up from his seat and leaned over the table, his large hat hiding his face from the room as the smile fell away. The hardness in Marziel's eyes took him aback for a second.

"Your bond is more significant than you're willing to admit. Don't make the mistake of abusing it. Now, I don't think that your punishment is over. You made a real mess last night, and we have more training to do."

Treylen nodded, finishing the last of his ale.

Marziel stood and spoke loud enough that the others could hear him. "Now get a coat and we'll go look for your horse." Then more quietly, "Bring your darks from the laundry, and your daggers. We'll leave your dragon here. I'd like to see this skill of yours for myself."

Chapter Twelve

THE CLEARING

Since the day that Rime had hatched, there'd been very few times that Treylen had been apart from him. Sometimes they argued and Rime would go a week without showing himself. But even then, he had stayed near.

As Treylen and his handler rode east along the main road, he'd felt that presence thinning. That same unexpected panic he felt in the dream set in again, as bit by bit, the dragonmind faded and that place just outside his own consciousness grew empty.

Clouds rolled in to cover the moon. Marziel stopped to light a lantern so the horses could see where they were going. Nobody was out this night, though the hardpacked road looked like it received heavy traffic when the Jaul were moving forces between Lome and the War Pass, with refuse all along it.

So far, he had only seen the elkbone soldiers, and wondered whether they were free to come and go from the army camps as they pleased, seeing as they were mercenaries and not conscripts. He kept his questions to himself, though, and waited for Marziel to announce that they'd gone far enough, instead focusing on keeping his nerves steady and trying to hold on to what faint glimmer of the dragonmind still hovered just out of reach.

They rode for another hour, until the moon came out, then Marziel took them off the road and into the woods. They dismounted and led the horses through the trees, tying them up once they were a short ways from the road.

"A little farther in," Marziel said. "Not too far. The deeper we go, the more likely that our trail will be picked up by the next ranger out looking for their friend."

"I hadn't thought of that." Treylen slipped his mask over his eyes and hurried forward. When the ground grew softer, he shifted his weight to the toe of his boot and adjusted his stride to match that of a running stag. It wouldn't fool anyone trained in wildcraft, but it might be inconspicuous enough for them to pass it over without bending to look. Marziel also changed his stride, following in Treylen's footprints.

"Well, aren't you a shite cart of surprises." Marziel laughed. "Apogee always told me that Bostra was a ranger at heart. Is this what you've been passing on to your students?"

They paused at a clearing of high grass with a great oak at its center.

"Do you know what became of them?" It wasn't something he was supposed to know. Assuming those Treylen had taught were still doing espionage, they would be expected to remain hidden—at least until the dragons were large enough to join the army. And even then, some stayed in hiding. It was possible the greatest assassin was not Rak'tsoro, but some unnamed shadow operating deep within Jaul.

"None of them are dragon riders yet, if that's what you mean."

"I didn't mean anything. Are you ready?"

Treylen shrugged. One hand went to his daggers.

"Okay, woodsman. How would you cross this clearing without the rangers in this forest seeing your path?"

"I wouldn't. I'd go around it."

"That's too bad. Because you have ten to climb that oak."

"Ten what?" Treylen asked.

"Nine…" Marziel hung the lantern on a branch.

"Oh." Treylen scanned the clearing. There wasn't much to see even with the lantern.

"Eight…" Marziel counted. "Better get up there. Seven…"

Treylen sprang into motion. It wouldn't be possible to cross the grass without leaving an impression. But as long as he didn't leave a trail, it wasn't likely to be noticed. He took a step back, then leaped into the clearing, landing halfway through and leaping again. As he did, he reached out for the dragonmind out of instinct, before remembering that it was gone. One more vault sent him toward the tree.

"Six…" Marziel counted.

It was a grand old oak. Older than any of the others and wider around. Shimmying up it was not an option. He pulled the daggers from his back, whipping them toward the tree. They sunk into it. He jumped, landed on the flat of the blade, nearly slicing his foot open again.

"Five…"

Without the dragonmind, he felt sluggish and clumsy.

"Four…" He caught the next dagger, which had wedged itself farther up. He was still sore from shoveling, but he pulled himself up again, the dagger bending under his weight. It wouldn't break, though. Not these daggers.

"Three…" Treylen threw himself into the air, catching the lowest branch and hauling himself up until he had his footing. He balanced and looked out over the clearing. It was empty. The lantern hung on a branch at the edge of the grass.

"That was well done." Marziel stood on the next branch over. "It puts you at a disadvantage for what comes next."

Marziel drew his daggers. Treylen backed away, pulling a small knife from his belt. Marziel leaped from his branch and landed on Treylen's, then darted forward, slashing. Treylen caught the branch overhead and pulled himself higher into the tree. Marziel swiped at his feet but missed him.

"You're running?"

Marziel ran up the trunk as if he were a spider, his feet sticking against the bark.

I've never seen that power, Treylen thought toward Rime again before remembering that Rime wasn't there. Marziel slashed and Treylen leaped again. There was no fighting against blades like the Queen's Fingers with a belt knife. Not in a tree anyway. Maybe on solid ground, in the daytime, with the dragonmind.

"You call this a fight?" Marziel was starting to sound angry. That was good. It might work to his advantage. "I came out here to test you. And you run from me."

Treylen fled higher, ignoring the taunts. He'd had enough practice with Aaron's jeers. And Marziel hadn't actually told him to stop. The fight was on, and Treylen had no reason to believe Marziel wouldn't kill him in the process. He would fight however he needed in order to stay alive.

Marziel seemed to defy gravity as he ran up the trunk again, and Treylen found himself on increasingly narrow branches. There was one glyph that might still work here. He scratched it into the bark as best he could in the dark, trusting practice. Without dragon sight, he couldn't know if he had placed it on a flow of magic, or whether all the strokes were right for this time of year, but if it was going to work anywhere, a tree would be the place.

Marziel was so intent on catching him that he stepped right into it.

"Crotus!" Treylen sliced the branch as he uttered the power word. Marziel danced backward, but he was too late. A mess of long, thin branches exploded from the bark like steam escaping a kettle and burst into leaves in an instant. Marziel was lifted from his feet and tangled in the mass of vegetation.

A hand with a dagger stuck out from the leaves and

Treylen seized it, wrenched the weapon free, and jammed it into them. Marziel grunted and his hand went still.

Treylen held the dagger steady, reaching forward with his other hand to push the leaves aside. The tip of the Queen's Finger pressed into Marziel's neck, just piercing the skin.

"You fight like Bostra," Marziel croaked. "Slippery bastard."

"We're finished?" Treylen kept the dagger steady.

"I am," Marziel said. "You need to learn to fight without tricks. That's why I separated the two of you."

"That wasn't dragonmind," Treylen said with a smirk. "Like you said, anyone could use crotus in this forest."

"I didn't bring you out here to see how clever you are. I want you to stand and fight."

"You didn't say to stand my ground," Treylen countered, though he already regretted saying it. Marziel's eyes hardened.

"I'm not going to disagree with a dagger at my throat."

Treylen eased the dagger away and gripped Marziel's arm, pulling him out. Marziel put pressure on his throat and fished into his kit for bandages while Treylen helped to steady him. He eased the older man down onto the branch, then stood and watched while Marziel wrapped his neck.

"Let's go again." Marziel rolled off the branch, dangling for a moment by one foot, then falling like a bat dropping from its perch and landing on the lowest bough. Then he stood, leaned against the trunk, and waited.

Treylen followed more carefully. When he reached the first branch, he walked out, balancing a few paces beyond Marziel. He held the dagger by the blade and offered it to him. Marziel shook his head.

"That trick with your daggers was clever. But those blades are worth more than your life."

"You said get up, I got up."

Marziel nodded, rubbing his neck.

"From now on, you're to assume that every tree in the

forest hides a ranger and every alley in the city hides a spycatcher. As deadly as a ranger, but with no other purpose aside from spotting you."

"Even Tabron?" Treylen asked.

"This close to Iverna…one in ten within the city guard will be spycatchers. You'll find out soon enough. Next time you need to climb, you'll use these." Marziel balanced on one foot and untied something. It had short iron claws with leather straps that attached to the left side of each boot. He removed the second, then tossed them both over.

So that was how he had run up the side of the tree like a spider.

"Keep them in your kit. Make sure they're on tight or they'll be worthless to you."

Treylen nodded and started to put them on.

"Put them away. We weren't supposed to scar this tree. There are rangers in these woods."

"We had to get up somehow."

"You should have been able to leap up here."

"Without Rime?" Treylen asked.

"You don't think after all this time, a little of the dragon-mind couldn't have rubbed off on you?"

Treylen chuckled. "Have you met Rime? He's a nasty little lizard. I'll take the speed, but I'd rather his mind didn't make any impression on me."

"No, the two of you are not the same. I had to fight him off of a roast yesterday and nearly lost a finger. It's strange, an assassin and his dragon not being of the same mind. You would be better together. In fact, I think that you would find him much more tolerable, if you should share a little of your own mild temperament. Although…" Marziel touched the wound on his neck. "Maybe you already are of one mind, and I just haven't seen your petulant side yet. Let's go again," he said, gripping his dagger. "You'll stand your ground this time. Understand? No tricks. Just bladework."

"I understand," Treylen whispered. He dropped into a fencing stance and held the dagger out between them.

"Interesting. You're just going to put it out there?"

Marziel stepped forward, one foot lashing out at Treylen's knee. When Treylen brought the dagger down to slash at it, Marziel jerked the foot back, spun with the other foot, and struck the back of Treylen's hand. The dagger went flying.

Treylen winced and staggered back, rubbing at his hand.

"I thought we weren't using dragonmind," he said.

"Did my eyes flash?" Marziel slashed at Treylen's chest, and he parried with the belt knife.

"Are you trying to get your fingers cut off?" Marziel slashed again. This time, when Treylen parried, Marziel let his blade slip down the knife and cut through Treylen's glove and into the flesh of one hand. "That's what happens when you try to fence with knives."

Treylen staggered back. The massive branch got narrower the farther out Marziel pushed him. Soon it would start to sway. Inwardly, he cursed himself, imagining what Rime would say about this sorry performance. He should have been better. How was this really any different from fighting with Aaron? He had been disarmed in their last fight and managed to keep up. But without dragon speed here, he couldn't do what he wanted.

Treylen led with a feint, but Marziel didn't commit, and it only led to Treylen being pushed back farther. Again, he lunged. Marziel countered. He leaned to dodge, but only succeeded in losing his footing. Marziel cut a gash across his shoulder before he'd recovered.

"This is pitiable." Marziel pushed forward again. Treylen deflected the blow, not able to change the angle and get around Marziel's blade, not willing to commit to a parry and risk his fingers again.

Another step and the branch started to shake. Leaves rustled behind him as he backed farther out over the clearing.

I just need an advantage. I need help with this. He spoke to Rime again, forgetting that he had lost connection to him. To his surprise, a reply came. It was faint and distant.

Use it, then.

Then he found it. That sense of the dragonmind. Like a single ray of sunlight on a winter day. He followed it, tracing out with his consciousness, feeling that void just beyond his own thoughts. For a moment, he felt it as something greater. Like the dragonmind from his dream, the connection to all the dragons, an ancient kinship.

Then the forest slowed. Marziel's strike came toward him sluggishly. And Treylen ducked it as easily as a branch on a trail run. He popped the wrist, struck the shoulder, and wheeled to strike his kidney with an elbow. Marziel tumbled, dropped the dagger, hit the branch, and slid, nearly flying off into the clearing before catching himself.

He cursed, feet flailing, a look of fury coming over him. Blood soaked his chin where his face had struck the bark of the tree.

"Aha!" Marziel shouted, his legs kicking as he dangled. "I knew it! You've been lying to me about the strength of your bond."

Treylen blanched. But he didn't move.

"I would never lie to a spymaster."

"Oh, don't be damned uptight about it," Marziel said, crawling back up onto the branch, his anger gone as quickly as it had come.

"But I really haven't," Treylen said, backing away.

"This is a good thing." Marziel clapped him on the shoulder and eased the dagger out of his still-shaking hand. "Do you know how rare it is to use the dragonmind over such a distance? He didn't follow you, did he? You wouldn't cheat, would you?"

Marziel tapped the tip of the dagger against Treylen's chest, a wild grin on his face.

"No. Never!" Treylen said, taking another step back until he bumped into the trunk.

"Then be glad. We're finished here. You have a strong connection to your bondmate. One of the strongest I have seen. Now I see why you're so dependent. It's too easy for you."

"I am trying not to abuse it…anymore," Treylen said, wiping the sweat from his forehead and slumping against the trunk as Marziel pulled the dagger from his chest and tucked it away. Once he was certain that the fight was over, he let his eyes close and caught his breath and held on to the tree to steady himself. "Are you alright?" Marziel asked. He pressed the back of a hand to Treylen's forehead. "You don't look well."

"Just a little winded."

"Get your horse and get back to the inn. I want Apogee to look you over." Marziel stepped back. He spat and wiped the blood from his face as he looked up into the branches, smiling.

"You aren't coming with me?" Treylen asked.

"I've got to hide the damage that you've done to this tree, so we don't bring every ranger in Lome down on our heads."

"I can help."

"You're done for the night. You've earned it." There was a finality to it that Treylen knew better than to ignore. He nodded, turning and dropping down along the trunk. As he did, he pulled his daggers free, then used that faint connection to the dragonmind to cross the clearing in a single bound, and hurried toward the road. Marziel watched with his arms crossed, grinning until Treylen had left before he began whatever work was needed to hide their presence.

The horses were where they had left them. Treylen quickly untied his, led it to the road, and headed back toward the inn. After an hour or so, he was close enough that he could feel Rime's presence more clearly.

Did you win? Rime asked.

I think I might have. What is Apogee doing?

At the bar. It's quiet.

Good. I need to see her.

It was late when he reached the inn, brushed his horse down, then staggered inside. Whatever crowd had been there had dispersed or gone to bed. Apogee was in the tavern cleaning up when he returned. She was not in character, however. She was just Apogee, standing at her full height, still wearing her barmaid's outfit and sweeping around the room. The fake cheeriness was gone.

The room was dark except for a low light emanating from the coals in the hearth. The candles on the dragon had been put out, the wax painstakingly cleaned away and replaced with fresh tapers.

"You don't look well." She put the last of the chairs into place.

"Marziel said the same thing. But I'm fine, really."

"Any new injuries?" Her hands moved to the cut on his shoulder, then to his hand, and she peeled away his glove to reveal the slice from the dagger. "Do you want me to stitch it?"

Treylen nodded, blinking back a tear from his eye when she prodded at the wound.

"This doesn't explain why you look so pale," she said, looking more troubled.

"I think my heel's torn open again. It was hurting on the way back."

"Again? Is it feverish?"

"I think so."

Her brow furrowed. "Then I'll have to speak with Marziel. Wrap them for now with plenty of salve. There's fresh water in your room. I'll wake you at dawn and we'll fix it more permanently."

"Don't tell him," Treylen pleaded. "It'll go away on its own."

"Don't worry," she said, seeing the look on Treylen's face. "You aren't a lame horse."

"Are you sure?" Treylen asked.

"We have plenty of horses, but you're the first trainee we've received in a while. He needs you more than he lets on."

"I should be training right now," Treylen said, even as a wave of nausea came over him. Apogee rolled her eyes and picked up her broom again.

"You'll start again in the morning. Go to your room and get some sleep."

"You're sure?"

"Don't worry, you'll pay for it tomorrow. Now go. I'm busy."

Treylen swallowed a nervous lump in his throat, then started toward his room. He was about to call for Rime when a thought came to him. He stopped and shuffled back toward Apogee, pointing at the dragon in the rafters.

"Whose dragon is that?"

Apogee's face remained flat.

"It isn't mine," she said. A long silence hung between them. When it became apparent she wasn't going to say any more, Treylen nodded.

"Rime hasn't seen Snarefoot yet. I know it's only been a day but…"

"Go to bed, Treylen."

"I will," he said. His head was feeling fuzzy, but he wasn't tired yet. "Just one more question. Do you ever miss the abbey?"

"All the time," she said. "When I was training there, all I wanted was to leave. Now I just wish I could go back."

"Yeah," he said. "I'm starting to miss it too. Don't tell Rime I said that."

Apogee put an arm around him and pulled him in, placing a decidedly chaste kiss on his forehead. She'd never comforted him before, but they'd all been close at the abbey, especially that year when Bos died.

"Nobody wants the kind of life that we live. You got to stay there longer than most." Her voice was as neutral as ever, but the pressure of her embrace told him it was sincere.

"It's just going to get harder, I guess," Treylen said.

"For a while." She spoke low into his ear. "But, you'll be surprised what you find out there. Now go on."

She shoved him toward the stairs and gave him a kick. Treylen caught the rail and stumbled up to the landing.

Are you back yet? Rime sounded tired, as if he hadn't slept since Treylen left. That was unlike him.

I'm back. Where are you?

Hunting rats in the attic. And you?

I think I'll try to sleep, he said, although he doubted it would be possible.

I will look in on you, bondmate.

"Are you sure we shouldn't stitch it now?" Treylen asked Apogee.

"I think we're beyond stitches. No, don't worry so much. Go to your room."

He should have resented a command like that, but tonight it was a relief. He wasn't sure if he could sleep. Maybe he was sicker than he realized. Apogee didn't seem worried, but she rarely had much emotion at all when she wasn't masquerading as the barmaid. It would be dawn soon anyway.

Treylen limped up to his small, windowless closet of a bedroom on the third floor and smeared salve on his wounds, wrapping them as best he could and collapsing onto the bed, still wearing his darks. At some point, Rime wriggled out from a gap in the ceiling and crawled into bed, curling up in Treylen's arms and watching over him until morning.

Chapter Thirteen

THE GRAVE

TREYLEN SLEPT OFF AND ON, WAKING AT EVERY SOUND AND never quite getting deep enough into slumber to feel rested. Apogee came into his room at first light, another bundle in her arms.

"Put this on and follow me." She threw the bundle at the foot of his bed and stepped out into the hall.

Treylen rubbed his eyes and sat up, pushing Rime to the side. His foot throbbed, but he stood anyway, took the bundle, and shook it out to find a long coat of bright silk. It was even more ridiculous looking than the hat they'd given him.

"Should I change?" he said, looking at the messy darks that he'd slept in.

"Just the hat," she said through the door.

Treylen put his assassin's jacket on, holding it open for Rime, who jumped inside and settled into the lining. Then he pulled the long silk coat over the top of it. He'd started putting on the fine leather boots when Apogee peeked in.

"Wear your old boots," she said, then pulled the door shut again. Treylen put on his assassin's boots and his toolkit, then pulled the silk jacket shut and buttoned it, covering his head with the Stone Kingdom hat. He opened the door and peered out before stepping cautiously into the hallway. Everything was smaller here than on the second floor—lower ceilings and shorter halls. These weren't the nicest rooms, nor the warmest.

Rather than leading him toward the stairs and down to the other floors, she and Treylen walked to the back. There she opened a closet, and moved a broom and some boxes aside to reveal a smaller staircase tucked away in the back corner. It was narrow enough that Treylen had to turn sideways to get past a couple of beams, and they reached a landing on the second floor. The narrow second-floor hallway was just as tight, as if tucked behind another closet wall. He paused a moment to inspect the joinery on the timbers between the walls. It was sloppy. Not unsafe, but not the work of a master craftsman either. Treylen would know—he'd watched his father inspect enough structures like this in the early years before his father became too important to do such things on his own. No, this was the work of the owner, someone not skilled enough to cut a perfect joint, but too proud not to have a hand in constructing their own inn.

"Let's go," Apogee called from below. He climbed over the debris from the second-floor closet and down a second staircase to the first floor. The passageway opened into a pantry in the kitchen. A low fire burned, warming a kettle, and from somewhere in that direction came the smell and sizzle of breakfast. Through the door into the tavern, he could see a couple patrons sitting and talking at the bar. He thought he got a glimpse of Marziel in the form of the innkeeper, going about his business.

Apogee gave a whistle, waiting at the back door. She cast a nervous glance in the direction of the common room and motioned for him to hurry. A small work yard sat in back of the inn, with stables on one side and a shed on the other. The houses crowded in on either side. There were no buildings between the back of the inn and the woods behind it.

They passed the way they had the morning before, when they were burying the bodies.

"What are we doing here?"

"You'll see." She kept walking.

Rime, will you go look around? He unbuttoned the jacket and Rime jumped onto a nearby tree and disappeared into the canopy. *Watch out for otters.*

When they reached the spot where they had buried the bodies, he found it just as they had left it. No new footprints or other obvious signs of them having come through. Even their initial footprints had been cleared away. Which made sense. Apogee had just as much training in wild craft as he did, and she knew just as much about the rangers here as Marziel. She would have erased any trace of them ever having passed.

She walked to the center of the clearing, stopping in the place where they had dug the hole, then sat on the ground. Treylen stood at the edge and watched while Apogee lowered herself to sit cross-legged on the center of the hidden grave.

"Why are we here?" Treylen walked out to stand across from her.

"Take your jacket off and fold it, then sit down."

Treylen crossed his arms, waiting.

"Do I have to drag you into everything, or will you trust me?"

"I'm just getting tired of surprises."

"We're here to fix your foot. Now take off your jacket so it doesn't get dirty, then get your boot off."

"Here?"

"Yes, here." A laugh slipped into her voice for a moment, and she smiled as she met his eyes, then her face went flat again. "Come on."

Treylen sighed, took the coat off, and bundled it, setting it carefully on the ground. He lowered himself onto the mat of leaves and branches he and Apogee had so carefully scattered a day earlier. Working at the laces of the boot that held his aching foot, he pulled it off. The gauze around the wound on his heel had a sickly yellow color mingled in with the blood.

Apogee blinked at the wound, shaking her head. She lifted the foot and looked more closely.

"I'm surprised you could walk on it."

"It's not that bad."

Apogee raised an eyebrow. She pulled a bottle from her pack, unstoppered it, and poured it over Treylen's heel. What he'd thought was water must have been brandy. He winced, gripping a handful of leaves.

When Apogee produced a small needle with no thread attached, he thought to ask her what she might be doing with it, but waited. Maybe there was pus in need of draining. A hot pain seared the flesh of his foot as she carved into it with the tip of the needle, but Treylen braced himself and bore it. A moment passed, and it should have ended, but Apogee kept working.

"Are you taking out the stitches?"

"No. They'd already come out. Keep it still," she said, such focus in her tone that it staved off any questions Treylen might have had. He nodded, took a breath, and forced his foot to lay still, biting the inside of his cheek to distract from whatever terrible needling she was doing. Another moment passed and the work continued. Apogee leaned closer, nodding to herself, and muttering quietly.

"It's coming along. Be patient." She jabbed at him again, scratching and scraping.

The needle moved around the outside of the wound, until Treylen wondered if the fever in his foot really had spread, and he was just imagining that the needle didn't have any thread in it. Maybe she was just stitching it up.

"What are you doing?" he said at last.

"I'm almost done." She peered up, then back to her work, scratching into his flesh for a moment longer. "There." She tipped another splash of brandy over his heel and fresh pain enveloped it. Treylen pulled away and raised his foot up to look at it, jaw falling open as he gazed in horror at the small markings chained around the bottom of his heel.

"That's an…" He stopped short of saying the power word. "A glyph that channels decay."

Apogee nodded. "I thought you'd be surprised."

Treylen pushed himself back, drawing his dagger out of instinct.

Apogee didn't move.

"It's to seal your foot up."

He stared, disbelieving. He had never seen an entropos glyph used on living flesh, but he'd heard tales of assassins turning their opponents into withered corpses with a well-placed glyph. He'd never really believed the stories. Why take the time to carve a glyph onto your opponent's chest when a dagger through the heart would do much quicker?

"I'm sorry. I knew it would scare you. This was how Marziel wanted it."

"What is it?" It was a strange pattern…not a single glyph, but dozens of minuscule ones carved into the flesh and linked together around the wound. They were also incomplete. The basic framework was there, but the crucial marks, those that needed dragon sight to draw correctly, had not yet been placed.

Apogee leaned forward, holding the needle out for him. "Go ahead."

Treylen sheathed his dagger and slid back toward her.

"You know what this glyph can do."

"If I wanted you dead, I'd have rubbed some poison into it. Trust me. This will work."

Treylen took the needle. He shuddered at the thought of using dragon sight here. Fresh graves had a different sort of magic to them. It reminded him of the shrines to the Dragon King, where the dragons lay down their bones, but more frenzied, more chaotic.

"Just finish them off," she said.

Rime ran over from one of the trees and sniffed at his heel, before crawling up on his shoulder to watch. Treylen put a hand on Rime, reaching the dragonmind in an instant.

The magic of death pushed up through the soil, seeping around the scattered leaves like smoke escaping and drifting across the ground in languid waves—settling into pools and dips in the earth.

Death magic was like that. Not so solid as the stable magic of earth, or as fleeting as fire. It hung around, settled, drifted when passersby disturbed it. That was why a place of old death still had such power. These seven bodies would decay the same as all the rest of the forest, and the magic they released, though strong now, would quickly dissipate as it was scattered by the life of the forest.

But places of death—cemeteries, crypts, temples to the Dragon King—were designed in such a way that they held on to it. A tomb was just as full of death as it had been when it was first sealed.

"Can you see it?"

"Of course. Lot of death here." Treylen shivered at the way the ribbons of magic whirled around the glyphs on his foot, looking for a place to enter into them. Treylen held the needle to the skin, still hesitant.

"It's not just death. The power word means entropy. It's linked to time, to settling…it's not the opposite of crotus—growth. They're two parts of the same thing. The magic of life unravels into the magic of death, and back again. I'm asking you to trust me. And when you're finished, close it with a crotus glyph." She looked at the forest that surrounded them. "The smallest that you can make. They're powerful here."

Treylen set his teeth and pushed the sharpened needle into his heel, dragging to open little slashes here and there. He followed the way the magic swirled, and as he struck the lines onto the glyphs, he saw it enter—seeping into the cuts on his heel like water into a channel.

"Crotus will be the power word. Softly, though…"

Treylen grunted. It didn't hurt nearly so much as it should have. The skin around the wound was so swollen and discolored, it had lost a lot of the feeling. How had he let it get this bad without noticing? When he finished, he drew the crotus, linking it to the outside of the chain.

"Will you do it?" he asked.

"Of course." Apogee leaned in, taking Treylen's foot gently in her hand so they both could see it. "Are you ready?"

Treylen nodded. He felt Rime's claws tighten on his collar. "No, but go ahead."

"Crotus…" She spoke in a whisper, touching one finger to the bottom of his foot. The magic of the forest siphoned in and swirled around them. When it found the glyph, a single rivulet of magic wriggled into it. The skin of his heel itched and bubbled, as it burst into warts and blisters all around the wound. But just as quickly as the flesh bubbled up, the entropos glyphs flared with dark energy, dissipating the crotus.

Apogee pushed the sides of the wound together as it shrank, flesh mending, oozing, then sealing together. The red faded, then the bruising, leaving behind a long, pink scar.

"That's it." Apogee grabbed the needle from his hand and slashed at the glyphs, cutting a fresh mark through them, and spilling the last of the magic out.

Treylen's hand was shaking as he brushed it over the now-healed skin. It was soft, like he'd never walked on it before. A few more veins stood out on his ankle and the nails on his foot seemed to have grown, then yellowed. It was as if the passage of time had healed the wound…perhaps too much time. It hardly looked like his own heel anymore.

"It's better than losing the leg," she said. "You might have a little arthritis in the heel now."

"Where did you learn that?"

"At the Wizard's Tower in Jaul. From a glyph scribe."

"I had no idea."

"That is one of the simpler glyphworks. The greater works would be…well, nearly impossible without a dragon. Which is one more reason why the Jaul are so keen on conquering us, so their scribes can finally put their wildest theories into practice."

Rime climbed off of Treylen's shoulder, crept up to his foot, and sniffed it, letting out a low hiss and darting into the woods again.

Watch for townsfolk. Treylen sent the thought after him.

"You spent a lot of time in Jaul?" He rubbed at the foot. A few bumps remained, but seeing the damage a tiny crotus glyph had done before the other glyphs suppressed it, he dreaded the thought of what would happen if a full crotus attack were unleashed on flesh. There would be nothing left of him but boils and warts. Of course, that would never happen in combat. Just like entropos, a dagger through the heart was far more efficient.

"Not long enough." She took his hand and unwrapped the cut on his finger. "This isn't bad. I'll stitch it."

"Are you sure?"

"You don't want to use that spell if you don't have to. Trust me."

Treylen nodded vigorously, and Apogee produced another needle, this one threaded, and dipped the string into a bowl of salve before dousing Treylen's hand in brandy, then smearing it with salve.

"Ouch." Treylen grabbed the bottle and took a slug.

"You whine too much," she said, then took the bottle from him. "You don't want that. You'll only spit it up later."

"Why?" he asked.

"You're training after this."

"I'm not pretending to be Mauridin's nephew?"

"Mauridin's nephew caught a chill last night. He's keeping

to his rooms." She jabbed the needle into his finger and pulled it through.

"Ouch. Rooms? Don't you think it's a little suspicious that Cren'pin's got these rooms, but every morning he comes out of a closet on the third floor?"

"Not so long as you don't bring anyone to bed with you and let them look around."

She jerked on the thread, then tied it off, cutting it and wrapping the wound again before putting the glove back on.

Once she was finished, she checked the stitches on his back. They were holding, and she smeared them with salve as well, then checked the cut on his shoulder. It was shallow and not worth stitching.

"What did Marziel say last night?"

"He asked me if Rime had followed you. But I told him Rime was following me around all night and stealing bits of boar. I've never seen a connection over a distance like that."

"I didn't think I could do it either, it just sort of happened."

"It certainly did," she said. "You've succeeded where you were expected to fail. Marziel is impressed with you."

That was little comfort. He'd been a teacher long enough to know that high expectations meant harder training would follow. Treylen pulled the sock back over his heel and laced his boot, then he stood and tested his foot. The pain was gone. He reached for the silk coat.

"Leave it off."

She pulled the barmaid's dress over her head to reveal her darks and bundled it up, setting it beside his coat.

"You're going for a run."

"Aren't there rangers everywhere?"

"Just the one for now. If you stick to the path along the river, you won't leave any trails when the others come looking."

"Last time I was at the river, I ran into some otters." He didn't think he needed to add that they were giant otters.

"They're to the north. You're going south from here." She tossed a sack into his hand. "Fill that from the apple tree. Bring it back here."

"Thanks," he said. "Don't think I don't appreciate this, but I can run back at the abbey. Isn't Marziel supposed to be teaching me?"

"Consider this a break. You'd better be careful. You exceeded his expectations last night, and I saw that sparkle in his eye when he got back. The better you do, the harder it will get."

"He shouldn't be that surprised. I was a trainer by the time I left the abbey. I had been for a long time, you know."

"I am aware of what happened. It's a shame how you were abandoned there. But you should consider yourself lucky. We all would've liked to have spent a little longer at the abbey if we could have. Now go get my apples. I want that bag stuffed, though. Now go on. Bring your dragon. He's eating everything in sight."

Let's go, he thought toward Rime. He left Apogee standing at the grave and headed through the woods.

Don't you think that I should stay back? Watch her? There was a gust of air as Rime glided from the trees, then landed on Treylen. *You don't think it's strange that she removed her dress before she sent you off?*

Well, she isn't going back into the inn without her dress, Treylen said.

Chapter Fourteen

THE ACCIDENT

TREYLEN HAD TIME TO THINK WHILE HE WAS RUNNING. Unfortunately, thinking at a time like this wasn't really to his benefit. What was there to think about other than the choices he'd made? He had known this day was coming, had yearned for it, and now that it was here, he felt doubts creeping in about whether he was truly prepared to hunt down Norris Duremo.

Maybe it was just the timing that was off. There had been a time when he was younger and fiery. He might have been more easily forgiven for his mistakes, and for his lack of training.

But he was old enough to have been a teacher…or at the very least a student who stayed on well past his time. Everyone else who'd trained with him had gone on to do something… maybe some of them were in the army now. Their dragons, not quite big enough to carry them, would be dressed in armor and fighting at their side. They would be making a name for themselves in the land surrounding the War Pass. Not tossed into the wilderness and forced to wait around some inn, learning spycraft.

It wasn't that he resented it. Only that he'd hoped he

would be good at it. He had hoped he knew everything that he would need. That his lingering doubts about Bos passing before he could impart his real wisdom would turn out to be unfounded.

Now, so many years after this life started, it felt like he was finally setting out on the real journey, only to find that he had missed his chance. He would have to speak with Apogee, learn more about what was out there. More about what lay before him. She hadn't said that it was all bad. There was almost a hopefulness in her voice when she spoke of her time in Jaul. It made him eager to get past this training. To see what came next. Still, he couldn't quite shake the feeling that what came next would be the death of him.

Your thoughts are loud, Rime said.

"Sorry," Treylen said out loud. "They weren't meant for you." He slowed his run to wipe his brow and drink from his waterskin.

I couldn't hear them. Just the noise they made.

"They weren't helping anyhow." Treylen tried to clear his mind and focus on the trail. He had to keep his eyes sharp for anything unusual that might indicate an ambush, or another test from Apogee. Rime was faster, racing through the canopy and gliding from branch to branch like a squirrel—he scouted ahead, looking for any trace of mischief.

His focus only lasted until the next bend in the river, when his mind wandered to the mission again.

Are you wondering if Marziel knows we're going up against a wizard? Rime asked.

We aren't going up against a wizard. I'm not afraid of a scribe.

Right. Rime didn't sound convinced.

Do you think that Marziel knows we're in a hurry? Treylen wondered.

I think he knows it all… Rime said. *But he wants Apogee in the dark.*

Why do you think that? He was starting to sweat now, letting his own muscles do the work, not dragon strength.

That's what you assassins do, you keep secrets.

Treylen couldn't dispute that. Though it wasn't how he'd done things at the abbey. He pushed himself to run faster. He needed to get this pointless exercise over with and get back to learning what was important. How to keep a disguise up, how to go undetected in a crowd and search for his prey.

Marziel knows what he needs to, Treylen said. *The queen trusts him.*

A bridge appeared ahead of them, as narrow and improvised as the path itself. On the other side of the bridge, the bright reds and greens of an apple tree leaned over the bank, branches heavy with fruit.

Careful, Rime said as they approached.

I'm watching for her.

Check the bridge, Rime said.

"Right," Treylen whispered, waiting until Rime had surveyed the riverbank, then kneeling before the bridge and borrowing dragon sight to peer across it. No trip wires spanned the gap. There wasn't much to it, a few shaped timbers, a couple of boards lashed together, but most of the treads were rough-cut tree branches that had been stripped of their bark. There was no railing.

Should I go first? Rime bounded up the edge.

If you want.

Rime hopped onto the first of the boards that made up the bridge. The river was picking up a bit of speed here.

Treylen watched the trees on either side as Rime went across and came back again.

All quiet.

He put a hand down and Rime ran up to perch on his shoulder again. Summoning the dragonmind, he stepped out onto the bridge, testing one section at a time.

"There's bound to be something," he whispered. No

sooner had he said it than a board creaked beneath his foot. A section of the bridge fell away, hitting the trusses. The whole bridge tipped over sideways.

Treylen ran along it as it fell. His feet hit the riverbank… and went through it, as he sank to his chest in the mud and sand.

Treylen thrashed against the silty mess, but it seemed to pull back each time he twisted away. He pawed at it, trying to dig, but it only flowed back around him like water. There was nothing to grab on to. The harder he struggled, the more the mud resisted him.

Treylen stopped to breathe.

He *wasn't* sinking.

He felt river rocks beneath his feet. This was just a bit of quicksand, and he knew that quicksand was rarely all that deep. Rime was perched in the apple tree, watching with a mix of amusement and concern. Apples littered the bank around him and floated in the sand beside him.

"You have to pull me out!" He wasn't panicked, but every moment that he spent here, he was vulnerable. Apogee's claim that this was a break and not another test was growing more dubious by the minute.

I can't do anything, bondmate. Lucky you didn't land headfirst.

"Just, hold on now…"

Treylen fished in his toolkit for a length of cord. It already had a loop in one end. He held it out of the muck for Rime, who snatched it and flapped back to the solid part of the bank. He draped the loop over the broken end of the largest branch, and did his best to toss the coil out. It unfurled, landing just short of Treylen.

"Can you fly it out to me?

If you want to risk me falling in.

"Okay, hold on." Treylen felt for his daggers, drew one, and leaned as far forward as he dared, nearly losing his footing. He managed to snag the end of the cord and pull it back to him, then put the dagger away and wrapped it around his arm, pulling it tight. Slowly, so that the muck didn't suck him back, he eased himself toward the rocks higher up on the bank.

There was a crack. The branch, heavy with apples, came crashing down on top of him.

Treylen reached a hand up just before it cracked him on the head. The weight of it drove him down into the quicksand. He got half a lungful of air before it pushed him under.

He felt a pressure against his back as it pinned him to the rocky bottom.

What are you doing? Rime shouted, as if this were somehow part of his plan.

I'm stuck.

Get out of there.

I'm trying. Treylen pushed against it, but the branch was pinned across his chest. He tried to move his feet, but the mud thickened around them the more he struggled.

I can't move. His mind was frantic. He flailed around, reaching for the cord, but that would do him no good. It was attached to the same branch that had just slammed into him. He twisted around and got an arm under himself, but the mud was too thick and the branch too heavy.

You're wasting time, bondmate. Rime sounded more impatient than worried now.

I can't breathe, Treylen said, fully aware of how panic-stricken his thoughts were, but too desperate to care.

Stop fooling around and use the dragonmind.

He wasn't already using it? No, he wasn't. He had become so accustomed to using dragon strength to move quickly, to leap great distances, that he forgot that he could use it for simple feats of strength. It hadn't helped him with the quicksand earlier. But now that he had something solid to grab on to, things had changed.

Letting his consciousness mingle with Rime's, he borrowed

dragon strength and pressed upward. Something snapped, then he was out from underneath the branch. Clinging to it like a snake, he pulled himself along the limb, snapping smaller branches that tried to entangle him, until his hand broke the surface. He sucked in a mouthful of air. It was mostly mixed with mud, but he sputtered, wiped his face, and breathed again.

He dragged himself farther until his body was out and his feet touched the gravel, then dropped to the dry riverbank and rolled onto his back, dragging a hand across his eyes to clear the mud away. He blinked up to see Rime winking down at him from the broken branch.

I think it's safe to say this was a test, Treylen thought. *And we may have failed.* He sat up, just long enough to make sure there were no more threats coming at him from the river or the woods above, then lay back again and breathed.

I think that maybe it is just a lesson, Rime said. *If it were a test, you would probably be dead. It is too bad you'll have to go back into the mud to retrieve the sack.*

"What?" Treylen felt around his belt where the sack should have been. "No, she wouldn't care. It was a trap."

No, Rime said. *She would expect apples. You had better get it.*

Chapter Fifteen

THE DRIFTER

It was midday by the time that Treylen had freed himself and all his gear from the muck, washed in the river, then filled the sack with apples and returned to the clearing. He was mostly dry from the run, and he found his new silk coat bundled where he had left it.

He slipped it on, then crept up to the edge of the forest, looking out to see which of the townsfolk were out. There were a couple of fields down the road, and a small mill where the road met the river. Treylen suspected most of the villagers would be out working, but a convenient row of hedges ran between the inn and the forest, giving him a bit of cover as he hurried across the yard to the kitchen.

Apogee stepped out the door, resting her hands on her hips as she watched him approach. She'd changed back into her dress, and Treylen couldn't see any sign of darks underneath it. Whatever she'd been up to, it was finished.

"How did it go?" She gave him one of the barmaid grins.

"It was good to clear my head." He handed the sack over. There was no hiding that it was wet and sandy. "What have *you* been doing here?"

"Speaking with Marziel. He had hoped to take the day to

teach you how to stage an accident. I told him that I think you understand accidents well enough. Wouldn't you agree?" There was nothing in her voice to give her away. Just like there had been no sign that anyone had tampered with either the bridge or the branch of the apple tree that had nearly crushed him.

"I think I understand the difference," he said carefully. "I'm good with traps. If I want to stage an accident, I just need to set a trap that doesn't look like one."

"Is that all?"

"If the goal is deception, then I guess the trap would have to be set in such a way that anybody looking into the death wouldn't find anything suspicious about it." She nodded at his answer.

"A little suspicion is sometimes okay. So long as there is no concrete evidence. This is especially true if the killing is meant to provoke a feud. Sometimes a suspected murder can create a deeper rift than a confirmed murder ever could. But I can talk you through some accidents later. Because of your good performance last night, Marziel has agreed to let you focus on your spycraft. You'll spend today working around the yard. There aren't many locals coming to the inn today, just a few soldiers passing through, so you won't be under quite the same scrutiny. I want you to put on the plain clothes I laid out. You aren't Cren'pin today. Come back to the kitchen and don't let anyone see you, then we will work on your face."

"My face?"

Apogee spoke in the bubbly voice of Amelia. "You know. Your face! I'll see you shortly, traveler." She skipped back into the kitchen, grabbed a tray, and disappeared into the common room.

I'm looking forward to this, Rime said, crawling up his leg.

"Of course you are, you get a nap in the rafters."

Only until I'm bored of it. Then I'll hunt rats in the attic.

Treylen used the passage between the walls again, slipping

into the pantry, and tiptoeing up the stairs. He could hear the sound of conversation on the second floor. Somebody in one of the rooms. It was the first that he had heard anyone besides himself and the other two assassins outside of the common room. The kitchen and the common room took up most of the first floor. Marziel and Apogee had rooms on the second, and he was alone on the third.

Rime had followed him into the pantry, but when he looked back, the dragon was nowhere to be found. Gaps at the top of the passage seemed to lead up into the attic. Rime must have wanted to get a start on catching rats. He peeked out the door into the third-floor hallway, then crept to his room. It was a lonely space to return to, with only the faintest bit of light creeping in under the door from the hall.

The new silks rested on the bed, neatly folded, and beside them a pile of rags that he would not have taken for clothing if he hadn't been told so. It looked like a beggar's clothing.

Treylen peeled off the darks and hung them to dry. The leather jacket had enough oil and wax on it that it was practically waterproof, but the lining was full of silt. The shirt and pants were half dry already. He reached for a rag to wipe a bit of mud from his chest, then thought better of it. The outfit they had given him was dirty already.

He shook out the brown tunic, then slipped it over his head. It stank like pigs. The breeches itched, and after trying to ignore it, he decided to take them off and put on a pair of underclothes. Over this, he put the assassin's toolkit and the shoulder straps that held his dagger, modified so that the handles of the daggers wouldn't stick out from the sides. Then he slipped on the breeches again and the long tunic. Underneath it all, he found an old oilskin skullcap shaped like the one Marziel wore when he was the innkeeper. Thankfully, there was no false beard to go with it.

There was no mirror in his toolkit, because it wasn't needed. The Queen's Fingers were always polished to a mirror finish. He drew the daggers and jammed them side-by-side into the wall, then stepped back, using a bit of dragon sight to make up for the darkness and look himself over.

It wasn't good. Nor was it much of a disguise. He looked like a filthier version of himself.

It was best just to get it over with. He yanked the daggers free, stuck them back into their holders, then tied a filthy belt over the pants, slipped on a pair of worn leather shoes he found by the door, then headed back to the kitchen by way of the secret passage again.

Now that he was alone, he noticed things he hadn't on his first pass through. One of the boards in the staircase creaked as he stepped on it—not a normal sound, but more like the chirp of a cricket. It screeched as he lifted it. Underneath, he found a metal prong, angled so that it rubbed against a coin that had been nailed to the casing of the stair. Carefully, he slipped it back into place.

He'd heard of the Jaul using these spycatcher boards in palaces, but he'd never realized how simple they might be. While he was alone and poking around, he decided to spend a little time on the second floor. There was a crawl space here between the second and third floors, and a hatch above the second staircase that led into another closet, maybe Marziel's.

When he reached the bottom and peeked his head out of the pantry, he found himself faced with both Marziel and Apogee, arms crossed, staring at him.

"Are you quite finished?" Marziel still wore the beard and clothing of the innkeeper, but they made a stark contrast to his full height and the commanding tone of his normal voice. Apogee was dressed the same and equally dour looking.

Treylen stepped out and stood with his back to the pantry door.

"What do you think?" Apogee asked Marziel, looking him over.

"I'm not sure he can pull it off."

"He will," she said, giving Treylen the faintest look of encouragement. He nodded affirmation.

"Tell me what to do," Treylen said, though his voice wavered, betraying his true feelings about the day so far.

We're starting, he said to Rime. *I'm not sure what we're doing yet.*

There was no answer, which probably meant that Rime was coming. Or sleeping. Or choking on a rat.

"Outside," Marziel said, peering into the common room, then leading them to the back door. Between the kitchen and the chicken coop was a spot of privacy. An outhouse and line of wash blocked the view from the rest of the work yard. Though he had survived the *accident*, Treylen couldn't shake the feeling that he was being led toward some kind of punishment.

"Okay," Marziel said, scanning the yard behind him. "Let's see something."

"What should I do?" Treylen felt like a court fool who'd been goaded into performing without his paint.

"Try smiling," Marziel said humorlessly.

Treylen forced the corners of his mouth up, and Marziel groaned, then cocked his head toward Apogee.

"Stand like Marcus," Apogee offered.

"His Marcus?" Treylen pointed at Marziel.

"Yes. The innkeeper. Hunch your back, push your shoulders down."

White sheets flapped around them, and the cold breeze cut through his threadbare tunic. He could feel their eyes on him, and half suspected one of the locals would come along soon, looking for the innkeeper. Treylen couldn't have been more uncomfortable if he were naked.

Slowly, he shifted his posture, pulled his arms together so his shoulders sloped. His lip curled up a bit out of instinct and he tried to distort his face.

Marziel and Apogee looked unimpressed.

"I feel like a fool," Treylen said, slipping out of the shape he'd contorted himself into.

"No, hold it there," Apogee said. Treylen pulled his shoulders down again and curled his lip. Apogee raised a hand to her chin and stared. At this point, Rime appeared, climbing up Apogee before bounding over to perch on Marziel and watch.

"You'd better stay hidden, little one." Marziel lifted the collar of his shirt and Rime scurried underneath, changing his color so that he blended with the fabric. "It isn't working," he said when he'd turned his attention back to Treylen.

"Could the dragonmind help?" Treylen offered. He'd been hesitant to bring up the dragonmind after being reprimanded for relying on it too heavily, but this exercise was getting them nowhere.

"It won't help if you don't know what you want."

Are you in disguise? Rime asked.

You can't tell humans apart by sight anyway, Treylen answered.

Why would I need to? You all smell so different from one another.

It must have been obvious that they were conversing, because Marziel turned to peer inside his shirt collar.

"Their bond is a strong one," he said to Apogee. "It's surprising."

"He could try the dragonmind. I'm not sure it would help if he didn't have an intention."

"Stop standing like that," Marziel said. "It won't do for you to copy mine. Not if you're to use it here." He reached into his collar and scooped Rime out. "Be him." He held the dragon in front of Treylen.

"You want me to be a dragon?"

"No, I want you to imagine what your bondmate would be like if he were human. Use the dragonmind if you like. It can't hurt."

"Alright..." Treylen tried to think of what made Rime so

different from the other dragons. It was mostly his abrasive nature.

"Start with the outside," Marziel said. "Think of what you're wearing. How would Rime wear it different?" Treylen looked down and thought of how he'd looked in these rags. He rolled his eyes, thinking of Rime's vanity. Of course, that was it. He raised the tunic and untied the belt from around the pants, knotting them to keep them up, then retied the belt over the tunic. He pulled his belt knife from his assassin's kit and tucked it into the outer belt, so it was showing. The leather skullcap had two flaps that came down over the ears. He tied them up, pushing the cap back so it sat at a rakish sort of angle. Then he unlaced the collar of the tunic, leaving it to hang open.

"How's that?" he asked Apogee, crossing his arms. "Do I look any different?"

"Make your voice harsh."

"Better?" He growled a little when he said it.

"Too much," she said. But Marziel nodded his approval.

"It's a start. Raise your upper lip. Let the bottom one droop, that's it."

Treylen did. He was starting to feel it. He focused on Rime more, pulled his shoulders back—let his belly sag just a little.

"He looks like a highwayman," Apogee said.

"I don't know if he's burly enough for a highwayman." Marziel narrowed his eyes. "But he certainly looks like a cutpurse. Now, use a bit of dragon stealth to aid the disguise."

Apogee reached into her dress and pulled out her dagger, holding it so he could see himself in the blade. It was something. Treylen wasn't sure that he could ever fool anyone simply by pulling a face and changing the way he stood. But he could feel the sense of dragon stealth come over him, the same way that he could almost feel the shadows wrapping around him when he moved silently in the dark. His features looked more sunken in the reflection, his false sneer more natural. He could almost have passed for a different person.

"I think that's it." Marziel clapped. Apogee looked like she was about to disagree, but Marziel continued. "He won't fool the local bard, or anyone else who's met him sober already, but he might fool our dear mayor, and those elkbones. Now I hope you are not too uncomfortable, because you'll spend the rest of the day like this."

He reached down and picked up a small stone. "Put this in your boot. If you can't change the way you walk, you won't fool anyone. Don't laugh—an assassin's gait is almost as distinctive as their daggers."

"Okay." Treylen took the pebble and slipped it into the old shoe. A muscle in his neck was cramping. "I don't know how long I can hold this."

"We'll find out," Marziel said. "Apogee will get you set up with some chores to take your mind off it. First, I think you'll fold the wash, then maybe some scouring, or have you not yet shoveled out the stables, Apogee?"

"A little of each, I think," she said.

"Whatever it takes." Treylen felt a flutter of optimism that a disguise had gone right. At least he would have the rest of the day alone to practice.

"I'll go back inside and let it slip I've hired a man to help around the yard. If anybody asks, you're a drifter. No, on second thought, if anyone asks, just walk away. I'll tell them you're a little strange. Just avoid speaking until you've got your voice down." Marziel handed Rime to Apogee, then bent over, taking on the crooked shape of the innkeeper as he loped toward the back door of the inn.

I think you passed a test for once, Rime said. *You don't look any different to me.*

"Rime doesn't think I look any different." He sighed.

"It's a start." Apogee tucked Rime inside her apron, then followed after Marziel. "Fold these sheets and leave them in the basket by the door. When that's done, you can shovel the stables. Don't look Marziel's horse in the eye, and if you bother my mare, I'll bury a pitchfork in you."

"Thanks for the vote of confidence."

"You're quite welcome, traveler," she said, slipping into her barmaid's voice again. "Take your persona seriously. It's weak and it will take practice to mature. If you can hold it while you're shoveling manure, you can hold it during interrogation. This is your training, you understand?"

"I think I've got it." He yanked a sheet down and tossed it into the basket.

"This will make you better. Come to me when you're done, and I'll help you with the voice. We'll find time to do some light bladework tomorrow. Marziel has asked me to help you stand your ground without the dragonmind." She said the last bit with a grin that told him she already knew he'd find it insulting. "Tonight, Cren'pin and his uncle can work on some sleight of hand."

Treylen pulled another sheet down and folded it, contemplating the next few hours. Already, he was cramping from the cockeyed posture of this new persona.

"You'll need another name," she said, pausing in the door. "Something better than Cren'pin."

"What about Trogan?" Treylen said. "It's Lomish. It's close enough to my own that you can say they misheard you if you say Treylen by mistake."

"I don't make mistakes. But it's good to see you're paying attention."

"Thank you," Treylen said. "For telling me what comes next."

"It's only the morning. You have a long training ahead of you. Unless, of course…your mission is too urgent for all of this."

I think that she wishes you could stay a little longer, Rime whispered in his head.

You just like the food here. He said to Apogee, "There's something…someone, I'm supposed to find in Tabron. I need to get down there."

"Or what?"

"The Jaul are up to something. Things aren't great at the Harvest Pass. They've lost a lot of riders. I'm the only eyes they had to—"

Apogee put a finger to his lips. The other hand went behind her back, to the slit in her dress—her daggers.

"Cut your tongue," she whispered, but it was soft—sympathetic even. "Do you know how much I wish I knew what happened in my homeland? Or what I would give to go back there? But you can't say these things here. If Marziel knew… Get to work. We'll train later. Don't speak of this."

She spun, shooing Rime out of her apron, and disappearing into the kitchen, leaving Treylen with an armful of sheets and an agitated dragon.

I think she's fond of you, Rime said, scratching at his chin before climbing into the basket and curling up between the sheets.

I think she might have cut my throat if I'd said any more. I just need to know that there'll be an end to this. We have a mission, you know. She and Marziel have to know it.

Rime yawned. *She's not too old for you, you know. No older than you are to Aaron.*

Now you're trying to get me killed. He piled another sheet on top of the dragon and moved on to the next one. A few more whites to fold, then it was off to the manure pile.

Chapter Sixteen

THE INTERMEDIARY

TRAINING SHOULD HAVE BEEN EASY, SIMPLY BECAUSE NOBODY was watching. Though a few locals passed, and a legion of soldiers marched by on the road, none stopped to question him. Staying in character, however, was its own kind of torture. Treylen had known the look was slipping from his face. The ache of a dozen small muscles in his neck and chin built into a throbbing pain.

At least that had made it easy to remember to hold the posture. In the end, he held it through most of the day with the help of the dragonmind. In the evening, Apogee brought him into the kitchen to coach him on perfecting the voice. She made him stand beside the door to keep the smell of manure from getting in the food, but by the time the meat pies finished baking and the sun had set, she'd helped him learn the Jaul accent and pronounced him good enough to try it on the locals.

Before she could arrange a test, the voice of Uncle Mauridin shouted from the bar.

"Good evening. Yes, he's feeling much better. Where is my nephew anyhow? Amelia? Where is the barmaid?" His head poked into the kitchen. "Amelia, will you go wake my nephew?"

"Yes, milord Mauridin!" Apogee sang. "That's your signal." She waved a kitchen knife at the pantry door. "There's a scented bath in the room. Have a good soak with plenty of soap. Mauridin's nephew can't smell like manure."

Treylen's heart warmed at the prospect of a bath—scented, no less. He removed his manure-covered shoes as he squeezed through the passage between the floors and practically skipped down the third-floor hallway to open the door. Rime was sniffing at the tub of bathwater that rested in the center of his small room. He tilted his head as Treylen entered.

It's cold.

His heart sank. Shuffling inside and pulling the door shut behind, he dipped a finger into the tub. The water was frigid. It smelled of flowers and strange scented oils. Hopefully, he wouldn't have to hide from otters or dragons anytime soon, because these smells would stand out in a forest.

Treylen set the shoes just inside the door. The rock was still rattling around in one of them. Then he stretched, unbelted, and slipped the tunic off, letting his posture shift back into what was natural. He fell onto the bed, rubbing at the cramped muscles in his face. Rime sniffed at the water again, sneezed, then raced up the wall and into a hole in the ceiling.

Can you stay out of trouble the rest of the night? Treylen lay on the bed and rubbed his face. His hands stunk of manure.

I had no trouble today, Rime said. Treylen could hear his claws scrabbling against the boards overhead.

It sounds busy downstairs. Just stay out of sight. I'll call you if I need you.

He sat up and stripped the rest of his clothing off, then regarded the wash basin. It was a large wooden tub—not an easy feat to carry something like that upstairs. A yoke with two buckets leaned against the bed. Apogee must have carried it up, then filled it for him. That was a kind gesture, even if the water wasn't heated to his liking.

Bright petals swirled on top of the water and stringent medicinal odors found his nose. Not unpleasant, but not any herb he'd known in Iverna. He approached the tub and dipped a toe in before pulling it back.

"Hellcaves!" It was more frigid than the river water had been.

At least it was clean. Maybe immersing himself was not the right way to go about it. He searched around the floor before he found a rag and soap, then dunked the rag, lathered the soap, and began scrubbing himself. The soap had the same oil in it as the bath. Treylen was methodical about it. If a leisurely soak was not in the cards for him, that didn't mean he couldn't take his time with the floral soaps. He wet his hair and worked the bubbles into it, luxuriating in the feeling of cleanliness and scents that he wouldn't have otherwise allowed himself.

Don't tell Volanti about the scented oils, Treylen said.

Do you think she'd be jealous? Rime replied.

Of the soap maybe.

At long last, he was covered in bubbles and there was nothing left to do but get it over with. He stood there for another minute to let the soap work against the smell of manure. Then he grit his teeth and took the plunge, stepping into the bath and kneeling to pour the cold water over himself. The abundance of soap added to the oils already mixed in with the water meant that he never quite got it all off. In the end, his eyes were stinging, his skin was slippery with a film of oil, and he stank like a flower merchant robbed an apothecary, but he was clean. He dressed in the new silks with a new hat to match, this one even more ostentatious than the last.

Marziel awaited him at the same table as last time, only this time he had a guest—a long-haired man in a well-cut shirt and shiny leather boots. The bard sat in his usual place beside the fire and strummed something light. He was joined by a girl, perhaps his granddaughter, who sat on the hearth and accompanied him on the ocarina.

It was not as busy as the noise had suggested. Most of the tables were empty—the locals must have only come in yesterday for the boar—but the mayor sat at the bar and the same table of elkbones was drinking and boasting at the bottom of the stairs. They were not quite as far along in their cups at this hour, but Treylen's hat drew a hearty laugh from them all the same.

A day spent practicing disguise had made Treylen more comfortable with the idea of spending the evening as Cren'pin, though he regretted the name every time he heard it and was determined to come up with something better for his second identity. Tonight, he felt he knew better what was expected from a minor lord of the Stone Kingdom and greeted Marziel loudly from the stairs as soon as he entered.

"Uncle Mauridin! Who's your friend?"

"My boy, Cren'pin!"

Treylen sauntered to the table, laughing at the elkbones' teasing as he passed. Marziel threw his arms around him, slapping him on the back. This time he didn't whisper anything threatening under his breath, another marked improvement.

"My boy, you smell fresh as a lamb. And you look much more yourself today…"

"Yes, I'm feeling much better, Uncle." Treylen pitched his voice higher.

"Good. There's nothing like a warm bath to take the chill off." Marziel kept one arm around his shoulder and directed him to the table. "Rebash Augur, meet my nephew, Cren'pin." The man rose from his chair and bowed to Treylen. His thin mustache and pointed goatee were dyed a dark brown that didn't match the graying hair over his shoulder.

"Milord Cren'pin, your uncle tells me that you're seeking to make a name for yourself in Tabron."

"Rebash and I go back a ways," Marziel said, squeezing Treylen's shoulder firm enough to serve as a warning. "He keeps the books for a trading company out of Tabron, and he has offered to bring you down when his wagons come through. He can help you make your introductions in the merchant quarter."

"That is quite generous of you, mister Rebash." Treylen returned the bow. Uncertain if he should remove the hat, he left it on. This was a lowborn man, merchant or not.

"But we can speak of that tomorrow, Lord Mauridin." Rebash took his jacket from the chair back and collected his tankard. "Say, milord Cren'pin, did you hear anything strange the night before last when you came in from the storm?"

"Did I?" Treylen looked to Marziel, wide-eyed. Marziel shrugged but gave the slightest shake of his head. "Can't say that I did," Treylen said. "But I was so shook up, I don't half remember it."

"Some mighty racket woke me, but I was loathe to go investigate. Now, the innkeeper and Amelia say nothing out of sorts happened that night, but I swear I heard something. Could it have been a hailstorm?"

"It could have been me," Treylen laughed. "You should have seen me, mud from head to toe and cursing my horse to hellcaves."

"Then I am glad that you have found some succor here, milord. There's not a better place in Lome to rest one's head, isn't that right, Lord Mauridin?"

"Quite," Marziel said. "A gem in the rough...right under the nose of the enemy."

"Hah." Rebash laughed. "If only the Iverans knew what they were missing." He bowed again as he backed away. As he passed the elkbones, he leaned to say a word to one of the elder mercenaries, and the man got up from the table, carrying his tankard and followed Rebash to a corner table on the opposite side of the fireplace.

"Now that is a man who can't be trusted," Marziel muttered once he had left. "I may have you leave with him at some point, but don't say a word we haven't coached you on."

"There's something about him, but I can't quite place it," Treylen said conspiratorially.

Marziel elbowed him in the ribs. "Keep your suspicion off your face, Cren'pin."

"Sorry, Uncle," he said, slipping around the table and taking his chair. "What's for dinner? Oh, hello, Lady Mayor!"

The mayor blushed. "Misses Mayor, milord, you flatter me. You look well this evening."

"I feel much better, thank you," he yelled across the room. Marziel smiled and made a gesture toward Apogee to bring them a round of drinks. Then tossed a coin to the bard, who struck up a rowdy tune to give them a bit more privacy.

"You do look better." Marziel spoke in his own voice.

"I feel better. Apogee helped me with my foot today. It was worse than I knew."

"So she has told me. I am glad to have her with me. Not just because it gets lonely here on the border, but her glyph-work is…" He stared at the bard, searching for the right words. "Beyond anything that I was taught. She spent time in, well, where she learned it isn't for anyone's ears but the queen's. But her knowledge is a real asset here. Don't think it goes unappreciated."

He spoke the last bit to Apogee as she came over to set two tankards in front of them. Then she hurried off to bring ale and food to Rebash and the elkbone, who had settled into their shadowy corner and were engaged in a very serious-looking discussion.

Treylen peered into the tankards. One held ale, the other water. Marziel grinned, then took the water for himself, pushing the ale in front of Treylen.

"Enjoy it now. You may regret it tonight."

"Speaking of tonight," Treylen began reluctantly, still not

convinced that Marziel had forgiven him over the previous night's mistakes. "I wanted to ask you something."

"Oh?" Marziel cocked an eyebrow.

"I wanted you to know I'm patient, and here to learn."

"That isn't a question." Marziel held his drink and waited.

"I can't talk about my purpose but…"

"You want to know when you can leave?" He leaned his chair back and swirled the water in the tankard. Treylen wondered how much of this show of good temper was for him and how much was because people were watching.

"Not that. I just wondered…well it would help to know what's in store for me tomorrow and the next day. Maybe even the day after that. I think I could perform better if I were prepared." When Marziel didn't answer right away, Treylen went on, though he wasn't sure that he should. "I'm used to being a teacher. Being a student again is hard for me."

Marziel sighed, then leaned in.

"I'll be honest, Cren'pin, I don't know what to make of you yet. You're far older than most that I get, and you're better prepared in some ways. But you're lacking in others. I can't tell you what's in store because I haven't got the measure of you. What I can tell you…We'll spar in the next few days. I think I'll keep you on the ground this time. I'll get a better appraisal of your abilities. Not tonight, I think. Tonight, there will be some climbing and acrobatics. Beyond tonight, there are skills I know you won't have practiced. Accents, interrogation, Stone Kingdom lore. We can start on those now during dinner. How's your sleight of hand?"

"My what?"

"We'll work on that too. I'm sure you'll take to it as quickly as you have to glyphwork."

"I already knew a bit of glyphwork," Treylen said.

"But no pickpocketing?" He seemed surprised.

"Nothing practiced."

"I think you'll find we're much less regimented here than

you were at your abbey. We take our training as it comes. Predictability is the death nail of assassins. Especially those engaged in spycraft. And I have a business to run. I wouldn't be a convincing innkeeper if I didn't put my patrons first. I care for these people of this crossroads, and my inn has become something of a fixture in the community. I take pride in it, you understand?"

"I think I do," Treylen said, but Marziel shook his head.

"I remember my training at the abbey. They take you away from everything and everyone you cared about and they teach you that the will of the queen is the only thing that matters. They make the world small. The abbey and the ones you trained alongside are the only things you believe in. You come to me out of that, and I have to teach you how to be a part of the world again. Maybe it's not as bad at Coops—you're the first since Apogee to come from there—but before you go and question why I have you shoveling shit…"

"I wasn't questioning," Treylen said.

"Before you do, I want you to know that I need you to be accustomed to a mundane life. Understand? I need you to be comfortable within this world. And I know your mission is crucial. Trust me, I have been made well aware of the urgency of your mission. But I can't have you going into Tabron with the queen's colors flying, letting every spycatcher from here to Jaul know where the queen's agents are operating. My position at this inn is more important than the success of any one mission. So I will keep you here until I deem you ready. Whether that be a week or until next summer is a decision I'll make once I have your measure. Until then, you will be tested. And I'm sorry to say, the course of the next few days will be unpredictable."

Marziel drained his water and waited. Treylen took a long drink of ale, letting Marziel's words hang between them. What more was there to say? He would be tested. He couldn't predict how, but he would give his best and hope that it was enough that Marziel would send him on his way.

Apogee returned from the far table carrying two empty tankards and a saltshaker, which she held upside down, a small trickle of salt spilling out of it. "Will you have the duck pie for dinner?" she asked.

"You're losing some." Treylen pointed at the salt.

"Sorry, milord." She righted it and put the little clay vessel on the table between them.

"Just vegetables for me," Marziel said. "My stomach is a touch unsettled."

"I'll have duck," Treylen said. Apogee nodded and hurried off.

"Let me see you complete a glyph script," Marziel said, glancing around to make sure that nobody was looking. He ran his finger through the salt that had spilled on the table, absently tracing the shape of a tiny aeris glyph in the center of it, then he made a circle of interlocking sestus glyphs all the way around the aeris. The final strokes of each glyph, he left undone, just like Apogee had that morning.

"Here's one that Apogee brought back and taught to me," Marziel said. "You'll find it's a useful addition to our repertoire." He glanced around the room again, then continued.

"I'd like you to finish this. Don't draw attention. And make sure to close your eyes when you summon the dragonmind. Everyone in Lome knows what the flash means. They would have the rangers upon us by morning. Sestus is your power word. Speak it quietly."

Treylen closed his eyes and reached for the dragonmind. When he opened them, he saw the magic moving across the patterns on the table. Salt that came from the earth produced a sort of sestus energy all its own. Aeris was much fainter in the smoky atmosphere of the inn, but there was always a little of it hanging around in the air. A few short strokes with his finger allowed the magic to enter the glyphs. Looking to

Marziel for confirmation and receiving a small nod, he whispered the power word and tapped the table.

"Sestus." Magic flowed into the salt, swirling over the table, then down along the small trail Apogee had left as she'd brought the shaker over to them, leading back to the table where Rebash and the elkbone sat. For a moment, Treylen worried that the wind would pick up, scattering the salt and drawing the attention of the entire room, but only the faintest breeze moved. With the dragonmind, he could see the shimmer of magic in the air between the two tables. Suddenly, there was another voice at their table, deep and brusque.

"Enough cud chewing. I've drank your ale and eaten your food. Out with it, merchant man." It was the heavily accented speech of the elkbone leader who sat across from Rebash.

Marziel put a finger to his lips, leaned around the table, and whispered in Treylen's ear. "The spell works both ways. We can hear them, but they could hear us as well."

Treylen nodded, then turned to watch. Marziel's hand grabbed his face and turned it back. He shook his head, then whispered in Treylen's ear again. "Watch the bard, not their table. If you give us away, then I'd have to kill the lot of them. I would rather not have any incidents with the good mayor around."

Treylen fished a coin from his pocket. It had been there when he put the clothing on. He placed it on the mantle for the bard, who started in on a ballad while his granddaughter took up the lute and plucked accompaniment.

"Good," Marziel whispered, then settled back on his side of the table.

Treylen turned his chair to watch the bard, then leaned back, so his ear was over the salt, and the voices came through clearly again.

"It's just two nights," Rebash was saying. "Stay and take a look at them."

"My crew have families waiting," the elkbone said. "They

need no more mouths to feed."

"You don't think your warlord would like more earners? These are lowsater fauns. Already fit to hold weapons. In a year's time, they'll be twice the size of your men. They'll bring in far more than what you paid for them."

"A child with a war hammer is still a child," the elkbone grumbled.

"All the better," Rebash said, his words as dark and oily as the mustache that issued them. "Children do as they're told."

Treylen stared at Marziel until his handler met his eyes, then mouthed, "What is happening?"

Marziel shook his head. Explanations would have to wait.

"Have you been to the badlands, trader?" the voice rumbled. "We are a free and wealthy people. We fight of our own accord."

"Then you would be doing them a kindness to buy them. If not you, then Jaul will have them. Should a few disappear along the way, who's to know? My wagons are paid either way."

"So you would make a jailor of me?" There was a racket as the old elkbone smacked his antlers against the wall beside him. From across the room came the nervous clatter of his companions rattling against each other's antlers. They couldn't hear what their leader was saying, but his irritation was easy enough to sense.

"Easy, friend. These aren't prisoners. They're conscripts, being carted off to do their service like every other youth in Jaul."

"The lowsater don't see it that way."

"The lowsater have writ their own misfortune. They should have surrendered."

"They do not deserve the cruelty that I've have seen," the mercenary said. Again, Treylen tried to meet Marziel's eyes, and again, he got no explanation.

"So take them on as wards," Rebash pressed. "It has to be

a better life than what Jaul has in store for them."

"Bah," the elkbone spat, and thumped the table. "I could turn you in for the coin."

"Friend," Rebash laughed, but there was an edge of fear to it, "we've done nothing but talk. My hands are clean in this. I'm just an intermediary, trying to make a few coins and help a good fellow out."

The elkbone growled, and Treylen turned his head to see him fiddling with the money that hung from the strips of leather sewn to his coat.

"There is no clean hand that has touched the coin of Jaul. At least I know where my blood came from." He yanked the coin free and slapped it on the table. "For my dinner." His chair toppled over as he stood, and one of his companions across the room jumped up, unsheathing his axe and moving toward the far table. Apogee appeared, cutting the man off and forcing a tankard into his free hand.

"Drink up." She flashed a smile, blocking the elkbone's way as the older man stomped back across the bar, leaving Rebash in his gloom. "Anything for you, warleader?"

"Whisky," he growled.

"I'll bring it in a moment. Don't make a mess now, my love."

He grunted thanks and took the younger elkbone by the arm.

"Leave the carrion for the crows," he grumbled, forcing the axe from his companion's hand, and guiding him back to the table.

As Apogee came up to their table, Marziel swept his hand across it, scattering the salt and causing the spell to dissipate.

"You'll not be going out again tonight, I hope?" She set a plate with duck pie and roast vegetables in front of Treylen.

"Maybe for a stroll," Marziel said. "We found my nephew's bags the other night. No horse, I'm afraid."

Treylen started on the food in Stone Kingdom fashion,

spearing the chunks of duck with his fork and tearing at them with his teeth. It occurred to him that even though he wasn't with the monks, he still only found the time to eat once a day. Marziel picked through the vegetables on his plate with a look of disappointment.

"Give my compliments to Marcus, will you? The food looks delicious, though you know I'm not afraid to pay a premium if that's what it takes to get fresh carrots here on the border."

"I'm sorry, milord, that's the only kind we grow, but I will look into it. Maybe I can bring you something from the pantry." She sounded genuinely offended, though Treylen was certain that Marziel was insulting his own cooking. He had been the one to roast the vegetables.

"You be careful if you go out," Apogee said. "The fog's creeping off the river. That's when the otters are out."

"Thank you, Amelia, but we'll be fine. I trained with the rangers, you know. Have I told you—"

"We've all heard the story." Apogee cut him off quickly. It seemed that Mauridin didn't have to be here long before he wore out his welcome. Even the mayor at the bar let out a low groan.

"I guess my exploits are known far and wide by now. I'm touched by your concern, though. A round of ale for the house. Rebash! Your drinks are on me, friend. It was good to catch up today." Rebash gave him a sour look, but forced a smile and raised his drink before turning back to stare into his tankard. The elkbones were hardly so moody. Half of them got up to clap their benefactor on the shoulder and clink steins with him. The leader who'd been so offended a moment ago seemed all cheer again. Hauling Marziel from his seat to embrace him, he mumbled something in the elkbone language that gave all the others a laugh, and made a show of checking Marziel's head for budding antlers before returning to his crew as the round of ale came out.

"Whew," Marziel breathed, and met Treylen's eyes with a laugh. "I think I'm an honorary elkbone now."

"Yes, they've adopted you." Treylen did his best to laugh, but his mind was too clouded with other concerns. Marziel saw the look, gesturing toward the bard again. The man picked his lute up and began playing "Rats of Oxbra'dal." They played it as a round and loudly enough to drown out any conversation from the tables. Treylen got the impression that the bard and Marziel had been at this game for a long time, and he half wondered if the man saw through the Mauridin facade. He gave no indication, which was in itself suspicious.

Marziel pulled his chair closer and put an arm around Treylen, like an uncle pulling his nephew in for a heart-to-heart.

"Speaking of adoption. You had questions about my good friend Rebash and his business."

"Were they talking about selling people?" Treylen asked.

"Some would call the lowsater people. Others call them half-men. Have you seen one?"

"They're like they elkbones, aren't they?" Treylen wondered. "I know they have horns instead of antlers."

"Horns, yes, but they're a true satyr…hooves and tail on the bottom, human on top, except the horns, and the fur, and the face. The face is a bit of both, strange looking. Called *low* for the noise they make, more cow than elk. Size of a cow too. Not man-sized folk. They've been on the run ever since the Stone Kingdom fell to the Jaul…"

"Is it all true?"

"True and tested. I've many a friend among the lowsater."

"Are they enslaved?"

"Not exactly," Marziel scoffed. "If there's one good thing the Jaul have done, it is outlawed slavery wherever they conquer. Which is why, I think, he hopes to make a sale to the elkbones. No laws in their lands, except what each warlord chooses."

"So what are they, then?"

"You heard him. Every citizen has a duty. And even though they've never formally surrendered, Jaul calls them his citizens. When the emperor catches them, those of a certain age are shipped off to do their duty. Of course, they are not a warlike people. Most refuse to fight at all. They wind up working in prison instead. Lowsater are exceptional stone carvers and smithies. Learned it from the dwarves in the old times. If you believe in such things."

"Sounds like slavery to me," Treylen said.

"That may be true, but there is a dignity in prison. A prisoner is never expected to accept their state. They may be held against their will, but that will is their own to hold in grudge. You and I aren't half so free."

Rime's voice popped into his head while Marziel was speaking.

I feel sorry for them. Somebody should kill that man.

I don't like it either, Treylen answered, *but it's not our mission. What are you doing eavesdropping? I told you to stay hidden tonight.*

I got hungry. And I'm still very hidden.

"Are you listening?" Marziel asked.

"I am," Treylen said. "The prisoners...what are you going to do about them?"

Marziel swirled the water in his cup. "What makes you think we should do anything?"

"What he's doing isn't right."

"He's right about something," Marziel said. "Those prisoners might be happier in the badlands. The elkbones would accept them and they would grow up to be mercenaries."

"He's not going to buy them," Treylen said. "But they're still going to Jaul."

"I don't like what Rebash does, but I can't stop the caravans. If I did, they would just put more rangers on this road.

Rebash will get what's coming to him someday. When I'm ready. For now, he's a valuable source of information. And a regular here. An inn's in need of regulars to stay in business."

"Well, Rime would like to kill him. He only says that about rats and pigeons."

"Oh, does he?" It had been an offhand comment, but Marziel seemed to give that more consideration than he had Treylen's own opinion. Marziel sighed and shifted in his chair.

"What do you say we eat and speak some more of the coast of the Stone Kingdom. That is where your alias came from. You'll need to know a bit of its history. Then we'll begin training."

"How will we start?" Treylen didn't mean to irritate him, but he was finding it easier to accept his training when he knew what to expect.

"I heard you've had your training in accidents." He smiled. "So we'll skip that. Before we leave, I'll have you lift the mayor's purse and put it back. Mauridin likes to play the odd trick on her. If she notices, she won't suspect any ill intent. If you are good enough, we may move up to pickpocketing the elkbones. That will have to wait until Rebash goes to bed. He's in a foul mood. I don't want to test him."

"And then?" Treylen pressed further. "What about tonight?"

"You'll see."

"I think I'd rather know," Treylen said, dropping any pretense of Cren'pin's cheeriness.

"If you must know…I was going to bring you out to that grave you made and use it as a training yard, but Apogee suggested it might be best to lay off of combat for a night. So instead, I'm going to see how you and your dragon handle ingress."

"What does that mean?" Treylen asked.

"Oh, you'll have to allow me a few surprises at least. Don't worry. You'll find out soon enough."

Chapter Seventeen

THE ATTIC

SLEIGHT OF HAND CAME EASILY ENOUGH TO TREYLEN. HE HAD never formally trained in it, but had spent enough time twirling daggers and performing feats of acrobatics to understand. So adept was Marziel at the skill that he managed to deliver a lesson on it in the middle of the tavern and nobody was the wiser.

They had stayed late after dinner and played the part of uncle and nephew, Mauridin regaling Cren'pin with stories of his old family home on the coast—simple fishing villages carved into the cliffs overlooking the ocean, and the imaginary life he used to live there, trading salt fish for textiles from the Salt Crescent and the lands beyond Ketaresk, and selling inland to caravans that visited great cities carved into the mountains.

Treylen listened in rapt attention, never needing to remind himself to commit these facts to memory. He could picture it as if it were his own story, his own family and homeland, and he knew he would remember just as clearly.

Marziel must have sensed his relaxation, because he'd leaned in to whisper to Treylen, "Don't become too fond of

Cren'pin. He is a means to an end. His concerns…his loyalties are not your own."

When the reminiscing had finished, Mauridin decided to regale the entire tavern with more stories of his own: hunting, sailing, training with the rangers when he served in the army. It was bland, boastful, and went on just long enough to make anyone in the common room regret they had not minded their own business.

"Now, my dear nephew, I think I'll retire for the night. I'm still a little sore from our adventure the other day. I fear I may have caught a bit of that chill you had this morning." Marziel bowed, and took his leave, but not before ordering another round of drinks for everyone. He leaned close to Treylen again, whispering.

"Take your time with your drink. I will meet you in the attic."

Mauridin retired upstairs. Shortly after that, innkeeper Marcus came out of the kitchen to help Apogee deliver the round that Mauridin had paid for, then Marcus disappeared again.

"All finished?" Apogee came over, clearing the table.

"I'm finished here," he whispered. "How do I get to the attic?"

"You'll figure it out. Wear your darks."

She sauntered off, holding her serving tray high and wading through the group of elkbones who'd abandoned their chairs and moved the tables to clear a dance floor for themselves and some newly arrived locals. The bard had sent his granddaughter away but kept the ocarina, playing a lively tune. Treylen took advantage of the distraction to slip away.

Rime, I'm going to the attic.

We're waiting, Rime said, lazily. So, Rime was conspiring with Marziel now. That didn't make Treylen feel any more confident. Or less alone.

He ducked into his room and got his darks on quickly,

along with the daggers and the toolkit. He cracked the door and peered out to make sure that nobody had followed him. Rebash had retired to his room on the second floor, but Treylen didn't trust him not to poke around. Once he was sure that nobody was lurking, he slipped out.

Any of the third-floor doors could have led to the attic, but he didn't try them. There was already a way in that he knew of.

He tiptoed down the hall to the closet that led to the passage between floors. He would have accessed the dragon-mind and used dragon stealth to blend into the shadows, but Rime, the little traitor, was already up there and might tip off Marziel to his approach.

Sure enough, a light shone from up above in the gap between walls. Treylen stepped carefully over the squeaking board and gripped the frame of the wall, shimmying out onto a support beam, then up another until he reached the narrow gap that led to the attic. Slowly, he pulled himself up and peered over the edge.

Lantern light shone warmly on a slanted ceiling, and a rough wooden floor led off into the shadows. Marziel sat on a small stool, the lantern resting beside him. In front of him was a dragon-shaped shrine, complete with pillars in the shape of serpents, and a small arched roof. It wasn't a genuine shrine to the old dragon king, of course. Those were larger and made of stone. It was roughly cut as well, not the work of an artisan, but the polish of the wood showed the degree of care its creator had put into it.

The platform at the center of the shrine held another carving. This one was in the shape of a small dragon roughly the size of Rime, curled in a circle with its tail draped over its nose and its wings tucked back. Rime lay curled up alongside the wooden dragon, yawning as Marziel scratched his belly.

"I didn't hear you. Well done," Marziel said, as Treylen pulled himself up from the gap just under the eaves of the inn.

He looked around. The attic was much larger than he'd realized. There was even a wall back in the darkness hinting at some other sections up here.

Marziel stood and pushed the stool aside.

"Most trainees wind up in the other part of the attic. You're observant."

"I saw Rime come up this way." Treylen walked over to stand beside him. He bent down and scratched Rime.

"Apogee tells me you were a stone carver."

"She remembered that?"

"Is that strange?"

"We didn't know each other long before she left the abbey."

"She's more intelligent than she seems."

"I think she seems intelligent."

"Exactly," Marziel said. Treylen laughed, but Marziel didn't find it funny.

"I was supposed to be an architect too. They couldn't quite make up their minds which of their footsteps I'd follow in, so they expected me to do both."

"I'm just a hobbyist," Marziel said, running his hand along the roof of the shrine. It looked to have been carved from a single piece of oak, except for the dragon, who was carved from ebony. "Do you still do it?"

"Never. I didn't want to do it in the first place." Treylen crouched down and inspected the smaller piece. "The detail is very good."

"Thank you. I think you'll find that a touch of artistry helps with your spycraft."

"You mean with disguises?" Treylen looked up. Marziel nodded. He was much more patient this evening.

"Staging traps, forgery, drawing maps…mind you, don't draw a map if you don't have to. Parchment is…"

"The greatest traitor," Treylen said, scratching Rime's chin, then running a hand along the carving of the dragon.

"Good, you're learning." Marziel sighed and watched him inspect the carving. "That's Kestrel."

Treylen drew himself up and met Marziel's eyes. When Marziel didn't go on, Treylen continued.

"Have I seen her?" Treylen asked.

Marziel gave the slightest nod, barely visible in the lamplight. "You've seen her in the rafters."

"How is that possible?"

Marziel turned away, stepping into the darkness.

"It shouldn't have been. She was injured on a mission. I thought that we could make it over the mountains. We landed here. She died in the mountains just north of here. Then I waited. I didn't bother eating. I knew that it was only a matter of time before I followed her into death. But something strange happened. I felt the dragonmind again. And it was like she was with me."

"That doesn't make any sense."

"You asked me how I know that you can access its power without having to take from your bondmate. This is how I know. It's not as powerful as it was when she was with me. But it's something."

"You'll teach me how you do it?" Treylen asked.

"I'll try."

"What about Apogee? Is she like you?"

"Hers isn't my story to tell. You have a lot of questions all of a sudden, you know that?"

"I've had nothing but questions since the beginning."

Marziel looked back, anger flashing on his face.

"Sorry," Treylen said. "I mean I'm sorry about your dragon. Do you miss her?"

Marziel stepped deeper into the attic, his face hidden. "They say it's grief that kills the bondmate. But if that were true, then I'd have died there on the mountain."

Rime's voice cut into his head. *I would miss you, bondmate. But I'm not sure that I'd die of it. Maybe they would let me stay here.*

Rime hopped up from the shrine and scurried over, twining around his feet before climbing up and burrowing into the cowl of his jacket.

"Don't let him kid you," Marziel said. "You mean more to him than he lets on."

"How do you know that?"

"We talk sometimes."

"You can talk to Rime?"

"It is one of the benefits I have discovered to having my own, solitary connection with dragonmind."

"Foxbane spoke to me," Treylen said.

Marziel nodded. "That's a little more common. It's not the same. Elder dragons can do it."

"Will you teach me?"

"I have been. It's not a fast thing. Not like last night when you managed to reach Rime from so far away."

"I've never done that before. I didn't mean to do it."

"I know. We've talked about it." He looked at Rime again. "Now come here. I have other things I'd rather teach you tonight."

"Right." Treylen glanced at the lantern on the floor, then stepped into the darkness of the attic after him.

"No dragon sight here," Marziel said. "That's cheating."

"I understand." Treylen reached for his dagger, but Marziel put a hand out.

"We aren't fighting."

"What are we doing, then?" he asked, stopping at the wall that separated this part of the attic from the rest.

"We're looking at this wall."

"What is it?

"This is the rear wall of Fort Spoils, just east of the War Pass on the edge of the badlands."

"This is the actual wall?" Treylen scratched his head, not quite comprehending. Rounded timbers, like the face of a palisade, lined this wall of the attic.

Marziel chuckled. "This is the wall as I remember it last I visited. Notice the tight spacing of the timbers. Go ahead. Touch it."

Treylen stepped up and put a hand on the wall.

"See if you can get a grip to climb it. Don't use the hooks I gave you. Most of the time when you are seeking ingress to enemy fortifications, you can't use them. The marks they make would let the enemy know that assassins were working among them."

"Why is it here?"

"I built it."

"Obviously," Treylen said. This got a laugh out of Marziel.

"You are just like your dragon sometimes."

Treylen figured it was best not to respond to that.

"Why did you build it?"

"I want to see if you can get past it."

Treylen cocked an eyebrow, looking into the shadows on either side. It seemed to span the width of the attic. And it stretched to the roof. There might have been a small gap at the top that he could squeeze over, but the timbers were so smooth and so close together that he didn't have a way to get a grip on them.

"Maybe with a running start"—Treylen pondered the roof —"but the real wall must have been taller than this."

"You're not going over it," Marziel said. "What else?"

"What part of the fort is this?" Treylen asked.

Marziel grinned. "The rear right corner."

"Is there a gate on the back of the fort?" Treylen asked.

"What an interesting question. Why would you ask it?"

"Because it's impossible to go under a palisade—the timbers go too far underground. But…" Treylen walked to the left-hand side of the wall, closest to where the gate would have been if this were the actual palisade.

"But what?"

"At the very least, there should be a gap in the wood here I can use to climb."

"True, but there are guards watching. You won't be climbing over this. Try something else."

"If I couldn't climb it, I would look here." He put his hand on the timber farthest to the left.

"Why that one? It doesn't look any different." Marziel walked over to stand next to him.

"A large gate might need more than a few timbers to anchor it. It probably has a stone foundation to support it."

"Maybe." Marziel leaned in.

"And, if there's a foundation surrounding the gate, that means the timber beside it can't go all the way into the ground like the others do. It would have to be cut short to accommodate the foundation."

"What would that mean?"

"It depends. If I were designing a secret door, I would put a hinge here, make the timber swing open." Treylen felt around the sides of it, searching for any sort of gap. There wasn't one.

"Or?" Marziel prompted. "What if you were loyal to Jaul and didn't intend to leave a secret entrance into your border fort?"

"In that case I would want to be sure the timber was securely in place and that the foundation was solid enough." Treylen bent to push at the floor just in front of the wall. A piece of it came up in his hand. "Solid enough not to do that."

The opening was just wide enough that he could squeeze down into the floor beneath the attic and crawl back up on the other side of the wall.

"Should I go through?"

Marziel nodded approval.

Treylen lifted Rime from his shoulders and set him on the floor.

Go look around, Rime.

I know everything in here, Rime said, hopping into the hole and disappearing on the other side.

"Is it clear?" Treylen whispered after him.

"You won't get any help from him," Marziel said. "I've already told him you're on your own here."

"Joke's on you," Treylen said, squeezing through the opening. "He isn't any help to begin with."

He came out into blackness. By the sound of it, there was another wide wall immediately after the one he'd just passed over. A door opened in the false palisade behind him and Marziel stepped through, carrying the lantern.

"I didn't see a door."

"It wasn't part of your exercise." Marziel shut the lantern, casting them in darkness again, but not before Treylen got a glimpse of the wall in front of him. The wall here was painted to look like marble. The floor was polished wood with red carpeting rolled out in front of it. A thin ridge of marble ran along the wall like baseboard. At the far end of the wall stood a red door. A sconce on either side of the door held an unlit candle. The door had a knob at its center with a keyhole just below it. Rime was gone—probably down in the kitchen stealing what was left of the duck.

"This is the hallway outside of Emperor Jaul's bedchambers," Marziel said.

"How do you know what that is like?"

No answer. Treylen changed tack.

"If we wanted to kill him and we knew where he was, why wouldn't we go in through the window?"

Marziel laughed darkly.

"You think he has windows? Emperor Jaul lives in fear of our Queen's Fingers. He sequesters himself deep inside and rules his empire from a coward's reach, just like his father before him and grandmother Jaul before that. The history of Jaul conquest is a history of cowards. His armies go far and wide, but he hides like a babe in his chambers. In my mind, that is already a defeat, don't you think?"

Treylen nodded.

"But we can't reach him."

"Not yet. But someday the queen will come knocking."

"How does the queen live? I guess she keeps court. I've known a few who have seen her…" Treylen was so caught up in Marziel's philosophizing about Jaul that he said it without thinking. No sooner had the words passed his lips than he felt the edge of a blade against his throat.

"Our queen does not live on your lips, apprentice. She is everywhere and nowhere. Whatever you know of Iverna, or think you know from your old life, must die in this room. It must not spread recklessly outside our borders."

"I understand," he whispered, too afraid to move. The knife disappeared and Treylen could breathe again.

"They always say they understand. But Jaul has ways of prying information out of ones like you. There was a time when we would have cut your tongue. Then Jaul started culling those who couldn't speak, and it was no longer practical."

"So I have to get through the door," Treylen said, desperate to change the course of the conversation. Thankfully, Marziel was happy to oblige.

"Yes, and quickly. Now get moving."

Treylen moved. He didn't trust the floor panels, instead leaping over them and landing on the narrow ridge of stone at the base of the wall. It was just wide enough for his toes.

"Interesting." Marziel tapped his foot.

Treylen had to move quickly before he lost this balance, shimmying along the base of the wall until he was near enough to put a hand on the door frame and steady himself.

"Now what?" Marziel asked. Treylen didn't dare try the handle. It would be locked for this. It was a large lock, so he brought out a couple of his larger picks, inserting them one at a time and getting a feel for it. He didn't press on anything just yet. In all likelihood, there was some trapped mechanism.

"Wouldn't I know the shape of the key by the time I got here?" he said as he worked.

"I suppose you might have seen it hanging from a belt loop." Marziel tapped his foot.

"Care to share what it looked like?" Treylen said, feeling around more. Sure enough, there were many tumblers. More than he would have expected.

"Long," Marziel said. "I guess if you were paying close attention, you'd have noticed three prongs on one side, with a wider gap between the top two."

That was more than he had hoped for. And it eliminated some of the more dubious tumblers that he could feel. In the end, Treylen still had to guess, and it took much longer to get a lever in place than it should have, but when all of the picks were in place, and the lever positioned just right, he turned with one hand.

Letting go of the frame, he reached out to take the handle, body stretching out in front of the doorway while his feet remained on the narrow stone ledge beside it. He turned the handle and it clicked. He pushed on the door...and nothing happened.

"Is that it?" he asked.

"Did it open?" Marziel said behind him.

"No," Treylen said.

"Then you aren't finished. Not much time now. He will have heard you."

He turned the knob again, giving the door another shove. It rattled but didn't budge, as if it were still barred from the inside. A long key...Treylen had assumed that just meant the tumblers were located deeper in. But what if it was even longer than that? What if there was a part of the key that extended beyond the tumblers and out the other side of the lock? Treylen slipped the lock picks back into his pouch, keeping the handle turned so the locking mechanism stayed open, then he pulled one last pick from his pocket. This was the longest. He stuck it through, not feeling around inside. Instead, letting it protrude out the other side of the door, where it wedged underneath a metal bar that sat across the door. The bar lifted up and the door swung free.

Treylen released the handle, reaching up to take hold of the candelabra. There was a click as the brace shifted on the wall and a twang and thump as a board swung down from the ceiling and cracked him on the head. He lost his footing and tumbled to the floor.

Before he could sit up, Marziel had paced over, one of the floor panels squeaking as he stepped across it, just as Treylen had expected it would. Marziel stopped and stood over him.

"Don't bother getting up. Your head is already rolling down the hallway."

Treylen rubbed the spot where the board had struck him.

"I had considered staying true to the original and using the blade of a broadsword. I'm glad I didn't. I would've been digging a lot more holes over the years."

"I could go again."

"No. You did better than most. I'm impressed with your lock picking. And quite pleased to see that my board still works. Most don't make it past the crossbows."

"Are those in the door or the floor?" Treylen groaned.

"Don't worry about it." Marziel opened the hood of the lantern again to light the room. "How did you know to stay off the floor? Something else you learned in your apprenticeship as an architect?"

"No," Treylen said, brushing himself off and searching for the lock pick, which had gone flying when the board struck him. "I learned it from your staircase in the closet."

"That's good," Marziel said. "I learned it the hard way. Shall we go through?" He held a hand toward the door.

"After you." Treylen did the same. Marziel raised an eyebrow.

"You're certainly jumpy tonight."

"Not as jumpy as whoever lights the emperor's candles." Treylen rubbed his head again.

Marziel chuckled, then stepped through and waited for Treylen to follow him.

"There's more?"

"I've been teaching here for a long time."

Treylen stepped through the doorway and found another wall that stretched across the width of the attic.

This one was black and made from rough stone.

"Hellcaves," Treylen said. "There's enough stone here to bring the whole building down."

"It's all painted wood, don't you worry, foreman. I wouldn't build a hideout that wasn't structurally sound."

"I would hope so." Treylen shook his head.

"This is a wall in Tabron. It was built before the Jaul came, back in the time when Lome and Iverna were doing a healthy trade with one another."

"It'll have a Ferrick door, then," Treylen said.

Troma Ferrick had been the most prolific architect on the continent in the time before the war. He'd also been loyal to the queen of Iverna, and most every building of that age had a Ferrick door somewhere. Newer buildings had their secrets, but the particular construction of a Ferrick door was difficult to hide in the early stages, and nowadays agents of the queen working among the Jaul had to be more subtle when planning their secret entrances.

"Do you trust it?" Marziel asked.

"It's difficult to set a trap on a Ferrick door," Treylen said. "They're so integral to the construction, there just isn't much room for traps. There might be a trap on the inside or outside, but I should be safe opening it. I don't trust this floor, though."

Treylen hopped over the floor again. The rough-cut stone

was easy enough to find a handhold on. He clung to it, then climbed sideways toward the far corner.

"You're like a frog on that wall." Marziel watched from the door.

"I've had a lot of practice," he said, finding the next handhold and sliding sideways.

"Most who come to me have only had a few years' practice. You've been doing this for much longer. I forget that."

"I could just climb over the wall," Treylen said.

"These guards would see you," Marziel answered. "Keep going. I'd like to see how well you fare climbing sideways here. You may not have trained in all the areas I would like, but you have many more years of practice than most, that much is clear."

"They kept me on as a teacher. I don't really know why they never sent a replacement for Bos. They say there weren't trainers to spare. Don't know what they're going to do now that I'm gone. I guess the ones I trained will take over." Treylen moved his hands across the rough wood that had been carved to look like stone. There was just enough of a gap between them to wedge his fingers in and keep moving sideways.

"They asked me to do it," Marziel said, "several years ago. Then the Jaul redoubled their attacks on the pass, and it became more important to keep a spymaster at this crossroads. Anyway, you aren't the only abbey that has lost a trainer. They are still in short supply. I hear that a few have even been pulled away to go back into combat. Ah, so you've found it."

Treylen put his hand on the keystone. All Ferrick doors had one somewhere. They were not always in the same place or the same shape, but he had learned to identify them because of where they sat and how narrow they were compared to the other stones.

He pressed it and a panel popped open beside him.

"I didn't take the time to sculpt the inside. Imagine it's a stone door sliding open." Marziel walked over to where he hung and stepped through the door, raising his lantern, and motioning for Treylen to follow.

"If you do find yourself entering the keep in Tabron, I'd be careful. I'm almost certain they've found this one. If it's not trapped, it will be guarded."

Treylen dropped down and hurried through.

The next room was made of smooth square blocks painted the color of white limestone flecked with blue.

"This is Iveran," Treylen whispered, following the light. It was not just any wall, though. There was no mortar used in the construction. At least that was the impression given by the wooden reproduction. The seams were so tight as to be almost nonexistent. And each block stuck out an inch farther than the one below it so that even if he could have gotten a handhold, his feet would be dangling. Flat relief carvings of gargoyles adorned each row of blocks, running up the center of the wall, a small opening in each of the mouths to let the water from the roof spill out. The center of this wall stretched up into the peak of the attic, where a narrow gap represented the crenellations at the top of the tower.

"It is one of ours," Marziel said. "You are an assassin of the queen, and you will go where she says and do as she pleases. You won't always have the luxury of killing enemies. Sometimes it is necessary to remove an ally as well. I would ask you if you understood, but that is not for you to contemplate."

"I understand well enough," Treylen said. True, it had been a very long time since he had thought about this aspect of the life he had chosen. He figured it was best not to think about it, and he put any doubts out of his mind, instead focusing on the construction. There was something familiar about this wall, though he couldn't quite place it.

"There aren't going to be any secret doors here," Treylen said. "You want me to go all the way up?"

"If you can. You'll have to leap to get there."

Marziel tilted his lantern down to reveal a gap in the floor. This part of the attic was unfinished, and it looked like he was peering down onto the ceiling of the third-floor bedrooms. There was a crack in the wood very similar to the one that Rime squirmed through every night when he went to hunt rats in the attic. The little traitor had known all along about the obstacle course up here and hadn't bothered to tell Treylen about any of it. He was probably getting a good laugh out of all of this right now.

He looked back at the wall, thinking. He was certain that he had seen a drawing of it before. The drooping jowls of the gargoyles sparked a memory of a diagram and his mother's workshop. Yes, she had been commissioned to carve something like this before. And if he recalled correctly, it had been specifically designed to ensnare climbers. Spikes set within the opening of the spout pointed inward, angled so that they would hook any stray hands slipped inside as surely as a weir caught stray eels. And if he correctly recalled, every curve and groove on the sculpture had a razor blade tucked in behind it. Every piece of the carving except for one.

Treylen got a running start, threw himself across the void, and collided with the nearest gargoyle. His fingers gripped the edges of the stone border that surrounded the carving. He hugged the wall tightly.

With his face pressed against it, he could see now little blades tucked behind every groove and nook within the gargoyle. The row of blocks above him stuck out from the ones below, and the stones above those stuck out farther, presenting an outward angle even more difficult to climb than a straight wall would have been, without any sort of handhold.

He recalled something strange, though. The stones had a

narrow ridge along the underside. It was subtle, and he hadn't seen the purpose for it at the time. It couldn't be seen easily so it wasn't decorative. But now it represented a possibility. If this was a perfect reproduction, the ridge would be there. He reached out to the lip of stone that hung above him, found the ridge, and pressed his fingertips against it. Bringing his feet up to push off the wall, he was able to get just enough friction to hold himself there.

"I've never seen this before," Marziel said.

Another gargoyle rested on the next level of stones. And the only opening that he could get enough of a grip on was the waterspout. He could see no other way.

Treylen released his pressure on one hand, reached up to the next gargoyle, and jammed his hand into the spout, only going deep enough for the hooks that he knew were inside to catch the leather of his glove. It held.

Treylen got another hand up.

Grabbing the top of the border, he pulled himself up, slipped his glove off, and got the other hand in place on the opposite side of the border of the carving. He found another ridge on the rock above him. His fingers ached, and his back was spasming. But he held tight.

There was one more gargoyle, and he repeated the process with the other hand, shredding another glove, but managing to get up without hooking any fingers. One final lunge, and he caught the top of the wooden parapet, hauled himself up, and crouched over the attic, peering down on the space below.

"Well done." Marziel clapped softly.

Treylen looked behind him to see the exterior wall of the attic. A slotted grate looked out from the peak of the roof, over the moonlit yard and the woods behind it.

"Come down from there," Marziel called. Treylen hopped down, landing on the floor of the attic as softly as he could. "Never before have I seen someone who knew what to do with this wall."

"I've seen it before. Somewhere. Which fortress is this in?" Marziel's brow furrowed.

"I will stop you there, apprentice. As important as it is for you to understand the defenses employed against our kind, and I commend you for what you demonstrated tonight, the location of this wall is not for you to know. I think I see now why the queen was so eager to have you in our service. I would be careful who you display your knowledge to. You become a greater liability, the more secrets you harbor. Put this out of your mind if you can."

He turned, directing the light of his lantern on the door behind them, and leading Treylen back through the series of walls to their starting point. Rime was sleeping again in the shrine. Treylen followed silently, taking in the series of obstacles that he had just navigated. How long had it taken to build such an intricate replica of each of these structures? And how accurate were they? He couldn't truly know what lay inside the hallway outside the bed chambers of Emperor Jaul. Could he?

If Treylen did go to Fort Spoils, or to this stone structure in Tabron, how accurate would he find it compared to the rough carvings of the master assassin? One thing he knew for certain: The final obstacle had been immaculate. Perhaps not as artistically symmetrical or as perfect as the gargoyles that his mother and artisans like her carved into limestone, but the details that mattered, the crucial handholds upon the wall, those were perfect.

"You have questions," Marziel said as he bent to light a candle, placing it lovingly on top of the shrine. "Keep them to yourself. I'm pleased tonight. I can tell that you have trained hard and with dedication for many years. Your knowledge in this area surpasses that of many who have come to me. It almost makes up for my disappointment at what you lack."

"What's next?" Treylen waited.

"I think I'm back downstairs. You listened well this

evening. Tomorrow, I'll ask you to repeat the stories of the Stone Kingdom back to me and we'll test you on your sleight of hand again. We will need to work on your self-awareness."

Marziel pulled one of Treylen's daggers from behind his back. Then reached into his pocket and produced a handful of coins, and some dried meat that Treylen had been saving for Rime. Then he pulled out Treylen's belt knife and set it in Treylen's hand with the rest.

"When did you take all that?"

"I've been lifting things from you since dinner in hopes you would notice. In the future, I hope you'll pay better attention to your own person."

"I'm sorry."

"I told you, what you lack in some areas, you have made up for tonight. As a reward, I'll leave you to your practice. I expect you to practice each obstacle until you can do it as fast in darkness as you can in the light. No dragonmind. Strive to match your dragon's speed without his help."

Treylen laughed and Marziel cocked an eyebrow again.

"Do it until one of us comes to relieve you. Make the dragon run through it with you. I'm fond of him, but you are right to call him lazy. And try not to make any noise."

"Right." Treylen nodded. He knelt to snag Rime out of the shrine and placed the dragon onto his shoulder. "Do you think we'll be finished before sunrise?"

He stood and looked back, but Marziel had slipped away.

"I guess we should get started." He scratched Rime's head.

I could nap a little longer, Rime said.

"I'm sure you can. But I would like to get some sleep tonight too. And if they catch us slacking, I won't be allowed any. Have you known all along that Marziel doesn't have a dragon?

I had suspicions.

"How is it possible?"

He bent to inspect the small carving of the dragon that rested in the shrine. It did look a little like Rime.

I don't know any more than you do. Only what they taught you at the abbey. And I was too young to remember most of that.

"I'm not sure I put much stock in the monks' teachings anymore," Treylen said. "I just wonder how much more there is that we don't know."

I suspect there is a great deal.

Treylen borrowed the candle from the shrine and paced back through the series of obstacles, resetting the traps, shutting the doors, and committing the layout of each room to memory before resuming the exercise.

Chapter Eighteen

THE WASHERMEN

SLEEP CAME EASY IN THE DRAGON'S HIDE. WHILE TREYLEN'S
bed was small, it was still larger than the pile of blankets in the
alcove by the abbey had been, and far softer. While the rooms
on the third floor were not as warm as the second-floor suites,
or the common room below, they were an improvement over a
drafty cave on a windswept cliff.

Unlike on the mountain—where every change in weather
brought sound and sometimes rain into their sleeping quarters, where the sun and moon shone in, and birds would come
to perch on the ledge outside and sing at all hours—Treylen's
closet-sized room was still and quiet as a royal bedchamber.

He slept heavily. What dreams came to him were patch-
work memories of a life imagined. Sunny days on the Stone
Kingdom coast, fleeting images of fancy hats and bright silk
garments blowing in the breeze as he rode a long, winding
trail through the Salt Crescent to visit his favorite uncle in the
north of Lome.

Treylen was jolted awake by Apogee at the foot of his bed
again.

"Wake up, you worthless bag of bones." Imitating
Marziel's voice, she planted a foot on his behind and gave it a

shove, then stepped back, grinning as Treylen scrambled to his feet.

"I'm up. What's happening?"

Apogee almost chuckled—it was the most humor he'd seen out of her since their reunion. She tossed a new pile of silks on his bed.

"You overslept again."

"There are no windows." He rubbed at his face and sat down, eyes searching for Rime. The only light came from the windows through the open door and down the stairs at the end of the hallway.

"What time is it?" he asked, clearing his throat. He reached for the silks she'd dropped on the bed.

"Those are for later. Leave them. It's morning. You've chores to do in your other disguise. Marziel has a surprise for you."

She turned and walked out, leaving the door to Treylen's room hanging open.

He heaved a sigh and fell back onto the bed. He had slept in his underclothes, and when he reached a hand out to grab his darks from the foot of the bed, he didn't find them. He bolted up again, searching the floor and still not finding anything.

Rime, where are my darks? He got a half-sleeping response from the dragon.

In the wash.

The peg on the wall where his jacket had been hanging was also empty. His daggers and toolkit were still where he'd put them.

The rags he'd worn earlier were piled by the door; Treylen cast a last glance over the silks on the foot of his bed. There wasn't much light from the hallways, but he thought they looked like an entirely different outfit from the last. A new hat rested beside them with a peacock's feather sticking up from the brim. He ran a hand across the bundle, before going to the door and slipping the stinking tunic over his head and the itching breeches on his legs. He tied the belt around his waist again and slipped into the old, worn-out shoes. They were oversized, stank, and without any stockings, they chafed his ankles and made it impossible to walk stealthily.

Dressed as Trogan the vagabond, he shut the door behind him, then clopped down the hall away from the light of the main staircase until he reached the closet that hid the passage into the kitchen. Treylen paused just inside of it. A faint bit of light illuminated the gap that he'd squeezed through to get up into Marziel's strange obstacle course.

"Rime. Psst," he hissed, then not hearing any stirring, climbed up to peer into the attic. Light seeped in through one of the gables, illuminating the wooden shrine. A few stolen coins, bones, and bits of jewelry lay beside it, but no Rime. He could have called for the dragon with a thought, but then he would miss the opportunity to catch him doing something he wasn't supposed to.

Treylen dropped back to the floor and crept down the narrow staircase, pausing on the second floor to listen. There was no activity from the rooms today, but sounds from the kitchen and the smell of bacon drifted up from below. He tiptoed the rest of the way down and peered out of the pantry into the kitchen.

Marziel was there, dressed as the innkeeper. He was stooped over and muttering to himself in the innkeeper's voice, despite the fact that nobody was here to listen to him. Treylen would have to ask Apogee if Marziel was a bit touched in the head. After what he now knew the man had been through, he wouldn't doubt it. How could anyone survive the death of a bondmate?

Treylen stepped out, shutting the pantry behind him.

"Took you long enough." Innkeeper Marziel studied him, then turned back to the cookfire.

"Sorry," Treylen said. "I'm used to sleeping in the caves—"

"I have something for you." He tossed a kitchen rag, which struck Treylen with a greasy slap. Treylen peeled it off, scowling at it.

"I've heard."

He winked at Treylen, his gaze twitching toward the door of the kitchen just as the merchant Rebash stuck his head in from the common room.

"Innkeep, is the breakfast almost ready?"

"Eat it raw, if ya like."

"Bah." Rebash scoffed. "Will you put the elkbones on my tab this morning?"

"Tell the girl." Marziel shook a spatula at him.

"If the girl was about, I'd have sent her back." The trader's eyes started to drift toward Treylen, when he realized he hadn't done anything to change his appearance. His face and posture looked no different than it had when he met the man the night before, as *Cren'pin*. Before Rebash could focus on him, Marziel barked and rattled his spatula on the oven.

"Here ya go. Cooked enough for ya?" Marziel grabbed a fistful of sizzling bacon with his bare hand, and a plate full of egg and creamed oats. He slapped the bacon onto the plate and tossed it into Rebash's hand so fast, the man almost dropped it.

As he moved, he shouted over his shoulder at Treylen, "What you standing around for? Get that rag washed with the rest of it."

Rebash staggered back, barely catching the plate, while Treylen bowed his head and ducked out the back door.

"Calm yourself, man, I'm not that hungry. Who was that?" Rebash craned his neck to look over the innkeeper's shoulder as he was pushed back out into the common room.

"Some poor beggar from the city, mister Rebash. Don't

worry, I keeps him out of the kitchen. He works hard enough. Now what will the rest of ya' be eating?"

Treylen pressed himself against the back wall of the inn and scanned the work yard while he caught his breath. The yard was empty, except for a bushel of dirty linens and another with a bunch of rags. The sleeve of his darks poked out from beneath them.

He saw something, Rime said.

Quiet. I need to focus.

Treylen sought the dragonmind. He still wasn't sure he knew what he was doing, but drawing upon the dragon's stealth made him feel more comfortable as he scrunched his shoulders and twisted his face up. He muttered a few words, trying to summon the voice that he'd used the other day.

As he focused, he saw Rime scurry out of the kitchen. The dragon hopped into one of the bushels of laundry and buried himself.

You should have warned me before you took my stealth away, Rime said. *I could've been seen.*

Oh.

He had forgotten that his companion might be hidden within the common room. Keeping his dragon from being noticed had not been part of life at the abbey.

I'll warn you next time, Treylen thought. *Did anyone see you?*

Just Marziel.

"Good," Treylen said, practicing the voice again. He bent down to adjust the rock in his shoe. As he leaned over, he caught sight of someone peering around the corner of the building.

"Marcus know you're back here?" Treylen turned to see the short, plump figure of the town's mayor coming up behind him. "Are you the man he hired? You had better be." She shouted past him at the door, "Marcus, there is a man back here!"

"Yes, I am," he said, his voice rasping a bit too much, and

shifting as he struggled to remember what accent he'd settled on the day before. As he stood, he rubbed some dirt across his face.

"I'd like to hear it from him, thank you. Marcus!" she shouted again, backing away as Treylen raised a hand toward her.

"Oh, what is it, love?" Marziel appeared at the door.

"I take it this man is skulking at your behest?"

"He's my man, for the day at least, and upon whose behest are you skulking?"

"I came to bring my wash to Amelia." She held out a bushel.

"Ah. Amelia's busy but leave it here. He's about to wash the sheets, I'm sure he can handle it."

"Where did he come from? You trust him?"

"Introduce yourself already." Marziel elbowed him.

The mayor's eyes fixed on Treylen, intently, and he hoped she had been drunk enough the first two times they had met that she wouldn't recognize him.

"It's, uh…Trogan…from…"

"He's from Old Westbridge, south of Tabron." Marziel nodded.

"I know where it is," the mayor said. "Are the old ruins still standing?"

"I, umm…" They had spent so much time talking over the places and people of the Stone Kingdom, they'd hardly covered Lome.

"He wouldn't know, Hilde, Trogan here hasn't been home since he served." He cupped his mouth with a hand and whispered, "Got the dragon shakes something awful."

Dragon shakes? Treylen wondered.

Never heard of them, Rime said.

"Is it true? Nerves shot from the war?" she asked, leaning closer and squinting as she looked him up and down again. Treylen nodded and took a step back.

"It is." Treylen drew more on his dragon's stealth, not quite sure what he was agreeing with.

"I suppose I can trust a fellow soldier. We all lent our flesh to the emperor, didn't we, Marcus?"

"Aye, we did, and not all of it came back." Marziel hitched up a pant leg to show a long scar down his calf.

"Oh, don't start with the scars, Marcus. I'll match you cut for cut. Ask my husband, he'll tell you."

Treylen watched the exchange, nodding.

"We've all heard. Hear this, Trogan, Hilde once killed a battle assassin!" He winked again.

"Brought him down with my hook and net. That was the autumn offensive, the emperor's father's time. You'd have been just a babe. The only thing that kept us from breaching Harvest Pass was the bodies were piled too high. Guts up to my knees and blood stained my eyeballs." The mayor's eyes were locked on Marziel's, a faraway look on both their faces.

"I was there, Hilde; you don't have to remind me."

Treylen almost laughed, then shuddered—of course they had been on opposite sides, the mayor just didn't know it. The one she had killed had likely been one of Marziel's close friends. She broke away from his stare and turned toward Treylen again, eyes glimmering, wiped the back of a hand across her face, then looked him up and down.

"You're a drifter now?" Her expression softened.

"He's a veteran looking for work," Marziel said. "Tabron didn't suit him, did it my boy?"

"No, sir," Treylen said, keeping his eyes on the ground.

"A soldier deserves a chance." She nodded, lips pressed tightly together. "Take care. My husband's best underthings are in there." She narrowed her eyes at him and bent to snatch a couple of dresses out of the bushel. She balled them up and tucked them under her arm. She made a sign with one hand and a fist with the other, thumping it against her chest. Treylen stared a moment, before Marziel caught his attention.

The man was bugging his eyes out so hard, Treylen worried they might pop from his head. He twitched at Treylen rapidly.

I think he wants you to do it back to her.

Treylen did his best imitation of the salute. The mayor frowned, then shook her head.

"Damn dragons…"

"He won't be stealing off with anything, Hilde, he can barely hold a broom straight. Go on inside now."

Marziel ushered her inside, then stuck his head out again.

"You know how to do the wash?"

"I've seen the monks do it."

Marziel shook his head.

"Just don't ruin the mayor's underthings, please. Now, keep your trap shut. Take all of that down to the river. I've a surprise for you there. And keep an eye out for otters."

Did you hear all of that? Treylen asked Rime.

A strange woman. Rime shifted in the basket, getting comfortable.

Everyone here is strange.

Maybe it is living so close to the war.

Treylen looked around the yard, not seeing Apogee. There was some activity in the distance. One of the locals working a garden, and the sound of an axe splitting wood, the crunch of gravel as a cart rolled by.

I guess they want me to learn washing on my own. Why must everything be so difficult?

I don't think washing is supposed to be difficult, bondmate.

It had never occurred to him to do his own wash. The monks were always there, they were always washing. They cooked, they cleaned, they washed, and they performed their devotions to the queen. Treylen was a killer in training. Killers didn't do the wash.

Please don't speak about this with Marziel.

Life would be easier if I couldn't speak to either of you, Rime said.

Treylen waited until the sound of the cart had passed, then stacked the bushels and hauled them toward the river.

A well-worn footpath ran behind the village, and Treylen followed it, past a few houses, to the water's edge. A wheat field lay on the opposite side of the river, and to the south was the wooded trail that Treylen had taken to find the apple tree the day before. Looking upriver to the north, he saw the mill, and a simple stone bridge of the emperor's road. It was low to the water, but wide, and as strong as anything he'd seen, better for the armies of Jaul to march across on their way to Harvest Pass. Beyond the bridge was the forest where he'd encountered the otters. The river was wide and shallow. A trio of wooden basins were set into the water's edge, each with a washing board and a bucket. Two washermen in broad-brimmed hats already knelt at the bank, knees on cushions, sleeves rolled up to reveal strong forearms, scrubbing away.

Treylen cleared his throat as he approached, but they paid him no mind. He searched left, then right. Not finding another basin, he threw the bushels down and knelt at the one between them, keeping his head down and his eyes on his work. There was soap here, and a wringer with a crank mounted on the side.

Stay low, he thought to Rime. *I know you hear them.*

I'm comfortable, bondmate.

It would have been best to start with his darks. If he was going to damage something, it was better his own clothing. But with the other two washers here, they would have to stay dirty. Instead, he grabbed one of the mayor's underthings. That turned out to be a mistake, as mud from the bottom of the basin quickly soiled the water. He did his best to clear it with the bucket. A slight chuckle from the washermen and his face reddened.

What did you do this morning? Treylen sent the thought to Rime, scrubbing again; this time it looked cleaner.

I was in the common room. Watching Marziel work. And that one called Rebash. I don't like him.

That's good. Marziel is going to test me on the Stone Kingdom tonight. But now that we're here, we need to watch everything.

I have been watching Rebash and his scheming closely. Treylen could hear the bristle in his voice. He didn't like the man any more than Treylen did.

You should let it go. Marziel said we're not to bother him. He's a good source of information.

He won't be bothered if he doesn't see it coming.

Treylen wrung the water out and tossed it into the bushel, starting on another pair of shortclothes. Rime filled him in on the details as he worked. Rebash had been working on the elkbones again, but to no avail. A new group had come through, but these mercenaries had spent all of their coin in Tabron. The cart he had just heard moving along the road was theirs, hauling goods back to their lands in the northeast. They stayed for food, then went on their way and had no interest in Rebash's scheme.

Marziel had changed into his Mauridin clothes and made an appearance before breakfast to let the townsfolk know that he and his nephew would be going out for the day to visit some nearby farms. One last effort to find the missing horse. Treylen knew that it was just an excuse to explain why neither of them would be around all day.

Treylen kept his head down and put his back into scrubbing. Rime had crept out of the wash basket and perched on the edge of the basin, watching with obvious amusement.

I think you've just made them dirtier, he said.

Treylen froze.

The sound of scrubbing on either side had stopped, both washermen seeing the dragon out in the open.

What have you done, Rime?

A jolt of panic knifed his spine, and Treylen sprang up and staggered back, eyes darting from one washerman to the next.

The two of them hadn't moved, their broad-brimmed hats hiding their expression, but both stared at the dragon perched between them.

What do we do?

Treylen's hands groped frantically for the hilt of his daggers, hidden under his rags.

Calm, bondmate, Rime said, a laugh in his voice.

Treylen blinked and took a breath, as one washerman backed slowly away. He pulled his hands back from under his shirt, unclenching them. They weren't screaming and running off, so perhaps they'd seen a dragon before. Surely, the feral fledglings who ventured into Iverna Valley from the Dragon Lands sometimes wandered out through Harvest Pass.

"Oh my, a dragon!" he said, not half as convincing as he'd hoped to sound.

The larger of the washermen grunted and held a soapy hand out toward it.

"Careful, fellow. Feral dragons take your hand off."

"Feral, huh?" the man said, gruffly. Treylen couldn't see much of him beneath the hat, but now that he thought of it, the cloak he wore was awfully similar to the rangers' green. And was that the bulge of a hatchet beneath it?

"All dragons are feral here." The smaller one had a croaking voice. "But you'd know that, if you weren't Iveran."

"Caught you!" The big one turned, pushing his cloak aside as he spun, dagger-in-hand. The hat tilted up to reveal a mad grin as he leaped, slashing so quickly that Treylen stumbled back, just barely getting his dagger drawn in time to cross blades with the man. Treylen was pressed back, his blade locked with his opponent's. But assassins always carried two, and Treylen's other hand snaked around, drawing his second dagger and bringing it up toward the man's kidney.

A small hand seized his wrist. The second washer had moved in a flash. They held no weapons, but gripped him with an unnatural strength.

"Careful," said a woman's voice. The hat had fallen away to reveal dark curls, and sharp, curious eyes.

"Volanti?"

"We got you good!" Aaron bellowed, pulling his blade away and laughing so hard he doubled over, sinking into Treylen, who dropped the daggers and embraced his friend. Volanti hopped into the air and threw her arms around the both of them, hanging there.

"You're a couple of bleeding idiots." She gave a muffled laugh, then pulled her face away to cough at the stink of his costume and fell on the riverbank.

A dark shape eeled through the water, then sprang out to land in her lap. Ketcher chirped and bounded off her, catching Treylen's sleeve and climbing up into his shirt, still wet from the river. Felicity crawled out of the river, shaking off before twining affectionately around Treylen's legs.

Aaron pushed him away, then gripped his shoulder and held him at arm's length.

"You stink." He plucked Ketcher out from Treylen's collar and dropped him on the bank. The dragons bolted, splashing after Rime into the water.

"Watch out for otters!" Treylen shouted.

Did you know all along? he thought to Rime.

Maybe.

"They should stay out of sight. Anyone could come along the road anytime," Treylen said, then smiled.

"You got a package," Aaron said, pulling a bundle from his pocket and handing it over. Treylen unwrapped it to reveal a needlepoint kit; the pattern of a small dog was drawn on the fabric in his mother's artful hand. Treylen shut the bundle quickly, and tucked it into his jacket.

"I wish my mother sent me crafts," Volanti said.

"Bah," Treylen scoffed, trying to keep his face from flushing red. "She should know that watchdogs are bad luck. Wait, can you be out with…" He grabbed a handful of curls and lifted to reveal a newly cropped ear…It was finely done, and the small stitching would be hardly noticeable once the swelling had gone down.

"Sister Ono's work? It's very good. Still should have been healed before you came." He checked the other ear. It was identical, if a little puffy. "I can't believe you're here. How did you get here?"

"Same as you." Aaron looked wistfully at the sky. Treylen wondered if that meant in a sack, or if they'd had a more dignified flight.

"Marziel knows?"

"It was his idea," Aaron said. "I guess you're doing well enough he thinks we can keep up too."

"Or so bad that he thinks you need our help," Volanti joked.

"Maybe a little of both," Treylen said, remembering his failure at the apple tree the previous morning and the struggle to learn disguise.

"I saw promise," Marziel said, climbing down the bank to join them, no longer disguised as the innkeeper. "I saw potential in you the other night, beyond what I am accustomed to. I also saw a glaring necessity for further training. As much as you have overtrained in wildcraft, it will never quite make up for the spycraft that Bostra Avex never had time to pass along."

"No, don't regret it now," he said when Treylen cast his eyes down. "I can't know what has become of your other students, but these two are well positioned for what I'll teach them. Now…" He glanced at Treylen's wash basin, then to Aaron and Volanti. "Will one of you please wash the good mayor's underthings? He's mangled them. While they're doing that, Treylen, I want you to go upriver."

He pointed the way Treylen had come when he'd first arrived.

"What's upriver?" Treylen asked.

"More surprises." He grinned. "You'll know when you see it."

Treylen looked to the others, but neither gave anything away.

"Now?"

"Get on with it." He waved Treylen off. "And bring your lizard."

"I still can't believe it," Treylen said. "How'd you send for them?"

"We'll tell you it all later," Volanti said, pointing dubiously toward the bridge. "You should hurry."

"Felicity will go with you," Aaron added.

Marziel lifted one of the bushels that Aaron and Volanti had washed, then trudged up the bank, his free hand reattaching his beard as he went. He stopped and looked back.

"Go on, then!"

Treylen clutched hands with the two of them, then pulled away and started upriver, his heart still pounding from the shock of it all. Rime and Felicity wriggled through the water. When he reached the road and the wide stone bridge, he debated a moment before ducking underneath. Better to be unseen and muddy than to risk running into the villagers or the mayor again.

It was low and shadowy and stank of rot. By the time he'd reached the middle, Treylen regretted the decision. He had to bend down, almost crawling as he crept along the mud bank. Rime and Ketcher swam gleefully, and their splashes echoed off of the rough-cut stone, but Treylen's eyes were fixed on something large and glistening near the far bank, low in the water. It was too big for an otter, too freshly wet to be a stone. It didn't move, but there was a presence about it.

Something's here, he said to Rime.

The dragons' play had faded, Rime and Felicity both disappearing below the surface. He kept a steady pace, so as not to alert the thing that he had seen it, but always keeping it in the corner of one eye. For a moment, he thought that it had shifted, but when he looked back, it was still.

A few steps more, and he was clear of the bridge.

Then a clawed hand seized him from above.

The gauntlets of the battle assassin tore his sleeve but stopped him tumbling into the river. Rak'Tsoro—in full leathers and dragon mask—crouched on the bank above. From behind, there was a bubbling sound, and the head of Foxbane emerged from the water, Rime clinging to his snout affectionately.

There was no such affection between the two assassins. Treylen found his footing in the mud, and she released him, glaring down like a gargoyle from a rooftop.

Treylen breathed a strained greeting, almost blurted that he'd thought she was an otter before thinking better of it, then clamped his mouth shut.

"The general wants a report," Rak'tsoro growled.

"There isn't much. Marziel says I'm doing well."

"A report of your mission. What of the scribe?" So Rak'Tsoro knew the mission. Somehow that was more chilling than reassuring.

"Marziel says I'm not ready for Tabron."

"He may have to accelerate your training. Our scouts have seen wizard sign at the fort outside the Harvest Pass." Treylen wondered what wizard sign could possibly look like, but held his tongue. "A new host is amassing as well…more than we're used to seeing at little Harvest Pass. And the main force at the War Pass has their own fight—they can't spare us."

"You want me to help you hunt the wizard?"

Rak'Tsoro frowned. "Absolutely not. I would rather you lived to complete the mission you were given. Before this wizard's host is armed with glyph-marked weapons. Tell your spymaster that you have one week to get to Tabron. Any longer and it may be too late."

"As the general commands."

"The queen favors you, Assassin Treylen." Her hard eyes softened a moment as she placed one hand on his shoulder, then drew it back, untied the gauntlet, and removed it to reveal a hand even more scarred than her face. She slipped her hand into a fold of her cloak and brought out something curious: like an abbey pigeon, but half the size, it lay in her palm, resting quietly on its back, feet in the air, eyes blinking slowly as if it had been asleep a moment earlier. A message cylinder was tied loosely to one leg. When it saw Treylen, it let out a soft coo.

"A pocket pigeon?" he whispered. He'd heard the monks at Coops Abbey speak enviously of the queen's exalted high-master pigeon keepers who raised birds so docile, they could be carried around behind enemy lines.

"The bird is homed to the Harvest Pass, where I am stationed," said Rak'Tsoro. "She's a fast flyer. From the time you toss her, the message should reach me in a matter of hours. Should you encounter the wizard that I'm hunting, you're to report it and withdraw."

Treylen nodded, gently lifting the bird from her palm, and slipping it into a pocket stitched on the old tunic.

"I can do that." He held his hand over the pocket in case the bird decided to flee. But it had settled into sleep already.

"I will find you if I need you."

She said no more, but glared at him until he lowered his eyes and turned to trudge back under the bridge. When he looked back, she and the dark lump that had been Foxbane were gone. Rime and Felicity splashed along, nipping at each other's tails as if nothing had happened, but for Treylen, it was as if a dark cloud had settled over him, even as he headed back to join his friends.

Three days was nothing. He'd hardly had time to get his bearings and get comfortable speaking with the Lomish people, who though not so different from Iverans, had a particular way of talking that he couldn't quite imitate yet. His friends had only just arrived, and now he was to leave again?

It was unfair, to the highest degree, as his father would have said. But it also was a childish impulse to complain about unfairness along the path of one's own choosing. There was nothing fair about the life he'd chosen, and if anything was unfair, it was that Treylen had been given the reprieve of being overlooked so many years, and not called into duty, while those that he had helped to train had been called up. How many of them, he wondered, had perished shortly after from their lack of proper spycraft?

He would never know, and that by itself was a small blessing.

"Are you alright?" Volanti said when he'd reached them. Aaron looked up and cringed.

"Didn't go well?"

"Better than last time." Treylen swallowed, and forced himself to focus on changing his posture and keeping his face twisted up enough; he still looked like the drifter, Trogan. Now, more than ever, he needed the practice.

They had finished the wash, and as eager as he'd been to catch up with them and hear every little detail he had missed at the abbey—from which birds were nesting where to the monks' petty squabbles over who was getting lazy in the kitchen—his conversation with Rak'Tsoro had put a damper on it all.

"We best get back there and see what he's planned."

They finished washing his darks and Treylen helped to load the baskets, Rime and Ketcher crawling into one together while Felicity took up one basket by herself. When they reached the yard behind the Dragon's Hide, Treylen went looking for Marziel.

"That was fast," Marziel said when Treylen peered into the kitchen. He was sweating over the oven with his beard and skullcap on. He raised an oversized wooden spoon and gestured toward the door.

"Get your friends settled in the stables. Then get washed and into your Stone Kingdom clothes."

"What's the cover if anyone asks about them?"

"The story," Marziel said, "is that Trogan came with two companions when he arrived, and Marcus, being a charitable old sot, kindly put them up inside the stables. He's hired them to help with the otter problem, but in the meantime, he'll put them to work around the inn. Now it's a little cold in the stables, but I'm sure you're all accustomed to it on the mountain.

"I don't mind," Treylen said.

"You have a second alias to mind, but don't neglect your first. I need you upstairs and changed to Cren'pin before dinner tonight. Be sure to wash that stink off of you. Splash a little perfume on."

"What should they do?" Treylen poked his thumb toward Aaron and Volanti, who were hanging sheets in the yard.

"You leave them to me," he said. "The inn's going to be busy tonight. I may have to test them early and put them to work. A word of warning, though. I understand the three of you are close…"

"We are."

"That grows the danger here." Marziel stepped away from the sink and stood to his full height, the innkeeper's voice slipping away for a moment. "You aren't playing any longer. And any loyalty you have aside from that which you owe to your queen is an affront to her sovereignty."

"I know that."

"Do you? Understand that Cren'pin is an alias that I must guard for you, because to expose it also exposes Mauridin, whose ties to the tavern could jeopardize my entire operation. Your friends have no such protection. If they're exposed here, there's little we can do to aid them. I won't slaughter these poor villagers to keep their secrets, and we won't be intervening should a ranger happen across them, understand?"

"I hadn't realized…but I do."

"Good. Now, don't look at me like that. It's the queen's prerogative. Too many losses have come because sentimental fools made some great sacrifice that wasn't theirs to give. Don't pout, I'm sure the both of them are capable."

"Right," Treylen said. "I'm sure they are." He had trained them, after all. He just had to hope that it had been enough.

Chapter Nineteen

THE BARDS

THIN SMOKE FILLED THE TAVERN AS TREYLEN DESCENDED—washed, perfumed, and dressed in the guise of Cren'pin—to find a crowded common room, and Marziel much too busy greeting customers and pouring drinks to tend the fire or trim the wicks of the lanterns. He'd dressed quickly, but it had taken some help from Rime to find an old cage in the attic, where he secured the pigeon before coming down.

The screech of a lyre set Treylen's nerves on edge as he scanned the unfamiliar crowd. No sign of Aaron or Volanti. There was a mix of locals between the bar and the tables. Three tables held what looked like off-duty legionnaires. A third table looked like they might be officers. There were two more tables of elkbones who seemed deliberately uninterested in the soldiers. Treylen was a bit disappointed that the group he'd become accustomed to seemed to have moved on. But for once, Treylen's arrival went unnoticed. A new warbard sat atop one of the mercenary tables, drawing most of the attention in the room.

She had one antler. The other had been broken off at the scalp, and her head was dressed with a bandage. She was bare from the waist up. A shawl of lace strung with silver coins hung over muscled shoulders. Her eyes were fixed upon a second bard, who was seated on a barrel between the two tables. Her companion belted out a rhythm of boastful syllables in the elkbone language and thumped on his naked chest as he acted out the motions of some great battle.

Treylen had been on the staircase, staring for a full minute, before a crash from the kitchen door pulled him out of it. The innkeeper and his friend, the elder bard, leaned at the end of the bar, glaring. Aaron—dressed in a new set of rags and a false beard—was bending over a mess of spilled soup and shattered crockery. He'd been looking at the bard when he'd walked straight into the counter with a tray in hand. Treylen shook off his stupor, coughed in the smoky air, and pushed past a couple of farmer-types and a flour-caked woman he took to be the town's miller, to join them at the far end of the bar, nearest the door.

"Pardon the commotion. It seems the soldiers have come to roost." Marziel moved frantically, taking mugs from a dirty pile, dunking them in a tub of gray water, then shoving them under the tap as fast as the beer would flow.

"No problem, Marcus. New help?"

"Aye, always hiring around here. Sop that up!" He grabbed a pile of rags and pitched them at Aaron's head. Treylen was relieved to see that Marziel hadn't made him take on any strange or complicated disguise on his first day. Aaron had always been a quick learner, but he was far too honest to be good at that sort of thing.

"Have you seen my uncle? I'm meeting him for dinner?" Treylen blinked to hide the flash in his eyes as he embraced the dragonmind, borrowing stealth as well as a little of his dragon's perception to cut through the din of the noise and the smoky haze in the air. Rime would be okay without it. He was probably already settled on one of the rafters.

"Why, didn't you see him upstairs, milord?" the old bard

said, though his eyes were on the two strapping warbards that were depriving him of his coin.

Marziel shot Treylen an evil glare. Clearly that had been the wrong question.

"Can I have an ale?" Treylen asked, drawing another scowl. Treylen was starting to dislike the innkeeper. He had to remind himself it was just a facade. Marziel thumped a tankard down in front of him. Treylen took a sip.

Water again. Treylen marveled, not seeing any water pitcher around that it could have been poured from. It was at least clean water, not from the dunk bucket.

"I'm afraid they are in your usual table." The bard pointed at the table where the elkbones gathered. "Should I chase them off for you? I'm not afraid of a few antlers."

"The young lord don't have a favorite table," Marziel croaked. "Miliness will find him something. You might as well pack your lute and go. I don't think there'll be much call for a third bard tonight."

"Not unless I strip down to my skivvies."

"I have seen it," Marziel said, meeting Treylen's eyes. "He was a great performer once."

"I'm as much a performer as I've ever been," the old bard said, a note of hurt in his voice. He seemed about to launch into some kind of story, but Treylen raised a hand and interrupted. It was rude, but it was what Mauridin would have done.

"Who is Miliness?"

"That would be me." A stout girl in a barmaid's apron sidled up next to Treylen and lifted the tray of mugs that Marziel had been filling. "I'll be back in a moment, and we'll get you a table."

There was a clatter as the bard stood on the table to sing, knocking tankards aside as she stomped a rhythm. Her sweaty partner struck a series of poses in front of the fire as he acted out the struggles of some elkbone hero—the song was in the common tongue, but he still couldn't parse the elkbone accent.

Treylen stared at the new barmaid as she delivered drinks to the elkbones, then crawled around collecting tankards under the table. She could have been the mayor's granddaughter from the look of her. He didn't think that he had seen her before, but there was a good possibility that this was Apogee. Or Volanti, with a great deal of paint on her face—a few wild curls poked out from the wrap on her head, and the corner of a pillow stuck out from her pants when she bent over. Why did Marziel have to make everything about spycraft? Treylen pretended that he hadn't seen the padding, and hoped that the rest of the room was too drunk to notice.

"Where is Apogee…" He had just gotten out the last syllable of the name when a mug slammed down on his finger. Treylen yelped.

"Pardon, milord." Marziel reached across the bar, dabbing at the ale he'd sloshed over Treylen's sleeve. "Did you say *Amelia*?" His eyes bugged out so hard that Treylen worried he might be having a fit.

"Yes, where is *Amelia*?"

"She had things to take care of. Sorry for the slow service, we're quite busy."

"Not at all." Treylen grabbed the ale that Marziel had whacked him with before he could take it back, leaving the tankard of water and eyeing the rest of the patrons at the bar as he followed Volanti to a small table by the door. His pulse quickened as he passed the tables of legionnaires. A few watched him, but none with anything bordering on suspicion. Their moods were dark, but they couldn't have rightly expected to win the battle at Harvest Pass. The officers had already been served and were fixed on their dinner.

"Will this do, milord?" She smiled and pulled a chair out.

"I suppose so," he said, then whispered, "Your stuffing is showing."

Someone waved at him from a table behind her, nearest the door, and Treylen heard a voice call to him.

"Master Cren'pin, sit here if you like." Rebash urged him over. It took every grain of Treylen's resolve to force a smile onto his face.

"I'm not obliged to refuse hospitality." He stumbled over the words.

"Not tonight in this inn, it might never come back around." Rebash laughed. He eyed the barmaid and added, "How is that drink coming along, my dear? Don't say you've forgotten me."

"Get the man a drink already," Marziel called from the bar before she could answer. "And bus the elkbones' table, you big ox," he shouted at Aaron. "I've no more tankards here. Curse Amelia, calling off on a night like this."

Treylen eased into his chair, trying for all he was worth to look relaxed. But should he be? Would Mauridin's nephew really want to spend the evening with some old trader? No. He probably wouldn't be very pleased with it at all.

"So what did you want with me?" He let the smile slip and took a swig of ale.

"Just passing the time, milord. Have you eaten?" Rebash rubbed his palm across the surface of the table.

"I'm waiting for my uncle."

"Of course." He leaned back, running a hand through his gray-streaked hair before tying it back. "Did you find the horse?"

"Pardon?" Treylen said.

"On your outing."

"Oh, no. No luck at all, I'm afraid." Treylen watched the bards dance in the firelight.

"About time we had some entertainment." Rebash scowled at the old bard who sat with Marziel, before turning his attention to the elkbone woman. "Much as I appreciate the comforts here, it gets very dull after a while. Your uncle is quite fond of going out for the day, isn't he?"

"I guess so," Treylen said.

What are you doing, Rime's voice cut into his thoughts, *sitting with that man?*

It was a bad idea, Treylen thought. *I don't have anything to say to him.*

So leave.

I can't do that.

Treylen stood, then fished a few coins from the pocket of his silks. They had already been in there when he put the clothing on. He walked to the table with the musician and leaned between two of the elkbones to slap the coin down beside her feet.

"Do you know any Stone Kingdom tunes?"

The woman nodded at him, impatient, then put a foot over the coins, drawing them toward the center of the table. One of the elkbones standing around grunted something in their own language—either that or this new group had thicker accents than the last. He held a hand out like he was expecting some coin for himself.

"I don't think I have any more," Treylen said.

The man spit ale as he laughed and slapped his hand on Treylen's chest.

"Oh. A joke. Yes, very funny."

Treylen forced a laugh, then turned and nearly collided with the bare-chested singer beside the hearth.

"Which Stone Kingdom song shall we play?" The man threw a sweaty arm over Treylen's neck.

"Any?"

"Ya must have a favorite."

Rime, what is the name of a Stone Kingdom song? He didn't expect that Rime would know, but maybe he could ask Marziel.

"Lower in the Hills," Rime hissed.

"'Lower in the Hills'?" Treylen said. A grin split the man's face and he slapped Treylen's back. "Aye, milord, 'Lower in the Hills,' then." The large, sweaty bard gave him a little shove back to his table.

Rebash picked up right where he'd left off talking.

"Your uncle is always out. And you like to stay in your room. It seems neither of you are around most days."

"Oh, he keeps busy. I think I'm just tired."

"I know what that is like. You know, I was like him once." Rebash pointed at Aaron, who was juggling an armload of tankards. "His kind try to better themselves, but they lack resolve to keep at it day after day."

Treylen grunted, thinking of what Rebash did day after day. As far as Treylen could tell, all he ever did was take up some of the nicer chambers in the inn and sit around waiting for his caravans to arrive, all the while complaining about the service and trying to make illicit deals with his clients' cargo before the shipment reached Tabron.

"Merchants really work all that hard?" Treylen said.

"Your uncle does when it suits him. I imagine you would be a little shaken up after your fall." His gaze passed over Treylen again, lingering over a training scar on his clavicle, then the bruise on his collarbone. Treylen already felt on edge —the noise and heat in the room, the smoke from the lamps, the ever-present threat of being found out—this man wasn't helping.

"Must have been quite a fall you took, though." He peered at the scar on Treylen's neckline more closely. Inwardly, Treylen cursed these silks; the cleaner and brighter they were, the more of a fraud he felt. And they were so light, he felt naked.

"You don't seem all that road weary."

"I took the inland road," he said.

"Still a long way. The Crescent's an unruly place, some- times forgets it's part of the empire. Good coin to be made there, if your porters understand discretion." Rebash winked, then drained his drink and raised a hand, beckoning Volanti to refill it. "How is food coming along?" he asked her.

"Quick as we can cook it, milord."

"I'm not a lord, darling." He winked at Treylen. "Just a humble merchant. I'll have that food as soon as it's ready. Ale now."

"Of course, mister."

Rebash shook his head. "And here I thought the other one was dim."

"She work here often?" Treylen asked, eager to change the subject.

"How would I know? There's always new folk in here. Did you see the wretch he's got shoveling the stables? Some rascal from the city. Marcus is getting gullible in his old age. Did you see him?" Treylen had thought that nobody had noticed him practicing his disguise the other day, but clearly Rebash was more observant than Treylen had given him credit for. Rebash was also the one who had heard the commotion the night that Treylen had arrived.

"See who?" Treylen took a sip and pretended to be watching the bards again. They had finished their tune and had their heads together—likely discussing the song he'd asked for. One peeked up and gestured toward him. The other nodded, frowning.

I don't think they like the song you picked, Rime. Where did you even hear it?

I don't know, Rime said. *Maybe Brother Ourbeth.*

The man bent over a sack and withdrew a large hoop drum, passing it up to his companion as he took up her lyre and bow. Out of the corner of his eye, Treylen caught sight of the older bard, still sitting at the bar stool, scowling, probably because the coin had gone to her instead of him.

Marziel was gone. Treylen hadn't seen him leave. Between the soldiers dining at the next table, the half-naked warbards, a new crowd of unruly elkbones, dinner not coming out, and every other distraction that came with a larger crowd than he'd encountered since before joining the abbey, Treylen's heart pounded. He couldn't shake the feeling he was about to be found out. And then what? Marziel wasn't about to poison a room full of locals. Would he? Treylen didn't know which would be worse, getting caught, or the things he would have to do to fix it.

"I said did you see that man he has working the back?" Rebash went on. "I think Marcus has him sleeping in the stables. I tell you. I should make him chase the man off. What if he's a highwayman? Part of a band. Could you imagine, poor Marcus, taken for a fool?"

"What is this about highwaymen?" a voice growled behind him. Someone new had entered the inn while he was watching the bard.

Treylen caught the polish of an axe handle from the corner of one eye. His blood ran cold as a green-gloved hand tossed a feathered cap onto the table, while a second pair of hunting gloves grasped his shoulders.

Chapter Twenty

THE LOWERING

THE DRAGGING OF THE BOW ACROSS THE STRINGS OF THE LYRE brought a droning wail from the instrument as the drum settled into a hollow rhythm. Treylen's hand went for his daggers—or where they would have been if they'd fit under his silks.

He raised his head and saw a woman with thin hair and pale eyes. Sunburned cheeks framed a broad smile that belied the ranger green of her hunting gloves. A thick-bearded man stood beside her, equally sunburned. Neither had the stature of the last ranger, but there was a hardness to them that Treylen had seen only in dragon riders. She gave his shoulders another squeeze, then removed her own hat and tossed it onto the table beside her friend's.

"Highwaymen on the emperor's road?"

Her companion pulled a chair out and settled at the table between them. Rebash shot to his feet.

"Milord ranger, lady ranger."

Treylen suspected a minor lord would not need to be quite so animated. He turned to nod at each of them. The woman kept her hands on his shoulders.

Her companion cracked his neck, then stretched. Tugging

his long gloves off by the fingers, he tossed them on the table, then ran a hand through his hair and smoothed his beard. He took a long breath, flashing a broad smile to match his companion's.

"Please." The ranger waved for Rebash to sit.

"Would the lady care to sit?" Rebash offered his chair.

She rubbed the fabric of Treylen's shirt between her gloved fingers, then moved around the table to settle into Rebash's seat. The trader stood a pace back between the two rangers, clutching his tankard.

Between the dulcet strains of the lyre, the bard sang in a low, bovine wail. So that was why the song was called "Lower in the Hills." The Stone Kingdom *was* full of lowsater. And what else would the lowsater language sound like, than mooing cows?

The rangers watched the singer for a moment. Rebash cast an impatient glance between them and then back toward Treylen, clearly irritated at having his seat taken, though his face didn't reveal the sort of panic that Treylen felt welling up. He forced a smile, though his brow was beginning to sweat.

The woman turned back toward Treylen.

"Guau? Auer mauo, hual'ah?"

There was a guttural tone to the words that matched the singing.

"I'm sorry?"

"You aren't from the Stone Kingdom?" Her smile was too wide.

"Cren'pin hails from the coast," Rebash said. "Or so I've heard from his uncle. Your uncle rarely talks of his home."

"It's a sore subject for him," Treylen said.

"That explains it. They don't speak the deep-tongue on the coast, do they?"

"You don't miss the lowsater?" the other ranger cut in. One hand went to his belt and undid the button that held his hatchet in place, withdrawing it and setting it on the table before bringing out a sharpening stone.

"Not really," Treylen agreed, not quite sure what they were talking about.

"What makes you think that I would allow highwaymen in my emperor's woods?" the woman said to Rebash.

"I didn't mean to imply. It was exaggeration. Just some drifter that was here," he stuttered.

"Who is this highwayman?" she asked. Both turned to watch Rebash, who waited politely, occasionally glancing at the empty table to his right.

"Just some wretch the innkeeper's hired to sweep his floors."

"You think he's trouble?"

"To be quite honest, lady ranger, I didn't get that close a look at him."

"Why do you suspect him, then?" She leaned back in her seat.

"In my line of work, you have to keep your wits about you." His eyes went to Treylen, who looked down at his ale. "The next turn of the road could always be your last, or your next big opportunity..."

So that was what Rebash was getting at. He'd probably heard that Trogan was a disgraced soldier and wanted Marcus to let him go, so he could hire him for his own illicit purposes.

"Where is this innkeeper?" the man asked Rebash.

Just then, the new barmaid came up with a tray.

"He's busy in the back getting the food out." Volanti smiled, handing Rebash another tankard, then looking at the table for a place to put his food. Treylen searched her face for any nervous tics or beading sweat, but to her credit, nothing showed, and she'd tucked her shirt to hide the padding that filled out her disguise.

"Over there, my dear, that way I will be out of the good

rangers' hair when they're tired of me." He pointed to the empty table beside them.

"Go to eat," the ranger said. Her companion nodded and waved Rebash away. "I would speak to the innkeep," she said to Volanti.

"After dinner," her companion said. "What is there tonight?"

"There's duck. There's stew…"

"Stew," the man said.

"Stew," the woman echoed. "And ale for us both." Then she smiled at Treylen. "Go with your friend."

"But don't leave the tavern." The man caught Treylen's arm. "We may have more questions for you and your friend."

"I won't go anywhere," Treylen assured him.

The door slammed open behind him, and he jumped. Wind and the beginnings of a rainstorm gusted in.

Stay calm. Rime's icy voice steadied him.

The two rangers were looking up, not at the door, but at Treylen.

The mayor and her husband ambled in.

"It's beginning to blow out there. Oh, good evening, my dear Cren'pin. Lord rangers, welcome."

The two nodded a greeting.

"Mayor." Treylen bowed slightly.

She moved past, chasing one of the locals out of her seat beneath the dragon chandelier. Her husband nodded to the rangers, then climbed into the stool beside her and began talking with the old bard.

"Good evening." Treylen gave a curt bow before they could press him any further. "I'll be around as long as you need me." Then he moved to the next table and pulled out a chair opposite Rebash.

"That was discourteous, don't you think?" Rebash muttered, peering over Treylen's shoulder.

"What was?" Treylen took his seat.

"Requisitioning our table like that. Highwaymen indeed, I feel I've just been robbed."

"It's only a table," Treylen whispered, not wanting to draw any more attention than he had already. He peered back to see the rangers were talking to each other. "I thought they worked alone."

"Supposed to. I've never seen these two. There's one comes in here sometimes. Big man. He at least keeps to himself. Doesn't chew my ear with questions."

"They don't scare you?"

"Scare me, milord? They protect us from *her*." He tilted his head toward Iverna. "And every other danger in these border-lands. They may be a couple of pricks, but two rangers—this is the safest inn in all of Lome. Does make my work a little harder." He said the last bit under his breath. Had Treylen not been using the dragonmind, he wouldn't have heard it. "Tell me, Cren'pin, what is your experience with the lowsater?"

That question was a trap if he'd ever heard one. Say yes, and he'd be tested further. Say no, and he'd prove he wasn't a man of the Stone Kingdom. Say nothing, and he might miss out on learning more about the merchant's dirty secret.

"Not much. I always kept to myself."

"Ah, the privilege of station. And the lowsater youths, no dalliances? No sweethearts?"

"You think my family would approve?"

"Of a lowsater in the family? What do I know of Stone Kingdom custom? It would certainly be hard on the furniture. It is a pity, though, you don't speak the language. That would have been some use to me when the caravan gets here."

"Oh, would it? What are you hauling?" There was a whistle from across the room. Marziel stood at the bottom of the stairs dressed as Mauridin. "My uncle said I might go with you," Treylen added, hoping to learn something more.

Marziel whistled again and gestured him over.

"Have a good evening, milord. Tell your uncle he's

welcome to join me." Rebash speared a bit of meat on his fork and shoved it in his mouth.

"I'm sure he knows."

Treylen pushed through the crowd of locals that stood around the bar and met his *uncle* just as the bards finished playing. Marziel threw his arms around Treylen and whispered to him.

"When I told you that attention could be a disguise, I didn't have quite this in mind."

"Neither did I," Treylen said. "Where did they come from?"

"What did I tell you about sitting with your back to the door? It was the first thing I taught you."

"Why are they here?"

"Who knows." He slapped Treylen on the back and scanned the room. "I'm hungry, aren't you?" He waved to the mayor and greeted a few of the locals. In the process, he also shooed them away from one of the central tables, leaving them holding their plates to eat standing up.

"Maybe we can take our dinner upstairs," Treylen said.

"Nonsense. You spend too much time in that room of yours as it is. Come along, don't mind the crowd." Marziel bumped his chair into one of the legionnaires and pretended not to notice the curses coming from the soldiers' table.

"Miliness!" He flagged down Volanti on her way to deliver the rangers' food. "Two of those please. And a drink for me."

He leaned closer and whispered to Treylen.

"This seating is not ideal, but we'll make the most of it. I'll watch your back, you watch mine. After we eat, we'll test your sleight of hand. Shall we go for the mayor's coin? Or the soldiers' daggers?"

"Is that wise with them here?" Treylen tipped his head toward the rangers.

"Two rangers? That bodes poorly for me if they sense anything amiss here. But…if I changed my plans every time there was an agent of Jaul poking around, I'd never get anything done."

"Okay, then."

Marziel watched Volanti as she ran from the bar to the tables, to the kitchen again. None of the tables had been cleared and half the tavern was waiting on drinks. Aaron had been helping, but was held up now struggling to tap a keg.

"Poor girl. It'll be a long night for her. Regulars know when Marcus goes to the shitter, he's there for the night."

"I'm afraid we may lose some business tonight."

"At least the rangers have their food." Treylen sighed. The two rangers had the same breathless approach to food and drink as the last one had, draining their tankards with ravenous gulps and slurping their stew without taking their eyes off the room around them.

"It's your doing, you know. They're here for their friend. Apogee is out laying false tracks for them and cleaning up some of the evidence of your mishap in the river the other day. By the time they leave tonight, there will be more than enough suspicious activity to the west to pull them away from here."

"How will they come across it?"

"When they ask us about the other night, when you were thrown from your horse, we'll tell them about a strange figure you saw in the woods, and how you and I came across a campsite while we were out riding today."

"They're suspicious of my other alias." Treylen was about to say more when Marziel put a hand up for him to wait. The bards had stopped playing their instruments. The open door had let a chill in and the woman stepped off the table to dress in her furs again. The man beside the fire didn't seem to mind it, though.

Marziel flashed some coin at his friend, the older bard, and the man hopped down from his bar stool and ran over.

"Lord Tromweft. Good night to you."

"And to you. Will you spell the young warbards a moment?"

"Certainly."

His chest swelled a bit, and he hopped back to his seat to take up his lute and played a dancing tune.

Marziel waited for the bard to start singing before talking again.

"That should be cover enough." He slid his chair closer and put his arm around his nephew. "Now, tell me why they suspect your brand-new alias whom they have never met."

"Rebash said he looked like a highwayman. And they overheard."

"That is…unfortunate. You'd better pray that you were convincing enough he didn't recognize you."

"He doesn't know it was me."

"We'll find out soon enough." No sooner had he said it than he felt a knife pressed against his back.

"First test of the night. Tell me, Cren'pin, where are your blades?"

This time it didn't intimidate him. What would he do, stab him in the middle of his own tavern?

No, the old man had his weaknesses as well. Marziel cared too much about these people.

"I left them under my mattress. They didn't fit."

"Did I tell you to leave them?"

"I assumed."

"From now on, you must always carry them. If you cannot find a way to conceal them, I will show you how. I wouldn't give you an outfit if there wasn't a way to carry a dagger with it."

The food came out, along with ale for the both of them. Marziel frowned when Volanti set a tankard in front of Treylen.

"Don't finish that. We can't afford mistakes tonight. Now tell me what you remember of the Stone Kingdom."

While they ate, Treylen repeated the stories he'd been told to memorize, speaking as if he were reminiscing with his uncle. He could talk more loudly, no fear of anyone over-hearing the tale of how he was born in the small seaside fishing village, how his uncle had made his fortune trading in textiles, before going off after his aunt and cousins were killed by a Ketaresk raiding ship. How he and his brothers and sisters had stayed home, with private tutors.

"Shouldn't I know more about lowsater?" Treylen asked, more quietly. Marziel answered loud enough for the rest of the tavern to overhear.

"Nephew, how can you know anything of the lowsater? Most of them were driven out. It wasn't as if you were side-by-side on the coast anyhow. Not like the inland cities."

"Do you speak the language?"

"Naturally." Marziel broke a chunk of bread and mopped at the last of his soup.

The air in the room shifted as a door flew open again, and a gust from the storm blew rain and leaves into the tavern. A small figure entered wrapped in furs—not the brown and tan pelts of the elkbones, but white and heavy, dripping with rain. A dark cape shed some of the water. Tucked under one arm was a black leather satchel.

"Change of plans." Marziel looked like he'd seen a ghost. "No training tonight. Don't talk to anyone. You're not feeling well."

He staggered toward the bar, grabbing hold of Volanti to whisper in her ear, then he slipped up the staircase before Treylen could ask what was going on. Volanti set her tray on a table, then stepped quickly behind the bar. She pulled Aaron down to whisper to him, and the two of them disappeared into the kitchen.

The small, white-robed figure shuffled inside, pulling the door closed behind them. Still dripping with rain, they waddled to the table nearest the door, where the rangers watched the new arrival with the same rapt interest as he did.

Treylen closed his eyes and summoned the dragonmind again, listening.

"Hold this." The figure in white tossed the satchel—wet—into the lap of the ranger, who caught and held it out to keep it from soaking his lap.

"Late to be traveling, isn't it?" The second ranger pushed her stew aside and leaned across the table, eyeing them.

The figure nodded.

"Piss and terrors." It sounded like a man's voice, but he couldn't be certain. They shook the rain from their sleeves before tugging at the lacing of their collar.

"You sound like you've come a long way, and yet." She paused to drain another tankard. "I don't see much of the road on you."

"Bah," the figure spat, and tossed their cloak to the floor, then began to unwrap their furs. "There's no groom in the damnable village."

The furs revealed a balding man with a potbelly, high collar, and tailored trousers.

"I'll give each of you a pittance if you can find someone to brush down my pony."

"Why not?" The ranger let out a booming laugh. "Now sit. We have some requests for you as well."

He went outside as his partner pulled her chair closer to the man who was settling reluctantly into his seat.

"Now, first, what is your business here at the crossroads?" she whispered. Treylen strained to make out what she was saying, but just as he summoned more of the dragonmind, a clash of metal rattled in his ears.

The shirtless bard had brought out a tambourine. His partner, tiring of her perch on the table, had settled into the chair by the fire—that was the spot that all bards seemed to favor. She'd put her bow away and plucked the strings of the lyre, humming, and crooning.

Marziel's bard seemed to have made peace with the loss of his spotlight. He put his feet up on the bar and produced a fife from within his jacket, playing along from across the room.

Treylen strained to pick out the whispered words, as the ranger leaned over the strange new arrival, agitation on her face. But the chatter of the room swelled. The easy concordance of the three musicians mingled with the smoky air, full bellies and heads high with too much ale—then the soldiers began to sway. The mayor tapped her feet on the sides of her bar stool, two of the elkbones crossed the floor to the bar to ask some village girls to dance—then they all were on their feet.

Shouts, laughter, music swelled, and the poor barmaid ran to-and-fro.

Treylen was drawing as much of the dragon's senses as he could, but it only seemed to increase the din. He was about to stand and try to dance in the direction of the door in order to get a better vantage, when the innkeeper appeared, tray in hand, and slammed a tankard on the table in front of him.

"That was fast," Treylen said. It never ceased to amaze him how easily Marziel could slip into the form of Marcus. Now that he knew there was no dragon's magic aiding him, it was even more impressive.

"Drink it." Marziel pushed a cup in front of him. "Quickly. Don't ask why."

A black liquid sloshed at the bottom.

Treylen grabbed the cup and tossed it back, drinking the sour elixir in a single swallow.

"Good. Now rinse your teeth." He slung a tankard in front of him, then threw his tray down and began to clear the table. Marziel spoke rapidly under his breath.

"I'm going to ask you to lie for me." He gathered their bowls and empty cups, including the one that had held the black liquid, stacking them on the tray. Sweat ran down his face, and Treylen realized his handler was nervous.

"What is it?"

"No time. Do you remember what I said to you about fools who suffer traitors?"

Treylen didn't quite, but he nodded. "You said it's against the queen?"

"Apogee has never been here," Marziel said. "You haven't seen her. We haven't spoken of her. The last you heard that name was at your abbey, long ago. You understand?"

"No."

"She wasn't here." One hand gripped Treylen's arm, eyes staring into his.

"Is this a test?"

"Not this time." Marziel tightened his grip. "You were close with your students? You cared for them?" he asked with a note of desperation.

Treylen thought of Aaron, Volanti, all of the monks, and every other student who had come and gone.

"I cared. More than I should have."

"Then maybe I have a chance." He glanced over his shoulder, squeezing Treylen's arm one more time, then grabbed the tray and rushed off, shoving the elkbones aside as he made for the kitchen.

Chapter Twenty-One

THE ACCOUNTANT

RIME WAS NERVOUS.

Treylen could sense it through the bond. He scanned the rafters, hoping his dragon wasn't moving around too much. The smoking lamps and shifting shadows from the dancing below would have hidden him anyway.

He took another drink to wash down the sour liquid and try to still his own nerves. The soldiers had gotten up to join in the dancing. Treylen was increasingly out of place at the center of it all.

Will you ask him what he wants me to do? If I'm to blend, and I think I should move.

He won't talk to me, Rime said. *He says that you need to make your own choices. Whatever that means.*

I think I choose to move. It's getting too rowdy here.

The small man with the potbelly had managed to get away from the rangers. He joined Treylen's table and opened a ledger.

"Excuse me?" Treylen asked. The man ignored him. He produced a pair of round, wire-rimmed spectacles from his shirt pocket and perched them on the tip of his nose. "You can have the table, I'm finished."

Treylen pushed his chair back and started to get up.

"Sit down, Treylen Corbel."

He flipped through a stack of papers and set them in front of Treylen. Then he brought out a small, rectangular box, placed it above his ledger, and opened it to reveal a metal quill and a bottle of ink. Unstoppering the bottle, he dipped his quill with his right hand, while his left shot out to seize Treylen by the wrist.

"What is this?" Treylen pulled back, but the man's grip tightened, ink-stained nails digging into Treylen's flesh.

"Routine accounting." The man didn't even look up from his ledger. "You're new." His grip tightened again.

"I'm here with my uncle...Mauridin."

"Yes, yes, and I'm your accountant, now please hold still. The ink contains a fast-acting toxin, you don't want to break the skin." He shifted his grip and Treylen saw a smear of ink where the nails had been biting into his wrist.

Rime answered, *Marziel says to be calm.*

The man scribbled a few notes in his ledger, one hand still clamped on to Treylen. The flesh on his wrist tingled a little where the ink was smeared. Treylen forced himself to be still, watching the man write. It looked like an inventory. A few words were legible: carts, goods, perishables.

He couldn't be an assassin. He had the domineering manner of Rak'tsoro, but no subtlety. He made no effort to hide what he was doing. And he certainly didn't have the build for it.

There was one way to get the measure of this man. Treylen could test him.

"Did you get your horse taken care of, traveler?" Treylen asked. "You'll find a brush and some grain in the corner of the stables where the sparrows nest."

"I have no time for assassins' code. We are past that already." The man's thumb moved to the inside of Treylen's wrist. "Answer my first question."

"I don't think that I can."

The pen scratched on the parchment and the man snarled.

"Treylen Corbel, I will say this only once. I am your accountant, I count for the queen. You are the one who will do her business, and I am the one who will follow behind, do you doubt me? No, don't struggle." His ink-stained nails tightened on Treylen's wrist. "One scratch and you won't make it up from the table."

Treylen wasn't sure he believed it, but his skin was beginning to itch.

"Why are you here for me and not Mauridin?"

"I will question him in due time."

"I saw you speaking to the rangers."

"Yes, they asked a lot of questions. Seems they are looking for one of their own who went missing."

"They told you that?"

"I have a talent for uncovering information, Treylen Corbel." Treylen cringed at the use of his name again. He looked around to make sure nobody had heard them.

"Aren't you worried they'll hear you?"

"The rangers? Bah!" The man didn't look up, he just kept scribbling in his book, one hand tight on Treylen's wrist. "Rangers spend their lives in the woods, hiding from the commerce of the world. There is nothing woodsmen fear more than accountants. And they'd gain nothing from me. My kind aren't taken alive."

"What did you tell them?"

"I told them I was here to do your uncle's books. Now quiet or I'll silence you for good."

Rime, is he telling the truth?

Marziel says yes.

"Your name is Treylen Corbel?"

"Yes."

The man nodded, shifting his thumb over Treylen's wrist.

"Good. Your mother is Laurelei."

"She is."

"Excellent."

"What are you doing?"

The man looked up long enough to meet his eyes. Candles glimmered off the glass of his spectacles. The fife and the tambourine filled the silence. "I'm seeking your base rhythm. The heart never lies. If you lie to me, I'll sense it. And then..." He dipped his pen in the poisoned ink.

Will Marziel at least tell me if this man is telling the truth?

He is, Rime responded.

That was all Treylen needed. If this was a servant of the queen, then they were the same. And if this *accountant* wasn't afraid of being found out, then Treylen wouldn't be either.

"Your father is Aldus?"

"Yes."

"Excellent. I have your heartline."

Something eased in Treylen after the first couple of questions.

"What are you writing?"

"These are your fictional uncle's local accounts. I'm balancing your books while we talk." He reached across and flipped a few of the pages that sat in front of Treylen, then transferred some numbers from the parchment into the books.

"I thought maybe it was a code," Treylen said.

"Do you believe that the queen keeps her accounts on parchment?"

"Parchment is the greatest traitor, says Marziel." Treylen ventured a smile, but the accountant only sneered at that.

"We shall see about that."

By now, the second ranger had returned and was sitting with his friend, laughing about something. Maybe he just liked brushing down strangers' ponies. One of them gestured toward Treylen again and he looked away, focusing on the bards and the dancers who jostled around his table. By now, most of the other tables had been dragged away to clear the center of the floor.

"Do you think we should move?" Treylen asked. The accountant seemed oblivious to the distractions, nose buried in his ledger.

"Your mother lives?" His eyes flicked up to watch Treylen's face with each answer. Maybe it was the poison on his skin, but he was beginning to feel ill.

"Yes."

"She still lives with your father?"

"Yes."

"Sleeps alone or in his company?"

"I'm not sure. Why does that matter?"

"It is not yours to decide which details must be accounted for. Are there any disloyal sentiments within your family?"

"No," Treylen answered.

The accountant put down his pen. "I'm sorry, Mr. Corbel, that is not an allowable answer. I'll forgive the lie just once, as I suspect you were mistaken. Try again."

"Disloyal sentiments?" Treylen asked.

"Take a moment. In the future, I will expect you to keep a better account before our meetings. Do you understand?"

"I'm beginning to." His voice wavered. He closed his eyes and focused on the same meditation that he used to clear his mind of pain. He pictured his fear and his doubts. Offered them up to the queen, to be burned away in the fires of the dragon lands.

Sometimes he pictured her there in Queenseat, looking up at those mountains, impassable to all but the strongest dragon riders. Those dragon lands were the source of the eggs, the bondmates, the queen's gift to him for his service. He was, after all, an extension of the queen. He was her hands, eyes, and ears. How could he lie to her?

That was not how he had been taught. For the queen's

own hands to cover her ears, to put out her eyes, that would be too great of a betrayal to bear.

"My father," he started reluctantly, "doesn't approve of my service. He says it's turning my back on the family, and all the work that he has done to elevate our standing."

"Your mother as well?"

"My mother…" How much really did he have to say? About the letters? About the subtle implications, the constant prodding? "My mother believes that I would better serve the queen if I were allowed to pursue my old career."

"Does she speak of this often?"

"No. She knows better than that. She sends me needlepoints."

"Do you agree with her?"

"Of course not. This was my decision."

"You don't think that the queen would receive more benefit from a skilled artisan then from another knife in the shadows?"

"That is not for me to decide," Treylen said.

"And yet it was your decision. You wanted it?"

"Yes."

"Good, now that's over with, we can get back to more important things." He turned the ledger over and opened the back cover to a page already full with lists.

Treylen scanned the cramped writing on this page for something more, but the lists inside were more of the same. He knew better than to voice the question on his lips. But he asked it anyway.

"Are they in danger because of this?"

"That is neither of our concerns," the man said. "I account for the queen's interests and her assets. Of which you are one. But since this is your first time, I'll put your mind at ease." He swished the pen in the inkwell again. "I have uncovered a great many traitorous thoughts on behalf of our queen. For the most part, the discovery of these weaknesses only further ingratiates her subjects to her. I suspect your parents will be fine."

He loosened his grip on Treylen's wrist. Some of the nearby patrons seemed to have taken notice, and no doubt thought them strange, but none were eager to interrupt.

With any luck, they would just assume Treylen was a student. And this man, an overzealous tutor. Like Marziel had said, most of the locals would not know any minor lords. Who was to say what lords got up to or what sort of books they kept?

"Thank you." Treylen watched Marziel again as he poured drinks, and the barmaid ran food out to the tables that were still seated. He knew what was coming. The question Marziel had warned him about. He also knew how he would have to answer it.

But why had he asked? And how could he ask Treylen to deceive a man that could read a line in his heartbeat? Rime was the only one who could get answers for him now.

Rime, you need to ask him why he wants me to lie about her. Get a real answer this time.

The accountant flipped the page. The tone of his voice told Treylen they were wrapping things up now.

"Your gratitude is noted. Now, who sent you into Lome?"

"General Bourin," Treylen answered. This was the sort of information that Marziel had threatened him not to reveal, even to his fellow assassins. But here he was spilling everything to a little man with a pen.

"And your point of entry?"

Rime's voice cut into his thoughts. It felt distant, his head foggy.

Marziel asks you to lie because Apogee is a deserter. If she is found out, she will be killed. And him for sheltering her.

That complicated things. Around him, the dancers wheeled. The music swept into a maddening, circular tune.

The lanterns flickered and smoked, still untrimmed. Treylen closed his eyes, struggling to understand it all.

"Your point of entry?" The accountant squeezed his wrist.

"Over the mountains just north of here."

"Not on foot."

Treylen shook his head, wiping his forehead with his sleeve.

"I was given a ride," he answered. Was it just his imagination, or were the soldiers staring now?

"By whom?" the man asked.

"Rak'tsoro," Treylen said.

"You met them alone?"

"Rime was there."

"Ah yes, the dragon." There had been a moment where Treylen wondered if this man were an assassin. A rider even, given his age. But the disinterest in his voice, bordering on disdain, told him otherwise.

"And since leaving your abbey, have you made contact with any of your fellow servants of the queen?"

What could he do, except tell the truth? There had to be another way. He would avoid mentioning Aaron and Volanti if he could. No point bringing them into this.

"Of course," Treylen said. "When I came here for my training." It was the truth. The accountant hadn't asked how many he'd encountered. The accountant paused, pen hovering over another inventory. For a moment, Treylen thought it might have worked.

"You haven't seen any other assassins since arriving?"

"None since the first night." Again, it was technically true. He had met Apogee *on* the first night, not after. Aaron and Volanti might have called themselves assassins, but until they received their first mission, they were trainees in the eyes of the queen.

The crowd around them parted as one of the military officers stepped up to the table.

"Dinner is over, good men. Your table is in the dance floor now." He had a booming voice, one hand resting on his sword. The accountant didn't even stop writing.

"Mind your soldiers, we've business here."

The tall officer blinked down at the spindly man.

"My men would like to use the dance floor. I'd say they've earned it, wouldn't you?"

"Oh, have they?" The accountant released the grip of death that he'd kept on Treylen's wrist and straightened his spectacles to sneer up at the man. "Are we in Iverna? Did you seize the Harvest Pass? No? Then tell your men to control themselves. I won't be long now. Shoo!" He waved him off, then gripped Treylen's wrist again.

The officer took a step back, as if he'd been struck. His face shifted, from shock, to anger, and back again. He half drew his blade, before finally letting out a strained laugh, ramming his sword back into its sheath, and staggering back to his table.

"That was bold," Treylen muttered.

"What?" The accountant hadn't even stopped writing. "That man is nothing. He'll die a miserable death in one of their pointless offensives, and I will trod his bones as I go home to our queen. Now..." He shut the book, looking Treylen in the eye. "There was a woman at your abbey. Apogee Suleyon. Do you remember her?"

Treylen choked and had to drink from his tankard.

"I do."

"Good." As he spoke, he tucked the pen away, corking the bottle and shutting the case. One hand still held on to Treylen's wrist, thumb on his heartbeat.

"She moved on some time before you did, yes?"

"She was only there a little while," Treylen said. "But I remember them all. Especially that first group."

"Have you seen her at all since she left?"

There it was again. There was no lying this time. But there had to be a way to talk around it.

"I had a dream once that we were on a training run together." It was true, he had once.

"That is not what I asked, Treylen Corbel. Have you seen her?"

Treylen sighed, eyes searching the dragon bones in the rafters. For a moment, he thought he saw the outline of Rime up there, eyes glimmering from the shadows.

He considered reaching for the dragonmind. Drawing upon just enough speed to give him time to think. But that might only throw his heart off.

He shook his head.

"She would have changed a lot since then."

Why had Marziel done it? Hidden a deserter. Betrayed the queen.

"We all change," the man said. "But you would know her."

"Yes," Treylen answered. "I remember everyone who trained under Bos."

What had happened to Apogee in that tower in Jaul? She was one of Bostra's. One of Treylen's own. Bostra didn't train cowards, so why would she become a deserter? And why come back here?

"So you haven't seen her."

"I don't remember her ever visiting the abbey again," Treylen said, hoping it was enough of the truth to get him by.

He waited.

The man kept his thumb on Treylen's pulse, the drum of an elkbone war dance pounding in the air.

"I expect a full accounting of your mission when it's completed. I don't suppose you have a lead on the missing glyph scribe yet?"

Treylen shook his head, quickly. The accountant released his grasp, wiping the ink from his fingers with a handkerchief.

"Time is short, Treylen Corbel." He stuffed his things back into his satchel. "And I believe I've worn out my welcome here. Tell your handler I'll meet him at the stables."

The strange man hopped up from the chair and moved toward the door. Treylen didn't wait to see him go. He slid back his chair, nearly falling, stumbled to the stairs and toward his room.

Are you alright, bondmate? Rime called to him, but Treylen pushed it away. Feeling his way down the dark hall of the third floor and pushing the door open, he plunged his hand into the cold wash basin to scrub the burning stains from his flesh. Sweat rolled down his brow to sting his eyes, tears stung his cheeks. Treylen was grateful for the darkness that hid his fear as he slumped down behind the door, pushing it closed and leaning his back against the rough panels to wait for whatever came next.

Chapter Twenty-Two

THE CONFESSION

IT WAS DIFFICULT TO REMEMBER HOW LONG HE'D BEEN SITTING in the dark. Footsteps, strains of music drifting up from the tavern below, and the throbbing of his head all spun together like carded wool.

Rime would speak to him now and then. He had relayed the message that Marziel was to meet the man in the stables. There had been other messages between them; something bad happened at the stable. Rime was calling for him. But it all was fuzzy. Treylen was increasingly certain that some of the poison had made it through his skin.

But Rime reassured him, told him to wait. Marziel would come. He would help.

He had tried to call his bondmate upstairs, to sit with him until the room stopped spinning, but Rime refused. He was watching, he said. There was much to watch that evening.

Fatigue crept over Treylen, but he fought it, sitting up, holding on to the dragonmind just for alertness—normally Rime would have put a stop to that, but not this night. He wasn't sure how much of the night had passed when his friends came for him.

Moments came in flashes. A knock on the door. Aaron

speaking from the hallway. The door pushing against his back as it was forced open. Hands gripping him under the arms. His heels dragging along the hallway, then the kitchen. Smells of spices, cooking smoke. Then the cool, damp smell of a grave. The light of a candle reflected off earthen walls. Marziel was leaning over him, pressing a warm mug into his hands.

"Drink this. The sooner you get it down, the sooner it'll be up again." He pushed the cup toward Treylen's mouth and tipped it up. It contained another foul mixture, but he choked it down until the mug was empty.

"Good, good." Marziel crossed the room to a table before a rack of weapons. There was clanking and the movement of shadows as he lit another candle and cleared a space on a workbench.

"Any minute now."

Treylen lay back, his head on the floor. Felicity perched on his chest and stared at him. Treylen tried to raise a hand and bat the dragon away, but his arms weren't cooperating. Then the room began spinning. His stomach churned, and he rolled over to retch on the dirt floor.

"There you go." Marziel chuckled darkly. "Almost through it now."

"Where are we?" Treylen wiped his mouth and rolled onto his back. His head was still too heavy to raise it. The room smelled of dampness, metal, and oil.

"In the cave under the subbasement."

"There's a basement?"

Marziel laughed again.

"Aye, and the one below it is even better hidden."

"Why did you bring me here?" He tried to push himself up again but failed.

"Just relax." Marziel knelt beside him and pushed another mug into his hands. This one was warm. Treylen tried to push it away, but Marziel wrapped his fingers around it.

"It's just tea." Marziel placed a hand behind him and helped him sit up. He took a sip, then coughed.

"It's bitter."

"It's powdered swift leaf and ginger root. You need a powerful stimulant to counteract the poison."

"He didn't scratch me…"

"No, that was snake venom in the ink. I poisoned you with black-cap mushroom in your drink. Now drink up, you need it."

"Why did you…" Marziel gripped Treylen under the shoulders and dragged him backward to rest against a wall.

"Because black cap has a calming effect. It slows the heart and the breathing gradually. I had to give you a large dose to be sure it would work quickly. You had better drink up."

"Why?"

"I think it's obvious, don't you?" He looked at Felicity, then shooed her off. When he was convinced that she was out of earshot, he continued. "I did it so you could lie to the man."

"He was reading my heart."

"Or attempting to. It's not a perfect art," Marziel said, "and they aren't all as good at it as they claim to be."

"Hellcaves, why didn't you just say so?" Treylen pressed his palm against his forehead. It felt like the bard was playing the tambourine inside.

Marziel crossed the room to a rack hung with swords and knives. A rag and a jar of blade oil rested on the table, among piles of parchment, odds and ends, strange tools that resembled the bits of an assassin's toolkit. All around him, the small room was packed with crates and barrels, rolls of fabric and leather.

"I didn't tell you," Marziel said, "because I couldn't be sure that it would work. If it didn't, your blood would be on my hands."

"Aren't you used to that?" He took another sip of the tea and grimaced.

"Failing the people who trust you is something that you should never get used to."

That jolted him awake again, his memory of the evening slowly coming back. He had the faintest recollection of Rime calling out to him, something about Volanti, and rangers, but it slipped away, solidifying instead around one frightening fact.

"I lied to the queen. You made me do this when you drugged me."

"That's not how the poison works," Marziel said. "I only slowed your heartbeat so it would stay even. Turns out I didn't even need to, crafty fox. You bent the truth so much you broke it."

"Why did you make me do it?"

Marziel was quiet, leaning over the workbench. Treylen sipped his tea. He could wait. It wasn't as if he could walk out anyway.

"It wasn't too long ago. Apogee had already moved on from here. I'd gotten word from the army that she was marked for elimination. I didn't know why." Marziel sighed, picking at the wax from the candle as it dribbled onto the bench. "One night, she came to me. The bar was busy, like tonight, or I might have killed her on sight. Probably should have. Instead, like a fool, I decided to listen to her."

Treylen groaned and Marziel looked back over his shoulder.

"Do you feel alright?"

Treylen held his stomach, then he doubled over and vomited again.

"Just keep sipping it. You need it more than you know."

Treylen dragged his sleeve across his mouth and picked up the tea again.

"Her bondmate had died. Maybe that's why I was so soft on her." Marziel got up from the bench and paced the small room. The ceiling was so low, he had to duck in parts of it.

"I knew it," Treylen said. "Rime would have smelled a dragon if she had one. How did it happen?"

"She was undercover. Deep in Jaul. Had gotten wrapped up with some young wizard. The two of them made plans to run away together."

The room had one exit. An old wardrobe trunk sat just to the side of it. Marziel stopped pacing and unlatched it.

"That made her a traitor. Or it would have if she had gone through with the plan. Young love makes us blind…"

He opened the trunk to reveal a collection of clothing hanging from hooks and racks inside of the luggage. On the inside of the door was a mirror, and what looked like an array of false beards, wigs, and spectacles. Everything a spy might need for a hundred disguises.

"She told the wizard everything. Revealed her dragon, her identity, her mission. They had a plan to get out. And it would have worked if the wizard hadn't turned out to be a spycatcher."

As he talked, he pulled things from the trunk and set them on the workbench. A false beard. A set of farmer's clothing. A bundle of silks.

"That night she woke up to the pain of her bond being severed, as her lover cut the head from her dragon. Never got to say goodbye like I did. They were just gone."

Treylen nodded. He had suspected something was off but never imagined this. Marziel dug frantically through the trunk of costumes. Maybe it was easier for him to talk about while he worked. A few items, what looked like signet rings and badges of authority, went back into the trunk. One sack he pulled from the trunk rattled like it was filled with small jars. He transferred some of those into a smaller bag.

"I'm adding these to your spy kit. Rouge. Powder. This is colored wax; there's an adhesive mixed with it for changing the shape of your face. You will need them soon. I'm to get you off to Tabron by week's end."

He held a jar out for Treylen to see, then stuffed it in the bag and cinched the lid.

"But we've a few days left to train you. I haven't yet decided if your friends should go. They still have a lot of work to do before they move on from here." Marziel shut the wardrobe trunk and leaned his head against it. "There's a lot in this world that our queen doesn't permit us to know. I may not have been the only assassin to survive the loss of a bond-mate. But I had to suffer it alone.

"Apogee didn't have to. She knew my story. She hoped that I could help her. Though at the time, I wasn't sure she even wanted to survive it. There wasn't much that I could do aside from understand her. Keep her eating. Talk her through the worst of it."

"But why do they want her?"

"Word got back she was a defector. Not sure how. May just be she missed too many check-ins with her handler, and they decided it best to cut her loose."

Marziel made a neat pile of the costumes and the kit. He wrapped it all up in a bundle and tied it off, tossing it into Treylen's lap.

"You'll bring that with you when you go. Take care of it."

"What's Apogee doing now?"

"I told you. She's out laying tracks to throw those rangers off of your scent. I assuaged most of their suspicions. But I don't trust them not to snoop around. They won't find you down here, though."

"I mean what's she doing here with you?"

Marziel shrugged his shoulders and kicked at the dirt of the floor.

"She's alive. She's getting better. We'll worry about what comes next later."

"She looks fine to me." He took another drink. Marziel seemed to have run out of things to do with himself. He grabbed a sword from the wall and started polishing it, speaking over his shoulder as he worked the blade oil into the weapon.

"Things have been good since you got here. Aside from the fact that you weren't supposed to know about her. She came out that night on her own, against my orders. If I've been angry at anyone, it's with her. But now you're a part of it." He glanced at the door where Felicity had gone. "I'm not sure how much your friends have guessed. Apogee was right about one thing. There's something different about you Coops Abbey people. If I wasn't in your debt for keeping your mouth shut tonight, I might call it a problem."

"What do you mean?" Treylen asked.

"The way you are with your students…everyone you trained under. It sounds like a family."

"Maybe," Treylen said.

"Families are a weakness. Every personal loyalty you have is a disloyalty to your queen." Something about the way he said it, Treylen couldn't help but feel he didn't believe it. Maybe it was just the hypocrisy of what he'd done tonight.

"The monks would say that. But I don't think they ever took it that seriously."

"I can't fault you for it tonight. But it still troubles me."

"What are you saying?" Treylen asked.

"I'm saying that one day we might be the only thing standing between the Jaul Empire and our home. Iverna and Ketaresk are the last free kingdoms of Pentearth. Every other land has been overrun. We can't afford weaknesses."

"So you're saying I should have turned you in."

"Yes. But I'm no traitor. And she's an asset. You've seen her glyphs. I think I can bring her back into service. When she's strong enough. Nobody has to know the rest." He slid the sword back into its sheath and hung it on the wall again, shaking his head. "It's a losing battle, trying to keep all of these blades from rusting down here."

"They'll question her too. Even if they took her back," Treylen said. "They'll know what you did."

"Apogee can handle that."

"What are we doing now?" Treylen tried to get to his feet again. This time he managed, holding on to one of the barrels so he could look around the cave. The walls were clay, the ceiling lined with boards.

"What is all this?"

"It's a hiding hole. They're all over the empire. Some have rations inside if you're lucky. Others are more extensive. You'll find them in attics, under bridges, in forests. I mark mine with a Queensberry bush." Marziel slipped his hand into his toolkit and pulled out a dried white-and-blue berry.

"You can't outfight every enemy you come across. But you can always outwait them. Drop a few seeds where you build your hiding hole. They'll grow anywhere, but you won't find them outside of the Iveran mountains. So if you see one, you know there's a hole nearby. Just don't eat them. They start to look good when you've hidden in a sewer drain for three days, but they're deadly poisonous."

Marziel dropped the berries next to Treylen's bundle. He pointed to a blanket spread over a row of crates.

"That's your bed for the night. There's water on the table. Bucket by the door. I'll get you in the morning."

He moved toward the small door, and Treylen put a hand out.

"I have more questions."

"And you'll have all night to think of more. Now get some rest. I have a mess upstairs."

Treylen nodded. His steps were shaky, but he reached the makeshift bed and rolled onto his side.

Marziel shook his head, picked up Treylen's mug, filled it from a kettle, and brought it to him.

"Drink it all if you want to live through the night."

"You poisoned me," Treylen muttered.

"We've already been over that." Marziel stopped at the door. It had come open a crack. "Where is the dragon of Aaron's?"

He looked around, then seeing a tail sticking out of a box of dried meats, snatched the dragon up and tucked her under his arm.

"Drink up and stay quiet. Don't bother Rime tonight. He's…busy."

Treylen wondered what that meant, but when he felt for the dragonmind, the pounding of his head increased and he had to lay back, taking another sip of tea. Marziel opened the half door and ducked through it. Treylen caught sight of a long, earthen tunnel with wood supports leading up into the dark. Then the door shut, and he was alone with the candles.

His eyelids were heavy and he wanted to sleep, but he knew that tea was more important. If he could get it down, then he could rest.

All he really wanted was to reach out to Rime.

Are you alright, Rime? For a moment, there was nothing, then he answered.

I'm alive, bondmate.

Will you come down? I could use the company. Treylen knew that Rime could feel his pain through the bond.

I can't right now. That was odd, if only because there was real regret in it.

But you're alright? he asked.

I am. It sounded pained.

You will tell me if something happens?

I will if you need to know about it. That was the answer he'd expected.

Don't forget which side you're on. I'm not sure if we can trust Marziel, Treylen thought.

He's put much trust in you, Rime whispered.

What about the queen?

No answer to that. Rime had never been all that fond of

the queen. He had certainly never participated in the devotionals or the meditation.

Fortunately for Rime, no one but their bondmates cared what dragons thought. Even those who knew that the bond granted human intelligence tended to underestimate them. The truth was, the only thing keeping dragons from flying off to the mountains was that they didn't care one way or the other about rules or what people thought of them. They stayed because they all cared deeply for their bondmates, and because the bond itself was a thing they craved.

He took another swig. This cup had steeped even longer than the first, and his head buzzed with it. By the time he finished drinking, the challenge would not be avoiding sleep, but finding it.

The room blurred again as the night dragged on. Treylen was beset by strange waking dreams—of mountain and forest, of wagons rolling down dusty roads and dragons sleeping deep within the earth.

He sat up, forcing the hand that held the tea to his lips, and drank again. It was cold now. The candle burned low and the hours passed. He had been vaguely aware of a presence for some time before he came to the hazy realization that it was Aaron. His friend had come down into the cave and was sitting up with him, one arm draped protectively over his shoulder.

Treylen heard a soft sound and looked beneath his other shoulder.

Volanti had wedged herself on his other side. There was a faint sniffling of her crying.

"I'll be fine," he said. "Don't worry about me."

"It's not you, Treylen," Aaron said. "They took Ketcher."

"What?" Treylen tried to get up, but Arron pulled him back. Volanti covered her face, tears slipping between her fingers.

"Whoa, whoa, you're not helping anyone. Rime's bad enough."

"What?" Treylen struggled again, but his movements were futile, and it was nothing for Aaron to keep him down. It upset Volanti, though, and she pulled away, rushing for the door, her barmaid's outfit hanging loose without the padding that had confused him earlier. She disappeared down the tunnel as he bit his tongue trying to make the words to call after her.

"Just sit back, Treylen. Calm now."

"What happened?"

"The rangers got him. Ketcher. Rime's okay; hurt himself trying to help, but he's upstairs with Marziel, and he's alright."

"She's...alright?" Treylen squeezed one eye shut, trying to focus on the door.

"I'm not sure..." Aaron said. "Just sit still. Try to sleep now. We've got you. You can help in the morning."

Chapter Twenty-Three

THE HANGOVER

THERE WAS SOMETHING COMFORTING ABOUT THAT CAVE IN THE bowels of the inn, the quiet stillness of the underground. But the tea had kept him awake anyway. He had only just managed to doze off when Marziel woke him. Aaron and Volanti were gone. Treylen stood, his strength returning, then Marziel let him through the small door and up a narrow clay tunnel.

It was a tight crawl, then they emerged into an earthen-floored room with stone walls. Marziel slid a stone into place and the passage to the hiding hole was hidden. One wall held a rack of weapons—some plain, others bore the stylized markings of authority.

A circle of soft earth ringed with white chalk filled the empty room. Treylen knew immediately what it was.

"You have a secret arena room in the basement?"

I would call it a pit," Marziel said. "I used to fight in one like this when I was younger. We'll start barehanded and work our way up to war hammers. I'd like to test you on each of these, eventually."

"I usually only care for knives," Treylen said. It wasn't that he didn't know how to use the others. He just preferred knives.

They let him use his speed, and their mirrored flash intimidated the enemy.

"You may not always have your knives. And there may be times when your disguise necessitates other weaponry."

Marziel pointed to each of the weapons on the wall and told their origin. There was the saber of a Seeran horselord, a Ketaresk admiral's cutlass, the axe of an elkbone warlord, a slim dagger with the royal sigil of a lowsater prince—far more delicate than anything he would have expected from the bovine people that had been described to him.

"Are you stalling because you don't want to tell me the truth about Apogee?"

"Maybe, but I wanted to talk to you about Volanti... Ketcher is still missing."

"Oh..." His head had been so cloudy that he thought maybe he'd imagined it. "What happened, where is he?"

"Last night after you went to sleep, there was an incident with the rangers."

"He's...dead?"

"No, no. He was lucky, I suppose, to be so small. He and Rime were foolish enough to follow them to the road, and they nabbed him."

"Where are they now?"

"Out setting a trap with him as bait, I'd suppose?"

"Where's Rime?" Treylen searched for an exit. A slim ladder leading to a hatch in the floor above was the only way out. Aaron must have carried him down on one shoulder.

"Rime is fine," Marziel said, pulling Treylen back from the ladder. He went up first and shouldered the hatch open, crawling up into another dark chamber before waving Treylen up. "Well, not fine. He's injured his wing."

"I should've been there." Treylen climbed up into the dark, confused for a moment when his head bumped against wood. The two of them had come out inside of a massive wine barrel. Marziel crouched and grabbed the bottom edge of the barrel, lifting it so he and Treylen could slide out from under it into a room.

Thin slats of light streamed down from the floor above to illuminate a cellar packed with casks of spirits and barrels of wine and ale.

"Welcome to my private wine cellar. There was a time I brewed my own, but I've long since handed over that responsibility to one of the locals." Treylen always detected a note of pride when Marziel listed the individual villagers his tavern kept employed, from farmers and hunters to the miller, the cooper, even the old bard whose name Treylen had never managed to learn.

"Over here are brandy. I bought these shortly after I built the tavern," Marziel said. "Many of the great houses of Lome keep their fortunes in barrels of brandy. It is easy to sell, hard to steal, and it only increases in value the longer it sits in your cellar."

The barrels were large, so much so that the room they were in must have been built around them because there was no way they would have fit through the door.

"You promise Rime is alright?"

"Yes, yes, he's in your room. Go to him now if you like. He's hurting a little, but his pride is a lot worse than that wing." Marziel slid the barrel back into place so that it fully concealed the hatch to the subbasement.

"I can't believe I didn't wake up. He must have called to me when I was out…What about Volanti?"

"Doing chores, and none too happy about it. But it's for her own good. If I let her sulk for more than a minute, she's liable to run off and do something stupid. Those rangers will have set their traps by now. It would be suicide for her to go to him. She hates me for it, of course, and for bringing them both here, but better hatred than despair, I think."

They moved out of the cellar, then passed through a false

wall and into a room with tarp-covered boxes, one of which was uncovered, and Treylen saw the glimmer of coin inside.

"Another tool of the trade," Marziel said, dipping into one of the boxes and dropping the coins into Treylen's hand. "Wealth is just another means to our ends."

They left the hidden chamber, then passed another false wall into a room stuffed with paints, pitch-pots, and other foul-smelling tools, before finally arriving in another cellar full of barrels—these seemed to be mostly ale. A wooden ladder led to a hatch in the floor. From the smell, Treylen guessed they were below the kitchen.

"So how do we get her bondmate back?"

Marziel sighed deeply. He put one hand on the ladder but didn't start up.

"Not by running into the woods after them."

Treylen crossed his arms. He didn't like the sound of that at all.

"There's five of us and two of them, and you're afraid?"

"Every ranger that we kill puts our queen's interests here in jeopardy." Treylen deflated a little at that. The queen's interests—that was something bigger than Volanti and her bondmate, or his feelings about the matter. Better to die than go against the queen's interest.

"Look at me, Treylen—we aren't abandoning him. If Ketcher was dead, then she would feel it. I suspect they've never seen a bondmate quite so small. They may decide he's feral and let him go, but if we go running in blindly, they'll kill him for sure. Besides, I've put Apogee on it, and she's trailing the rangers as we speak. She'll find Ketcher."

"I have questions about Apogee."

"Good." Marziel put a foot on the ladder and started up. "You can ask her when she gets back. In the meantime, let Apogee worry about Ketcher. Now do your friends a favor and keep them focused on their training. You can all blame me if it's easier for you."

He shoved the hatch open, then crawled out into the kitchen, leaving Treylen staring up at the open hatch. Somewhere not far off, he could hear the sound of a broom, and Aaron cursing as he dragged a table across the tavern floor.

He would go to them in a moment, but what comfort could he hope to offer to someone who was separated from their bondmate? First, he'd check on his own and get Rime's account of what had happened, then consult with Aaron about how best to help Volanti feel better.

All he really wanted was to get Ketcher back for her.

Chapter Twenty-Four

THE CLOCK

WHILE IT WAS THE MOST PAINFUL INCENTIVE IN THE WORLD, Treylen couldn't deny that Ketcher's disappearance had improved Volanti's skills tenfold. Rime was injured, but not permanently, and his account of that night matched up with what Marziel had told him.

Two days had passed since the incident and Apogee still hadn't returned.

Marziel had seemed unbothered at first, but on the morning of the second day, there was a shift in him, and Treylen knew it was because she had been gone too long. By noontime, he had packed a bag and taken the horse he rode when he was playing Mauridin, saying nothing, but riding west along the queen's road.

The inn felt oddly quiet now, in his absence. The air was sticky from an impending storm. Even Rebash was not in his usual room. He'd disappeared at the same time Apogee had, and Treylen wondered if he'd given up trying to find an elkbone buyer and gone off to meet his caravan. Treylen found himself hanging midsummer bunting along the hearth and honing knives in the kitchen—perhaps sharper than he should have—before eventually giving in to Volanti's request for a fight.

They'd been training all afternoon, while Aaron minded the bar. Treylen was pretty sure dinnertime had come and gone without any patrons. He'd figured they could take a break after Volanti had let some of her anger out. So far, she showed no signs of tiring. She moved fluidly, as if she were in a dance with the elements. He'd never seen glyphs formed so seamlessly. He'd also never seen so many straw men set on fire.

"Try something else," he gasped eventually. "What if your opponent has perfected crotus magic?"

Volanti snatched a spear and vaulted over the makeshift barrier he'd made out of empty cider barrows to replicate the hedge of vines that even a rough crotus glyph could summon in these woods. Treylen blocked her strike, but his heel buckled and the tip grazed his rib.

Treylen knew he was training too hard as well. But Marziel was right. What use would he be against a wizard if he relied on borrowed power?

Volanti swiped at his face. He ducked and pushed her sweat-drenched chin back, bringing a knife to her ear. She snarled and grabbed his wrist, rolling backward. He flipped with her, but she kept turning. His face was half-mashed against the mat, and he struggled to call out. Any more pressure and his wrist would shatter.

He was not going to use the dragonmind.

Through the murk of pain, he saw her eyes narrow. Her grip tightened as her lips pressed into a thin line.

Was she really going to do it?

Aaron's face appeared in the hatch. "Upstairs. Quickly!"

Volanti released Treylen, offering no apology. He massaged his hand as they followed Aaron up.

The tavern was filled with Iveran soldiers. The queen's blue of their cloaks stood out like a beacon behind Jaul lines.

"What in the hellcaves, Aaron?" Volanti appraised the men's wounds and disheveled attire.

"Captain Greythorn." A tall, redheaded soldier with an arm in a sling gave a deep bow and stepped forward. "I hate to intrude on Marziel like this, but we had no choice."

"What happened?" Treylen asked.

"We were clearing the mouth of the pass with the regular army, but somehow got turned around and ended up south. Cut around a lake, figuring we could make it back to Iverna that way." Greythorn glanced at his troop. "It was the strangest thing. A fog came from across from the other side, like it was moving directly for us. I ordered the troop to hide beneath some boulders. But our youngest cadet approached the mist. There were roars, and screaming. A minute later, it dispersed like it had never existed. Nothing left of the cadet but a stain on the rocks. We've been running for nearly three days straight since then, and now there's a ranger on our tail."

Treylen shuddered. Was this what Rak'Tsoro meant when she said spoke of wizard sign? Damn Marziel for being away tonight of all nights. The group looked at Treylen expectantly.

"Basement, all of you, and—"

Lightning lit up the path outside. A figure was approaching the open front door, wearing the telltale cap of a ranger.

Volanti unceremoniously elbowed the troop down the stairs, except for Greythorn, who'd stayed with Treylen. Crossing to the kitchen now would put him in full view of the ranger.

Treylen opened the grandfather clock. "In."

The captain obeyed without hesitation, wedging himself in with the movement and tugging the hatch closed behind him.

Spurs chimed as the stranger entered. With a grimace, Treylen grabbed the spaniel puppy needlework that his mother had sent him and sank down on a stool. Aaron slid over to the bar.

"Evening," the ranger said. His voice had that belittling quality that made a speaker instantly dislikeable, even if they weren't hunting a group of Iveran stowaways. There was a strange glyph-marked hatchet tucked into his belt, and next to it, a bellbird whistle. Bostra Avex had often carried a whistle just like it. The small, shy birds built their little mud nests under every eave in the village and all through the forests. They made nary a peep, but a single cry from one would be repeated for miles around.

Treylen needed to warn the others. Starting a fight with this one would be a mistake if that whistle could summon any ranger in five miles, not to mention any nearby Lome troops.

Aaron murmured a greeting.

Treylen realized he had accidentally added a red stitch to one of the spaniel's eyes.

The ranger lifted a mirror to inspect the wall behind it. Finding nothing there, he let the mirror drop, the glass shattering.

"What's the commotion?" a voice called sweetly.

Treylen's breath caught. Apogee had returned and was wearing a golden silk gown that looked like it had been plucked from fireflies. On her head was a crown adorned with small white candles that flickered brightly.

"Are you here to celebrate the night of lights?" she asked the ranger.

"No, my lady." He surveyed her and hastily kicked some of the shards of mirror beneath a rug. "Ranger Thorn."

"A ranger? You must stay and drink to the solstice!"

Before he could protest, Thorn was guided expertly to a table. Apogee took a candle from her crown and brought it to his pipe. As it flared, Apogee gave Thorn a smile, but her eyes fell on Treylen's. Predictable as the rest, she seemed to be saying. She must have read his response too because her smile widened, her gaze turning deeper.

Treylen forgot the soldiers, the danger they were in.

She'd narrowed the rest of the world to a pinpoint. Even the simmering resentment, which had been turning his stomach ever since he learned she was a traitor, was forgotten for a moment.

Something distantly crashed.

Treylen cursed himself. He should have snuck away to help the others when he had the chance. Thorn brought his hand to his hatchet.

Volanti appeared in her maid's outfit, eyes red. "I'm so sorry, mistress. Your favorite vase." She offered some shattered pieces of floral crockery in her apron.

"Clumsy girl. Be careful next time." Apogee's annoyance seemed too real. Perhaps the vase had been hers. Though she didn't strike Treylen as the floral type.

He really shouldn't be worrying about this now.

Aaron shuffled out from the kitchen with a slim decanter and a flute of cherry wine balanced on a tray.

"Apologies it isn't the traditional blueberry kind," he said, bending down to set it on the ranger's table.

Thorn cupped a hand under Aaron's jaw, thumb digging in. "You didn't get these scars from pouring ale. Or these muscles."

Treylen noted the stripe on the man's sleeve: a golden zigzag that—according to Marziel—denoted the highest rank a ranger could receive, and a six-point star to indicate northern territory. Not good.

Aaron held a bored expression. "Did a summer overseeing the legion's oxen. Brutal things."

Apogee tutted. "Since he arrived, he's spent half of his time brawling in the yard. So hard to find good men, you know, with the war taking the best of them."

"I've heard about this inn. Has quite the reputation for turnover of staff." Thorn knocked a glass of wine back. "You wouldn't mind if I took a look around?"

"Be my guest."

The ranger stood from his table and disappeared up the stairs. When he was out of earshot, Treylen hopped from his chair and raced to Apogee's side.

"What are you doing here?"

"I was out tending to some business on the road when I saw this one coming your way. I thought you might need a hand with him."

"You know Marziel's out looking for you. Things went… bad the other night."

"I had an inkling"—Apogee frowned—"but trust me, they would have been worse without the work I'm doing. The woods are crawling with rangers."

"And who are you supposed to be anyhow?" Treylen gestured at the gown and the wig of blonde hair.

"Oh this." She twirled, then straightened the candles that adorned her head. They made a striking parallel with the candle-lit bones in the rafters behind her. "This is Lord Mauridin's daughter, Pouline. Her father is a well-respected patron of the inn, and having an eye for business, she has been known to drop by and watch over it when the good innkeeper Marcus is out provisioning."

Treylen blinked a moment, pondering the lengths to which Marziel and Apogee had gone to deceive a handful of simple villagers. But perhaps that was how they had managed to keep the safehouse running and confound the local rangers for so long.

"Sometimes, my dear, a bit of class is needed if you want to properly shoo off someone important."

Apogee waved a hand and floated up the stairs after the ranger. Thunder punctured the creaking of floorboards as Thorn went from room to room, then came back downstairs. Apogee followed behind as he tossed the kitchen. Treylen raveled and unraveled a knot in the embroidery thread. Eventually, Aaron motioned Treylen into the hallway under the guise of fetching a cask of ale.

Thorn was peering down at the basement hatch. It appeared blackened with a newly adorned sort of mold around the edges. It was, in fact, the residue from all the straw men Volanti had been burning. Volanti pretended to do the dishes and surreptitiously scrubbed at her dirtied fingernails.

Thorn bent down and gripped the handle, but the hatch didn't budge.

"If you could get that open, it would be a great service," Apogee said. "Cow herder over here's been a little useless with it."

Thorn looked like he didn't favor his odds against Aaron's muscles. "Perhaps next time." He let go, then straightened and paced to the grandfather clock, tweaking the hour hand.

"I look forward to that meeting," Apogee said.

The ranger didn't leave.

Tension grew with every second that the clock didn't tick.

A distinct smell had filled the air when Thorn had arrived. Treylen had been puzzling over it. Now it clicked. Apple and clover, with a deeper musk underneath, stagnant and strong. That third scent reminded him of a new recruit nearly slipping on the abbey walkway, or Volanti the night when Ketcher disappeared. It was the sort of smell that only years of using the dragonmind had taught him to detect.

Fear.

And the ranger certainly wasn't afraid of them. That begged the question: What were the emperor's forces planning at the pass?

Aaron etched a hatchet and whistle into the dust on top of the cask he and Treylen were slowly hauling. Treylen tapped on the hatchet drawing and pointed at himself. He spread his fingers in a countdown: five, four, three—

"Hullo!" The mayor walked in, shaking off her rain-soaked cloak. "Saints of the Sky, a ranger! And what would your quarry be?"

"Soldiers," Thorn said curtly.

"You don't say! But I saw a group heading west not an hour ago!"

Thorn bolted.

"Oh dear." The mayor watched him go. "Always in a rush, those hunter types, aren't they? Blueberry wine please, if you have it. Nothing better on midsummer, even if the skies won't cooperate."

As the others headed over to the bar, Treylen made a mental note to ask Marziel if the mayor was quite as unobservant as she seemed.

It had been too close. One call of that bellbird whistle and it would be over. They couldn't keep taking in every stray that wandered in from the crossroads. How much longer could their work at the Hide remain undetected? Treylen was due to start hunting the scribe in Tabron in less than a week. They had to keep their heads down until then. Nothing else mattered.

"I don't wish to be a bother." Captain Greythorn's voice came from within the clock. "But I do believe there's a rather angry mouse in here with me."

―――――――

Just before the moon came up, Treylen ushered the soldiers out a second-floor balcony overlooking the oak tree so that they could make their escape without leaving footprints. There was no guarantee that Thorn wasn't hiding by the road somewhere, staking out the inn. Treylen hung back and watched the soldiers creep expertly through the emerald canopy, dropping quietly onto the roof of a nearby shed before making for the river.

"Thanks for the hospitality. Here." Captain Greythorn handed Treylen a small copper medallion engraved with a small "M" that looked like a valley between two mountains. "See this symbol? Give that to the owner of any building in a

Lome city that has the emblem on their porch. They'll help you with what you need, no questions asked."

Apogee came in and began to fill a pitcher of black tea, humming softly.

The captain stilled. "Anyway, thanks again," he told Treylen, adjusting his sling and clambering up the branch.

"What was that?" Treylen asked.

Apogee caught one of the falling leaves that the captain had dispersed. "I think he was the one who betrayed me to Marziel. He doesn't seem to recognize me now."

He had been waiting for her to return so he could confront her about her treason, and how he'd been made to lie for her. Treylen figured he was entitled to hear the story from her own lips. But how to start?

"Captain Greythorn? He seemed nice." He had probably done nothing more than honor his duty and pass the intel along, but Treylen didn't dare say as much in front of her.

"Treylen," she said. "When you meet enough people in this world, you learn that nice is a hollow coin. It's a disguise to put on. Cherry wine in the dark."

He wanted to say that he understood, but the truth was he'd never known loss. His friends were alive. Even his grandparents were happily retired in Lakehold. For all his training as an assassin, he knew very little of death—not spilling your guts death, but death that followed you after it was over. That gave you that haunted, dark-circled look that Apogee always wore, like something chased her at night.

The moment that he should have said something passed, and Apogee went out onto the balcony, plunging to the ground in a perfect roll before walking in the direction of the yard. Treylen and the tea were left behind.

"Treylen, will you help me downstairs?" Aaron poked his head into the room, looking tired but wide-eyed.

"What is it now?" He hadn't slept that night either.

"The mayor apparently doesn't have the stomach for cherries, and she's been throwing up for the past twenty minutes. And there's news. It's Volanti's bondmate."

Treylen nearly tripped over his own feet. "Apogee found Ketcher?"

"Sort of. She said that when the rangers bagged him the other night, they didn't keep him. That snake Rebash bought him off of them."

"What?"

"And guess who just came in the door bragging about all the coin he made at an illegal trading den in Tabron?"

"Then we have to go get him. Damn, why isn't Marziel back? Is she okay?" Treylen thought again of the way she had looked when Ketcher had gone missing…

"I'm not sure she'll wait for him. She can't go alone, Treylen. Rebash says even the worst of Tabron criminals avoid the Under Den."

"Funny, it didn't stop him."

"He says they run lowsater fights, hire out killers across the city. Says half the poisons assassins use have been traded through it at some point."

"Rebash said all that?"

Aaron nodded.

"He's giddy as a skunk. Must've made a fortune. But he's telling the truth. No way is Volanti getting near the place alone, let alone getting out…We have to help her."

"Marziel wouldn't like us racing off," Treylen said. "He would want to get in touch with his eyes and ears in Tabron, feel it out first."

"Well, she's gone to the basement. I think I heard her punching things down there."

"You sure she's not packing?"

"I had Rebash and the mayor to deal with. Will you come and help me?"

Treylen followed him down and found that Rebash had mercifully taken his wine back to his rooms. They cleaned the mayor up and carried her upstairs to a vacant room to sleep it off. Once the tavern was empty again, Treylen felt comfortable slipping out of his Stone Kingdom silks and into some working clothes to dress as Trogan. Marziel had decided it was time that Treylen's second alter ego get some rags that weren't shit stained so he could help out in the kitchen without turning stomachs.

He thought about going down to comfort Volanti but decided to wait until Apogee returned. She could help to form some kind of plan in Marziel's absence. He and Aaron scrubbed footprints and removed any evidence they could find of the soldiers. When he finished, he went upstairs to check on the mayor again. She was sleeping soundly where they had left her. Treylen heard the tap of a claw on the glass and found Rime asleep on the outside of her window, injured wing crooked against the windowpane. The dragon had grown fond of the woman—always watching her from a distance. Treylen considered shooing him off, but there was little chance the mayor would wake anyhow, and even less that she would remember much of anything.

Rime normally moved so much it fooled you into thinking he was bigger. Now, he appeared as a tiny collection of leather and bones. Only a hint of breath fogging the glass suggested he was alive.

Treylen kicked himself again for the other day. He should have been there for Ketcher too.

Maybe it was time for Volanti to speak to Apogee about how she had survived the loss of her dragon. The idea hurt in a way that Treylen couldn't articulate. But all the more reason to prepare her now.

Treylen leaned his forehead against the cool window frame. It was a hazy night, and the moon leaked into its indigo backdrop.

Something moved below. A figure was leaving the inn.

Treylen cursed, grabbing a cloak and his knives before

heading outside. The grass was wet underfoot, as though already drenched in blood.

"Don't try to stop me," Volanti growled, the hem of Apogee's silk gown whipping behind her as she strode ahead. She stunk of jasmine, her curls yanked up in an elaborate knot. She was dressed as a wealthy heiress, Treylen realized with a jolt—an attempt to copy Apogee's performance from earlier in the night. Whatever her plan was, it wouldn't work. She looked like a teenager playing dress-up.

"The general gave me strict orders." Treylen followed her, hating himself. "We can't alter things in Tabron. We can't even let them know we were there. If we mess this mission up, we could jeopardize everything."

"You think I care about the mission? Ketcher could be having his claws removed as we speak, or his wings ripped away. He could be thirsty. He's not meant to be in a cage. He wasn't even meant to be here. He belongs in the mountains."

They reached the roadside and paused, listening for any late-night travelers.

"I'm going to the Under Den," Volanti said. "If Marziel tries to stop me, I will burn him, and I will burn you, and every citizen of Lome until I find Ketcher."

His hand curled around his dagger. Volanti reached for her own.

He thought of Apogee's face, her haunted eyes.

"All right. But I'm coming with you." Apogee would just have to watch over the inn herself tomorrow, assuming she came back from following the soldiers before the night was over.

A wooden bow clonked his forehead. Aaron emerged from the stables, the reins of the mayor's horses in his hands. "Always unprepared, aren't you, Treylen? Come on. Reckon I can reach the city in half the time you can." He ushered a third horse from the stables. It was Apogee's.

Treylen stifled a groan but eased into the saddle, nevertheless. The stallion pricked its ears but seemed content to be out of the stables at least.

As the three of them rode off, Treylen tried to work out a plan. Maybe he could delay Volanti when they arrived in the city. Send word to Marziel, somehow.

But after a while, all he could hear was the rush of blood pounding in his ears, and the general's warning: stay in the shadows, don't leave a trace of your presence. Don't let yourself be seen.

Too soon, the lights of Tabron were before them, flickering like the candles in Kestrel's skeleton.

Chapter Twenty-Five

THE CITY

TRAVELING WITHOUT RIME ALWAYS FELT STRANGE.

Treylen knew that with an injured wing, it was for the best that he left Rime behind, as he didn't want to risk another dragon getting trapped and dragged off into the Under Den, but that didn't make it better. Still, he'd been telling himself that he needed to use less of the dragonmind, rely more on his training, and to be ready for the mission, so perhaps this was one more test that he could put himself through that would help determine whether he was truly ready for the mission—and convince Marziel.

For his part, Rime had been happy to keep napping when Treylen had reached out to tell him he was leaving. Felicity was another story. Treylen would be lucky if she hadn't shredded every silk he owned out of spite by the time they got back. But she was simply too big, and too inexperienced, to stay hidden in a city.

"Don't suppose you know much about this city," Aaron said as they reached the outskirts of Tabron.

It was early, and they were tired, but from the look on Volanti's face, Treylen doubted they'd be able to rest until she had a chance to look through all Tabron to see if they could find any sign of Ketcher.

"Just what the general gave me a few hints about," Treylen said with a bit of a shrug. "Dangerous place, but it's a city without the queen's protection, so it's going to be dangerous."

"We don't have anywhere like this," Volanti said, her voice soft. It wasn't entirely true. This was a small city compared to where Treylen had grown up. But there was chaos and disorder here that was much harder to find in Lakehold. So this was how people lived when the queen's assassins weren't watching their every move. It was dirty, but it also called to something in him.

Volanti had fallen increasingly quiet during the journey. Treylen hoped some of that came from her realization of just how foolish this was, or maybe she was thankful that she hadn't needed to come alone. Not like he and Aaron would have forced her to come out here by herself. Not that she couldn't protect herself from any of the usual dangers of this sort of city—but there were spycatchers to worry about.

"No. No place like this," Treylen agreed. "I don't suppose you can, you know, feel Ketcher?"

They paused near a dingy stone building that looked as if it were covered with rotted moss. Other nearby buildings had the same layering of foul dark crawling along the walls, reaching the eaves, before fading completely. It looked as if some wizard—or more likely, dragon—had come through here blasting with fire as it ripped through much of this part of the city.

The streets themselves were uneven cobbles, and he nearly turned his ankle once on a particularly broken stone. Aaron had slipped in what they hoped was mud, but everything along the edge of Tabron stunk, so it was difficult to know. Only Volanti danced along the broken stones with ease, though she was quiet and withdrawn.

"If he was very close, I would know it. I don't know if

there's anything that I'd feel. It's not like you and Rime," she said, looking over to him. "At least, not yet."

Treylen wanted to warn her that she shouldn't want it to get to that point, but knowing Volanti, she'd ignore him anyway.

"Then this Under Den." Aaron turned in place as he looked around the streets, managing to keep his expression neutral—something that Treylen found impressive. "Where do you suppose a place like that would be found in the city?"

Treylen wanted to tell him that he didn't know, as he wasn't from Tabron, and that the Under Den hadn't been his mission, but decided that would only irritate them. While he was less concerned with irritating Aaron, Volanti remained on edge, so he needed to be careful with her. One wrong word could send her racing into danger—something that Treylen knew he had to avoid.

"I doubt a place like that will be hard to find," Volanti piped in. "You just follow the filth. Then it finds you."

It was sage advice, but a place called the Under Den wouldn't be easy to find. It was a place that required a person to know their way around Tabron to find it. Rebash had mentioned the entrances, but not where to find them.

"People don't build tunnels to do illicit deals in. They use what's already there. And the homes here have open sewers," he said, covering his nose and gesturing toward the center of the city. "We need to go deeper."

The cobbles grew more level and tighter together as the buildings crowded in, and before long, they reached the city wall. The gates were shut this early, but an old guard waved them over to a small door on the side. Treylen hadn't taken time to grab his darks or a change of clothes. He and Aaron wore the same stained kitchen wear he had been in when they had left. They had removed most of Volanti's makeup and jewelry—enough that she looked less like a stage actor and more a sensibly dressed minor noble out on an errand.

"Your business?" Their disguise must have been passable, as the guard didn't get up from his seat.

"Market," Treylen said, working the rough character back into his voice. He kept walking as if the guard was only a minor convenience.

"Haven't seen you two before." The guard tipped his spear so that it crossed the doorway. He didn't stand, though.

"I see your ugly mug often enough." Treylen stepped to the edge of the door, stopping just short of moving the man's spear for him.

"They will behave themselves if they want to keep their jobs," Volanti said, pushing to the front.

"Let's hope so, my lady." The guard stood and bowed his head as he pulled the spear aside to let them through.

"See, that wasn't hard," she whispered.

"Don't be sure," Treylen said, peering back to see the man's eyes on them. "We need to hurry."

It was still early and people were about. He could tell that made the others nervous, but it worked to their advantage. Plenty of suspicious characters to keep the spycatchers searching. And there would have surely been more questions from the guard if there were others waiting to pass the gate. They did as Volanti suggested, following the filth.

Not the smell, though Tabron certainly had its share of that, at least in this part of the city. But the three of them had trained long enough to be skilled observers, and when Aaron noticed a few men disappearing down a darkened alley and not returning, they had their first hint of how to find the Under Den.

"What do you think?" Aaron hissed from a vantage across from where the men had gone. While they watched, a pair of older women, both with ragged gray robes and carrying a large leather trunk between them, stepped out of the alley.

"I think...I might feel something..." Volanti said. "It's faint."

"I think we've found one entrance," Treylen said.

"Then let's go find Ketcher. The longer he's there—"

"I know what you're thinking, but we have to do this right. What has Marziel taught us?"

Neither of them said anything, but he could see the question lingering in their minds, the same way that it did for him. Marziel would want them to take the right approach, and in this case, it was not fighting through a place called the Under Den.

"We're exotic-creature merchants," Treylen decided.

"Volanti and I don't look old enough for merchants," Aaron said, "and I'm not buying you as one either."

"We're searching on behalf of our master, Rebash. We appraise the goods, then decide if it's worth his time and money to return. We just need to find Ketcher, then we can break him out."

"Why would Rebash be buying back the dragon he just sold?"

"He wouldn't, but if they know that much, then we've found his buyer."

He kept his gaze on Volanti as he said it. She'd need to be calm during this, he knew, but worried about how well she could stay calm.

"I can do this," she said, as if reading his mind.

"Good. Now walk with purpose and let's look like we belong."

They started down the alley.

At the end, there was what looked to be an iron wall, but with a bit of a push, the wall swung open, revealing stairs heading down into darkness. Treylen took a deep breath before starting down.

The Under Den was a sprawling network of twisting passages, hidden alcoves, and shadowy corners, located beneath the bustling city. The air grew thick with the scent of smoke and sulfur. The torches that lined the walls flickered and cast eerie shadows on the rough-hewn stone. The sound of clattering metal and murmuring voices echoed off the walls, giving the impression that the Under Den was alive with its own strange energy.

They pressed forward, and it didn't take long before they reached the true marketplace. The stalls that lined the passageways were a strange mix of exotic and dangerous. Cages filled with all manner of creatures lined the walls, from tiny fireflies to massive wolves. Creatures from far-off lands could be seen peering out from the cages, their eyes glowing in the dim light. Merchants sold strange potions and powders that promised to cure any ailment. Other stalls sold exotic foods, strange artifacts, and valuable treasures that had probably been looted during Jaul's conquests. Some stalls sold weapons, poisons, and other contraband. In dark corners, groups of rough-looking characters huddled together, eyeing the trio with suspicion and hostility. As long as they were thugs and not spycatchers, Treylen wasn't particularly concerned.

"Oh!" Volanti sucked in a breath. "I can hear him!"

"Great, where is he?"

"He isn't sure how to say," she said. "He's still so little…"

"Well, this looks promising," Aaron muttered, sweeping his gaze around him as he looked at the different stalls. "Exactly the kind of place where you can find what we're looking for. Now, how do you propose we start?"

"There," Treylen said, nodding to a man with a cart resting in front of a caged-off stall. "Looks like he's got some interesting things for sale. Let me do the talking."

They elbowed their way through the crowd, though none of them wanted to get too close to any of the other customers —or the merchants, for that matter—as they approached the man at the stall selling exotic creatures. Treylen had been drawn by the sight of a small, bright red lizard perched on a branch in a cage resting on the counter. The merchant, a thin, wiry man with greasy hair and a crooked nose, looked up as he approached.

"Good day, sir," Treylen said, keeping his tone neutral, realizing almost too late that he wasn't exactly sure how he should communicate with someone like this.

The merchant narrowed his eyes, sizing up Treylen with a suspicious gaze. "What do you want?" he asked, his voice rough and gravelly.

Treylen gestured to the lizard. "I was just admiring your creature. What kind of lizard is it?"

The merchant grinned. "It's a firetail lizard, native to the tropical jungles of the south isles. It's got a venomous bite and can run up to thirty miles per hour. A fine addition to any collection, or for other uses."

Treylen resisted the urge to ask what those other uses might be. "That sounds dangerous. Why would anyone want to keep a creature like that?"

The merchant shrugged. "Some people like the thrill of the danger. Others just like to show off their wealth. Either way, I don't ask questions. I just sell the creatures."

Treylen nodded, still eyeing the lizard warily. "Do you have anything a little more exotic?"

"More than a firetail? Bah." The man waved a hand, motioning toward the lizard. "Doubt that you're really a collector, then." He frowned at the stained, drab clothing that Treylen wore.

"You're right. I'm not. Our master, however, very much is."

The man frowned at the mention of *master*. "Is that right? Anyone I know?"

Treylen shrugged, leaning to the side so that he could look behind the man, though not really expecting to be able to see anything. The man, and the cage on the counter, made it difficult for him. "Depends on who you know."

"I'm as connected as any in Tabron, boy. We've had quite

a few interested shoppers looking for exotics of late. Seems to be a trend for such things these days."

Treylen suppressed his sudden worry. If they were too late for Ketcher...

He didn't know what Volanti would do. But she had sensed him. He couldn't be far.

"That right?" Treylen sniffed. "I suppose we will see about that. Maisey," he went on, motioning to Volanti. She took the name and the sudden attention in stride, as he knew that she would. "See if you can't slip past the counter here and get a look at a few other critters for Master Rebash."

The merchant's eyes narrowed immediately, but he did nothing to keep Volanti from sliding past him and peering into the stall. It didn't have to be her looking, but she could search for Ketcher more easily than he.

"Rebash, you say?" the merchant said. "I might have a few more exotics. I hear that man has some...interesting...tastes. But I didn't know he was buying."

"Can't sell if you don't buy. We're looking for only the most unique," Treylen said. "And whoever helps find it gets a reward."

The merchant licked his lips. "Most unique? Anything he's in the market for in particular?"

"Lately it's been lowsater fawn, mountain sloth, dragons..."

He was careful with the last. Treylen didn't want to get too eager, but he wanted to leave it out there for the merchant to bite. Once he had a nibble, then Treylen could pull the hook.

"I've got none of them here," the merchant said.

"Ah, well, we'll keep searching." He motioned for Volanti, who dutifully slipped back behind the counter, and they started to turn.

"If I offered my assistance..."

"You might be rewarded," Treylen said without turning back. "If the creature is worthy. I would make sure Master

Rebash knew you were of assistance. He is a good man to know if you've got merchandise to move."

The merchant hurried toward them, scurrying to position himself to stand in front of them again. "Not many down here are worth a damn, but there's a few...oh yes...a few where you might find exactly what you're looking for."

"Just show us where we need to go. And if it works, then we can see what sort of contract you will be deserving of."

The merchant looked as if he wanted to argue with him, before smiling tightly. "Ignore the first few stalls up ahead. You're going to have to get into some of the darker reaches of the Under Den. But I can give you a few names. Oh yes, I can give you a few names."

Treylen glanced at the others. It was a start.

Now they had to use it to find Ketcher.

And hope they weren't already too late.

Chapter Twenty-Six

THE CAGES

THE MERCHANT WAS RIGHT THAT THEY SHOULD IGNORE THE first few exotic-animal dealers. Treylen and the others stopped at several of them regardless, having seen a few different creatures that had drawn their attention, and had wanted to take an opportunity to test whether Volanti might detect anything to reveal if Ketcher was there. So far, there had been no sign of the small dragon.

The inside of the Under Den made it difficult to navigate easily. The air was foul, and the deeper they went within the maze of corridors, the thicker it seemed to be. Treylen found his attention drawn in a dozen different directions at times, including at one point where he saw a small stall with different glyph-marked items. He froze.

"What is it?" Aaron asked, practically colliding with him as he came to an abrupt stop.

"This." He nodded to the stall. The old woman working at it was talking to a hooded man, their voices low and in a whisper. He couldn't see much about either of them, but he suspected that if he were to go and investigate the glyphs on some of the items that he would see that they bore the scribe's mark. "It's my assignment."

"I thought your assignment was to find—"

Treylen raised a hand to cut Volanti off before she said anything out loud that might betray the overall mission. He'd filled them in on the basics when they'd arrived to help. Finding Ketcher was certainly important, and it was something that they all felt was essential, but Treylen had a real mission that he'd been given, and he could not fail.

"The mission was to find him," he said, keeping his voice low and careful, "and things like this might lead me to him. I hadn't considered coming to the Under Den to search for evidence of him."

For his part, Treylen hadn't given much thought about how he was going to even find Norris, though he wasn't sure that he was ready for that aspect of the job yet, anyway. Seeing evidence of glyph-marked items within the Under Den only served to prove the point of the danger that someone with great power and no loyalties could pose.

"You need to get back here," Volanti said, grabbing his arm before he pushed too far ahead. He caught himself and hesitated, shaking his head to clear it. She was right. He was getting ahead of himself. It was dangerous to do that.

He had already started toward the stall and didn't have a plan in place for how he would position himself to ask the kind of questions that he needed.

"You're right. Find Ketcher. Then we can go about seeing what else we might uncover here. There has to be a way of tracking all of this back to him."

"Maybe there's more than one scribe involved," Aaron suggested. When Treylen looked over to him, he shrugged. "Or maybe none of this even works. You are acting as if this is some huge find, but if it was all that functional, don't you think there would be more people buying it?"

"He's not wrong," Volanti said.

Treylen nodded and dragged himself away. There was no point in staying there, and no point in getting caught up in it, as he could return once they dealt with finding Ketcher.

They stopped at a few more of the stalls, checking for different strange animals, before making their way into some of the darkened side pathways the first merchant had suggested they try.

They hadn't gone far before sounds of fighting caught their attention. It came from down a narrow, darkened hall, where the air smelled especially foul. Someone cried out and was silenced.

When Aaron looked in his direction, Treylen shook his head. "We stay on task. This task."

Aaron nodded, but his gaze kept drifting back toward that hall, as if he wanted to race down and save whoever was getting assaulted. At another side hall, several young women beckoned toward all three of them, making suggestive comments that could only be ignored. Volanti paled. Aaron blushed. Treylen had learned to lock that side of himself away long ago, through harsh training and devotionals most of the time, at least.

"Maybe this was a mistake," Volanti said.

"If we find Ketcher, then there's no mistake."

They passed a dozen more different merchants, though none had glyph-marked items like the ones that Treylen had seen. He kept looking for anything useful, knowing that ultimately, he would have to return to Tabron to complete the mission, but other than that singular stall, he didn't have much of a lead.

First Ketcher, then go after Norris.

That wasn't the reason they had come to Tabron this time. But he remembered his meetings with Rak'tsoro and the queen's accountant. The clock was ticking. If he could try to find a little extra information, maybe he could make it useful, nonetheless.

It took a while, but they managed to find one of the names

the first merchant had given them. Treylen took the lead again, and as before, he played it up as if they were serving their master, inquiring about different exotic animals that might be for sale. It went better here, especially as they now knew for certain that Rebash had something of a reputation here. Hopefully, it was of the good sort.

"Oh, I've dealt with him before. Don't remember any of you three, but he gets new blood through quite often," the broad-shouldered older man said. He had scars on his hands that looked as if they'd poorly healed. "Can't say that I have anything he will be particularly excited about."

"You don't even want us to look?" Treylen offered.

"I know old Rebash well enough to know that I don't have what he wants. Not this time. Now that I know that he's ready to buy again, I might make a point of ensuring that I have the right supplies the next time."

Aaron nudged Treylen to go. He was tempted to, as they had other names, but he hesitated. "Know anyone else here who might?"

"Only one. You're not going to want to go back there, boy. Too dangerous."

"What makes it too dangerous?" Volanti asked.

Treylen wanted to caution her against asking too many questions, but couldn't do that without drawing the wrong kind of attention. Unfortunately, the man leaned forward, regarding her carefully. Too carefully.

"You're a young one to be working with ol' Rebash. Where did he buy you?" He pinched the hem of her sleeve between his thumb and forefinger, as if testing the quality of the silk.

To Volanti's credit, she didn't flush, and she didn't even hesitate. "A small village near the Iron Range, sir," she said, her voice lower than a whisper, and making her sound as if she were deferential. "Told me that I could earn my keep, he did."

The Under Den merchant just snorted. "You keep telling yourself that, girl."

"Where might we find something?" Treylen asked. "As you said, we are still new to Master Rebash, and need to make a good impression. We can make it worth your while."

"Oy? What are you three having that you think could make it worth my while?"

"First sale opportunity," Aaron offered.

The man looked over to Aaron, sizing him up. "Young man like you looks like he has a bit of experience with some of these little beasties. All right. You go down until the next left, and keep going. You'll know it when you reach it."

"How will we know?" Treylen asked.

The man grinned, flashing a mouthful of yellowed teeth. "Oh, you will know."

They followed his directions. As they reached the next intersecting hall, Aaron grabbed Treylen and motioned Volanti to stop. "We have to think about something. Let's say we do find Ketcher," he said, though there was a note in his voice that made it clear to Treylen that he wasn't completely convinced that they would find much of anything. "How do you intend for us to sneak him out of here?"

"Well, that's not so much a matter of sneaking as it is a matter of us just creating a distraction for her. Besides, we are assassins, aren't we?"

"Not really," Aaron muttered, shaking his head. "Not until we make the first kill."

There was some truth to that. But they had their bond-mates, which meant they held the title. They served the queen. They would not fail.

They headed down the hall, and it became readily apparent as to what the last merchant had suggested. There was a distinct odor that grew worse the farther that they went.

"Yuck," Volanti said, covering her nose. "What do you think that is?"

"Animal shit," Aaron said. "And a lot of it."

Treylen figured he was right. And they found that the hall widened, and at the end of it was a single door. Behind the door was the stench.

"Any thoughts?"

"Well, I've got quite a few thoughts," Aaron said, "but none of them are good."

Volanti was bouncing on her toes. "He's here. I can feel—"

Volanti didn't get a chance to finish what she felt.

The door popped open, and a short man with a knobby cane peered out at them. He had wide eyes, almost too round, and slightly pointed ears with a bit of tufted hair on the ends of them. The rest of the hair on his head was thinning, completely gray, and Treylen could count speckles of age spots on his scalp. Dirt coated his face and exposed arms, and the stench that they had picked up on seemed to waft away from him.

"I'm not selling," he said.

He started to pull the door closed, and Treylen hurriedly reacted, grabbing for it. The man smacked him with his cane, and it was almost enough for Treylen to jerk his hand back, but not quite. Volanti stayed on her toes next to him, and Treylen could practically feel her eagerness.

"We didn't even tell you what we were interested in."

"Same thing everybody's been interested in. I've got a buyer, and I'm not selling."

"Can we at least take a look?" Treylen asked. "We need to know if it's a good specimen."

The man still tried to pull on the door, but he seemed to realize that he wasn't going to get past Treylen that easily, and he eased back. "I told you, I have a buyer."

"And we just want to take a look at the specimen," Treylen said, flashing his most winning smile.

The man snorted. "Gawkers. Not even buyers."

"We are here to buy. We work with Master Rebash."

The man's eyes narrowed.

"Is that right?" the man asked. "In that case, why don't you come inside?"

He stepped forward, leaving the door ajar.

"Something's not quite right," said Aaron.

"What?" Volanti asked. "He said we could come inside and see the specimen."

Treylen couldn't place what it was that bothered him, but the moment they had mentioned Rebash…

"Oh, hellcaves. I think we just made a mistake."

"What's that?" Aaron asked.

"Rebash was the seller. We were supposed to change our damned story."

Aaron's eyes widened. "No choice but to finish off."

"Let's go find Ketcher," Treylen said.

They stepped inside.

The stench was phenomenal. There were rows of cages, all made of a dark metal, and inside each of those cages were different animals of different species, some small, some large, and some that he couldn't even fathom from where they stood.

Volanti immediately was drawn forward.

Treylen had to grab her arm, keeping her from racing toward Ketcher, but she was already gone.

"Go get her," he hissed.

Aaron darted away, chasing after Volanti.

The old man stepped toward Treylen, a long, slender snakelike creature slithering along his arm, up around his neck. It wasn't exactly a snake, as it had small, stunted wings that made it seem as if it could be a dragon, but no dragon like Treylen had ever seen before. Heat seemed to radiate from the creature—little tongues of flame curled from its mouth like a dragon puffing fire. Somehow, the man was not bothered by it.

"Left the other two outside, did you?"

Treylen blinked. Did he not realize that they had gone running in here?

That was to their advantage.

"I just want to see the specimen."

"Here you go," he said. "A salinasar. A mature one, at that. Rare enough, especially here."

Treylen smiled tightly, feigning interest. "It's a lovely specimen, but we both know that's not what I came to see."

"No. And I told Rebash the sale was final," the man said, confirming Treylen's suspicion. "If he's found another buyer, they can come to me. It must be a significant offer for him to go to such trouble. I'm happy to pay a finder's fee."

"Of course. And he wanted us to come to ensure that the precautions were being taken to keep the specimen in good condition."

"I'm sure you do. Since you intend to steal it back from me!"

The strange merchant didn't give Treylen an opportunity to answer.

He flung the salinasar at Treylen.

The strange snakelike creature might not have been able to fly, but it certainly floated just fine, gliding right at Treylen.

He shielded himself, wishing that he had Rime with him, and spun to the side.

Only for Volanti to shout. Ketcher came streaking forward, snapping the salinasar out of the air, and throwing it to the ground. The old merchant took a step toward Ketcher, raising his cane, and pointing it. A glyph along the surface of it began to glow. Treylen stumbled, eyes on the weapon. Just how busy had Norris Duremo been? Volanti had already reacted. A streak of flame shot from Ketcher, catching the merchant in the chest.

"Time to run," Aaron said, jogging from the back of the room.

"Why?"

"Distraction," he said, his eyes flashing with amused light. "Isn't that what you said?"

"Well, I said that we needed a distraction to get out of here." The man was trying to get up, leaning on his cane. Glyphs didn't typically glow before their power word was spoken. Treylen worried about what would happen if he managed to activate it. "I didn't expect for…Wait. What is that sound?"

"Our distraction."

Aaron grabbed Treylen by the arm, pushing them off to the side of the doorway. Volanti, knowing what was coming, moved to the other side of the door.

A small, squat stonelike creature lumbered forward, saw the opening in the doorway, and then went racing through. It didn't take long before shouts began to ring out down the hall.

"Do you even know what that is?"

"What? I thought it looked cute. Now, let's get out of here. If you see more of Norris's work, you can grab it along the way, but if not, let's just get back to Marziel and regroup."

Aaron sounded confident, calling the shots—but this went against everything they'd been warned about, and it undermined the mission. As much as Treylen wanted to argue, the best they could hope for now was a swift escape, especially now that they might have Rebash trying to figure out who was pretending to work for him.

As they raced through the Under Den, finding evidence of the strange creature having destroyed its way to freedom, Treylen saw no further signs of Norris's glyphwork. They may have saved Ketcher, and made Volanti whole—something that Treylen knew was necessary—but he still had a mission to accomplish, and Treylen wasn't sure how he was going to accomplish it.

Chapter Twenty-Seven

THE CLUB

TREYLEN KNEW THAT MARZIEL COULDN'T PUNISH VOLANTI for the mess in Tabron. She had succeeded, after all, and done what was necessary at a time when he'd been missing. He was also far too angry at Apogee to let the blame fall on the rest of them. She had never returned that night, or the morning after. By the third day, he seemed to have stopped waiting. Aaron and Volanti took over most of her duties at the inn, while Treylen's training in the pit had intensified. Rime's wing recovered, and everyone was happy to have Ketcher back.

It was dinner when the news arrived that Rebash's wagons were due to arrive later in the night. Their delay had been a source of great frustration for the man. A caravan filled with prisoners was expensive to maintain, even if those prisoners could live on hay and grasses, so each day they were stalled had eaten into his share of the profits.

The Jaul rate for prisoner transport being low, it was far more lucrative to sell a few of the prisoners off to someone.

He was in rare form that evening, when shortly after the news had come, a greasy-haired nobleman from northern Libbat, and the son of an elkbone warlord who had just got in from the badlands for another attack on the Harvest Pass, both agreed to take a look at what he had to offer.

Rebash had bought a round of drinks for the tavern, and the table where he sat with his new associates was heaped with meats and cheeses. The mayor and her husband joined another group of legionnaires, along with a recently arrived band of poor Lomish soldiers, to toast the merchant's generosity. Treylen's drink sat in front of him untouched, as he watched from Cren'pin's usual table in the far corner by the stairs. He picked at the bones on his plate and waited for Marziel to signal that it was time to descend to the training ring, where he and Marziel had been slowly working their way through the wall of weapons.

"Look at him." Aaron growled, leaning in to whisper as he brought a tankard over from the bar. "The things that bring a man like that joy." Ever since the Under Den, Aaron had been seething.

"I don't like it any more than you do," Treylen said.

"You don't think something should be done about him?"

Treylen did agree. And though he wasn't practiced in assassination, he was fairly sure he could have brought himself to kill the man if Marziel would allow it.

"It's not part of our mission. If it were up to me, it would be. But it's not my decision."

"You haven't even spoken to Marziel about it," Aaron whispered.

"Because he wouldn't agree to it."

He didn't need to ask to know what Marziel would say. Rebash was too valuable of a contact, a source of too much information, and as a criminal, he was more of an enemy to Jaul than to Iverna. Besides, there was no good reason to harm him, aside from their desire to get revenge for what he'd done to Ketcher.

I agree with Aaron, Rime said. *Marziel poisoned you. He asked you to lie to the queen. Who is he to tell you what to do and what not to do?*

Of course, Rime didn't care about lying to the queen. He just knew how to pluck Treylen's stings. But Treylen had already chosen to accept what he'd done for Marziel. There was no going back now.

I can't just kill people because I don't like them, Treylen thought.

You don't want to help others by getting rid of him?

That wasn't our mission.

Rebash stood again and raised his tankard.

"What say you, Cren'pin? Will you leave with us this night for Tabron?"

Treylen forced a smile and raised his drink.

We should go with him, Rime hissed in his thoughts. *Cut his throat and leave him on the roadside.* As the training had grown more intensive, Rime's aggression had as well. He was still angry that he hadn't been able to stop them from taking Ketcher.

Behind the bar, Marziel gave a small shake of the head. Their original plan had been for Treylen to accept the offer and travel to Tabron with him. But now that they had spread the merchant's name all over town, they had drawn far too much attention. Treylen would be leaving soon, but not with the merchant caravan.

"I would leave this moment, but I think my uncle has other plans for me."

"Your misfortune, then," Rebash said, still holding his drink aloft. "I'm sure I could have found a place for you. Is he taking you on his next run?"

"I think he might." Treylen drained his tankard—only water now, he trained too hard for ale—then pushed his chair back to stand.

"Gentlemen. A good evening to you. Lady Mayor." Treylen bowed his head to each. "And Marcus, if my uncle comes down again, will you tell him I've turned in?"

Rebash pushed his new companions aside and crossed the tavern. Now that things were going his way, he was all cheer again.

"I'll be gone in the morning, lad. I will see you again, certainly." He clasped one hand on Treylen's shoulder.

"Perhaps," Treylen said. "And I will give your goodbyes to my uncle."

"Of course. Give my best to Mauridin."

Treylen broke away and went upstairs. He changed in his room—that was all he used it for anymore—then threw a silk jacket on to cover his darks and went to the subbasement, eager to blow off some steam.

Are you coming, Rime?

I'm going to stay here and watch these three, Rime said. *Marziel is coming, though. He's told them he's stepping out to the toilet.*

That was the most common excuse for the innkeeper's frequent disappearances. The patrons were used to the old man's irregularity. The inn had a separate outhouse in the back that he reserved for himself.

That's fine as long as Marziel allows it. Make sure you're watching all of the common room. Not just the merchant.

I see everything.

That was far from true. As sharp as the dragon's eyes were, he had a tendency to fixate upon one thing to the exclusion of all else.

Let him know I'll be here when he's ready.

Treylen dropped from the ladder into the pit, surprised to see a candle already burning at the edge of the sand. Volanti knelt beside it, Ketcher in her lap. The two of them had not been apart for a moment since his rescue the other day. Mood had only marginally improved. She had that tortured look in her eyes as if she still could not quite believe that Ketcher was safe.

"I thought I was fighting Marziel. Aren't you changing the linens tonight?"

"Marziel says we're leaving tomorrow," she said, stroking Ketcher.

"I think so," Treylen said. "You don't seem excited."

"It feels like we have unfinished business. Did Aaron talk to you about Rebash?"

"You too?"

"What do you mean me too?" Volanti sprang up, yanking Ketcher under one arm. "You saw what he did with him." She shook her dragon at Treylen.

"I'm not killing him for you. You aren't the queen."

"Treylen…" Volanti made a sound like it pained her. "I have…an idea. It isn't as good as killing him, but I've been thinking, what if his caravan never makes it and those poor lowsater he wants to sell all got away…"

"I think that would be a bigger problem than if I killed him."

"I'm serious, Treylen. I want to do something to him."

Treylen groaned. "Then train. You're lucky that Ketcher is still alive."

"It's your fault we're here. You couldn't help me the night they caught him. You owe me this."

We should do it, bondmate.

Treylen glared up at the hatch to see Rime, peeking through.

"You were supposed to stay upstairs." Rime dropped down to land on his shoulder.

She has a plan. You should listen.

"Rime says you have a plan?" Treylen asked.

"It's easy. You just have to tire out Marziel tonight. Fight him hard and he'll let you turn in early, then we can go out and hit it before it gets here."

"Tire out Marziel? He's a monster."

"He's an old man, Treylen."

"Okay, then what?"

"We steal the lowsater."

"And do what with them, sneak the lowsater down here?"

"Maybe," she said, sounding strained. "They'll be grateful. Maybe they can help us with your mission. I don't know, I just want to get at Rebash somehow…"

"Don't be ridiculous." He could tell from her wild, wide eyes that she wasn't thinking clearly. Captivity had been terrible for her bondmate, and whatever trauma he'd gone through was seeping over through the bond.

Treylen laughed at the thought of a bunch of orphaned lowsater running around Tabron for him. But it did give him an idea. Maybe there was a way to hit the caravan with Marziel's permission. If nothing else, it would ease whatever pain still clung to his friend.

"Okay…maybe," Treylen said. "Be ready, and we'll see."

There was a rattle up above and Marziel appeared at the ladder just a few moments later.

"I thought we might get started early," he said. "I'd like to be up there when Rebash's caravan comes through."

"He said that it wouldn't be passing until later."

"The bar will be open later. And Marcus will be there pouring drinks. Did you think I go to bed after we train? Volanti, don't you have linens to change?"

"I do." She grabbed the ladder as soon as Marziel hopped down, then hurried out, glaring down at Treylen one last time.

"I wanted to talk to you about Rebash," Treylen said.

"Don't start. I know what you're going to say. You've been staring daggers at him since you met him. You need not worry about having to go to Tabron with him. We'll send you separately."

"That wasn't what I was about to say," Treylen objected. "Volanti wants to kill him."

"Oh, I'm aware." Marziel laughed.

"She's told you too?"

"And Aaron, and I'll bet Rime too. Dragons approach every problem the same way. But Rebash isn't a rat in the attic. He's my informant. You understand. He is not to be harmed. In fact, you're to avoid him at all costs."

"That's the other problem," Treylen said. "In the Under Den, we saw glyph-marked weapons. I don't know that Rebash is involved, but if he knows something about them, I might run into him again. I don't want to go against your orders but…"

"If my orders conflict with your mission, then you do what you must in service of your mission. Now, we won't talk of this anymore, do you understand?"

That was the answer Treylen was looking for.

But it might be enough that he could give Volanti what she wanted. After all, what better place to start looking for glyph-marked weapons than a merchant caravan that had just passed through the Jaul army's camp on the way to Tabron? And given how Marziel had strongly encouraged Treylen to manipulate the truth in his reporting to the accountant, he could hardly fault him for doing it again.

"Now, what will we train in?" Marziel strode to the wall and placed his hands on his hips. They had trained in most of the weapons already. Treylen got up and stood next to him.

"We haven't trained in that yet," he said, pointing to a pair of sturdy wooden implements about the length of his forearm. One side was slim and carved into a handle, the other was just slightly wider and resembled a polished tree limb.

"Ah, the humble club." Marziel stepped forward and took the weapons off their hooks. "Favored weapons of high-waymen and lawmen alike. This pair came from the western border, where Lome meets the Salt Crescent."

"What is special about them?"

"Well, for one, it's slightly more difficult to accidentally kill your opponent. Not everyone is cut out to be a killer. And those who don't have trust in the restraint of their underlings tend to give them clubs. Although I find the more deadly a weapon you carry, the less likely you are to need to use it.

Whereas clubs…they demand employment." He flipped one over in his hand and held it out to Treylen. "Shall we begin?"

"Maybe we can finish early?" Treylen asked. "I can get some sleep for once."

"We'll see," Marziel said, stepping into the ring and beginning to circle. "First I'll take you through the range of nonlethal strikes. You know most of these in your hand-to-hand already. Then I'll show you what the humble club is really capable of."

Chapter Twenty-Eight

THE LOWSATER

It felt good to run again. After so many days training indoors, even Rime was eager for the exercise, leaping down from Treylen's shoulder to sprint with him and Volanti along the west road.

Most of the time, Treylen carried him, drawing upon dragon strength to speed them along as quickly as possible. In one hand, he clutched the club from that evening's training session. Volanti carried the other.

He couldn't know where the caravan would be, but they would need to be as far from the inn as possible when they laid ambush. When the fires of the Jaul army encampment came into view, Treylen decided they had gone far enough. Up ahead, the road split. One direction continued westward to the coastal city states known as the Salt Crescent. Another went north and became the Harvest Road. At one time, it had continued all the way through the pass into Iverna before reaching Lakehold and Queenseat.

Once they found the camp, they doubled back. There would be no benefit to laying ambush so close to the army. It would only put them at greater risk of being interrupted by a military patrol. The land was clear of forests here, likely to make it more difficult for any Iveran incursion to go unde-tected. The grass had been grazed, so there were no patches to hide behind. Fortunately, the sky was overcast, so they had only to sit down on a small mound just off the road and wait for their prey to come along.

A chill breeze raked the fields, bringing with it smells of fire and fresh mowed grasses. Rime ducked inside his collar and pressed against him for warmth. It reminded him of camping out on the mountain just before he had been given his assignment. Treylen put his arms behind his head and closed his eyes, keeping his focus on the sounds around him.

"What now?" Volanti asked.

"Now we try to sleep. If Marziel finds out what we've done, we won't be getting any more tonight."

"Do you think he will?"

They had slipped out shortly after Marziel ended his train-ing. He'd made sure to choose a weapon that would fatigue and batter his training partner. A sword or a war hammer might have been heavier, but with those, he was expected to exercise some restraint.

With clubs, he could get away with landing a few more strikes. And each time their weapons clashed, the impact had rattled the bones of the hands holding them. He could push hard and punish Marziel with his dragon strength. Of course, he had lost the fight because of that. But his aim had not been to win. It had been to exhaust Marziel early.

Once the victor had gone upstairs to lick his wounds, Rime and Treylen had pretended to turn in for the night, then snuck out when Marziel was preoccupied with serving drinks. Rebash and his companions were committed to staying up and drinking until the caravan arrived, and they would likely keep him busy until the small hours of the morning.

Marziel had been avoiding Volanti ever since the Under Den, perhaps out of guilt that he'd not been the one to help her, so he wouldn't notice she was gone. That left Aaron tending bar with him. Though he was not too keen on sneaking out, anyhow, and seemed more than happy to be left behind this once.

"I don't know what Marziel will think," Treylen said. "I'm surprised you even care."

"I don't have to like him to care," Volanti said.

I like him, Rime said. *But I don't like being told what not to do.*

Rime poked his head out, then scampered to the top of the hill and stood on his hind legs to look around.

The truth was it didn't matter if their handler found out. He had granted them permission to begin pursuing goals that served the mission. And there was good reason to believe this would serve their mission.

The way Treylen and Volanti figured it, even the best glyph scribes would struggle to create something that wouldn't lose its potency as the seasons changed and currents of magic shifted.

So wasn't it likely that every caravan passing through the Jaul war camps would be asked to haul a shipment of the glyph-marked weapons back to Tabron to be replenished? And if this Norris Duremo was in hiding, wouldn't it be far easier to track a shipment of weapons to the scribe than to wander Tabron aimlessly, hoping to catch a glimpse of magic?

Add to that the glyph-marked weapons they had seen in the Under Den. It was hard to imagine a man like Rebash would let the opportunity to skim a couple off the top pass him by.

That was how he intended to justify it. But if he staged this attack correctly, it would look as if a gang of highwaymen had done it, or that a couple of bad seeds within the Jaul ranks took it upon themselves to rob the caravan after it passed their camp. Or maybe the Iveran army would catch the blame. They were near enough to the pass for that.

They're here. Rime's hiss brought him out of his drowse.

Treylen sat up, blinking. The dark shapes of wagons rolled along the road just in front of him. Volanti was just below, crouching beside the road already.

How long was I out?

Don't worry, bondmate. I have been watching.

Treylen crawled forward, staying low to the ground and looking over the wagons as he approached. There were six of them, larger than he'd expected, each pulled by two oxen. Low-burning lanterns hung beside each of the drivers. The first two were covered by arched canopies, and the last four were open. Sullen figures of the lowsater were chained to them.

They must have been in a hurry if they were making the oxen walk through the night. Two of the carts were already past him.

I'm in place, Rime said.

Is it just the six of them? Treylen gripped the club and straightened his disguise, a set of brown working clothes he had borrowed from the trunk in the basement.

Aside from the lowsater. I can't see inside the first two carts.

Good. Wait for my signal.

He crept up beside Volanti as she took Ketcher out from her shirt and set him behind her.

"You stay out of this," Treylen whispered, though he wasn't always certain that Volanti's dragon understood him.

He pressed low against the dark roadside and massaged his arm. It still ached from the blows he had taken with Marziel. The grip of the club felt clumsy in his hand, but he had practiced with it earlier that night. He was comfortable with its use, though he was not confident in its ability to silence his victims. How easy it would've been to cut a couple of throats. But he was limiting his exposure here. Cut throats would indicate an assassin, and this was to be something simpler.

As the last cart crept past, he slipped out into the darkness behind it. There was a grunt in the dark. The glimmer of a dozen sets of bovine eyes reflected the faint light of the driver's lantern.

Treylen stared back at them and put a finger to his lips. He had to hope they wouldn't frighten and give him away. He heard a few low murmurings, but they stayed quiet.

Creeping up beside the wheels, he peered into the driver's seat. Volanti popped up on the opposite side. The man's head was slumped against his chest, sleeping. It seemed almost unfair to strike him, but necessary.

Treylen grabbed the edge of the seat and hauled himself up in one swift motion. He wrapped his arm around the man's neck as he clapped the other over his mouth as he struggled. He held it there until the man sunk down in his seat again. Then he pulled from his belt a length of rope he'd cut in advance and Volanti bound the man's hands to the seat, before stuffing a rag in his mouth and tying it off. The man let out a low moan, but it was hidden below the squeaking of the wheels and plod of oxen.

"Stay silent and you'll live," she hissed. "Scream and I will cut your throat."

The man breathed and then nodded.

"One down." He let the reins rest on the seat and the oxen plodded on as if nothing had happened. He slipped down from the seat and raced to the next wagon in the line. More startled lowsater watched him from inside. He heard the clink of chains as they shifted in their bonds, but they didn't betray him.

Coming up alongside the next seat, this driver was alert, as if he had heard something. He turned his head to look back at the other wagon, his eyes fixed upon Treylen. Volanti vaulted up from the other side, striking the man on the back of the head with a muffled crack. Treylen caught him before he could tumble from the cart, then they quickly bound him as well.

The lowsater in the cart in front of this one were making noise. Treylen hopped down, raced up alongside it, and sprang into the driver's seat without waiting. The man saw him jump up but hadn't had enough time to raise alarm. Treylen struck him, and he cried out. Another strike on the side of his head and he fell unconscious. No time to bind this one. Treylen lifted him up with dragon strength and tossed him into the back of the cart, where the shadows of the lowsater came together to batter him and pin him down.

Now there was shouting. Volanti darted past, toward the next cart.

It's time, Treylen said to Rime. He hopped down and raced to the next cart. A deep, soft voice called to him from the back of it, and a hand reached out to him, palm up. It had three thick fingers and was covered in fur. Black nails on each finger resembled the cloven hoof of a deer. Metal shackles clasped around the wrist.

He didn't need the help, but why not?

He grasped the hand and the palm closed around his, hauling him up. A face like that of a shortened cow bent down to look at him. It snorted warm air, then it released him and moved back to sit along the rail. More crowded in around him, but with a wave of a hand, the one who had pulled him up motioned for them to make way, and they cleared a path down the middle of the cart.

Treylen gave a quick nod, then darted up the cart, leaping over the back and into the seat, where the driver was looking frantically from side to side. There was a weapon in his hand, and he stabbed at Volanti, who peered out from underneath. Treylen had no time to waste. He whacked him on the side of the head and the man went over, falling into the road. Now there was more noise—someone moaning from the cart behind him. The driver of the cart up ahead raised a crossbow and loosed a bolt. Treylen dove away as the arrow sank into the seat.

Along the side of the road came a flash of light. A small campfire flared up, its light falling onto the front two carts. The driver spun and fired at the flames. But Rime had already moved on to light another pile of sticks and brush farther up. It was important to make it look like this was the work of a group of assailants. Two attackers taking out six men would be suspicious.

Good enough. Now keep hidden. If any of them saw the dragon, the ruse would be a failure.

Volanti raced up the side of the road and flung herself into the fourth driver from behind, knocking him off the seat. He heard a jingle from the man's belt as he fell. He jumped down and ran to him, then reached down to find a loop of keys, snatched it up, then ran to the third wagon again. The same hand reached out to him, those gigantic, dark eyes seeming to track him even when he was in the shadow. Behind them, the second wagon had started to veer off the road, and there came the low mooing of oxen and lowsater alike. The massive palm seemed to swallow up the ring of keys as it disappeared into the shadows of the cart.

"Get the front." Treylen pointed ahead as they jumped down, and Volanti raced ahead to the first wagon while Treylen approached the second. He heard the crack of a whip, and the shake of reins as the lead driver urged his cart forward. Volanti yelped and tumbled out the back of the cart.

The second driver in line wasn't nearly as much of a coward. He had jumped down from his cart and drawn a sword. Treylen rolled beneath the wagon, then padded up behind him soundlessly, twisting the sword from his hand and cracking his face with the butt of the club. Before the man could recover, he seized him by the front of his shirt and tossed him into the back of the cart. A massive hand wrapped around his face, and he was gone beneath the press of fur and bodies. Treylen raced to where Volanti had fallen. She was on her back, hands clutching her head.

Ketcher was at her side already, sniffing at the trickle of blood.

"You're hurt."

"He's getting away," Volanti mumbled, pointing at the last cart.

No wagon could outrun an assassin. Treylen took a moment to make sure her bleeding wasn't bad, then chased after it and caught up a short ways down the road, leaping inside. He waved his weapon around and pulled on dragon sight. It was empty of people. Crates and boxes filled the space covered by the canvas. He peered through the flap at the front of the wagon. The driver leaned forward, lashing at the oxen with his whip and urging them onward. He held a short-sword in one hand.

Treylen drew his head back inside and looked around the wagon. If he wished for it to look like a robbery, he would have to take all these valuables. He had no way of doing that. Better to let this man get away. But there was the issue of the enchanted weapons. Treylen bent over one of the boxes and pried it open. Inside was cloth and jewelry. The next box held fine wool, and the sack beside it had more fabric. A small chest in the corner held coins, more jewelry, and other items that looked like they might have been taken from the prisoners.

Finally, shifting a pile of tarps, he heard the clank of metal. Unrolling the fabric, he saw a familiar blade marked with glyphs. He had been right after all.

There weren't many of them, but these were the blades he was looking for. He would leave these. He could follow them later, maybe even press Rebash for information.

He was about to jump off the back of the moving cart when he changed his mind. This man couldn't be allowed to reach the inn before he did. He crept back, swung his club, and hit the man from behind. The man slumped over and tumbled off the side of the cart to fall onto the road.

Without the man's lashing, the cart began to slow. Treylen kept it steady in the center of the road, then tied the reins off so the animals would go on their own for a ways before they stopped.

It just had to go far enough that it was believable when they found it had not been plundered. He hopped off and ran back.

Volanti had crawled off the road, and lay in the dark ditch at the front of the wagons. Rime and Ketcher crouched beside her, wide-eyed.

"Are you still with us?"

"I'm..." She sat halfway up, then rolled onto her back again, clutching at her head. "All I see is spots."

"You're be alright. Don't go anywhere." He pointed to Rime and Ketcher. "Don't leave her." Treylen crept out of the ditch onto the road again.

The large figures of the lowsater were everywhere. The first group had freed the others. They were chasing down the runaway wagons to calm the oxen, whispering to them as they stroked their coats and worked to get them free. On the ground near the front wagon were the bloodied wagon drivers. A few were sitting up, but most lay limp in the road. He would not be adding any knots to the cord that he kept for Aaron, though it was possible a few might die.

It wouldn't do for the drivers to see him, so he stopped just out of sight. He was about to call out to the lowsater when a group of them broke off from the crowd and approached him. It seemed that their vision in the dark was just as good as his dragon sight.

Treylen had seen the massive arms, bull-like heads, and broad, fur-covered shoulders as they sat in the wagon. They were easily head and shoulders taller than Aaron, and twice his weight.

And that was just the children.

The lead lowsater who approached him now was twice the

height of a man. It was nearly tall enough to look inside the second-story windows of the inn. Outweighing the oxen, this one must have been chained within the covered wagon, or he would've seen them earlier. He was covered in fur the color of coal, with scattered patches of white like stars on a cloudless sky. A thick skirt of pleated leather encircled his waist and a vest of fine linen hung over his shoulders. It stopped just before him, stones crunching under large, iron-shod hooves, then crouched down, head lowering until it was level with his own.

Clouds of steam rose from its nostrils as it breathed in the cool night air.

"Lomish man…"

The voice seemed to reverberate through him like a rumble from deep in the earth.

Rime hopped out of the dark and clawed up Treylen's back to stand on his shoulder.

You were supposed to stay with her, he thought.

Rime stretched out toward the lowsater, who recoiled a bit, then raised one hand to touch the dragon's nose, before leaning in again, bringing his face close to Treylen's. His breath smelled of sweet grasses.

"Iveran, we are in your debt." The smaller lowsater youths knelt beside him, murmuring in the lowsater tongue.

Treylen peered past them to see a small crowd of young lowsater tending to the wounded drivers. The oxen were loose and milling about.

"You aren't safe yet. If you go north until you reach the mountains, then west, you'll reach Harvest Pass. Just stay off the roads."

"Is it guarded?" the lowsater asked.

"There'll be patrols. But the army is here at the crossroads. Reach the wall and the Iverans will take you in."

Are you sure they will make it? Rime asked.

No, but they won't fit in the basement.

In truth, it would be nearly impossible to get through the pass undetected. But it was a good deal wider on the Lomish side. The army couldn't guard all of it. If they reached it before daybreak, they might stand a chance.

We could hide them all, Rime said.

Don't be ridiculous. This is their best shot.

The lowsater nodded and blew out of its nostrils. "What is your name?"

Treylen hesitated. He hadn't planned to give one. It seemed wrong to lie in that moment.

"I'm Treylen. And this is Rime."

The lowsater bowed more deeply.

"I am Uberetus Oua Tuhaug, and these are my children, Noulea and Brome." Two of the youths bowed as he indicated them.

Treylen returned the gesture.

"Your companion is injured," he said, looking down the road.

"I can get her to safety. You take care of yours."

"We are in her debt, as well." The lowsater bowed again. "If we could be of any help…"

"Actually, I do have a request of you," Treylen said, and the lowsater raised his head attentively. "I wasn't here. If the Iverans ask or if the Jaul catch you, it was highwaymen that attacked the caravan to rob it. You freed yourselves and chased them off."

"We are artisans. Not soldiers."

Treylen suppressed a chuckle, looking them over. "I don't think anyone will question it."

"Understood."

"Take what you can from the wagons, so it looks like they've been robbed."

He nodded again, then waited, breathing heavily in the quiet night air.

"Good luck." Treylen took a step back as the lowsater stood, looming over him again.

"May your good fortune run deep," Uberetus said.

They parted ways, the lowsater lumbering back to the wagons before heading north across the fields, and Treylen carrying Volanti as he raced back toward the inn.

Chapter Twenty-Nine

THE BREAKFAST

THAT NIGHT, TREYLEN DREAMED OF LOWSATER AND THE HIGH walls of the Harvest Pass as it wound through the mountains into Iverna. The peaks loomed over him, dark and foreboding. The farther he walked, the higher the cliffs became and the darker the path ahead. It seemed no matter how long they walked, they never reached the end of it.

But Uberetus was at his side, the herd of young lowsater behind them. They walked stubbornly onward, bones of ancient battles crunching underfoot and the distant flap of leathery wings over the wall ushering them forward until morning.

There is bacon.

Treylen had expected to be awakened by a furious Marziel demanding to know what he had done last night. He had made it in without being seen, leaving Volanti in Aaron's care. She was feeling better already. Then he'd returned the clubs and the clothing to their place within the basement, but thought surely Marziel would see through his ruse anyway. When nothing had happened, he had retreated to his bed and slept heavily.

Treylen sat up, shook off the last memories of the dream,

and sent a probing thought out to Rime.

What is he doing? What time is it?

He would like for you to come eat.

That was odd. Rime could be short, but he was rarely evasive. Treylen wiped the sleep from his eyes and stood up.

What do you mean there is bacon? He doesn't cook me breakfast.

No answer.

Treylen dressed in the previous day's silks and made his way down through the secret passage. Carefully, he opened the pantry door and peered out. Marziel was at the stove. Aaron and Volanti sat at the counter in the center of the kitchen, a plate of food in front of each of them.

Quietly, he shut the pantry, stepping toward the door to make sure none of the patrons were about.

"So you're awake," Marziel said, not bothering to disguise his voice.

Treylen backed away from the door and stepped up to the counter, startled when he realized the dragons were in the kitchen too. Rime, Ketcher, and Felicity, perched on the shelf above the wash basin, all three watching him intently.

"Sit down."

He pulled out a stool and sat between Aaron and Volanti. Marziel flipped the eggs in the skillet, then transferred them to the plate beside a slab of bacon and some fried bread, then placed it down in front of him. He gestured toward the utensils, and Treylen picked up his fork and knife but didn't eat, still uncertain what was going on.

"What is this?"

"You're leaving today." Marziel turned away and began cleaning the skillet. "I thought the three of you might appreciate a parting meal."

"So you'll miss us after all?"

Marziel grumbled to himself and scrubbed harder. Treylen looked at his friends. Neither had said a word yet, nor touched their food.

"What's the trouble? Did Rebash keep you up all night?" Treylen forced a laugh.

"You know damn well that he did."

"What do you mean?" Treylen grabbed the fork and tried to eat while looking natural.

"Queen's shadow! Damn it to hellcaves." Marziel threw the skillet into the sink with a clatter. Treylen put the utensils down again.

"What happened last night?" Treylen asked.

Why pretend? Rime hissed in his thoughts. *You had good reasons. He knows what you did anyway.*

"You know damn well what happened." Marziel scrubbed furiously in the wash basin. He paused to look back over his shoulder, glaring at Volanti. "You, take out the wash."

Volanti stood, steadied herself, and made two steps toward the door before she stumbled. Aaron caught her and helped her back to her seat.

"Sit down. Now eat the food."

Treylen ate. Marziel washed in silence. Volanti tried to eat, but halfway through, the food came up again and Aaron had to help her out the back door.

"You're leaving now. I've packed a bag and put it on your bed. You are going to Tabron. You will commence with your mission as planned."

"Just me?"

"It's clear to me now they're holding you back."

Treylen glanced at the back door. Volanti was vomiting around the corner. Aaron had his head turned the other way; one hand held the back of her shirt to keep her upright.

"They're good assassins. Aaron can fight as well as I can. And you've seen Volanti's glyphwork."

"That may be, but sometimes, a handler needs to do what's best for the network. The three of you are bringing far too much attention on the inn. The rangers. The Under Den. Whatever last night was."

Something shattered in the sink, and Marziel cursed under his breath before giving up and grabbing a towel to dry his hands as he came to stand opposite Treylen.

"You are more than capable. In some areas, you are far more advanced than most who come through here. And in the places where you're lacking, you have made progress."

Treylen nodded, still not quite awake, not quite understanding either.

"You'll keep them here, though? You won't send them back?"

"Finish your damn breakfast." He pounded on the table.

A voice called from the common room, and Marziel ran to the door, fixing his beard as he did, then stuck his head out and spoke with one of the regulars in the voice of Marcus. He straightened to his full height as he returned to the counter.

"This is not the end of your training, only the beginning. You'll report back to me when you are finished with the task. Perhaps you will have learned to keep a lower profile by the time you return. I do hope that you will return."

Treylen nodded again, swallowing a chunk of egg whole. Marziel placed a tankard of water in front of him.

"The sun is up, and I have work to do. You and your dragon will go to your room. You'll take the bag that I have packed and you will walk to Tabron."

"Walk?"

"You think I would lend you a horse after last night?"

Treylen kept his mouth shut. If Marziel wanted a confession, he would need to pry it out of him.

"What about them?" Treylen looked to Volanti, who was sitting up. Aaron seemed reluctant to let her go, lest she topple over.

"I will deal with them."

"There. You've finished." He snatched the plate away, before Treylen could get the last of the bacon. "Congratulations, you have completed your first round of training. Now get out of my tavern and don't come back until you and that dragon of yours have remembered your discipline."

He threw the plate into the washbasin, where it shattered, then stormed out into the common room without a second glance.

How did it go? Rime asked, no longer on his perch. *I couldn't stand to listen anymore.*

It could have been worse. Treylen stood from the counter and drank the water that Marziel had placed in front of him. *Unless he's poisoned breakfast.*

Let's hope not.

I hope you ate your fill, dragon, because it's the last you're getting for a long while.

Not a problem, Rime said. *Marziel has packed me meat for the road. He would not want for me to go hungry just because of you.*

Treylen left Marziel to stew and went outside. He knelt before Volanti.

"I'm very sorry," he said, putting a hand on her shoulder.

"My stupid mistake," she said, eyes half-lidded.

"She'll be alright by tonight. I've been hit worse."

"And look what it did to you." Volanti laughed, swaying again.

"Maybe this is for the best. I'm not sure either of you are ready for Tabron either. I'll see you here when I'm finished. I don't believe he'll send you back. He needs the help."

"But will you be back, with a new mission?" Aaron asked.

"That's up to General Bourin, but I think so." He put a hand on each of their arms. Take care of each other…and try not to make any more trouble for Marziel. He's a good man, you'll see. Be careful what you trust to Apogee, if she comes back."

"We'll be alright here," Aaron said, looking in the door again. "Marziel is alright. You'd better get moving, though, before he kicks you out."

Chapter Thirty

THE ROAD

THE ROAD SOUTH OF THE FOREST WOUND BETWEEN SPRAWLING fields of wheat and lush pastures, still green even this late in the year thanks to the mild temperatures and rich soil that gave the country of Lome its name. Homes were far between, and Treylen had to wonder how they even found the time to harvest it all.

Maybe Jaul sent laborers up to help Lome with the harvest. It was clear that farmland hadn't always stretched this far north, for all along the road, thick patches of trees and large stretches of forest still remained, especially across the fields to the west. This begged the question: Just how foolish was Iverna for not sending its armies out to burn these fields that fed the Jaul army?

Treylen barred the thought from his mind. The queen was not capable of being foolish, and the generals of Iverna did not make mistakes.

Treylen wished that he could have caught a ride with Rebash that morning, but from the sound of things, it was a somber procession once he had learned his wagons were raided. The sun was warm this day and the road was dusty. Rime made a wheezing noise and buried his head in Treylen's shirt. Treylen wore a bright silk shirt and pants with another wide-brimmed hat. A ridiculous traveling cape of even brighter silk completed the look.

True to its name, the pigeon he had been given seemed content to rest inside of the pocket of his jacket. He kept the pocket buttoned just in case.

The silks should have given Treylen some relief from the heat. But the assassin's darks layered underneath meant the silks gave little comfort. At least the boots were soft and the cape covered the bulge of his daggers.

A gold-embroidered pack held his assassin's boots along with a few other necessary supplies, and an unnecessary quantity of other silks, hats, and foppery that only a Stone Kingdom noble could appreciate. It was light, but after a day of walking on hard, dry soil, even silks began to feel like boulders to him.

"Don't you want to get down and look around a while?" he said to Rime. The dragon only squirmed deeper under the cape.

Nothing to eat but field mice.

"You love chasing field mice." He reached behind his back and seized Rime around the waist, dragging him out and dropping him to the road. "You need to stretch your legs."

You're just tired of carrying me, Rime hissed.

"I didn't want to carry you in the first place. How much longer do you figure it is?" Treylen brought a hand up to shield his eyes and squinted down the road toward Tabron. No buildings stood on the horizon. The road stretched on between trees and fields for the next mile or so, disappearing behind a low hill planted with wheat.

Why would I know? You're the one who's been this way.

"Dragon senses?"

Well, I don't sense anything, aside from too much sweat. Are you sour about your training?

"Not really. It's over now anyway."

Not over for good. You still have much to learn.

"I'm learning that. I'm sure there'll be plenty more training when we've finished in Tabron."

Do you miss them already?

"They weren't ready." Treylen kicked a stone down the road. He looked backward. A trail of dust rose along the road behind him, more than a single horse would make. "Someone's coming. Get in my pack."

The dust plume came closer, until Treylen caught sight of an enclosed carriage. As it drew near, Treylen stepped off the road. He stopped to inspect it as it passed.

It had two horses and a lone driver. The man was well dressed in gloves and boots, and he kept a large sword on the seat by his side. It was an enclosed wooden carriage, well built, but not ostentatious, with a simple red paint on the outside, and curtains covering the windows.

The driver gave him a suspicious look and lashed his horses as they passed, but a hand reached out to pull aside the curtain and another set of eyes watched him through the window.

Hail a ride, Rime pestered.

No, Treylen responded. *We'll have trouble enough when we get to the city. I want to keep to myself as long as I can.*

Treylen coughed in the dust and covered his face with the cloak as the carriage passed. It had only gone a little ways before the driver leaned over, turning his attention to the window. Words were exchanged and he nodded, drawing the carriage to a stop.

Stay quiet. Treylen hopped back onto the road and started toward the carriage.

"I'm sorry, milord, I didn't see you there." The driver was all smiles now.

"That's fine. I'm quite alright," Treylen said, pitching his voice up so he sounded more like a young noble. He was about to tell them to get on their way when the curtain opened and a young woman greeted him.

"I love your hat," she called down to him, flashing a pearly smile. Light hair hung loose beneath a jeweled headband, and painted fingernails gripped the edge of the window. She leaned out intently.

"Thank you, milady." Treylen swept the hat.

"Have you walked long?" Her grin widened as she took in the cloak and the pack on his back.

"Not long, milady. My horse threw me near Harvest Pass. Ran off, I'm afraid. I'm bound for Tabron."

"It's not far now," she said brightly. "You're Stone Kingdom?"

"So they tell me," Treylen said with a laugh. The clothing certainly saved him a lot of time explaining.

"Isn't that to the south?" she said. There wasn't any suspicion in it, only curiosity. Treylen heard a grunt from the driver, but when he looked up, the man was in his seat, eyes fixed on the road ahead of them. One of the horses whinnied.

"I come by way of the west road. Through the Salt Crescent. My uncle is a trader here; he's found a position for me in Tabron."

"The west road! Well, I must hear more about that."

"Milady"—the driver leaned to the side—"I'm to get you home."

"Yes," Treylen said. "Don't let me stop you, milady, I'm quite alright. You haven't run me over."

"Don't be silly. You'll ride with us the rest of the way."

"Your parents would not approve, milady," the driver grumbled.

"Don't worry about him, he's always this way. He won't lift a rein until I tell him. Besides, we're about to get some much-needed weather."

"Are we?" Treylen looked up. There were rain clouds

growing on the horizon, though it was still unseasonably hot and sunny here on the road.

The driver grumbled again but didn't contradict her. The door popped open, and a jumble of skirts spilled out before the lady gathered her dress and moved away from the opening.

Treylen cast a reluctant glance toward the driver, who scowled back at him. The sword that had been sheathed at his side now rested across his lap.

"If you insist." Treylen grabbed hold of the carriage frame and hauled himself up. It was bright inside, with tasseled fabric across the ceiling and plump cushions lining two wooden benches. Treylen settled in the front of the carriage, facing the lady.

A growl made him jump, and Treylen found the red-orange fur and bared teeth of a vulpine form perched on the seat behind him.

"Rexhus! No!" The fox's teeth sank into the fabric of Treylen's pack, and a faint hiss came from inside. The lady snatched the animal in both arms, holding it as it yipped and pawed at the air.

"I'm Pravaida, this is Rexhus." She dropped the fox on the seat beside her, then put a hand on its head to keep it in place. The fox's ears went back, but it settled down, never taking its eyes off Treylen's pack.

"Cren'pin Tromweft," Treylen said, borrowing his fake uncle's surname. It would not be unheard of for a young man in his position to take his mother's maiden name, especially if he were seeking a fresh start in a new town with the help of his Tromweft uncle. Also, Eelbucket was absurd.

The carriage lurched into motion and bounced along the hardpacked road. The young woman smiled, as if waiting for more. She wouldn't get it. At least not easily. Of all he'd learned at the inn, one thing that would stick with him the longest was the importance of keeping his mouth shut when others asked questions. Silence couldn't betray you. At least not any more than words could.

"Are you here alone, milord Cren'pin?" She tipped her head and leaned against the opposite window frame.

"I am," he said, smiling just enough to seem cordial and keep himself from being tossed out of the carriage, but not so much as to get himself drawn further into whatever designs this inquisitive noblewoman had.

"The Salt Crescent," she said. "I hear that it is quite beautiful."

"Hmm," Treylen nodded. "The west road was uneventful." He looked out the window and pretended to enjoy the view.

"Was it not remarkable? My mother says it's quite lovely." She kept one arm on top of the fox and stroked its nose. The creature's focus was centered entirely upon the bag, which Treylen had removed and tucked behind his feet. Inside, Rime was still, but Treylen could sense his excitement about the presence of the fox.

"It is quite lovely," he said, then thought that the best way to get to Tabron without running out of things to say was probably to keep his new companion talking about herself. "Tell me about yourself."

"Oh, there isn't much to tell," she said. "We oversee the farms just west of Harvest Pass. Grandfather says it was once the most dangerous holding in the empire, but…well, I don't know how much you know of life on the border. We have a lot of soldiers pass, but the Iverans haven't come this far out from their mountains since his time. It's not quite as exciting as it sounds. I might prefer the city."

Treylen nodded but didn't comment.

"Oh, you must tell me of the great cities. Are they really carved into the mountains?"

"I couldn't say," Treylen answered. "I'm from the coast.

I've never seen the stone cities. We have to watch out for the Ketaresk navy. I guess that would be the most excitement."

"It must be quite terrifying."

"It is," Treylen said, not really sure what life would be like for the people on the coast north of Ketaresk.

"Tell me of this uncle, Lord Cren'pin. Would I know him?"

"I think not," Treylen said. "He doesn't spend much time in the city."

"We don't either," Pravaida said. "Does he have land here?"

"No, I don't think so."

"You don't know?"

"He's a trader, he's back and forth."

"Surely he must have land somewhere." She looked at him critically. "Where is he putting you up?"

The fox lunged for the bag. Treylen caught it, but it bit him on the finger.

"Rexhus, don't do that."

Keep quiet, he thought toward Rime as he put his legs between the bag and the fox. It growled and worked to get around them.

"Come here, you rascal." She bent to pick the fox up at the same time as Rime decided to let out another warning hiss. She shot back into her seat.

Her eyes said everything. She knew that something was in the bag. She'd lost interest in his stories of the Stone King-dom. He should have done what he'd been trained to do and talked a bunch of arrogant nonsense to keep her from asking questions.

"What is in there anyway?" she asked.

"Nothing for foxes," Treylen said.

Before she could press further, there was a knock on the roof of the cart. The driver's voice called from the window.

"Soldiers in the road, milady."

Chapter Thirty-One

THE RIVER

"Oh." She pulled the curtain aside and stuck her head out the window, keeping one hand on the scruff of her pet. "It looks like we're being hailed."

Treylen leaned back in his seat, keeping away from the curtain. From her open window, he could see the tops of legionnaire helmets, but the individual who came up on horseback to lean into the window wasn't one of them.

He wore a pointed green woodsman's hat with a long feather in the brim. His long features were hidden by a wild and untrimmed beard that seemed out of character with the clean hat and the crisp green collar of his shirt. Treylen knew this man. Long, green hunter's gloves went halfway up his forearms. He rested his arm on the edge of the window as he leaned inside.

"Good day, milord ranger." The young woman pulled back from the window but didn't seem particularly frightened of the man.

"Good day." He looked around the inside of the carriage. The fox squirmed in her grasp. The opposite curtain was pulled open, and another ranger leaned inside, this one a woman. Treylen knew her as well. Stringy brown hair hung down on either side of her face, and the skin of her lips was sunburned and peeling, but her uniform was as crisp and well-maintained as the man's.

It meant that they had just come from a barracks, after spending the last week or so hunting the roads. They were supposed to be solitary. Not only were these two working together, now they had a retinue of soldiers at their command?

The driver had just finished relating to the rangers the location of their country manor, and which farms the family oversaw.

"Bound for Geldshare house in the garden district," he said.

"Mmmh." The woman looked at her companion across the carriage, then her eyes went to Treylen.

"And the Stone Kingdom man?"

"Picked him up just around the bend, milord ranger. Says his horse threw him and run off."

"Doesn't look like he's been thrown," she said, eyes roaming Treylen's outfit, before darting to the fox, who yipped at the bag behind Treylen's feet.

"Says it was back at Harvest Pass, milord ranger. He is bound for Tabron. Has an uncle there."

"He does look rather too clean," she said. "Does he look familiar to you?" she asked her partner, who nodded. "You were at the inn. Remind me, Lord. What is in Tabron for you?"

"My uncle is sending me there," Treylen said. "He's a merchant with a trading company that operates out of the city."

"Names?" the second ranger said. "Yours, his, and his company."

I have a bad feeling. Rime's thoughts echoed Treylen's own. He closed his eyes a moment and opened his thoughts to the dragonmind, pulling first upon dragon speed, just to give himself an extra moment to think while the world seemed to slow around him.

They know, Rime said.

They aren't certain, Treylen answered.

The small, musky one knows. He sniffed me out.

The fox isn't talking, Treylen said.

He knows. He will give us away.

What can I do, then?

We should kill them, Rime said.

That's always your answer.

Treylen opened his eyes once the flash from the dragon-mind had passed. The world around him moved just a little more slowly. The rangers stared at one another. One tilted her chin up to look at her companion, then she looked back over Treylen's outfit again.

Rime was right. His spycraft was useless here. They were already looking for someone. They were going to search him no matter what answers he gave them. Then they would find his daggers, and Rime.

Did he really want to give his fake uncle's name first before the fighting started? It was better to get it over with now, before he gave them any more information that would cast suspicion on the Dragon's Hide.

Alright. We'll do it your way.

Treylen drew on more dragon speed, as the look on the face of the ranger slowly shifted from impatience to suspicion.

Don't hurt the lady or the driver, he said.

Which of the rangers shall we kill first?

We're just getting out and into the woods, Treylen thought. *They were kind enough to give us a ride. I'm not killing anyone in front of them if I don't have to.*

I don't see why not, Rime said. *Don't you want to see if you can do it?*

Not particularly.

Treylen turned his head to look at the male ranger and

watched as his expression shifted. He'd moved too quickly, and he had seen his unnatural speed. The look spreading across the ranger's face told him everything.

If they didn't know before, they do now. You go left. He ripped open his pack and Rime shot out toward the ranger who'd leaned into the carriage. Pravaida grabbed her fox and scrambled back as Rime flew past onto the face of the ranger, who tumbled from his horse. The other ranger had started to draw her axe when Treylen kicked. She also tumbled, the soldiers behind her catching her.

"Thanks for the ride," Treylen muttered as he gripped the door of the carriage and swung out the window onto the roof. He rolled and was starting to get up when he saw the flash of metal, and the broadsword belonging to the driver came down on him. He rolled again and narrowly avoided it.

He was reaching into the bag for his daggers when an axe sank into the roof beside him, and the ranger used it to pull herself up. Still holding on to dragon speed, Treylen planted a foot on the ranger's neck and sent her tumbling to the road.

"Sestus!" The male ranger pulled a new weapon from his belt. It was a hatchet like the others, but it looked newly made. Power seeped into the glyphs. A chain of aeris and crotus glyphs funneled the energy into a whirlpool that blurred the air around the ranger. As the spell finished, the man threw himself onto the carriage. He no longer seemed sluggish in comparison to Treylen's dragon speed. He swung his hatchet for Treylen's legs, and it was all that Treylen could do to back away and get clear. He found himself at the front of the carriage again and gave the driver a mule kick before the man could impale him with the broadsword.

Duck! Rime's voice echoed in his head. Treylen flattened himself against the carriage top just as an arrow flew past. Three more of the legionnaires were leveling crossbows at him as Rime landed on his shoulder.

"To the trees," Treylen said. He leaped from the top of the carriage and over the soldiers' heads to land in the wheat field.

The male ranger was already sprinting toward him. Back on the road, his partner drew a dagger from her belt, shouting, "Sestus!"

Treylen didn't wait to see if the spell would work. He ran. Rime wrapped his body around Treylen's neck.

He's keeping pace with you.

"I know," Treylen grunted. Glancing over his shoulder, he could see the ranger not far behind. He pulled on more dragon strength and pumped his legs, dashing through the chest-high wheat field.

The soldiers are slow. But they're coming as well.

"I know."

You might as well kill them.

"Not yet," Treylen said. "Too many. Which way should I go?"

I'll see. Rime took to the air. His flight was clumsy, and he wavered for a moment before landing on Treylen's shoulder again.

River is to the right. Forest there.

"That's it, then."

I don't think you can hide from rangers in the woods.

"I just want to separate them," Treylen panted.

The soldiers have already fallen behind. They're wearing too much armor. But there's four on horseback. And those are gaining.

Treylen gasped for breath. *I'm not worried about the legionnaires. Just these two. Did you see their magic?*

They are still using it. You're too slow. He's about to catch you.

Treylen pulled the daggers from his pack. He slashed at the tall wheat in front of him. He didn't have time to judge the strength of the fire energy around him. He would have to hope that the chaff of the wheat and the relentless heat of the midday sun was enough to take a spark.

"Flavus!" Small embers spread out around him as he

carved a second glyph, cutting the shape of it into the dust that filled the air.

"Aeris!" Wind blasted outward, feeding the flames and setting the field ablaze. The ranger shielded his eyes and fell back.

It wouldn't blow for long, but it was just enough. Treylen could see the trees now. He bolted toward the edge of the field as the wheat behind him blazed.

Is he still coming? Treylen thought.

He's stalled, Rime answered, *but the other has leaped over. The horses are looking for a way around.*

That's okay. We'll make it to the woods.

Treylen reached the trees just as the horses came back into sight. It wasn't the soldiers he was worried about, though. He would lose them the second he entered the forest. The rangers, however, might be at an advantage here. Losing sight of them now might only give them more time to catch him by surprise. No, he needed to confront them and end it. But not before they had gained some ground between them and the soldiers. If he were lucky, he might even be able to separate the two or draw the chase out long enough that the spell which granted them their speed dissipated. But there was no way to know how long that would be. The glyph chains they had used were unlike anything he'd seen before. But, like the weapons that the Jaul had used at the Harvest Pass, it was something that should not exist.

Are you watching the rangers? he asked Rime.

I'll trail them. Rime leaped into the first tree as Treylen fought his way through the thick undergrowth at the edge of the forest.

Just don't let them see you.

They won't.

Rime's colors shifted and he disappeared into the canopy overhead. Treylen followed the slope of the land downhill until it intersected a game trail, then raced along it.

They've reached the forest. They're together.

That's no good, Treylen said, moving faster. If he couldn't split them up, then he needed to create more distance and find a place to set an ambush.

The game trail split in two, one path heading toward the river, the other moving straight ahead. If he left tracks here, they would know in an instant which way he had gone. But if he didn't, they might split up. Carefully, Treylen stepped off the path, tiptoeing behind a bush and doing his best not to disturb the thick underbrush.

Are they moving quickly? he asked.

They have found the trail now.

He didn't have much time, then. Crawling to a fallen tree, he tucked himself underneath it. Leaves and thick bushes surrounded him. The bird in his jacket let out a muffled squawk, Treylen slipped a hand into his pocket to run a finger over the bird's feathers.

"There now, I'm not going to crush you," he whispered, hoping that it was the truth. Then he sent a thought to Rime.

Tell me their movements.

They are still on your trail, Rime said. *They're getting closer to the river. There's a fork in the path. They don't know which way you were going.*

That's what I was hoping, Treylen thought, holding his breath.

They're parting ways. One going up, the other going down.

Perfect. Treylen loosed one of his daggers.

Which one should I follow? Rime asked.

Whichever one goes toward the river. Once they've passed me, I'll slip out and attack the upper path. It'll take longer for help to come.

They're moving very slowly, Rime said. *I don't know why.*

It's because they don't see my tracks.

Bondmate, I think they know. She's looking at something on the side of the trail.

Damn.

The ranger whistled, then Treylen heard a crack as she muscled through the undergrowth. From up above, he could hear the second ranger charging into the brush. They were converging on him.

What now?

He could wait and hope they didn't see him, maybe take them by surprise when they got close. If they saw him first and he was on his back, they would have him at a disadvantage.

It's time, he said to Rime, then rolled from his hiding place and drew his second dagger. The ranger was four paces to his left. Her partner was ten paces uphill and to the right. She threw a hatchet the moment he appeared. The blurring energy of the spell she had cast was still swirling around her.

Treylen closed the distance first, lunged with his dagger, then backpedaled as she drew an arming sword and parried him in a flash. Her off hand still held the glyph-marked dagger that granted her speed, and she used it to block his own and open him up for another thrust from the sword.

At the same moment, Treylen caught sight of Rime racing through the canopy.

Stay back! These are hunters.

Rime didn't listen. He streaked down from the trees, colliding with the ranger and sinking his teeth into the back of her neck, tearing out a small strip of flesh. She lashed out with her sword, but he had already sprung away and disappeared into the brush. Treylen took that moment to slash at the ranger's off hand. The thick hunting gloves spared her fingers, but the swirling energy around her dissipated as the glyph-marked dagger fell from her hand.

Treylen was about to go in for the kill when Rime shouted.

Look out!

He rolled as the second ranger came up behind him, chopping with the hatchet. The first ranger had already recovered and came at him again, still moving almost as quickly as she had with magic. It was all he could do to roll backward, finally getting to his feet.

They gripped their weapons, circling.

Treylen slashed at each of them in turn, like a cornered animal—keeping both at bay for a moment. It felt oddly similar to what Marziel had trained him for. He had been preparing him for this. The moment he would be up against enemies of such training that he was evenly matched, and couldn't get away.

Trained or not, he didn't like it. This was a fair fight.

There had to be a better way than fighting fair.

I'm getting out.

Sparing a quick glance to make sure Rime wasn't leaping into the fray, he drew as much dragon strength as he could, bent his legs, and launched himself upward and back toward the trunk of the nearest tree. Both rangers lunged, but he was just fast enough that their blades missed his heels. Colliding with the tree, he kicked off and landed on a branch overhead. Then he swung, rolled to the ground, and began to run.

Treylen raced downhill. He burst out onto the game trail and ran down it toward the water—just as Volanti had that night he'd caught her in a snare back at Coops Abbey. There wouldn't be any traps here, would there? These were rangers, after all. Who knew where they might have been before they set up the roadblock?

Rime glided out from the canopy and landed hard on his shoulder.

They're right behind you.

Thanks. Now, I need your sight. All of it.

Treylen gave the warning, then drew on as much dragon sight as he could. In the daytime, drawing upon that much dragon sight made his head spin. The colors became sickeningly bright, and trails of life magic wriggled through the air. Only the slightest distortion showed the snare laid out across the path.

He avoided three in succession.

I got lucky.

Treylen raced onward. The strain of using dragon sight at the same time as he used speed and strength to keep ahead of his pursuers was wearing on him. They were gaining ground.

You're going to have to fight.

I know, Treylen said. *I'm just looking for my advantage.*

Then he saw it. At first, he thought that it was the mark of an axe on a tree, and he eyed it warily. As he drew closer, he realized it was something different.

"Stay with me," Treylen said, dropping most of the dragon sight so that Rime could see, then cutting into the forest beside the trail. It was thicker near the water's edge. But running up the length of a fallen tree let him get clear.

Treylen followed the sound of running water, bursting out onto a stony riverbank. He dashed into it, hoping to the queen that he didn't land in quicksand again. The riverbed was hard, and he slipped, falling into the knee-deep water, before getting his footing.

A large rock sat in the middle of the river…the perfect place for a giant otter to sun itself. If he was right, and the markings on the tree had been from otter claws, he would have to hope they wouldn't come out until after he'd crossed. Treylen grabbed the rock, just as the pair of rangers splashed down behind him. One charged ahead, swimming toward him. Her partner stopped, drew a strap of leather from his belt, and loaded a stone into it.

The water swirled beside him. No time to think about the sling.

"Sorry for this." Treylen put a hand over the lump in his jacket where the bird was tucked away. He took a half step, then threw himself as far as he could toward the other bank of the river.

The stone struck the back of his head, and everything

went dark for a moment. Then he came to, sputtering and pushing himself onto the far bank.

There was a terrible yell behind him.

Move! Rime shouted into his thoughts and hissed from up the bank. Treylen's arms moved, dragging him up the rocks. Rime guided him to a low-hanging branch, which he gripped, and hauled himself up and over the bank. A damp squawk came from within his jacket.

Looking back, he caught a glimpse of swirling red water and a single feathered ranger's hat floating down the river.

Move! Rime hissed again, landing on his shoulder and lashing out to bite him on the back of the head.

Treylen yelped but sprang into action. He could hear them growling, their claws dislodging rocks as they scrabbled up the riverbank.

He raced through the woods west of the river.

The details of the chase grew fuzzy. He remembered leaves and branches, scrapes and stumbles. He remembered Rime shouting, biting, scratching at him to keep him moving. Always behind him were the grunting, bleating sounds of bloodthirsty boatsnatchers.

Treylen wasn't sure when they'd stopped following him. He wasn't sure how long he'd run or how much time he'd spent wedged beneath the rotten stump of a burned-out tree until his senses returned.

He stared up through the hollow trunk and watched the clouds roll in and rain begin to fall, wondering what had caused this tree to die in the first place and why the inside was charred as if it had been burned away. Maybe it had been struck by lightning years ago or hollowed out by blight, and the char had come from some long-ago traveler who'd build a campfire inside.

The unseasonable heat disappeared, and a chill crept back into the air with the rain. A campfire might not have been such a bad idea—if he could force himself to sit up. He stared at the circle of sky overhead, wiggling his toes in the wet leather boots. Without looking himself over, he counted the number of scrapes he'd received, trying to guess their severity by how much they throbbed. It was too early yet to move his head. He feared that if he did, he would lose his stomach and what little he had eaten that morning.

Every so often, a plume of smoke drifted overhead, and Treylen wondered if the fire he'd set in the field was still burning and whether the rain would put it out.

Are you back with me? Rime asked, perching on his chest, and sniffing at a wound on his neck. He started to send a thought in return, but decided that might make his head hurt even worse.

"The rangers?" Treylen groaned.

I saw them both go under, Rime said. *They did not come up.*

"They might still be out there." He groaned again, then started to raise his head before dropping it down when the world seemed to lurch to the side.

Don't move, bondmate. You took a head wound.

"The otters…We have to go…"

They've had their fun, bondmate.

"You're sure?"

It hardly matters. You aren't fit to walk anywhere yet.

"But we have to." He felt himself over. He was uninjured. So too—surprisingly—was the bird in his pocket. It let out a soft coo as he fumbled with it.

I am watching, bondmate, Rime said, hopping from his chest, then slipping off into the forest. *You must sleep. I will wake you if anyone approaches.*

I can't sleep. Treylen forced the thought out to Rime. *It's dangerous to sleep.*

You have already been asleep and awake, bondmate.

Don't let me sleep again, Rime. I'm serious.

Even as he said it, Treylen felt a weariness pass over him, his eyes drifting closed. Then a pain shot through his hand,

and he jolted awake. Looking down, he saw Rime gnawing on his finger.

"Thanks," he said, pulling his hand away.

Happy to help. Rime licked the blood from his fangs, then scampered off into the trees again.

Please don't tell Volanti about this.

No answer to that. Treylen turned his eyes back to the circle of sky and focused on what he would do next. The disappearance of two rangers and the noblewoman's story of a traveler from the Stone Kingdom who turned out to be an assassin were a snag in his plans.

Each mistake that he had made would make the task of blending in within Tabron and searching for the scribe more impossible than before. There was one consolation, however. The damage had already been done. Even if he wanted to, Treylen was in no condition to chase down the carriage and round up every soldier that had seen him.

Any hope he'd had of playing Cren'pin and entering the city that way was gone. And that was something of a relief. There was still his second identity. He could enter the city in the guise of Trogan the drifter, then roam the streets looking for Rebash and his wagons—however many of them had got their oxen back and finished the journey. Or he could go back to his old ways. His first plan had always been to sneak in and hunt Norris under the cover of darkness.

With little knowledge of the city and few clues on where to start, skulking in the shadows was unlikely to yield the information he sought. But the opportunity to give up on this foolish spycraft and fall back to his more reliable talents was a tempting proposition.

He wished that Aaron and Volanti were with him.

He had lay there half a day, waiting for his head to stop aching, keeping himself awake by planning his next move and worrying how little he knew of what the future had in store, when he heard the horse approaching.

Chapter Thirty-Two

THE NOBLEWOMAN

TREYLEN HEARD THE HORSE COMING LONG BEFORE IT REACHED him, slow and deliberate hooves crunching on the forest floor as it wound its way down the side of one slope and up another, before turning and ambling around the bushes that hid the base of the hollowed-out tree that was his hiding place.

His head still throbbed, but he could sit upright, then move to a standing position inside the tree. Bracing hands and feet on either side, he shimmied up so his feet couldn't be seen in the hole at the bottom.

What's out there?

He hadn't heard from Rime in a while. The dragon should have let him know that somebody was coming. Had the rangers' traps got him? No, Treylen would have felt it.

Hoping that the rotten bark of the tree was enough to hold him, he shimmied higher until he reached a notch to peer out from. The walls of the tree flexed little when he pressed on them. If he tried to go any higher, his arms might pop out the side like a surcoat, and he'd be stuck up there, a sitting pigeon. Any sudden movement and the thing might snap, and he would go tumbling down.

A long-haired girl in a beautiful emerald gown of silk and spun silver rode aside an elegantly barded chestnut mare. The horse whinnied as it picked its way into the thicket, and she leaned forward in her saddle to pat the animal on its flank.

She was unarmed, not properly dressed to be in a forest, and about the least threatening thing he had expected to encounter. Treylen was about to come out and ask her who she was and what she was doing so deep in these woods with their otters and other dangers, when another horse appeared behind her. The hair on the back of Treylen's neck stood on end and a chill ran through him.

The second rider and his horse moved like a ghost, soundlessly across the litter of the forest floor. A third and a fourth glided swiftly after him, joining the woman as she pushed through the brambles. Their small, elegant horses barely rustled the brush as they picked their way leisurely along.

The first one was a man, lanky and middle-aged with fine, white hair. The other two were also slight of build and wore helmets made from a pattern of silver buttons stitched onto soft leather.

Unlike the woman, the man had pointed ears, and for a moment, Treylen thought they were Iveran, and his heart leaped at the idea of Iveran soldiers riding freely through Lome once again. But the silver-spangled leather that they wore was unlike any Iveran uniform that he'd ever seen. And there was something wrong with the ears. They weren't just pointed, they were long, almost unnaturally so.

Once they were through the brush, they split off from the woman to circle the hollow tree.

Stopping just before his hiding place, the woman's horse whinnied and turned about. The rider looked from the opening at the base to the top, where Treylen kept one eye pressed against the crack and watched.

She stared right at him, then let out a bright laugh, like the chime of a wineglass. She hopped to the ground and tied her horse's reins off to a bush nearby.

"Come out now, cousin. You aren't fooling anybody."

Treylen stayed completely still, not so much as blinking. The woman crossed her arms and tossed her hair.

I don't think that you have to worry, Rime said.

Where have you been? Treylen didn't try to hide his irritation.

I've been watching.

Treylen rested his head against the inside of the tree. What was the point of having a lookout if the lookout never warned him?

He loosened his grip and slid down the inside of the old tree, landing in the ash at the bottom. He drew his dagger before kneeling to squeeze out of the hiding place. He rolled out, sprang to his feet, and almost fell on his face again as the forest seemed to lurch and his balance went out. The noblewoman lunged to catch him by the arms and Treylen instinctively raised the dagger as close to her throat as he dared.

"Don't be a brat, cousin. I'm here to help you." There was a twinkle in her eye as a sly grin crossed her face.

"Apogee?" he whispered, eyes darting to the riders who'd completed their circuit of the small clearing and waited a respectful distance from the two of them.

He looked back to her again, eyes searching. That was right, this was the disguise she'd worn on the night of lights, but it was even more complete now. Her face was unrecognizable: sharp features, long cheekbones, and a bit of rouge. She looked almost too slender in the silk dress to be the woman that he knew. No, it couldn't be.

"Don't tell me you don't remember your cousin, Pouline." She laughed. "But you can speak freely around the elves. They know who I am. And they wouldn't understand you anyway."

"Elves?"

The man dismounted and extended a hand toward him.

Treylen gripped it, marveling at the man as he got closer. He looked just like an Iveran, except longer, leaner, and of course, there were those ears...The man spoke a greeting in a language he didn't understand. The words were like music. What had at first seemed to be almost formal armor was indeed a supple leather patched with bits of finely tooled metal.

"How did you find me?" Treylen asked.

"My friends here saw your confrontation on the road and sent for me. It just so happened I was working nearby. I would have been here sooner, but we had to clean up some of the mess you made."

The man turned and spoke a few words to Apogee, who smiled and gave a graceful curtsey. Then he mounted his horse and the three of them rode off without a sound. They weren't a stone's throw away before they passed behind a copse of smaller trees and disappeared entirely. Treylen squinted through the forest but couldn't find them again.

There was a chattering noise as Rime sprang out of the bushes and raced to greet the fair noblewoman, nipping at her hand before perching on her arm to inspect her.

"I wouldn't have recognized you."

"Who else could I be? Marziel?" She beamed at him with that uncharacteristic smile.

"Please, will you drop it?"

"If you wish."

She wiped the rouge on the back of her hand and gave the hair a slight tug. Her wig came loose to reveal her own hair tucked into a bun atop her head. Reaching back, she snapped a clasp beneath the dress and sighed as whatever artifice she had been using to correct her posture relaxed. She even grew taller and broader, her sloped shoulders squaring off. She looked ungainly and ill-suited to such a bright and flowing sheet of silk. Finally, she reached up and pulled the top of her nose off—it was a lump of putty, painted with powder to match her complexion—rolling it between her fingers, then tossing it away.

"Better?" All but the faintest trace of cheer was gone from her voice. That was the Apogee he knew. Treylen nodded, though even the woods around them seemed to dim with the shift in her.

"Pouline is Mauridin's estranged daughter. We don't care much for each other, but that's no reason she and Cren'pin shouldn't get along."

He nodded, storing the information away for later. "What are you doing here?"

"I could ask the same of you."

"You first." Treylen realized that he was still holding the dagger in one hand. He put it back in its holder.

"I was working to keep the local rangers distracted and away from the tavern," she said matter-of-factly. "You make quite a stir wherever you go."

"You know, Marziel would like for you to check in with him. Who were they?" He pointed to the place the riders had disappeared.

"Just friends." She shrugged like it was nothing to prance around the forest with elves in tow. Treylen had to wonder just how many other Iveran tall tales and ghost stories were commonplace here on the other side of the mountains.

"You have strange friends," he said.

She stared after them into the forest, sighing. "When things went bad on my last mission, I couldn't come back right away."

"Yeah?" Treylen said. He wanted to confront her about what he had learned from Marziel and the queen's accountant. He was angry at her for lying, even if he was sympathetic to the loss of her bondmate. But he wouldn't let on that he knew any of that just yet. First, he would see just how much she was willing to give away.

"I had nowhere to go. I remembered Marziel told me that

he used to spend time in the mountains between Jaul and Oara Valley, when he was younger and still went on missions. It sounded like a nice place to hide out for a while."

"You skipped out on your duties?" He was dangerously close to the truth now.

"I suppose. But I was in a difficult position. I was troubled, and I was wounded. The elves were kind enough to take me in. There are more of them in the forests near Jaul. But now that they know me, I can find them most anywhere. They have been good friends ever since, and a good help, wherever I go."

"Does Marziel know about these friends of yours?"

"Come on. We're going. There are still soldiers out here looking for you." She lifted Rime from her shoulder and placed him on Treylen, then bent over and looked in the hollow tree. "What are you doing hiding in here anyhow?"

"I was resting my head." Treylen rubbed it and held his palm out to show her the blood caked in his hair. "Marziel kicked me out without a horse. There were rangers looking for me."

"I noticed." She paced around, inspecting.

"I guess I drew too much attention."

"At least he taught you a thing or two first." She pointed to a flowering Queensberry bush that grew beside the tree.

"I guess he did." Or maybe Rime had spotted it. It was all sort of a stew in his head.

"Usually, they're better hidden than this. It may be that there's a cave nearby with provisions and the tree's just a decoy." Apogee peered around at the forest floor, and the tree once again, then shrugged and walked over to her horse.

"Get up on the back." She spread her feet and bent her knees to stoop over, then held her hands out, fingers interlocked to provide a step for him. It was a preposterous pose to strike in a gown like that.

"I'm riding?"

Apogee nodded.

"I can get myself up." He took a step toward the horse, then faltered, catching himself on the animal. Apogee raised one sharply painted eyebrow and waited.

"Fine." He placed a foot in her hands so she could boost him up, and sat on a pillow just behind the saddle. There was not much padding, but he was in no state to argue. Rime leaped from his shoulder onto the horse's back.

"No!" Treylen tensed, expecting the mare to spook and buck him off. But she only tossed her head, then ignored the creature perched on her.

You can't just jump on the horses like that, he scolded Rime privately.

It doesn't seem to mind me.

"This is a good horse," Treylen said.

"It will take more than a dragon to startle Frewa."

Apogee untied the reins and led the horse out of the thicket before mounting up herself.

"This is your horse?"

"It is," she said, settling into her seat and leaning over to put the wig and some of the jewelry into her saddlebag.

"This horse wasn't in the stables."

"No, she wasn't." She kept her focus on the forest, as if the soldiers that were hunting him were closer than she had first let on.

"But this is your horse. Obviously."

"She knows me."

He could tell from the way she said it he wasn't getting further answers about where the horse had come from. They rode down the hillside and down a winding trail in the same direction as the river. Every so often, he thought he spotted someone through the trees, but even with dragon sight, he couldn't discern whether they were being followed.

"Where have you been all this time?"

"He didn't tell you?" she asked.

They followed the river just a ways before another shallow

place appeared. They were much farther south than where he'd encountered the otters and there hadn't been any scratchings here.

Still, he was nervous.

"He told me you were off leaving trails to lead the rangers astray. But that was…days ago."

"And it had been working until you went and bumped into them again."

When he thought about it, that was probably true. They had left the inn without bothering to track down his alter ego to question him and hadn't returned. Ranger Thorn had done the same. "I've never seen an elf before."

"Most people haven't. They aren't in Iverna." She scanned the water before urging the horse across.

"But they're here?" Treylen asked. He had to pull his feet up to keep them dry. The horse did not seem to mind. The water here was flowing slowly, and the deepest spot was passed quickly enough. "I thought all the elven kingdoms disappeared a long time ago."

"Disappeared?" She looked back over her shoulder, like Treylen had just made a poor joke. "Iverna never disappeared, did we?"

"We aren't an elven kingdom."

"Maybe not anymore. But the kingdom never fell. It just became more human. We're what's left of the elven kingdom, we just aren't that elven anymore."

"How's that even possible?"

She looked back again, rolled her eyes. "If you don't know how children are made, I'm not about to tell you…"

"But what about the ones with you? Where did they come from?"

"They live in the forest." She said it as if that was all he needed to know. The horse made it up the opposite bank out of the river and into the woods again. There was no trail, but she seemed confident in where she was going and the horse picked its way through the woods as if it had grown up in them. They were moving southeast now. Toward Tabron, it seemed.

"What do you mean the elves live in the forest? All forests? I've never seen them."

"There aren't enough trees left in Iverna. Anywhere there's a decent-sized forest, you'll have elves. They don't have a kingdom anymore. At least not since Jaul took Oara Valley as his hunting ground. There was something like a kingdom there, but the emperor wanted it, so the elves moved."

"He conquered them?"

"I'm not sure conquered is the right word. He has never been able to find them long enough to wage war. Even when they live within his own lands. Even his rangers leave the elves to their own."

"So they're on our side?"

She sighed and leaned forward in the saddle, resting her arms on the back of the horse, scratching at Rime with her forefinger. "I'm not sure they realize there are sides to be taken. I get along with them well enough. They are stubborn in their ways, and wary of showing themselves. But one of these days, I will convince them they are a force to be reckoned with."

"You're telling me that elves are everywhere, but Jaul can't find them?"

"They aren't everywhere, but they're always somewhere."

"Is that where we are going? Where are you taking me? Why are you even here? Does Marziel know?"

She groaned and sat up in the saddle again, reaching back to pull one of his eyelids up and stare at his pupil. "You're talking a lot. That can be a symptom of an injury to the head."

He crossed his arms to pout and nearly fell off the saddle before catching himself. Maybe he *was* talking too much.

"Does he know you're here?" he asked again.

"I think he would like for me to stay away awhile. I think you know why, now."

He had a pretty good idea now. She thought she could just show up here without answering any questions. But perhaps she was right about the head injury. Just thinking about it made his stomach tense again, and the trees around him seemed to swirl. He was about to ask if they could stop so he could run behind a bush for a moment, when the trees opened up and they were on a hillside overlooking a broad vista of wooded hills and rutted wheat fields. Beyond that were the drab stone walls, central barracks, and sprawling outer village of the city of Tabron.

"This is where you wanted to go, isn't it?"

"Yes." Treylen nodded. Rime hopped off and disappeared into the trees to look around.

"What does the queen have you doing here?"

"I'd rather not get my throat cut for telling you that."

"You spoke with the accountant who came the night I left?" Apogee turned to look at him again as the horse kept walking. Her expression was unreadable.

"I did."

"And we're both still alive."

"I guess so."

"So what's one more secret? Tell me what you're here to do. I'm not ready to go back to Marziel yet. Maybe I can stay and help you."

Chapter Thirty-Three

THE TOWER

TREYLEN KEPT HIS MOUTH SHUT. THEY RODE ALONG THE hillside, circling the city to get a better vantage. He wouldn't turn down the ride, not in his present condition. But he had made enough mistakes lately. He was in no hurry to add another by trusting the queen's secrets to this deserter.

After they had ridden for a while, the ruins of an old tower appeared on the wooded hillside, overlooking some of the fields that separated the forest from the city.

"What is this?"

"I thought that you could use a base of operations that was outside the city. We both know you aren't good enough at blending in to do it Marziel's way." She slipped off her horse and helped Treylen down.

"I'll have you know I've gotten much better at spycraft. It's Aaron and Volanti who haven't quite grasped it." He sighed. "I still wish they could have come."

"You've got me now."

"Why are you helping me with this?" he asked, once he'd gotten off the horse and steadied himself.

"Why shouldn't I?"

Leading them into the trees behind the tower, Apogee

found a place with some grass to tie her horse, then Treylen helped to unsaddle and brush it down while she got a bit of grain into a feed bag, as well as a bit of dried meat for Rime.

What did you see? Treylen asked when the dragon dropped down from a branch overhead.

It is empty for now. Somebody was camping inside.

"Marziel told me you were a deserter," Treylen said to Apogee.

He had expected a reaction, but she didn't give anything away. She only bent down to check her horse's hooves, focusing on the work.

"I don't believe he would've put it like that. He knows what happened to me. He's helping me to get back into the queen's service."

"By lying to her. What do you think you can do? She won't just take you back. You need to get away from here."

"You sound like Marziel," she deadpanned.

"I'm serious. What plan could you possibly have?"

"I'm just trying to get past what happened to Snarefoot. I don't have a plan for getting back into the queen's good graces."

"Her graces? Queen's shadow, she wants you dead. She'd want me dead if she knew I was talking to you."

"One thing at a time. Should we go in?"

There was no roof, just thick, circular stone walls that ended twenty feet up. At first, he had thought that it was collapsed, but looking closer, it seemed more like it was unfinished. There was no rubble, and any scaffolding that would have been inside had long ago rotted away.

"What was this place supposed to be?"

Apogee shrugged. "A lookout tower, I guess. It's not near the road so it's not guarding anything. Maybe a signal tower."

"I wonder why it was never finished."

"Must have been early in the war," she said. "We've held

Harvest Pass for so long, the people here barely remember the fighting."

"Except for the skirmishes at the crossroads." Treylen had reached the back corner of the tower when he encountered a small fire pit and a tarp stretched over an alcove to keep the rain off. An old, rusted axe leaned against the wall.

"Is this where you been staying?" He looked back at her and she shook her head.

"This is a ranger's den. Don't worry. I think the otters got this one."

"So you want me to move into it?"

"Do you really think you would fare better trying to blend in around Tabron?" she asked.

"Are you sure no one will come here?"

"I'm sure they will eventually. Just as the two who came after you were looking for your friend, there will be two rangers whose territories overlap with each of theirs, and those four will come looking for them. And on and on it goes. It almost makes you feel foolish the way we work alone."

"I have Rime looking out for me."

Apogee frowned, her gaze going distant. He knew she must be thinking of Snarefoot.

"Sorry."

"Anyway," she said, "you'll be gone before they come looking here. If you let me help you."

Treylen narrowed his eyes at her. It was hard to look stern with his head still pounding.

You might as well, Rime said. *Can't make any more trouble than she has already.*

Dirt rained on his head as Rime scrabbled along the top of the wall, exploring the tower. There was something familiar about its construction, beyond just his familiarity with the methods. Rough edges aside, this was almost Iveran in nature. He stepped out from under the tarp and joined her in the center again. Leaves littered the old stone floor, crunching underfoot.

"You can come along," Treylen said. "But I'm not telling you anything."

"I've done more with less." She unpinned her hair and shook it out before tying it back. "Will you at least tell me what we're looking for?"

"I'm looking for the wagons that belong to Marziel's friend, Rebash. You remember him?"

The scowl on her face was answer enough.

"That's all?" she asked.

"That's all I can tell you. But you can come if you want."

She sighed, then nodded.

"You have no idea what you're getting into. Of course I'm coming." She stepped up to the wall and peered out of an opening overlooking the fields leading up to the city. "When do you need to start?"

"We need to go now," he said. "Once they've unloaded the wagons, it'll be too late."

"That's good." She pulled her head back into the tower, then turned to look up at the trees, where the sun had already begun to set, a smile creeping across her face. "If Rebash is who you want, I think I know where to look for him. You can leave your disguise behind. Get your darks on. Marziel's good at what he does, but we're going to do this how Bos would have done it."

Chapter Thirty-Four

THE SEARCH

WHILE THE WALLS OF THE CITY OF TABRON DID RESEMBLE THE one he had practiced on in the attic of the Dragon's Hide, Apogee assured him there was no need to look for a Ferrick door. They weren't guarded heavily since the city extended out from the walls. Still, the gates were closed each night.

They had waited until the last rays of the sun cast an orange gloom over the drab, wood-shingled rooftops before setting out. Before they had left for the city, he had made a small cage for the pigeon out of piled stones, hidden in the corner. Apogee had asked about it, but he wasn't going to tell her any more than she knew already. Their silk cloaks covered their darks as they emerged from the forest and headed down a winding shepherds' path that led through the fields to the outskirts.

Rime had tried to run off on his own, but Apogee snatched him up and tucked him into Treylen's jacket.

"He can scout around," Treylen had said.

"Would either of you know a spycatcher if you saw them? Can Rime tell the difference between a pigeon's nest and a dragon-snare? Stay behind me and don't wander off."

Small, clustered buildings soon gave way to muddy streets

and modest hovels. It was not unlike the small town of Signet Lake that he had visited when he was living at Coops Abbey.

The dirt streets gave way to cobblestones, and the cottages gave way to clustered homes built side-by-side. By the time that they had reached the wall that separated the center city from the outer sprawl, there were rows of houses and various shops shuttered for the night.

At times, they would pass a street or alley and would catch sight of lit lanterns and throngs of people, but the section that she had taken him through was sleepy, residential, and mostly empty this time of night. There were more guards on the streets than he'd seen in the daytime, but here again, Apogee showed her expertise, always pulling him into alleys or turning down a side street well before they crossed paths with any of these.

The last alley dead-ended at the city wall. Treylen approached the wall and felt along it for a climbing hold. Apogee's hand on his shoulder bade him stop and look back. She shook her head, then reached out to push Rime's head back into Treylen's jacket and button it up.

"Not yet."

She walked up to a house and knocked, then pulled a marker like the one Captain Greythorn had given Treylen from her jacket and slid it under the gap in the door.

A moment passed. The light of a candle shone underneath. There was a click as the door was unlatched. The light disappeared.

"Why did the general say we didn't have people in Tabron?" Treylen asked.

"We have people all over," said Apogee, stepping up to the door and trying the handle. It opened. The hall inside was dark. "But not enough like you and me."

She ducked inside. Treylen followed after. He had expected to see somebody, but the first floor of the house was empty.

She moved to the back of the house and into a kitchen. Beside the pantry was a white marble countertop flecked with blue—the queen's colors. She pushed it aside to reveal a hole leading into the city wall. She knelt and crawled through the stone tunnel. Reaching the other side, she pushed another counter out of the way. Treylen followed and they emerged in the kitchen of another house, presumably on the opposite side of the city wall.

He slipped the counter back into place, then followed her up two flights of stairs into a small study. She paused to grab a bag from the corner, pulling out a four-pronged hook with a length of rope attached, as well as a pair of metal claws like the ones that Marziel had used to run up the side of the tree on the night they had fought in the forest.

Watching her strap them on one side of her boots, Treylen pulled out his spikes and did the same.

They tucked their cloaks away. He had been waiting by the door, but they weren't going back downstairs. Instead, Apogee went to the window and threw it open.

The streets below were narrower. Three, sometimes four-story buildings lined either side, with their upper floors built outward so that they leaned over the street below, nearly touching the upper floors of the buildings opposite.

This was similar to the buildings within the walls of Lakehold, the largest city in Iverna. The wealthy wanted to live as close to the center of their city as possible, but there was only so much room within the walls, and no matter how great their wealth became, there was nowhere to build except up. Of course, where Tabron had three and four stories, the great houses of Lakehold were five or six, each upper story larger than the last. And down below, the cellars, too, were expanded, just like the cellars of the Dragon's Hide, to hold investments in wine and liquor. As the wealth of the homeowners grew, the basements were dug deeper.

There was the neglect of age to the wood-shingled buildings here. As important as this land was to the Jaul empire, the farmers and merchants who traded their goods never earned quite so well as when they had fed the great country of Iverna. They were forced to sell their food to the Jaul armies and the other states within the empire at whatever price Emperor Jaul told them to.

"Are you ready?" She slipped her dragon mask over her face and Treylen did the same. Then she tossed the hook, and it caught on the chimney of a house across the street. "Send the dragon out first. Tell him to lie low. This close to Iverna, there's always a spycatcher lurking somewhere."

She grabbed the rope and swung out, climbing onto the rooftop before tossing it back to him. Treylen followed.

He looked back just in time to see the shutters being closed. Whatever unseen helper had let them in had come in behind them to remove evidence of their passing.

He used dragon sight to spot his tower on the distant hill and commit this location to memory.

"This way." Apogee crept along the lower edge of the roof, avoiding the peaks wherever possible. When she did reach the peak of a rooftop, she stayed low, rolled over the peak and quickly down to the other side.

The city was divided on a grid pattern. As they moved, they encountered more narrow roadways where the overhanging floors made it easy to leap from one to the next, and for every five or six of these narrow roads and alleys, there was a larger one, the main thoroughfares of the city that they couldn't simply leap across. Here they dropped down into alleys, waited until the street was empty and then walked across, careful not to move so fast as to draw attention. On the far end of the city was the garrison. He could see the wooden watch towers on either side. Marziel had described it to him in one of their late-night sessions. This was where the army trained. It rested just outside of the city wall, and the land beyond it was occupied by a sprawling military camp.

Treylen thought that she would take him there or to the Under Den, but instead they veered away from it and toward the northern gate of the city. Just inside the gate was a marketplace, and on the outskirts of the marketplace an upscale stable. Just beyond that was a warehouse. Marziel had told him there were many warehouses on the northern and southern sides of the city outside the wall, but this was one of the few still located on the inside. That meant what it traded in was likely far more valuable: jewels, antiquities, other rarities and valuables. The sort of thing that he had seen in the lead wagon of Rebash's caravan.

When they stopped on a low valley between two rooftops just opposite the stables that serviced this warehouse, he was not at all surprised to see a covered wagon parked just within the open doors of a large building. There was no sign of the other wagons. Either they hadn't made it, or without any cargo, there was no reason to bring them in.

"That's it. How did you know what I was looking for?" he asked, crawling to the edge of the roof and looking down.

"I just know who he trades with," she whispered. "It looks like they haven't unloaded it yet."

Rime hopped up and perched on Treylen's back.

"I don't see him here."

"He doesn't own the wagons. He just manages them. That's why he's so keen to earn some money on the side."

"You knew what he was doing?"

Apogee crawled away, laying down in a low spot where the two roofs came together.

"We may be here a while. Get comfortable. Keep an eye out for whatever it is you're looking for. Since you won't tell me what it is." Rime ran up the roof to look around again, and Apogee rested a hand on Treylen's arm. "Don't let him do that."

You heard her. Treylen called Rime back. The dragon returned, flopping down beside him and curling into a ball.

I thought we were going to see the city, Rime complained.

Not if we don't have to. This isn't a friendly place.

We should have come in disguise. We could have gone where we pleased.

You don't have a disguise, Rime.

I could dress as a tomcat.

Treylen suppressed a chuckle.

Maybe we'll try disguising you as a rooster sometime, he said. *We don't need to do it Marziel's way tonight. Apogee's way is quicker.*

Rime huffed and buried his face under his tail. *Wake me when something happens.*

Chapter Thirty-Five

THE MANOR

They waited until it was nearly morning. At dawn, they would have to either return to the tower to wait for the next night, or change into disguises and operate from the streets.

Apogee's reluctance to consider that option suggested that blending in might be a more difficult task than he had first thought. Maybe he, Aaron, and Volanti had just gotten lucky the first time. Treylen's leg itched and he tried to offer his discomfort up to the queen, but it wouldn't go away. Whenever he thought of the queen, he thought of his betrayal of her. How he'd lied for Apogee.

"They're unloading." She nudged him and he sat up. A strange group crowded around the wagon. Some were workers at the warehouse. Others looked like they had just come from a tavern. They wore drab, dirty clothing and had disheveled hair. And they all wore the same style of boots that didn't fit with the rest of their appearance.

"They're legionaries," Apogee confirmed.

"Off duty?"

"In disguise. Whatever they're carrying, they're doing it in secret," she whispered. "Are you sure you don't want to tell me what we're looking for?"

"I think you know enough." He crept closer to the edge to see the street below, then pulled back.

"There's someone in the alley."

"Wearing darks?" she asked.

"I think so."

"That would be a spycatcher. We should get out of here," she whispered, peering over the edge for a moment. "He'll be coming up here soon to check the rooftops."

Treylen could still see the inside of the warehouse. As the cart was unloaded, the workers removed the bundle of weapons, handed it to one of the incognito soldiers, then ushered them out, shutting the door behind them. They were four, not counting the spycatcher who trailed behind them as they moved down the street. They had turned the corner and headed toward one of the residential districts when a hook, not unlike the grappling hook that Apogee had used, clattered to the rooftop beside Treylen.

"That would be him." Apogee motioned for Treylen to follow her up the roof and onto the other side, wedging herself behind a chimney and pulling him close against her. She smelled of the road, of horses, and just the faintest hint of citrus. Leaning closer, she put a finger to her lips. The soft tread of footsteps passed beside them, pausing on the peak of the roof.

The spycatcher let out a short whistle. A sound like the squeal of a rat responded from the street below. Another whistle echoed from one of the city walls.

"I told you they were all over," she whispered.

"We have to follow those soldiers."

"We'll follow him," she said, pointing at the spycatcher. "He's their shadow."

"Are you sure?"

"Rime can follow the cargo."

Where are you? he asked Rime, who let out a soft growl from the chimney above. *Get down there and follow the soldiers. If you have to cross the street, try to look like a rat.*

A rat? I would never.

Swallow your pride and get it done.

Rime hissed, then leaped off the chimney, gliding behind the spycatcher unnoticed, and down into the street.

Careful. There's four of them down there.

They followed at a distance. The spycatcher moved like an assassin, racing from gable to gable, like an owl's shadow. Apogee followed as if all eyes in the city were seeking her, and Treylen did his best to imitate. Gradually, the spycatcher got farther and farther away, but not before they had followed him to a distant corner of the city wall. It was an affluent area with carriage houses and courtyards next to mansions.

The spycatcher stopped and whistled; one whistle came in return. Then he waited, on a rooftop. Cobblestones here were polished and neat, the lanterns more brightly lit, leaving little room for shadows on the street below. A guard strolling along this road had been the one to return the whistle. He seemed disinterested in the presence of the spycatcher above. That alone hinted how commonplace they were within the city.

There was no trace of the four soldiers they had been following.

Where are you? He sent a thought out to the dragon.

I'm watching them. We are still moving.

Tell me when they stop. Be careful. The spycatcher is still up here. Guards on the street.

I see them all. Just don't steal my vision, bondmate.

Before long, the four figures appeared on the street, one of them carrying the bundle of weapons. They stopped at one of the manors and entered the yard by a side door.

"We'll have to get down there," Apogee said.

"Are you sure?" Treylen looked at the spycatcher.

"We don't have a choice. We'll have to kill him. Can you do it? Quietly."

"Yes." Treylen broke off from her and crept down the edge of the roof. The spycatcher was three houses away, alert. He perched at the high point, scanning the rooftops every few moments, but focused on the manor. Treylen wished that he had brought a bow along. Aaron would've had no trouble silencing this one with his bow. But Treylen hated carrying the things, as they were too ungainly to move easily the way Treylen preferred.

He waited until the man's back was turned and then darted out, racing up the ridge of the roof. He had nearly reached him when the man spun and drew a dagger. He lunged at Treylen just as Apogee shoved her dagger into his neck. Wrapping her arm around him, she eased him down onto the rooftop.

Blood ran down the shingles and dripped in the gutter.

"I've never seen somebody move that fast without dragon speed," Treylen said. "Aside from Marziel."

"They're all this quick," Apogee muttered.

"No," Treylen said. "I mean you." Her hand tightened on her dagger. "I'm sorry. I know you must miss her."

"Let's get over there. Quick, before they come looking for him." Apogee leaped off the roof, landing hard below, then rolling and scaling the side of the building to perch on top. Treylen followed, the fall nearly knocking the wind out of him, but he made it out of the lamplight and scaled the building before the next guard appeared on the street. Once on top of the manor house, they crept up to hide behind a gable and peered out into the courtyard.

The figures approached a door in the back, knocking on what looked like the carriage house. Treylen jumped as Rime landed on his shoulder.

The door opened a crack.

"Why are you here?" the woman said through the opening.

"We're here at the lord's invitation. We come to return a gift."

"Good. You're late. I'll let him know." The door slid shut again.

Crossbows appeared in the windows, pointing down into the courtyard. Another spycatcher crept out and drew his knife just behind the four visitors.

"We need to get inside." Treylen leaned forward. Apogee grabbed the back of his shirt and pulled him back from the edge.

"I could be more help if I knew what you were looking for," Apogee said.

What did it matter? They'd come this far already.

"A glyph scribe. I only need to find him."

"That simple?"

She had a point. Something didn't feel right. The weapons had drawn his attention to the wagons, and the wagons had brought him to the soldiers who had brought him here. It was all too easy.

I think we've found the scribe, Rime said.

Treylen looked back to the carriage house and his mouth fell open.

In the doorway was a red-robed figure with a long white beard. A pointed hat sat on top of his head.

"That isn't him…" Treylen said. It showed just how little attention Rime paid to humans The man was far too old, and far too important looking to be Norris Duremo.

"That's a wizard," Apogee said, eyes darting about as if she might run.

"Why would he be that obvious?" Treylen rubbed his eyes and borrowed Rime's sight to see more clearly. The answer came with the dragon sight. All along the hem of the man's robe was gold embroidery in the shape of glyphs. With the dragon sight, he could see the trails of magic as they swirled around the hem of the robe, and all along the staff the wizard carried. He wasn't casting any spells, but he was surrounded by finished glyph chains, one power-word away from casting.

These trappings weren't just a uniform. They hummed with power.

The man ushered the four inside.

A hooded figure sat at a workbench just inside the door, dressed in similar robes to the wizard's, but more modest and without the eccentric hat or staff. Quill in hand, they bent over the counter, scrawling intricate script onto a sheet of parchment. They looked up just for an instant as the door shut.

"There he is," Treylen said. "That's the one I'm looking for."

"The scribe?" Apogee sounded distracted. "Did you not see the wizard?"

"My mission was for the scribe. There was no mention of a wizard."

"They would never send someone like you to hunt a wizard," she said grimly. "The fact that one is here means this is an even bigger problem than anyone realized."

"You don't know my mission," Treylen said. These weapons had not appeared until this scribe defected from Iverna. Frightening as wizards were, they were irrelevant to the matter at hand. "The wizard isn't the target."

"Hellcaves, Treylen, do you know who that is?" Apogee said, a shiver in her voice. "That is the wizard Paz'terrum. I know him."

"How?" Treylen demanded. Apogee dragged him back from the edge of the roof.

"Paz'terrum is one of Emperor Jaul's advisors. And the overseer of the Wizard's Tower."

"What is that supposed to mean?"

"It means," Apogee hissed, "that your target is beyond your reach so long as Paz'terrum is with him."

Treylen glared back at her. He could feel a growl welling

up inside him. He focused on his meditation, offering his anger up to the queen. He breathed, then answered.

"We'll watch, then, wait until he's alone and take him quietly. I want his books too…"

"I don't think you understand," she whispered. "Paz'terrum is the most important Jaul official outside of the royal family. And he is a wizard. If your scribe is under his protection, you won't get anywhere near him and live to tell of it. And if you did, the queen would kill you for letting Paz'terrum escape."

"So we get them both," Treylen said. "While they're sleeping."

Apogee shook her head. "Can't sneak up on wizards. They have spells in place. You fight them head on, or not at all."

"So how do we do it?" he asked. "You know them."

"We don't," she said. There was a finality in the words. "It's time to swallow your pride, go back to Marziel, and ask for help. He can send word back to Iverna, and they can send someone more qualified to deal with it." Treylen scowled at her again, peering over the roof and into the yard. There hadn't been any movement yet. A faint light shone around the edges of the door.

"What if there was a way to bring in a wizard hunter without bothering Marziel or the others?"

"The bird?" she asked. Treylen nodded.

"Rak'tsoro."

"Now you're thinking clearly," she said, but her eyes still darted to the courtyard, and she shuddered. "There isn't any time to waste, then. Let's get out of here."

The door opened again, and they slipped away while the attention of any nearby spycatchers was drawn to the courtyard.

They leaped from the roof and crossed the street to the alley, where the blood from the dead spycatcher dripped from the eave and pooled in the gutter.

Scaling a drainpipe, they climbed out and left the alley.

"This is a problem," she said when they reached the roof. "If they find the body here, they'll move your scribe."

Together they carried him as best they could across the rooftops. It was a slow process, and the sky in the east began to grow light. As dawn crept into the sky, they reached the location near the warehouse district inside the wall. They dropped the body there after emptying his pockets to make it look like he'd been robbed.

"That's not going to fool anyone for long. But it might buy you enough time for Rak'tsoro to do whatever she needs to do."

They passed out through the same hidden passage in the home and raced across the fields just as the sun made its first appearance in the sky. They wore their silk cloaks. They'd removed their dragon masks, but had their hoods up, and Rime let himself be carried. If a farmer caught sight of them, they might not know what to make of them, but assassin wouldn't be the first thing that they guessed.

The sheep were coming out to the pastures as they reached the forest edge, then crept along it until they found the tower. Treylen threw himself down, panting once they were safe inside. Rime burst out of his jacket and scurried up the rocks, perching on top and looking out.

Apogee settled beside him. They lay there a moment side by side and caught their breath, then she sat up, reached out, and gave his knee a squeeze. "Don't be discouraged. If this leads to the killing of Paz'terrum, it will be a greater victory than we could have hoped for."

Treylen stared up at the sky.

"You think they'll take you back then?"

She laughed at that.

"Oh yes. Just tell the queen that you had some help from the traitor that Marziel has been harboring in his safehouse. It should go over brilliantly."

"I understand the difficulty," Treylen said. "But isn't that your goal eventually?"

"They aren't going to know that I was involved," Apogee said, then went over to the things that he had stowed in the back of the tower. The pigeon was still there. She reached into its improvised cage, then brought the bird over, handing Treylen the canister that had been attached to the bird's leg. He opened it to pull out a rolled slip of paper. Apogee retrieved a small quill and a vial of ink from her assassin's toolkit. She waited for Treylen to sit up, then pressed the implements into his hand while she cradled the pigeon, stroking it with one hand. Rime peered down at the bird and flicked his tongue at it, then ducked away when Apogee noticed him.

"There's no goal where I'm concerned," she said as Treylen began to write. "Though Marziel might think that he can help, sooner or later he'll have to accept that there's no future left for me in Iverna. And I'll have to find something else to fill my time."

"What would you do with yourself?" Treylen said, squinting as he tried his best to squeeze the crucial details onto the strip of paper—the scribe, the workshop, the wizard Paz'terrum.

"How should I know? I'm not even supposed to be alive," she said, sighing and looking up to watch the clouds. "I suppose I'd go west, hop a trade ship in the Salt Crescent, where they don't ask questions and they don't much care which way the war goes."

She leaned over his shoulder to put a finger on the parchment.

"You don't need to say the street name. We use a grid system for tracking locations. It's the second house of the third block, third street. That's good enough."

"You're sure?"

"I haven't been out of the loop that long."

Treylen finished writing. There was just enough space on the small slip to say he would wait in the ruined tower west of town.

"She's not going to come for you," she said, peering over his shoulder again as he finished.

"What do you mean?" Treylen asked.

"I mean if you think Rak'tsoro will come and get you to share in the glory, you are mistaken. She will go straight to the wizard, take him out, along with your scribe, then she'll go back to Iverna, before anyone is the wiser."

"So we should go back and stake out the wizard?" Treylen asked.

"You just want to sit around with the spycatchers until she gets there? And how long do you think that will be?" She had a point there. As foolish as it would have been not to call in the wizard hunter, it was even more foolish to think that he could take part in her hunt if she didn't want him there. Treylen sighed and stepped up to the window.

"Then I'll wait to see that it's done. If Rak'tsoro needs my blade, I'm here." He slipped the parchment into the tube, handing it to Apogee.

"So you've figured out that I won't be waiting around for the wizard hunter." She gave a wry smile, then tied the tube back onto the pigeon's foot, handing the bird back to Treylen.

"I'll give her your regards," Treylen said.

"I know you're joking." She brushed the leaves off her darks and began to take her hair down and unlace her boots.

"I will see you at the Dragon's Hide. We won't speak of this. You can take the full credit for it." She slipped her boots off and her jacket, then retrieved the noblewoman's garb from her pack.

"I don't care if he knows that you helped me. You're going now?" Treylen felt a slight pang at the idea she was leaving so soon. He'd only just been reunited with the woman, and he felt like for the first time she was opening up to him. Was there anything more to it than that? Rime probably would have said so.

"I think I've stayed away for long enough. Besides, the old man will be even angrier if he has to run the inn by himself."

She stepped outside to saddle her horse.

Treylen stepped back to the window again. After checking the skies to make sure no hawks were about, he released the pigeon and watched it go toward the Harvest Pass.

Apogee came back dressed in her silks.

"Thank you, Apogee. I don't know how I could've done this without you. It's a service to our queen, you know."

She nodded.

"I never lost faith in our queen," she said. "She lost faith in me."

"Well, maybe someday I can put in a good word for you."

"Don't stick your neck out for me, Treylen. It'll only get cut." She thrust a hand out toward him and he grasped it. "May that you see me next we meet, Treylen."

"You'll see me tomorrow," he said, looking back the way the bird had gone. There really was no way to know how long Rak'tsoro would take. "Three days at the latest."

"Be careful here," she said. "And don't linger. The rangers will come looking soon. Don't do anything here that you weren't ordered to. Remember your mission. Don't stray from it."

She's one to talk about missions, Rime joked.

She made one mistake. Since when do you care anyway? He waved goodbye, then she led her horse along the woods line and back toward the path that they had taken through the forest.

I don't care about the missions, Rime said. *But I watch her. I think that you do too.*

Treylen turned away and looked out over the fields, to the distant city. Beyond it, he could see the shapes of the Iveran mountain range.

His role may have ended, but the mission wasn't over until the scribe was dead.

There was nothing to do now but watch. A part of him hoped that he would be allowed to take part in the hunting of the wizard.

Another part suspected that he would regret it.

Chapter Thirty-Six

THE OATH

WIND FROM THE WEST SWEPT OVER THE OPEN FIELDS surrounding Lome. Shepherds kept their cloaks pulled tight as they sat in the pastures of the slope below the ruins of the tower and watched their flocks.

Rime was silent, perched on the top of the wall, while Treylen sat below, peering out of an unfinished window, eyes fixed on the horizon, keen for the faintest hint of dragon. It occurred to Treylen that in these times of great anticipation, just like in times of combat, he and the dragon were finally of one mind. For all their disagreements, when it came down to necessity, they were united.

Rime looked like a stone, and Treylen like a statue.

He knew he wasn't the only one watching. They were on the border, after all. Surely someone on those walls was watching the same mountains, noting every passing hawk, every strange cloud in the sky. It was an ideal day for dragon flight, but not if one wished to go unnoticed.

Of course, a skilled assassin would never let themselves be seen until it was too late. And then he would be stuck here two…three days longer. How long would he wait before he assumed it had been done and went back to his handler? How was he to know when it would be finished? Should he go into the city to see if it had been done? If it took much longer, he would have to abandon this perch. Soon the rangers would come looking.

For a city at the border of a great war, not much happened. There were more wagons moving along the southern road—the one that connected the city with the rest of Jaul—than there were along the road he had come in on. But it was no great mobilization of forces. He knew that things would look much different in the northeast, along the War Pass. But even there, he suspected that Jaul only sent a large enough army to keep the Iverans busy. Jaul required conquest. And conquest was easier in the south of the continent.

First, it had been Libbat and Lome. Then the Salt Crescent, Seera, and the Stone Kingdom and Southern Kysik. The latest to fall had been Midden, the upper half of the Ketaresk Peninsula.

That was the price that Iverna paid for this languid stalemate at the Harvest Pass...the Jaul were free to push elsewhere. If only Iverna were to play the aggressor. If the army that held the pass were to push out, to take Tabron. There was the crossroads to think of. And the garrison here. Still... how long could they expect the mountains to hold? What would happen when all of the continent had fallen, and the Jaul finally brought the full force of their united armies to Iverna?

Treylen shut the thought out. That was treasonous. Who was he to question the wisdom of his queen? If the queen's wisdom was to hold them at the mountains, then that was what they should do. After all, it was common knowledge that empires like that fell apart just as quickly as they came together. What did it matter to the queen how long it took, so long as the enemy stayed on the other side of the wall? And besides, it was not as if Iverna didn't send aid to its ally

Ketaresk. Her aid just came in the form of assassins. And assassins did their best work unseen.

By midday, Treylen was getting sore. Rime could be still all day so long as he was in the sun, but humans needed to move. His head still ached from the previous day, and he had been without sleep for too long. The dragon promised to keep a sharp eye on the city so Treylen could move around for a spell.

He got up to relieve himself, strolling through the surrounding woods and pausing to check a couple of tripwires that Apogee had set for him on her way out.

Before he took his position again, he walked around the outside of the tower, inspecting the masonry. It was admirable work—a shame it had never been finished. He searched around the foundation until he found the mason's mark. It was not any that was familiar to him. Whoever had laid the stone had not also operated in Iverna.

But the architecture was familiar. In fact, looking at the placement of the interior supports, the way the windows were positioned in a spiral upward, how the openings narrowed at the top, the subtle curve of the inward-facing blocks, and alternating sections of single and double reinforced walls, this wasn't just familiar styling. It was his family's style.

The rest of the day passed quietly and without incident. The winds grew colder, clocking toward the north, and a light mist began to fall. Soon the leaves would change, harvest would come, and the Jaul attacks on the pass would slow for the winter.

When the sun grew low behind them, and the peaks of the northern mountains glowed with the last light of dusk, Treylen released what little dragonmind he had been holding on to.

Are you watching the sky?

If I don't see them, they can't be seen.

There wasn't much to see in the city. The dusky outline of the walls, the sprawling buildings that spilled out from it, gradually giving way to farmland. It was a large city, nearly half as large as Queenseat, and as the evening waned, the faint glow of streetlights illumined smoke trails drifting up from hearths and cookfires. Treylen's eyes were trained on one unassuming corner, where any moment now, the most dangerous agent of Jaul in the north of the continent was about to get his due at the hand of his queen.

It was a momentous thing to be a part of even from afar. Through the connection, he could tell even Rime buzzed with anticipation. He still held out hope that she would come for him first and he would get to be a part of such a great victory.

The sky grew darker, and the stars came out. The night became still as the wind died down. The mist that had been falling tapered off as the clouds broke. They watched together in stillness, senses opened to the world before them, smells of wood smoke and wool drifting across. Soon the moon would rise and cast its white light over the languid fields and drifting plumes from the chimneys of the city.

They waited like that for most of the night. The bond hummed, Rime's focus bolstering his own. They were separate in their perches, but together in mind and intention. His bondmate felt it too, and it reassured him. This was how life was supposed to be after the abbey—the two of them, on assignment in a foreign land. Here on the edge of the woods, senses open to the world around them, they were in their element and on their own. No handler watching every move, no training every moment. Just the pair of them, the trust the queen had placed in their abilities, and the knowledge that they'd succeeded…

The first inkling that something had gone wrong came as a cold presence in the depths of Treylen's consciousness. It was just a feeling like a weighty blackness. But that feeling swelled in the shadows of the hollow tower behind him. Treylen didn't dare make any sudden movements. They weren't alone. The hairs on the back of his neck stood on end.

Rime let out a low growl, and Treylen's hand moved to his dagger.

A smell like a gut-shot stag hit his nose, and a wail burned through his mind. There were no words, only a quavering howl of soul-rending fury.

It struck with such a force that for a moment the bridge between he and Rime was shattered. His bondmate shrieked from his perch overhead, and Treylen threw himself to the stone floor.

A low utterance emerged from the end of that howl, like the last stones of an avalanche settling into the rubble of a single name.

Rak'tsoro…

Treylen forced his eyes open. The dragon standing over him showed no outward sign of distress. But a long gash across his belly oozed a bloody ichor.

"Foxbane!" Treylen pushed himself up and rushed forward to inspect the wound. Foxbane didn't flinch.

There is no time for me.

He turned and exited the tower, tail lashing at the carpet of fallen leaves. Treylen followed.

His boot made a squelching sound as it sank into something. Foxbane circled around to face him, leaning protectively over a smaller form. His head bent down and nudged it.

Treylen didn't need the dragon sight to know it was Rak't-soro. As soon as he summoned it, he wished that he hadn't. Red burns and oozing blisters marred the flesh where her armor was torn away. Residual patterns of fire magic swirled over the charred wounds. A slash across her torso showed the bones of her ribs and exposed muscle.

"Rak'tsoro!" Treylen dropped to his knees. "What happened?"

Treylen felt for a pulse. It took some effort to find a patch of skin on her neck that wasn't burned away.

Rak'tsoro seized his wrist. "Was it you?" she growled, letting out a wheezing breath.

"You're hurt," Treylen said. She laughed at that, bloody foam flecking her lips.

"No." She coughed. "Too much of a fool."

It was a mortal wound. As were the burns. The spell that Apogee had cast on his heel came to mind. But even if he could draw a glyph chain to encircle such a large wound, there were no graves out here to draw upon. "If we can get you to the inn…"

"Hellcaves." Rak'tsoro grabbed Treylen by the collar and pulled him closer. "Listen to me." She struggled to get the words out. "It's undone."

"What?" He craned his neck to look up at Foxbane, but the dragon stood with his eyes on the horizon.

"You'll finish it. I charge you, assassin." She clutched his shirt, pushing her mask up off her face. "It must be done tonight, or you will lose him."

She brushed her dragon's cheek and closed her eyes. Foxbane rested his head beside hers. Rime crept forward to sniff at the pair of them, then slunk away, pausing to look back at Treylen.

Come away, bondmate. It won't be long.

Treylen squeezed her hand, then let it go, backing quietly into the ruined tower to sit beside his bondmate and watch the fields as Foxbane and Rak'tsoro shared their final moments.

Chapter Thirty-Seven

THE ERRAND

No one must know of it. We go alone.

Foxbane the Elder dominated the center of the old tower, looming over Treylen and Rime with a dark energy that seemed to make the starlight shrink away.

The dragon wouldn't allow him to inspect the wound that gaped on his side. It didn't matter, he said. Only the oath. It did not seem to be bleeding much anymore.

"We can't do it alone. You're hurt. I can't fight like her. Rime's not killing anyone. There have to be others at the Harvest Pass who can help."

They were prepared for us. Someone in the chain of command alerted them to our mission. Your spymaster is not to be trusted either.

"Let me plan something. We can set a trap for him."

He looked up at Rime, who'd perched on the wall and was watching the fields below for trouble. So far, the night was calm and quiet.

We must go now, Foxbane said. *They will move the wizard in the morning.*

"You're in no shape to fight."

I will bring you in, then draw their arrows. We must do this now, and we must do it alone.

Treylen shook his head, thinking.

"If you're well enough to fly, then go to the Dragon's Hide and bring Aaron and Volanti here. I trained them. If you trust me, you can trust them."

Foxbane bared his teeth.

There is a traitor in our ranks.

"I go with them, or I go alone. But I don't need a dragon. You'd only draw attention."

It wasn't a lie. Treylen had seen the archers in the windows. The spycatchers on the roofs. The dragon could get them to the courtyard, but the wizard would be long gone by the time they fought their way inside. That, and his injuries.

Foxbane heaved a massive sigh and turned away, walking back out toward the body of Rak'tsoro.

I will attempt it, not because they have my trust, but each minute we disagree, I grow weaker.

"Can you make the flight?" Dark wings beat air, and Foxbane disappeared into the night.

Treylen glanced at Rak'tsoro, who lay beneath a tree on the edge of the woods. Then he went back to sit alongside Rime.

"I don't want you to come with us." He ran one hand idly across the dragon's back.

Rime looked up at him but didn't say anything.

"When we go in. Wait here. If we don't make it out, you can stay with Marziel."

I don't think I can do that, bondmate. Rime crawled into his lap and curled up again.

"I'll still have the dragonmind."

You fight better with me.

"We might not make it out."

I'm not afraid.

Treylen turned back to the fields.

They sat and watched the city a while longer. The guards

weren't on alert as far as he could tell. Every so often, he could see a soldier pacing along the top of the wall.

At some point, fatigue overtook him and he drifted to sleep. It had grown even colder by the time he woke, and the moon had crossed the sky. The night was almost over, but that wouldn't matter.

It didn't matter how angry Foxbane was. They weren't going to fight their way into the wizard's compound. They'd failed at that once already.

The way Treylen figured it, if the wizard was moved to another compound during the night, then they'd lost him already.

But he was safer in the compound than on the streets at night, so it was more likely he would stay hidden until morning. And if he thought he had succeeded in fighting off his attackers, there was a chance he might not move at all.

In any case, the guard on him would be doubled, and he would likely be hidden somewhere within the house. He wouldn't be back in his workshop until morning. That gave Treylen an hour or two to prepare while he waited for Foxbane to return.

He would need a weapon not associated with an assassin.

The only one available was the rusted woodcutter's axe left behind by the ranger who had used this place. That was ideal really.

He climbed down a moment to gather the axe, then began to scratch out a series of glyphs. The dead wood had little magic in it, but it wasn't about the scratches. He could add materials into the grooves he had created later, just as he suspected the wizard had done to make the enchanted weapons. Dirt for a little sestus magic. A bit of fresh ash from the body of the fallen battle assassin to summon fire magic. Cold blood for entropos.

He could not do anything as complex as the long scripts that he had seen on the weapons carried by the rangers, but by linking a few simple chains together, he could put on an impressive display all the same. It was more important that the weapon looked authentic.

First, he had to clean the weapon, scouring it with a bit of sand, and a rag, then scraping the tougher bits. It still looked rough, but not rusty. A little water with a rag and the handle was clean as well. Then he carved a pattern up the handle, then went down to retrieve the materials he would use to fill it. There would be some interference between the material and the wood it was embedded in, but with luck, it would only enhance the spell. Etching the head of the axe wouldn't work, but it was still possible to paint the material over the surface—help from the paints in his disguise kit, and it would look almost as good.

When it was finished, he cut the tarp down from the corner of the tower and wrapped it.

He was just finishing when the sound of wings behind the tower caught his ear.

Is that them, Rime? He set the bundle down, then drew his daggers, pressing himself against the wall and edging toward the opening.

It is. I didn't see them approach.

He must be weak if we can hear him.

Treylen sheathed the daggers just as Aaron came around the corner. When he caught sight of Treylen, he grinned ear-to-ear.

"I see you there."

Treylen stepped out of the shadows and approached his friend. Aaron threw an arm around him.

"It is good to see you." He clapped Treylen on the back.

Up on the wall, he could hear Rime scuffling with Felicity.

"You too." Treylen pushed his friend off and looked him over. Aaron had dressed in his darks. Now that he had a plan, he realized that darks might not work.

"Foxbane has filled you in?" Treylen asked.

"He's told me what he knows." Aaron's face fell. "Which isn't much. How did you get yourself into such a mess?"

"Rak'tsoro charged me with finishing her work. I have to honor that, even if I don't think I'll survive it. You can stay out of it if you want."

Aaron grimaced but nodded. "I'm surprised you sent for us." He looked back and a second figure appeared around the corner, a small dragon perched on her shoulder.

"She's feeling better?"

"I'm well enough. Foxbane said you had nobody you could trust." She crossed her arms, then glanced behind her.

"He still didn't trust Marziel?" Treylen asked.

"He couldn't carry us all," Volanti said. "Marziel will come when he can. We are to go without him."

"Damn, well, you heard what I said to Aaron. It's not too late to change your mind. "

Volanti shook her head.

"I always wanted to meet Rak'tsoro."

She may come and have a look at her. Foxbane made a rumbling noise, and Volanti nodded. Ketcher hopped down from her shoulder and they both disappeared into the trees. Aaron looked back.

"What will you do with the body?"

"Foxbane will take her to Iverna." Treylen looked him over again. "Did you bring any clothes that aren't darks?"

"I wasn't planning a holiday."

"Right."

"Volanti has a cloak."

"That's a start." Treylen unwrapped the axe and tossed the tarp at him. "Put this on. We've got to get moving. I'll tell you the plan on the way."

Chapter Thirty-Eight

THE DISGUISE

THE SHEEP HAD JUST BEGUN TO FILE INTO THE PASTURES ON the outskirts of Tabron when Treylen, Aaron, and Volanti walked out from the tower and into the city. Volanti was wearing the cloak she had brought to ward off the cold during their flight, and Aaron had wrapped himself in the tarp, carrying the glyph-marked axe underneath. None of them wore their dragon masks. If anyone noticed them, they were just a few shepherds who had been out looking for a missing sheep.

Foxbane watched from the tower. Though he'd seethed for vengeance, the elder had been fading since he'd returned. It pained Treylen to see it, but Foxbane had agreed with his plan, and there was no room in it for a full-sized dragon, injured or not.

Each of the smaller dragons was hidden inside their bond-mate's cloak. While all were stealthy, none of the dragons had extensive experience with sneaking through the city. And Treylen had shared Apogee's warning about snares disguised as pigeon nests and other dangers.

They made it to the house near the wall without incident. Treylen knocked on the door, then pulled the marker

Greythorn had given him from his spy kit and slipped it under.

It took a little longer, but after a while, light appeared. He heard the bolt slip, and then the light faded. The front room of the house was empty. He waited until the others were inside, then closed the door.

"Who does this belong to?" Volanti asked.

"She wouldn't tell me. Come on."

Guiding them through the house, he was careful to stick to the same path he had taken before. It wouldn't do to intrude on the lives of the queen's supporters any more than necessary. He was also wary of passing through here without permission.

Through the tunnel and up the stairs was the room where Apogee had returned the grappling hook on the way out of the city. Treylen took it.

What he really needed was a disguise. He had lost the outfits he'd been carrying when he ran from the rangers. The clothes they wore weren't going to be enough to get inside of where he needed to go. Fortunately, a search of the cupboards revealed exactly what he was looking for. Clothing, the kind a farmer might have worn, hung on hooks inside of a closet.

He pulled a set of clothing for each of them, then stuck his legs into the scratchy wool trousers and slipped an old vest over his back. His arms were a bit too tightly muscled even for a soldier, so he slipped the vest off and tried a loose shirt instead. This one had a bit of lace around the sleeve and collar. Perfect for what he intended.

Turning around, he found Aaron struggling to button the tight waist of a pair of ugly brown breeches and Volanti entirely swallowed by a stained wool tunic. Treylen helped her roll the sleeves and belt it so it fit a little better. Then he retrieved the disguise kit from his belt of thieves' tools and set it on the table. Reluctantly, he put the tools away, keeping just a single lock pick, which he slipped into his boot, as well as his belt knife, which he tucked into his waist. The daggers, too, went into the cupboard.

"Are you sure about this?" Aaron watched grimly as the blades were shut away. "Marziel said never leave them behind."

"Not at all. But I think it's the best option. I won't fault either of you if you don't want to go through with it. This is my oath. You can walk out now and wait with Foxbane."

"No." Aaron hissed at the dragons, who had been scratching around in the corners of the neglected room, looking for rats and roaches. They quieted down.

"We're with you." Volanti placed her daggers into the cupboard alongside his. "But you haven't told us the full plan."

"I'll tell you on the way. See if you can find any boots that aren't assassins' boots and anything you can carry as a weapon that won't give you away if they search you. Just give me a minute to powder my hair and put my beard on. Then you'll need to bind my hands and take me prisoner."

Chapter Thirty-Nine

THE RUSE

AARON AND VOLANTI MARCHED TREYLEN THROUGH THE streets of Tabron and up the cobblestone walk to the nicer residential district where the wizard's lair was hidden.

The whole gambit relied upon these two making a show of having captured him and presenting him to the guards at the wizard's manor. Yet Treylen wasn't certain that the city watch was aware of Norris and Paz'terrum or the soldiers who brought shipments to them, so they sent the dragons ahead to make sure the streets were empty. There were a few crafts-people working already. Shops were opening for the day, and housekeepers used their scouring stones to strip the night's soot from the steps of their homes.

The dragons moved on the rooftops, keeping away from the peaks. Ketcher was small enough that anyone who saw him might mistake him for a rat or a pigeon anyway.

Treylen's hair was powdered with gray. A goatee and mustache were affixed to his face, and a thin gum had been smeared on the corners of his eyes to deepen the wrinkles there. A wedge in the heel of each shoe made him taller and added a stoop to his back. No friend of Rebash would have mistaken Treylen for the merchant, but whatever agent of Jaul had hired him to ferry weapons back to Tabron might. Treylen was counting on the man's dislikable nature to work to his advantage.

Aaron and Volanti were disguised as close as possible to the soldiers who had brought the bundle of weapons to the manor. They'd had to cut Aaron's hair quickly. Volanti had to let hers down to hide her ears, which were mostly, but not quite, healed. The woman soldier had been gaunt and older than her, so a bit of boot-black thinned with oil under her eyes and on her cheeks was the best Treylen could do. He didn't have the skill with it that Marziel did. It would have to be enough.

They passed into the neighborhood without trouble, though more than once, Treylen thought he saw the outline of a spycatcher following them from the rooftops.

Despite the imposing facade of the manor that abutted the street, a small door in the side wall opened when Aaron tried the handle. A path around the side led into the courtyard. Already embracing the dragonmind, Treylen heard the arming of crossbows as they entered. Boots on the roof overhead told him that at least one spycatcher lurked up there. Even a pair of gardeners stopped their work when Aaron and Volanti entered, hands going to swords at their belts. Volanti dragged Treylen along behind her, gripping him by his shirt and kicking the back of his knee to force him down, while Aaron knocked at the door of the carriage house.

Treylen feigned distress and craned his neck to look around the courtyard. Two more windows opened as they waited, two more crossbows trained on them. One of the spycatchers hopped down from the roof behind them.

Where are you? He hadn't heard from Rime since they'd entered the neighborhood.

We are in the next courtyard over.

Stay there. There's spycatchers on the roof.

Treylen wished the dragon would have let him go alone.

He didn't want any harm coming to Rime, even if he himself didn't make it out. If anyone could survive the loss of a bond-mate, it was Rime.

He was equally bothered by Volanti's presence. She was still a trainee, and he had no desire to be responsible for her death.

The door opened just a crack and a woman's face looked out.

"What do you want?"

Aaron cleared his throat and stepped aside to show Treylen.

"We are here at the lord's invitation. We come to return a gift." Before she could object, he added, "The delivery felt light. I went back on a hunch. Found him in possession of this." He raised the bundled axe, lifting the fabric just enough to show the glyphs carved into it. The woman's scowl deepened.

"That is not one of ours." She made a gesture. The two nearest gardeners dropped any pretense of managing the yard and drew swords. A soldier stepped from the bushes and ran his hands over the three of them. He removed a sword that Aaron had found in the house earlier. He also inspected the knife Volanti carried before returning it.

"Where did you get this?"

"I found it in the woods, milady." Treylen pitched his voice down and forced it to sound older and raspier. "These high-waymen have no right to it. This is robbery."

"Be quiet." Volanti kicked him. She was even more convincing in her disguise than Treylen was. Treylen had only just explained the technique as he helped them with their makeup, but she had taken to the idea of using her dragon stealth to empower her disguise as quickly as she had taken to spellcast-ing. She was meaner, and her features were more weathered.

"Who are you?" The woman narrowed her eyes at him.

"I am Rebash Auger. I brought your last shipment. And my caravan was attacked on the road because of it. Now, if you don't mind, I'm going to leave, I won't stand for this interrogation." He started to get up and Volanti kicked him again. Hard.

"Stay on your knees, traitor."

Treylen felt his mustache come loose a bit. He caught his head in his hands and fixed it before looking up.

"You were suspicious?" She looked at Aaron, then at the weapon again.

"The delivery felt light," he repeated.

"And you went back?" she asked.

He nodded.

"But it wasn't light. This is not one of ours. You were with him?" She looked at Volanti.

"There was something strange about the delivery," she offered. Nodding to Treylen. "They were acting strange."

"Well, which was it? Was it light or they were strange?"

"Something was off," Aaron said. She frowned at that with a look of suspicion.

Treylen remembered what Marziel had said. Sometimes attention was the best disguise.

"Well, I don't see I need to be here anymore. You have the axe. You'll be hearing from the magistrate over this." He started to stand up and got a knee in the back from Volanti.

He didn't have to fake the growl he let out as she twisted his shirt collar and forced him back to the flagstones of the yard. He couldn't help but feel proud of his student. She wasn't holding back.

"We're all going to wait right here," Aaron said. "Don't try anything." He seemed like he meant it too.

"And what if I do?" Treylen tried to get up again. This time, Aaron joined Volanti in forcing him back down.

"Calm yourself."

"Indeed." The woman scowled at Treylen again. "Rebash Auger, you said?"

"Yes."

"You manage the caravan."

"I keep the books."

"Quite involved for a bookkeeper, aren't you? Out here with your carts."

Treylen swallowed, trying to channel the merchant's rueful anger. "As I am entitled to be. We suffered great losses on the road, lady. It was an ambush. As you no doubt have already been informed. Someone must take stock of it, and your people are keeping me from my work."

"Be quiet!" Volanti balled her fist and struck him on the side of the head. This time Treylen's beard began to peel off, and he caught it as he fell to the ground and wrapped his chin with his hands, pressing it back into place as he squirmed in the dirt.

"Enough of that. Don't move." The woman at the door signaled the soldiers behind them. Swords were drawn. All Treylen could do was send a message out to Rime.

Keep everyone calm.

"You will answer to Paz'terrum."

She disappeared inside, sliding the door closed. The carriage house didn't look all that large, but there must have been a passage from there into the main house or one of the adjoining properties, because she was gone for a long while. It was early enough that the wizard might have been sleeping.

The cold of the morning seemed to stifle the sounds out of the city. There was no motion in the yard, aside from the fog of their breath and the rustle of the gardeners returning to their work.

Lanterns were lit inside the carriage house. The door slid open to reveal Paz'terrum with his robe askew and hair on end. It was clear the man had been sleeping. The room behind him was still arrayed with workbenches and racks of weapons. Bits of arcane paraphernalia lay about, scrolls, books, charts with glyphs written on them. A half-dressed glyph scribe shuffled behind him, rubbing at his eyes and yawning. That was more how Treylen had remembered him looking in their early morning lessons. Close, there was no mistaking it—this was Norris Duremo.

"What is this about?" The aged man raised his rune-adorned staff toward them.

"We are here at the lord's invitation." Aaron bowed. "We come to return a gift."

"Be quiet, you fool. What is this?" He grabbed the axe out of Aaron's hands and pushed him away with his staff before shoving the axe in Treylen's face. "You claim you found this in the woods?"

"I did, milord, honestly."

"I find that when a man must use the word 'honestly,' he has already been dishonest with me."

"I meant no offense, milord." Treylen shuffled forward on his knees. He was almost close enough to touch the wizard. If he had his daggers, he could have finished him already.

"Tell me, mister Augur, in which woods did you find this?"

"I'm not sure that should matter. I found it. I should keep it."

"Is this one of yours?" He handed the axe to Norris, who squinted blearily.

"There is no craftsmanship in this..." said the scribe. He turned it over, inspecting the glyphs. "These are glyphs, though. I will have to test their accuracy."

Norris brought the axe back into the workshop. The wizard turned and took a step in. Treylen poised to lunge for him.

"Bring him in. I will put him to the question myself."

Volanti and Aaron hauled Treylen to his feet, each holding one of his shoulders.

"Not you." The woman who had first received them

stepped out and put her hand up. "You two may go." She took Treylen by the collar and pulled him in toward two waiting soldiers. "You did the right thing by bringing him here. Now run off."

Volanti shot Aaron a questioning look. Treylen twitched his head to the street, praying they would go. He might stand a better chance if they attacked the wizard now, together, but his friends had swords at their backs, and crossbows trained on each of them. If he followed the wizard in, alone, then he would fight alone…He might not get away then, but Aaron and Volanti would, at least.

They let him go, troubled looks on their faces. The soldiers that had come up behind them interposed themselves between his companions and the door, then the door was slid shut.

The bondmates are upset, Rime warned him. *What is happening over there?*

*I'm inside. I've got him alone, mostly…*His eyes went to the woman who had answered the door. And a pair of soldiers who shadowed him. The only real threat was the wizard, and he was an old man wearing glyphs…more of a mystery than a threat.

Treylen followed him as close as he could. It had been the right choice leaving his daggers, he told himself. If they had searched him and found them, the fight would've started before the wizard revealed himself, then they would've had to kill everyone in the courtyard before searching the buildings. Paz'terrum almost certainly would've gotten away.

Treylen eyed the weapons, trying to decide which one he could grab the quickest and plunge through the wizard's heart. Do that, and he could leave without fighting the others. The axe in the man's hand was still the nearest.

Norris held it close to his face, inspecting the markings Treylen had made.

"This was made recently. When did you find this?" He stopped between a workbench of metalworking tools and a shelf with jars filled with lumps of metal and wood. One of the guards gripped Treylen's shoulder before he could step any closer. He hoped they wouldn't look too closely at his powdered hair. The wizard stood to the side, watching him as he watched Norris.

"That look...do you know what these markings mean?" He snatched the axe out of the scribe's hands and shook it toward Treylen. "Do you know why I'm here in Tabron? Hmm, I have heard a thing or two about you, merchant. Not all of it good, yet...perhaps I could make use of a man like you."

What might he ask Rebash's wagons to carry? Treylen had stumbled into a position to acquire the exact sort of intel that General Bourin had wanted. How disappointed the general would be if he didn't wait until the wizard had spilled his secrets before putting an end to him.

But he had sworn an oath to Rak'tsoro. With a twist of the arm, he broke free of the soldier's grip, surged forward, and touched the axe, shouting the power word.

Chapter Forty

THE SNARE

"Flavus!"

It was the most complex spell he'd ever rendered, clever enough to make even Volanti jealous.

When he'd planned it, he wasn't sure what flows of magic would be nearby to draw upon. He'd made up for this by adding elements to the grooves. The most potent of these was the charred blood of Rak'tsoro. The magic in it was still fresh.

Flames burst out of the handle, and when the spell reached an entropos glyph under the wizard's hand, time seemed to slow, holding him in place as fire blossomed. Small crotus glyphs splintered the wood, and tiny leaves pushed their way out, bursting into flames.

The patterns painted onto the head of the axe flared with a swirling aeris glyph, whipping the explosion into a fiery tornado, engulfing the wizard entirely. Norris Duremo screamed and went behind the workbench.

Treylen staggered back. Something glinted, and he ducked a slash from one of the soldiers. With a kick, he sent the man crashing into the wall. The second guard had only just reached for his sword when Treylen grabbed a glyph-marked dagger from the wall and plunged it into his chest.

He cast a warning glare at the woman behind him, then spun back to finish off the smoldering wizard...only to find Paz'terrum untouched. The glyphs on his robe pulsed with a fiery energy. The last of the flames fizzled out as they were drawn down and into the pattern, disappearing.

Treylen lunged with the dagger.

The wizard struck his staff against the stone. "Sestus!"

A pattern flared on the staff. His dragon sight caught the energy flowing up from the stones, through a sestus glyph on the base of the staff, then out through an aeris glyph at the top. Treylen's blade struck the air between them like a blunt knife on cold butter. He pulled back and lunged again, two hands on the weapon. The wizard struck the ground again, shouting another sestus, and Treylen slammed into the barrier with a soundless impact. The glyph on the staff flared and sizzled.

Another heel kick set the guard behind him sprawling again. He dropped and spun to slice the other guard's feet. Someone pounded on the door, but the fools had barred it when they'd entered. Treylen lunged again.

"Sestus!" the wizard screamed. Treylen hit the barrier again. It was weaker this time. Again, the glyph seemed to glow and spark. They were weakening.

"Flavus!" The wizard ran a hand across a glyph to his sleeve, and flames shot out from it. It struck the workbench next to him and the jars of powder shattered, letting out another fiery plume. Somewhere underneath, Norris screamed. Treylen ducked and rolled beneath the table. Drawing upon Rime's strength, he launched himself into the rafters, caught one faster than the old man could follow, and swung around to land behind the wizard.

He thrust his dagger toward the wizard's heart, just as one of the shadows detached from the ceiling, the black-clothed figure dropping down onto Treylen, kicking his weapon hand aside, and planting a boot on his face. Treylen rolled clear from his attacker, diving aside as a rack of glyph-marked weapons came tumbling down on him.

Springing to his feet and grabbing a second dagger off the wall, he struck a fighting stance.

"You can breathe now, Treylen."

Apogee stood at the center of the smoke-filled room. She had no dragon mask, but wore the hardened-leather greaves and spiked gloves of a full-fledged battle assassin.

The scribe crawled out from under the bench and was about to unbar the door, but Apogee raised her hand toward him, and he stopped. Paz'terrum scowled, unmoving.

"What in hellcaves are you doing here, Apogee?" Treylen breathed.

"I needed some time away." She had a dagger in her hand, but it wasn't raised.

"Don't joke with me."

Soldiers came down the passage leading to the main house.

"Hold!" she commanded them, then turned to Treylen. "We've got a lot to talk about."

"Why are you here?" Treylen kept his knives in place. The wizard didn't make any moves, only scowled and twisted his staff.

"What was I supposed to do? Go back to the kingdom that disowned me?"

"So you went to Jaul? They killed your bondmate."

"That's what I told Marziel. Because he wouldn't believe the truth."

"He said you tried to run off with a wizard and they turned out to be a spycatcher."

"I knew what they were. I didn't care. We were in love. But the queen found out and sent another assassin."

"So you were a traitor…"

"I hadn't done anything yet. I had good reasons, but the

queen doesn't care. You'll see…You won't know you've failed her until they drive a dagger into your bondmate."

He didn't care for the sound of that. Emperor Jaul was supposed to be the cruel one. The queen acted out of necessity. His mind went to the other night. The lowsater he had liberated. How would they be received upon reaching Iverna? Surely it couldn't be any worse than what Jaul had in store for them.

Behind her, the wizard tapped his staff. "Get on with it."

"No." Apogee tossed the order back like an old apple core. The wizard snarled and Norris made a choking sound, but she ignored it. "I told you he's with me. Treylen, you have my word on this. Put the blades down and we'll talk. If you don't like what I have to say, you can go back to Marziel."

She could've killed him; he knew that much. She could have done it any time in the last couple of days. But she'd trusted in him. And the bond they shared. Marziel was right, Coops Abbey was different. Bos had taught them differently than he was meant to. Maybe that was why they'd been so easy to lead astray. But if Apogee had intended to sway Treylen, then she should have done it before betraying Rak'tsoro.

"You used me to get to Rak'tsoro."

She had even told him what to write on the slip. It was entirely likely that the location he had given to Rak'tsoro was a different house, one better suited to killing a battle assassin.

"I didn't want to. But the best trap is the one that brings home dinner."

There was more that he wished to say. More questions to ask. But when he opened his mouth to speak, he found only the power word.

"Sestus."

The daggers flared to life. That same thrumming power that had surrounded the rangers when they chased him off the road spread over Treylen. It was like dragon speed, but not. When he did pull on the dragonmind, taking Rime's speed on top of the enchantment, the world around him slowed to a spider's crawl. Apogee's eyes widened, as she understood what had happened a moment before anyone else had.

She moved just fast enough to turn his dagger aside. If he'd aimed to kill her, it might have landed. But the only blood he really wanted was the wizard's. He slashed her arm, and she moved sluggishly out of the way, before falling backward. Treylen cut down a guard who had come up behind him, then looked back to see the wizard duck out the door into the courtyard, with Norris close on his heels.

He raced after them—ready for the rain of bolts that would follow, but no longer caring. He had only to drive the blade through the wizard's heart before the archers brought him down.

Out in the courtyard, he braced for a barrage from the crossbows.

Instead, he saw Rime, Ketcher, and Felicity ripping an archer from their window, and tossing them down to join two others broken on the lawn. A guard lay with one of Aaron's arrows buried in her neck, while Aaron and Volanti danced on the wall of the courtyard in fierce combat with a pair of spycatchers. They were nearly to the house.

Treylen closed the distance, seizing the scribe by the hood of his robe and driving the dagger through his back. Norris issued a faint gasp as a glyph-marked scroll fell from his hand. Whatever power word he'd been readying died on his lips as he sank to his knees.

"Corbel?" he wheezed, and for a moment Treylen pitied the man. Were they really so different? Both had abandoned their path in life in search of something else. Power? Freedom? Both had waited for too long to be recognized for their talent. But only one had betrayed their queen…The last thought drowned the others.

Treylen gave a final twist, then removed the blade as a spray of crimson sluiced onto the steps of the manor. He looked up as the door slammed shut and heard the thunk of a bar being dropped. That hardly mattered. There were other ways in.

Treylen had almost reached the window when a screech came from the roof, and a dragon dropped from overhead and pounced onto him. Snarefoot had always been large—big enough to wrestle a hound by the time that Apogee had left Coops Abbey. She was the size of a draft horse now, with a snaking neck that had an old scar across it, and a tail that whirled like a ribbon.

The air fled from Treylen's lungs, and he felt the dragon's talons pierce his arms. Both daggers clattered away. His head struck the ground, and the throbbing pain from the previous day returned. Rime screeched from the manor, and even the soldiers in the courtyard cried out in surprise.

"You're alive?" He gasped for the words. Terror warred with relief at the sight of the dragon he'd once known as a friend. It was almost like seeing Bos's bondmate Windfell again, and a smile forced its way onto his lips.

It faded as her back foot raked at one of his legs, cutting a gash along it. Snarefoot cocked her head to the side. Recognition went both ways.

Apogee rushed past Treylen and knelt beside the corpse of the scribe.

Treylen struggled in vain. Even drawing upon Rime's strength, he was no match for Snarefoot.

"It's too late." Apogee looked toward Treylen before turning away. "He's already chosen his side."

Snarefoot spared him for a moment, regret in her eyes until the inner lids narrowed. Her jaw opened and smoke spilled out.

A pair of garden shears sailed through the air and lodged into the dragon's eye.

The gardener who'd been cowering in the bushes shouted, "Crotus!"

His cloak fell away to reveal Marziel in his full darks, mask covering his face. Magic flared along the raked ground surrounding the manor, vines bursting forth and snaking up the front of the house to entangle a pair of soldiers coming down the back steps.

One of his Queen's Fingers pierced Apogee's shoulder as the other slashed a long wound across Snarefoot's flank. The dragon reared, pawing at her eye. One of Aaron's arrows sank into her neck. Hot blood splashed across Treylen's face, and he scrambled back.

Snarefoot's wings beat as she shrank backward. Apogee cursed, spun low to sweep one of Marziel's legs out from under him, then ran for her bondmate and caught the strap of her saddle as the dragon took flight. Aaron loosed another arrow and the dragon shrieked, but they found their way into the sky and disappeared over the rooftops.

Marziel dispatched the guards and hauled Treylen to his feet.

"You certainly taught them to fight well enough." He nodded at Volanti, who had just set the last of the spycatchers alight with a fire spell. Aaron fired another arrow, striking one of the archers that had fallen from the windows. Rime dropped down to land on Marziel.

"The wizard, he's getting away," Treylen said, starting toward the manor again. Marziel seized his arm.

"Not that way. Let's bring him out here."

Marziel struck the ground and a second set of glyphs flared to life around the hedges. The vines surged up the wall of the house, curling over the roof, then tearing inward like two hands splitting a pomegranate. The walls shuddered, then with a rending snap, tore asunder. The innards of the house spilled out into the courtyard. At its center, halfway up a winding staircase that now led to nowhere, the startled wizard

Paz'terrum held his hands out—a string of glyphs on the sleeve of his robe held the pieces of the home that were nearest to him in a capsule of force—paintings, plaster, and chunks of wall. He lowered his arms and the debris clattered away.

"Sestus!" the wizard barked, then dashed to the top of the staircase, as the swirling winds of two glyph chains spiraled up from his boots and hastened his movement. He perched at the top of the broken stairs and looked out over the ruined courtyard.

"Not yet." Marziel kept a hold on Treylen's arm. "This is a high-value target."

Hold back a moment, Treylen said to Rime, wherever he was. Ketcher and Felicity were on the walls around the courtyard, where Aaron and Volanti still perched, catching their breath and watching for the next wave of guards.

"Paz'terrum!" Marziel shouted. "By the authority of Queen Olysya Rewenis Ivera, I offer you pardon. Throw down your staff and come with us. You will be received in Queenseat."

"Throw it down?" The wizard chuckled. "Oh, I think I will. Flavus!"

"Now we go!" Marziel said, bounding forward.

Paz'terrum hurled the staff like a spear from the top of the broken staircase. It struck the ruined manor in a ball of fire that burst and spilled out to engulf the wreckage. Marziel sprang backward, landing on a chunk of the upper floors. Treylen landed beside him, looking for a path through the flames.

The wizard pulled a slender chain from inside of his robe. All along the chain, clay tablets dangled. The wizard bent over, scratching a glyph onto the back of one with his fingernail. Treylen didn't wait to see what he was trying. He leaped past Marziel, onto the top of a broken wall, and ran along it as the fire raged on either side. There was a flutter of wings as

Rime glided over the fire, landing on Treylen's shoulder as he ran. The wizard spoke the power word and the tablets began to burn and smoke. He swung the chain just as Treylen leaped from the wall toward the wizard's perch. An arm of smoke and flame reached up from the inferno, following the motions of the chain, and it batted Treylen from the air like a fly. Rime shrieked and fell down into the fiery ruins. Treylen lost sight of him, and it was all he could do to cover his face, as the wind and crackling ash swatted him down. He caught the edge of the other wall and hauled himself over, out of the flame.

The short cape that trailed from his cowl flared up and Treylen tore it from his jacket before the fire could engulf it, rolling free. He caught sight of Volanti leaping across the yard, and looked up just in time to see Marziel dodge a similar arm of fire.

Rime, are you alright? There was no answer.

Marziel landed on a broken door in the center of the flames, sprang out just as quickly, and scaled the outside of the staircase. He'd almost reached the wizard again when the man reached into his cloak, pulling out a scroll of parchment and tossing it down. It unrolled, and another chain of glyphs flared to life, a wall of force swirling to wrap the wizard in another cocoon of force and air. He raised the chain of smoking tablets and the fire surged up from below, engulfing everything. Marziel sprang backward, landing in a broken bedroom and scrambling up and away from the manor, falling into the yard.

Rime, are you alright?

I may be if you don't distract me, Rime growled. *I am trapped beneath.*

Treylen clutched the edge of one broken wall, peering over into the inferno. He thought he saw the lithe shape of his bondmate wriggling between the beams of a flame-licked crawl space.

"She sent four of you? What luck!" The wizard laughed as one of Aaron's arrows flew toward him. It stuck into the wall of force, then fell away. Holding the chain in two hands, he thrust it out before him, and the flames surged out of the ruin and down each of the walls of the yard. Aaron and Volanti were forced down, together with their bondmates. Marziel ran to Treylen and helped him up, looking back as the other two scrambled to get away from the flames, their young bond-mates clinging to them. The wizard brought his arms together and the flames came together to encircle the back. The smoke from the burning tablets drifted out to mix with the fire, funneling it into a swirling torrent that spread down the walls and into the yard as the flames leaped higher and higher.

"First Rak'tsoro, and now her lackeys. Today will be a great victory for Jaul."

Do you trust me, bondmate? Rime asked.

Of course, Treylen said, relieved just to hear his bondmate's voice again.

Attack him now!

Treylen didn't hesitate. There wasn't time for it. He held the dragonmind and launched himself through the flames, landing on a beam that stuck above the house before leaping again toward the wizard.

Paz'terrum chuckled, narrowed his eyes at Treylen, and brought the chain up leisurely. Another arm of smoke and flame rose from the inferno.

Something darted from the wreckage below, and up beneath the wizard's robe. He let out a yelp and twisted aside, beating his hands against himself. He spun, crying out and calling power into another glyph, but it was no use on the inside. Rime's head burst from beneath the collar of the robe, jaw wide. His teeth sunk into the neck of the wizard.

Paz'terrum thrashed and tugged him away as a spray of blood soaked the robes. Rime slipped from his grip and dove into the red, snarling. Treylen leaped and landed on the stairs, hit the wall of force, and pushed his dagger into it. Inch by inch it sank, as if through melting ice, and then his arm was through. It plunged into the wizard's side, and he staggered. The parchment at his feet tore, and the force wall dissipated. The wizard sank to his knees as Treylen pushed the dagger deeper. The chain fell from his arm and the smoking tablets shattered on the stairs. Treylen pulled the dagger free, and let the wizard crumple. Rime raced up Treylen's arm to his shoulders, eyes wide as the fire, no longer controlled by the wizard, climbed higher around the stairs.

There was a crash and a great gust of wind and fire as Volanti cast a spell to push the flame back. Marziel sprang through the gap to land beside him.

"I think we're done here, don't you?" Marziel coughed and covered his mouth.

"I'm glad you made it," Treylen said.

"Just came down to see how much of a fool Apogee had made of me." He stared in the direction where Apogee had disappeared. "I take it you've done what you came for?"

"And more." Treylen took a step back as the fire surged and Volanti cast her spell again to fight it back.

"Then we'd best be going." Marziel bent and reached into the wizard's robe, pulling a book out of a pocket and cutting loose the pouch that held a ream of scrolls. "It's boar tonight. And the inn's short-handed."

Chapter Forty-One

THE LAST CALL

They reached the Dragon's Hide by the end of the day. The four assassins and three dragons had maintained a well-practiced jog, ducking off to the side anytime another traveler appeared on the roads.

They had passed through the house to retrieve their daggers, then made a quick stop at the tower overlooking the city. Foxbane was gone, along with the body of his bondmate. The group stayed long enough to stitch a couple of wounds. Aaron and Volanti had the worst, as they'd struggled with the spycatchers. The gash on Treylen's leg was another concern. Twice, they'd needed to stop jogging to fix the bandage. But the bleeding was manageable, and there was always the healing spell that Apogee had taught him at the gravesite.

Treylen hoped it wouldn't come to that.

When they made it back, the poor mayor was trying to run the inn for Marcus, serving drinks while the old bard helped by roasting the boar and lighting the lamps.

Marziel snuck them through the kitchen and into the cellar, then returned to the tavern to take over while the assassins did their best to clean their wounds. Before he left, he told Aaron and Volanti not to bother with their old disguises and for Treylen to dress the both of them in silks from his wardrobe, then join him in the common room.

Treylen thought that was a bad idea but did as he was told. As unlikely as it might be for friends of Cren'pin to show up out of nowhere, so far from their home, the air of nobility would win them a measure of privacy from the locals who had already begun to crowd the tavern.

There were no soldiers in the tavern when he entered later that night. The old bard was in his rightful place beside the fire. The mayor and her husband were enjoying their dinner. Every table was full, but Marziel had saved them three stools at the end of the bar, each with a full tankard. Treylen was too tired to wonder if there was poison in this one.

Treylen chatted politely with the mayor and a few of the locals, deflecting any questions about his two *new* friends as tactfully as he could.

"Eat well and turn in early. You'll all sleep in the basement tonight. I may have to wake you if word of what happened has already left Tabron. Depends on what became of Apogee, and how many others knew of our operations here. Don't trouble yourself now. Eat. Drink. Have a dance with the good mayor." He slipped back into the innkeeper's voice and spoke loud enough for her to hear.

Hilde grinned and leaned across an empty stool to clap him on the shoulder.

"I think I'd rather have a dance with your tall friend, my dear." She winked at Aaron, who smiled back politely.

Volanti sat at the end of the bar, staring at the dancers, the bard cast in the warm light of the fire, and the bones of the dragon with their flickering candles. Marziel set another drink in front of Treylen, then went off to check on the kitchen. Aaron held up his tankard.

"What should we drink to now?"

"To my friends, for coming to my aid?" Treylen murmured.

"How about to Foxbane?" Volanti said. "And his bondmate."

"To Rak'tsoro," Aaron said, raising his drink higher. "And to Foxbane. Wherever he is."

Treylen and Volanti joined him. Afterward they fell quiet, watching the dancers before retreating to the hiding hole beneath the subbasement. Marziel had laid out blankets. They sat a while in the dark with their dragons, talking about old times and catching up on the events of the last day before turning in to sleep.

The smell of brandy woke him.

Aaron and Volanti were gone, and all the dragons. Treylen grabbed his daggers and toolkit, then put on his darks before creeping up through the narrow passage from the cave to the basement. Mud squished beneath his boots as he passed through the training arena and up the ladder to find the barrels of fine brandy broken open.

The kitchen was dark, as was the common room, the door to which hung open. Borrowing a little dragon sight, he could see Rime scurrying about, following Volanti, who held a bucket in her hand and tossed it, dousing the walls and the bar top. The stink of brandy was just as strong up here.

"Good. You're up." Marziel exited the pantry. He wore heavy traveling coats over his darks. A leather hat covered his head and a bag hung over his shoulder. A wooden carving of a dragon's head poked out of it, taken from the shrine in the attic. Marziel grabbed a chunk of ham, holding it out to Treylen. "Here. Eat something."

"What's going on?"

"Last call," Marziel said. "Have an ale if you like. Do you have all of your things from the basement?"

"Everything that matters."

Aaron appeared from the secret passageway. "It's done." He noticed Treylen. "Good morning. Are you feeling better?"

"My head still hurts a little."

"This should help." He handed a bucket to Treylen. A bit of brandy sloshed at the bottom. Treylen set it aside.

"What's happening?"

"She was here," Marziel said. "I suspect it happened even before we returned from Tabron. I found evidence around the grave. She may have used her magic there to heal herself and the dragon."

"Apogee?" Treylen asked, and Marziel nodded. "Why would she come here? There had to be closer cemeteries."

"Her rooms were cleared out. Some things of mine are missing. Important things."

He shouldered his pack, took a last look around, and stepped out the back door, motioning for the others to follow. Treylen walked back to the bar. The inn was empty. He found the coin that Marziel had given him on his first night here. He pulled the cord free and contemplated adding a few knots to it, before tossing it on the floor. He left the coin on the counter.

Outside, it was still dark. Treylen went to stand beside Marziel, looking up at the proud inn and the two old trees that stood on either side.

"Are you sure about this? You could send me away. I'll work in Tabron."

"It's not you. I don't know that Apogee would give me away, but I can't be sure. She may have been reporting on me all along."

Treylen wondered if he should tell Marziel the whole story. How Apogee had not been attacked by her lover, but by another agent of the queen.

The scar he'd seen across Snarefoot's neck was unmistakable. It had been meant as an execution. Maybe Apogee's magic had helped her survive.

"You've seen what's in the attic. There's more that you haven't seen." Marziel tugged his jacket closed and pulled his hood up. "We can't chance any of it falling into Jaul hands."

The four of them stood in a row, looking up at it. One forgotten bedsheet flapped on the line. Someone had opened the door to the chicken coop and the rooster was out, scratching around the yard. They waited there in the dark and the growing winds, nobody wanting to speak before Marziel, until at length, a fifth appeared.

The old bard, whose name Treylen had never managed to learn, stepped out from behind the shed. A bag was over his shoulder with a lute strapped on top of it, an old legionnaires sword in one hand, and an oil lamp in the other.

He grinned at Treylen as he crossed the yard to join them, touching Rime on the snout before putting one hand on Marziel's shoulder.

"We put on a good show, Marcus."

"We always do." Marziel made no pretense of trying to sound like the innkeeper. He took the lamp from the bard and tossed it.

Fire flared in the kitchen, then the windows of the second story lit up as the flames wicked along the brandy-soaked carpet and stairs. They watched until the fire reached the attic, smoke and flame licking from the vent in the gable.

"Come along." Marziel snagged Treylen and Aaron, giving Volanti a nudge to get her moving toward the river. The bard watched it burn for another moment before jogging to catch up, his lute thumping noisily against this pack. Then the five of them, reaching the river, followed it north to the bridge then over, toward Harvest Pass and Iverna.

Chapter Forty-Two

THE WINTER

WINTER AT COOPS ABBEY WAS A TRYING TIME EVEN FOR THE bravest of trainees.

As the new recruits had yet to get their footing, Marziel had ordered that they all be tethered together when they made the perilous climb to and from the abbey.

"I don't know if this is the way, Marziel," Treylen said, pointing at the largest one at the back of the line. "If he goes down, he's bringing the whole class with him."

"Then they should have anchored before he came across." Marziel stood on the wall that connected the great hall to the dovecote tower and separated the courtyard from the sheer drop below. Aaron sat on the wall beside them, Felicity on his lap, feet dangling over the ledge.

"I don't disagree," he said, "but it's hardly a learning experience if none of them survive to absorb the lesson." He scratched the dragon under her chin.

"Who is the teacher here?" Marziel crossed his arms, though Treylen detected a hint of relief when the last of the trainees made it to the courtyard.

Aaron let out a sigh. "I'm just glad it isn't me."

The trainees filed into the courtyard, Volanti leading the drill while Rime and Ketcher followed, nipping at their heels.

"Rime's going to be upset when he learns he's leaving," Aaron said.

"Is it time?" Marziel asked.

"Bird came in this morning," Treylen said. "We've been summoned to Queenseat in the spring."

"That's good." Marziel's chest swelled. "I remember when I first met the queen. That would have been her mother, I suppose."

"That is a while off yet. I'm still your handler for now. You've both improved, but Aaron's disguises need work. And you still rely too much on the dragonmind."

"I'm getting much better about it. Ask Rime." Treylen chuckled. "But I'm happy to play dress up. Should I show up to dinner as Rebash?"

Now it was Marziel's turn to laugh. "I don't think your Volanti would appreciate that. That swindler is still out there. If I'd known I was leaving, I might have removed him myself. Oh well. The queen's shadow take him. Was there any news from the Harvest Pass?"

"Sister Ono says there was another attack," Aaron said, standing and tossing Felicity, who glided down into the court-yard. "No magic weapons. It seems like Treylen may have put a stop to it, for now."

"There will be more. As long as they have Snarefoot and Apogee's dragon sight, the wizards of Jaul have too much power. The queen's been made aware of her collusion. She'll have agents hunting—not only Lome, but all through the empire. Do either of you have an assignment yet?"

"No." Treylen waved at Ourbeth and Cenna down in the courtyard, who beckoned the three of them to come inside. Sister Ono had prepared another early dinner, and the courtyard was filled with the smells of smoked meats and baking bread.

"All the more reason to be prepared," Marziel said. "And to enjoy your time here while it lasts."

The doors of the great hall were propped open while the hungry-looking recruits finished their exercises. The sound of a lute drifted out. Smoke from the hearth curled up from the great hall, swirling around the overhanging cliffs before drifting away on the mountain winds.

Treylen turned away and sat beside Aaron. Rime scurried up the wall to perch on his back.

Treylen decided he would wait until dinner to tell Rime. At that moment, there was no place he would rather be than here at the abbey. But with the promise of an audience, there was nowhere other than Queenseat he'd rather be going.

Together, they looked out from the mountain and watched the snow fall over Iveran fields, the sun dropping low, and the faint glimmer of the distant towers of the capital, just below the Dragon Lands.

Don't miss the next book in The Shadow's Dragon: Dragon Lands.

Treylen never thought he'd be hunting his own people. Least of all, family.

In the mines of Wetherdin, a foul plot is unfolding. Someone's stealing dragon eggs for the Jaul, and it's up to Treylen, Aaron, and their dragons to infiltrate and root out the traitor.

This time he's ready. His spycraft is stronger, his bond with Rime is better than ever, and his mentor has come along for the mission. Under the guise of visiting nobility, they'll have all the comforts of a cozy mountain lodge while untangling the mystery at their leisure.

But when Marziel disappears on the night of a murder, and his own family gets caught up in the intrigue, a dire deadline is set. Treylen is faced with a choice that the abbey never prepared him for. And the solution will take him deeper into the caves of the Dragon Lands than he'd ever imagined.

Printed in Dunstable, United Kingdom